MIRACLE MAN

NOLAN
RYAN

THE AUTOBIOGRAPHY

# MIRACLE MAN
# NOLAN RYAN
## THE AUTOBIOGRAPHY

## WORD PUBLISHING
London · Vancouver · Melbourne

MIRACLE MAN: NOLAN RYAN, THE AUTOBIOGRAPHY

**Library of Congress Cataloging-in-Publication Data**

Ryan, Nolan, 1947-
    Miracle man : Nolan Ryan, the autobiography /
Nolan Ryan with Jerry Jenkins.
    p.   cm.
    ISBN 0-8499-0945-7 (hc)
          0-8499-3507-5 (mp)
    1.  Ryan, Nolan, 1947-  .   2.  Baseball players—United
States—Biography.   I.  Jenkins, Jerry B.   II.  Title.
GV865.R9A3 1992
796.357'092—dc20
    [B]                                              92-4973
                                                     CIP

*Printed in the United States of America*

3 4 5 6 9

To Ruth

You've been more than I could
have ever wished for, and I
couldn't have done anything
without you.

# Contents

# Acknowledgments

Thanks to John Blake and the Texas Rangers public relations department for the latest statistics, and to John D. Miley, Jr., president of The Miley Collection, Inc., for selected career highlights on tape.

# The Nolan You Don't Know

Seems like everybody who writes about me makes a big deal about how soft-spoken and modest I am. Well, I guess that's true. I never had a goal to be in the spotlight. But what happens when you leave your image to other people is that they make something out of you that may or may not be all true.

My life story's been told and retold so many different times that I want a chance to say some things my own way. I know my image is of a laid-back country guy, and I don't mind that. But just because I believe in traditional, conservative values and try to treat everybody the way I want to be treated doesn't mean I don't have opinions.

We placed all the career statistics in the back if you like that kind of thing, and I'll tell you about a lot of the baseball stuff that hasn't already been hashed over a million times. But if you really want to get to know me better by what I've got to say about things, you picked up the right book.

I like being known as just a regular guy. I'm not perfect. I have my likes and dislikes, my pet peeves, and, like I say, my opinions. You may not like me as much when you read them, but at least you'll have a better idea of who I really am. If you get tired of me or mad at me or disagree with me so much you can't take any more, just pass this book on to somebody else. Maybe they'll appreciate it. I'd rather have you not like me for who I really am than like me for who I'm not.

Nolan Ryan
*Alvin, Texas*

# 1

## No Lone Ranger

*S*ometimes I think my whole life is made up of numbers. They tell me I even hold a record for records held. I know some of the numbers, but I don't keep track of them the way a lot of folks do. The most important number in my life is *one*. There's one woman in my life, and Ruth has been the only girl I ever wanted to be with since the time I was a teenager. That's never changed. I consider her the best friend I have.

In this day and age it's pretty rare for a marriage to last a lifetime, let alone for the couple to still like and love each other after all those years. I confide in very few people, and I don't confide in anybody the way I confide in Ruth.

People who look at our lives might think Ruth has it made. She's the wife of a famous person, and she can have just about anything she wants. But the one thing she can never have again is her husband all to herself. She'll probably never have the privacy she'd like either. And her identity will almost always be tied to me. Besides what it can do to a family to have your husband and father gone half the time, a woman with any kind of self-worth has to sacrifice and become unselfish to be a so-called star's wife.

Ruth was the prettiest girl at Alvin High School, and I'm proud that she's still great looking and athletic. But the things a young boy looks for in a girl aren't always what makes the best wife. There're a lot of good-looking, in-shape women who have no business being wives. As a young man, you have no idea what you need in a wife, so it's no wonder so many mistakes are made.

Ruth has always been a good listener, and when we started dating, I thought that was just a nice bonus. But that stuff becomes more important over the years. Now I know that it's her looks and all that which are just bonuses. Her character is what really sets her apart.

Like most guys, especially athletes, I had to learn the hard way to treat Ruth right. Before we had kids, she was stuck in New York while I was on the road with the Mets. When I got home, I wanted to stay; she was ready to go out. Traveling and eating out looks glamorous until you do it for a while. It wasn't until we both learned to be sensitive to the other that we started compromising on things like that.

The biggest adjustment comes when you have children. I don't think anybody has any idea of the impact kids have on your marriage and your life in general. Men sure don't. If they're not careful, nothing changes for them. They just keep doing what they've been doing, and their wives end up with all the work. Ballplayers especially push the obligation of the children off on their wives. Everybody has to learn sooner or later how the time and effort that have to be put into raising children restrict a woman's life. I had to understand that I was not the only person in the marriage and that Ruth had desires and dreams and goals too. That's not an easy lesson for someone who's become the center of attention almost everywhere he goes just because he can throw a baseball.

Our kids are growing up; Reid's in college and Reese and Wendy are in high school. But I still have to work at making my marriage and my family a priority. Most men are out of the game at my age, but my career seems to have taken off because of my longevity, because of the records, and because I've become kind of a folk hero to middle-aged people.

The demands on my time are greater than ever, so working on our marriage is a constant, everyday deal. I've had to learn to be understanding and sympathetic and caring. I have to remind myself that I need to carry my load at home too; it isn't just Ruth's responsibility.

It shouldn't be surprising that so many marriages break up when you think that most people don't understand the commitment that goes with it, especially if they get married while they're young like we did. If brides are anything like us grooms, they're in a kind of shock and not thinking about what they're really saying when they make their vows.

I went to a relative's wedding late last year, and I looked around the congregation while the couple was saying their vows. It seemed like half the people I looked at were divorced. There's nothing like young love, and you wish and hope and pray for the best for the beautiful couple that seem so committed to each other, but you look around and you have to wonder, How long will this one last?

If you ask me, the divorce rate just shows how screwed up our society is. Those vows before man and God are legal and sacred, but they must have had more meaning when my parents got married and when I got married. There are so many prenuptial agreements now that you just know people are saying, "Hey, if this doesn't work out, no big deal." Ruth and I believed we had made a commitment, and we decided to work together under whatever circumstances came along and work through whatever problems we faced. There were no strings attached to that commitment, no contingency clauses. Part of the commitment was figuring out what had to be done and doing it.

Our marriage has not been perfect. Like any other couple, we've had our ups and downs. I'm sure Ruth's had a lot more frustrations than I have, trying to put up with my schedule and lifestyle and demands on my time. Maybe there've been times when she wondered if it was worth it, but I sure never have. I'd like to think that I get better at this marriage business as I go along because I learn more. Only trouble is, once I think I've got things pretty much under control, more demands complicate my life, and I have to look at my priorities all over again. Ruth and I have worked through that, and the particulars are nobody's business but ours.

People's private lives ought to stay that way, but a lot of professional athletes think they are above any system, that they don't have to conform to the laws of the land, and that they're entitled to do whatever they please without answering to anyone. It's disgusting.

Take Lenny Dykstra's book. He's with the Phillies now, but he was on the Mets when they won the World Series in 1986, and he came out with a book so filthy and full of obscenities that I was appalled. You know that book should have been written for youngsters, teenagers, and young adults, but it was done in such poor taste that it showed the caliber of person Lenny was. I found it very offensive. I understand Lenny has grown up some since he got in a wreck after drinking. I just wish he'd write something about what he learned from that. People seem to want the dirt more though, and that's a sad commentary on our society.

It says something about us too that a superstar athlete with the AIDS virus is made into a hero. Magic Johnson was already a hero, of course, because of his ability and his personality. I've never met him, but like anyone else, I was shocked when I heard the news. I had no reason to think he would ever become a victim, and I'm not one of those who wishes him anything but the best. But I can't say I'm surprised that AIDS is finally starting to spread into all of society. It was just a matter of time before a prominent person who wasn't a homosexual got struck with the disease. We have a major problem here that needs more effort toward a solution. Maybe Magic Johnson's impact will help accomplish that and put things on a higher awareness level.

But I still think Magic is a hero because of what he did athletically, not because he's so courageous and outspoken now. It's good he's doing that, of course, and I'm glad to see he's even starting to say that the only real safe sex is no sex outside of marriage. But I have a problem with making a hero out of him because of AIDS.

I don't often find myself agreeing with someone who defends her bisexuality and has said that this country is so conservative that she might be better off going back to live under communism. But Martina Navratilova made a good point about Magic Johnson. She said that if a woman athlete had announced she had AIDS and that she had slept with a couple hundred men, she would not be considered a hero at all. She would be called a tramp.

Martina's got a point. It could be that she believes that neither a man nor a woman should be criticized and that both should be called heroes. All I know is, you stay married to and sleep only with one person who does the same, and you're not going to get AIDS through sex. It's just sad that it takes someone like Magic Johnson's sacrificing himself before we get around to getting something done about the problem. If Magic had done that on purpose for that reason, then maybe he would be a hero to the cause of AIDS research.

Now we're at a point where if somebody doesn't come up with some kind of miracle vaccine, we're in deep trouble. You can educate people about safe sex and all, but most of them think things like AIDS happen to others. That's just human nature. The morals of our country have fallen to where you're not going to get people to abstain from sex outside of marriage. It's scary. When you look at the numbers and think about your children and what they're exposed to, man . . .

So many innocent people can be affected now. Our attitude used to be that it was a disease of the gay community and that if those people chose to participate in those activities, that risk was part of the price they paid. I think that's the way people viewed it when Rock Hudson died. That's why his tragedy didn't have the impact that Magic Johnson's does, because Magic is looked on through different eyes by the public. But of course, even though Magic was not gay, he wasn't really an innocent victim because of his lifestyle.

Sacrificing someone to get something done is sort of like our country's foreign policy. We give away billions of dollars overseas, but we don't spend much here trying to do some of the things our own people need done. That's what's got President Bush in so much trouble now. And I'm a Bush fan. I've known him since back in my days with the Mets when he was our ambassador to the United Nations. I campaigned for him when he was running for vice-president. I see him a couple, maybe three times a year around Texas, and Ruth and I have been to a state dinner and stayed overnight at the White House. I even went to Honduras with him once.

But I still have to say I'm not real pleased with the way things have gone domestically. I feel that Congress hasn't tried to work with the administration in the best interests of our country. The president's interests have been worldwide, which is good, but we need to address the problems and concerns here. I'm not saying you ignore what goes on in the rest of the world, because it definitely has an impact on us. But we should put the same energy and invest the same monies here in our country. I don't see that happening.

I'm not an advocate of war, but I felt like what we did in the Persian Gulf was justified. We did what we needed to do, but still we bobbled the ball on that deal. We should have gone ahead and finished it off and not have to still be dealing with it. Why we didn't do that, I don't know. What we did accomplish only shows that we could have handled the Vietnam War differently.

People have never quite gotten over the tarnished image we have over the beating we took in Vietnam, and now that we've had time to reflect on it, I think our country is also embarrassed by the way it treated its people who served over there. A lot of people didn't speak out or take stands on what was going on because it wasn't the popular thing to do. They took the position that it's best not to get involved. I'm not saying the war was right, but I know our approach to it was wrong. When we went in there we didn't make a commitment to get a job done. We just sacrificed a lot of money and lives and for what? We still wonder now.

That's where politics comes into play. Politicians will play with lives; they'll play with money. What's really disgusting and hard to understand is what the human race does to itself. Sit down and look through history at what we're capable of doing to each other. It's staggering.

I think we've become too image conscious, too worried about what the rest of the world thinks of us. That's why we didn't finish off Iraq. Other world powers don't worry so much about international opinion, and how has it hurt them? It hasn't. They do what they want, project a bully-on-the-block image, and everybody fears them. We have the mentality that we want to be loved worldwide, but the only people who even pretend to like us are the ones who get handouts from us. They only want our money, and we're gullible enough to think they respect us for it. That's just amazing.

In our own country we don't put enough emphasis on education. That struck home with me one year when I was with the Astros and we were playing the Giants on the road. At Candlestick Park they were honoring the top ten students in the San Francisco Bay area. Seven of them were Asians, one was black, one was Latino, and one was Anglo. Minorities were in the majority when it came to excellence in education. You had to be proud of those families. But what does it say about the rest of us?

We Americans who have been here for generations take education for granted. When the Asians and others see the golden opportunity in this country to develop their minds and excel, they take advantage of it. The majority of the population figures education is something they don't have to work for; they're entitled to it. I just hope our society and lifestyle doesn't rub off on our newer citizens. We've brought ourselves down educationally. I may sound pessimistic, but these are things that bother me. These are the kinds of problems I think we need to be addressing.

The next presidential election, in my opinion, is going to be important. I'm going to see who the candidates are and listen to their attitudes and proposals and evaluate them against what George Bush has done. He's done a lot of things right, and I like him as a man. But even though I usually lean toward the Republican side of things, I'm not locked in.

You won't see me running for office, even though I've been approached about being the commissioner of agriculture for Texas. I gave it a lot of thought in 1989 when I thought I might be getting out of baseball. The more people I talked to and the more I investigated it, the more I realized what it means to run for office. Because of the scrutiny of your personal life and the amount of time you spend raising money, it's no wonder we don't have better candidates.

What's most disheartening about our politics is how, unless we're really threatened, we're always fighting each other. Democrats against Republicans, Congress against the president, all that. They can't address an issue without looking at what impact it has on them and their future. They put their individual careers ahead of good common sense unless it's truly a crisis. Then they pull together like they should all the time. That's why I'm not a big political player.

Most people in their right mind wouldn't want anything to do with it. The way the game's played now, they were talking about spending a million and a half dollars or more just to run for commissioner of agriculture of Texas. I could see that much of my time would not be running to get elected but going to fund-raisers. That sounded like a never-ending deal. It's all become dollars, and it looks to me like a guy we need doing agriculture business spends more than half his time running for office and paying for that.

Maybe that's why politics in my state and in the country is in shambles. The last Texas governor's race got to be such a mud-slinging deal that it was embarrassing. I don't know how anybody, winner or loser, could have been proud of that election campaign. And I don't know who I'd have voted for if I'd lived in Louisiana, the racist or the criminal? I guess I would have viewed that as one of those rare occasions when there's justification not to vote. Actually, there are a lot of races I don't vote. I won't vote if I don't know the candidates, and I don't vote if I don't approve of them.

Like I said, I'm basically a Republican, but I voted for Jimmy Carter his first time running for president because I was fed up with the way things were going. My attitude was that Jimmy Carter had to be better than what we had. Now as I look back on it, I honestly don't believe he was. I don't believe he was suited to be president. He tried, but he didn't have the ability. That's my opinion. I didn't vote for him a second time, and I've been real careful ever since if I don't know much about a man.

Ted Kennedy hasn't helped my attitude toward the Democrats either. It killed me to see him sitting up there at the table next to Joe Biden in the Clarence Thomas hearings. That kinda gives you an idea of where we are with our politics in this country. I couldn't believe what I saw on television and what went on in those hearings. If that doesn't wake us up, I don't know what will. The bottom line is you don't know the truth in that situation, but the media sensationalized everything. It came down to people making statements and accusations about each other that couldn't be defended. Once someone says something about you and it's been written, published, or put on the air, it doesn't matter a bit whether it's true or how many people believe it or don't. They never forget it, and you live with it the rest of your life. It casts a shadow on you and your family and on your relationship with everybody. It's a crime.

And in those hearings, that went both ways. Once Anita Hill's private charges were made public, then charges against her were made public. Then people were split right down the middle on who was a liar and who wasn't. It was a nightmare. The moral fiber of this country has to change. Too many people have strayed so far from traditional values that it's become every man for himself. What we need are people who stand by their commitments and return to moral living.

We have to take a different stance in our judicial system, too. We protect criminals while the victims, whose rights have really been violated, have no protection. Someone told me that in Texas the average stay in the penitentiary for a convicted murderer is two and a half years. We're so worried about everybody's rights that we've done a 180-degree turn, and we protect the criminal. Sure, okay, protect the person's rights when he's been accused, but once he's been convicted what would be so wrong with depriving him of his rights?

That might sound extreme, but I think we need to take a hard line on that. Anybody convicted of a violent crime with a weapon, or rape, or murder should lose his rights. He's had his opportunities; why should we continue to protect his rights? We deny him his freedom—for at least two and half years—and he doesn't get to vote. Why don't we go further and put some teeth in the sentencing and keep these people away from the rest of society? They are the ones who have denied law-abiding citizens their right to life, liberty, and the pursuit of happiness.

I'm not talking about denying due process or creating a police state. I'm talking about getting serious about convicted criminals. Something's screwy when murderers are getting out of prison in two and a half years, and a guy who turns himself in on a minor misdemeanor gets hammered for an honest mistake. That actually happened. A hunter accidentally shot a whooping crane he thought was a goose, so he turned himself in to the Texas authorities because cranes are an endangered species in this state. He could have walked away and no one would have ever known. That wouldn't have made it right, but he was being honest, living by his conscience, trying to do the right thing. He was sent to prison for six months and fined $30,000! We do that to him, and we wink at people who have never ever abided by the law! We have so much corruption in our system that it's slanted toward criminals and those who have money.

Well, now that I've offended just about everybody, let me take on the attorneys. We have way too many, and now they're making the laws. I know that's a real unpopular thing to say and attorneys don't like to hear it, but there's a lot of truth to it. What's happened is that there are so many lawyers in our system that they have to find ways to make a living. They're out stimulating business, and that's why we have so many lawsuits. Insurance premiums go up, people settle out of court, and lawyers have nothing involved but their time.

Now let me be clear: I have friends who are attorneys (at least until they see this!), and I'm not saying all attorneys are that way. It's just like the other problems we have in this country: nothing gets done until it becomes financial. Our pollution problem is not going to be solved until it really starts to hurt the income of big business. It would be nice to think we'd clean it up just because it's the right thing to do for us and for our descendants. But it will come down to the dollar just like most everything else.

We had a gas shortage in the 1970s and everybody got serious about conserving because their lifestyles were affected. Now we're more dependent on foreign oil than we've ever been, but because nobody's suffering, we'll just rock along and pay for it.

Well, I didn't mean to depress you. Would you believe, in spite of all that, I'm basically an optimist? That's because there's one thing about this country: it's resourceful. It finds ways to rise above some of the problems we develop. Sometimes I feel like a dying breed, being part of what has become the minority—people who still believe in old-fashioned hard work and common sense and treating people right. But then I realize that we're probably still in the majority. We just don't make as much noise as the other guys. We're considered out of step or out of date, and we sure aren't as newsworthy as the ones making all the trouble.

You look at all the television shows about crime and about entertainers and about tragedy and you see what the producers think we all want to see. Nobody wants good news and stories about solid values. At least that's what Hollywood and New York think. But the people I live and work with haven't changed. There are still a lot of people all over the country who remember what made it great. You can still be an optimist in spite of all the problems if you know you're not alone. And you're not.

# 2

## Of Images and Reality

*T*here's so much competition in the media nowadays that you can't trust anybody. Nothing's sacred anymore. You can't confide in a reporter because there's so much pressure for those guys to break a story first that they have to figure out some way to get it into print. That's just business. They may promise not to write something you've told them, but they might tell someone else on their staff and then the news gets out from the other writer. I might be talking off the record about something or somebody because I think I've established a friendship with the writer, but once I see that come out in print somehow, I know our personal and professional relationships didn't stay separate. I've learned that lesson enough times that I should know better by now.

In spite of that, I've been fairly well treated by the press. I've had my run-ins and there are people I don't like to talk to, but generally I get along all right. There are always going to be some reporters whose writing I just don't like, or some who get into what I call a negative mode, where they seem to enjoy writing about all the things that are wrong with your team. The doom-and-gloom writers have a tendency to complain more when things are going bad, and they take advantage of players who are doing that too.

Anybody can dig up that kind of stuff if he wants to. Bad news travels fast. They start talking about the shortcomings of a ball team and speculate on what the club needs to do—who they need to trade or fire or whatever, and it creates a lot of discussion and interest. All you have to do is lose a few games in a row and then tune in to one of those post-game radio talk shows. Everybody's got an opinion, a gripe, a complaint, a suggestion. That makes some players say things they maybe wouldn't say otherwise, and of course the writers quote them in the papers and that gets added into the mix. I have a problem with the attitudes of writers like that, and I try to keep from reading their material. I don't want it to affect my attitude and my relationship with them.

It's a lot easier and safer for a writer to predict that a team is going to lose rather than win its division, because there are only four teams who will do that. The writers say that all we players want is for them to be cheerleaders, but their big deal is to be objective journalists. Like this is international politics or something. I don't mind them being honest, but when every writer comes off like an expert or a manager, it gets tiring. I admit most ballplayers don't want anything negative written about them whether it's the truth or not. So, sportswriters aren't in an ideal position. Overall, I feel like they've treated me fairly and I try to give them as much time as I can. All I ask of them is that they do their homework and that they ask reasonable questions.

Sometimes they try to get you to criticize one of your teammates or the management. They ask you a leading question or get you into a situation where you have to start explaining yourself, and you end up talking yourself into a corner. If I feel that I pitched poorly, then I will admit that and so state. If I stunk, I stunk. What really irritates me is when

you've won and the team did well, but the fi̶̶̶̶
tion you get is about something negative. Tha̶̶̶
me nuts because I think it shows what track̶̶̶
minds run on.

Maybe I pitched a low-hit game and we won
by a run. A sportswriter will ask me if I thought I
was lucky to get out of the third inning when a guy
hit a line drive right at somebody with a man in scoring position. Or he'll ask how I evaluated the seventh inning when I threw twice as many pitches as
any other inning or walked a couple of guys or
something. That kind of a question tells you something about a person. When you deal with them on a
day-to-day basis as we do, you don't even have to
read their articles. They tell you about themselves
just by their conversations and by what they ask.

I normally just look at the box scores and read
the summaries of the other games. I don't read our
game stories. I see our games, and I figure writers
have a tough job. They have to come in and ask you
questions, and just because you may have had a bad
game doesn't entitle you to be ugly to them and
make their job harder.

Naturally I've become friends with some writers because of the time we spend together on the
road and in the clubhouse. Others, because of their
personalities or their interests or the little time they
spend with us, I don't get to know as well.

The national media are a little different. They
tend to be a little more star struck, and when they're
doing their first story about me, they have read all
the stuff about my ranches and my banks and my
family and my down-home values, so they have a lot
of preconceived notions. If they think I'm a country
bumpkin, then unless I say something dramatic that

their mind, that's how their story's going to
...t. If they think I'm a soft-spoken gentleman,
...bably won't do anything to change their opinion. But sometimes I'm surprised at the difference
between the image and who I really am.

Advertising has exposed my face and my voice
to more people, so a lot of folks who have only seen
me pitch on television now know what I look like
and what my accent sounds like. When I said on a
commercial that when I take Advil my headache is
"long gone," nobody where I'm from gave it a second thought. But I guess because of my Texas accent
on the o's, I started getting mimicked all over the
country. I don't mind that. I don't hear my accent,
but it doesn't surprise me that I sound like where I
come from. I'm certainly not ashamed of it.

Because I stay in shape and have done some
Wrangler Jeans ads, some people call me a sex symbol for my age group. I don't view myself that way
and I never have, and honestly the first time I ever
heard anything said like that was when the Wrangler poster came out. That bugs Ruth, and I suppose
it would bother any wife to think her husband is being looked at by other women as some sort of an
object. I'm proud of the way she looks, but I
wouldn't want her to be considered a sex symbol.
As for my being one, those kinds of things never
cross my mind. It hits me as kind of silly because I
don't see myself that way. I think everybody feels
like they'd like to improve their looks in certain
ways. My kids tease me about losing my hair, and I
just tell them that's the way the Lord wanted me so
I don't worry about it.

I have teammates who spend a lot of time on
their hair and then worry when they see some of it

coming off on their comb. I figure whatever hair I've got or not got is all part of the package. I'd never wear a hairpiece, I'll tell you that. You don't fool anybody but yourself if you think people can't tell. I'd rather have people know I'm losing my hair than that I'm wearing a wig and trying to hide it.

I don't spend a lot of time analyzing myself because I think, like most people, that I'm not any more complex than anybody else. I don't want people to have to try to figure me out. If I say anything at all, I just tell you honestly what I think. With me, what you see is pretty much what you get. I'm pretty sure most people don't much care what everybody else's opinion is, so I usually don't offer one unless I'm asked or I'm in a business situation where what I think means something.

Sometimes this image thing makes me think about who I really am, and like I say, I'm no mystery. My parents had the biggest influence on me, and I think it says a lot about how I feel about them and about this part of the country that I still live a few miles from where I was raised. Alvin is no tropical paradise, but its people and their values make it all-American. My parents—like most people around here—were dedicated to raising their kids and doing the best job they possibly could with us. They hardly ever spent any money on themselves. Everything they did hinged on the best interests of the family. That was instilled in me. It wasn't preached to me in any way, but I feel their impact on me every day in the way I see as the proper way of doing things.

My dad worked two jobs to put his four daughters through college, and when I find myself wanting to deal honestly with people, I sense his influence.

Besides working all day, he was a distributor for the *Houston Post* to fifteen hundred homes over a fifty-five mile route that took four hours, starting at one o'clock in the morning every day. From the time I was old enough to help, that was my life: waking up at one o'clock and rolling papers, tossing them for four hours, and getting back to bed before dawn.

You learn responsibility that way. You learn hard work. My dad did that to give us kids opportunities he never had, a chance to better our lives. Naturally I have the means to do a lot of things he didn't because of the success I've had in baseball, but everything Ruth and I do is with the same attitude our parents had. Just about everything we do is centered on our family. We hardly ever go off on vacation, especially not for an extended period, without the kids.

My basic philosophy of life came from my parents: Treat people the way you want to be treated, with honesty and integrity. I've never really gotten caught up in doing glamorous things. I'm very conservative. My dad never had to deal with extra money, because there never was any. But no matter what kind of resources I have, I treat them the way he treated what little he had. Baseball is a fleeting thing, which may sound strange coming from a guy who's been in it for so long. But I've never known how long I would be in the game. You don't know from one season to the next, one game to the next, even one pitch to the next. Because of the way I was raised I always believed that no matter how successful you are, it should not change you as a person. It doesn't entitle you to treat people any differently than if you were just another person trying to make a living. I believe I should treat the fan in the bleachers the same way I would treat George Bush—with respect.

Where I come from, treating people that way doesn't make me anything special. That's the way people are raised and, for the most part, that's the way they are. Of course every town has its share of bad apples, but I like a place where trying to be a good person doesn't make you stand out from the crowd. Treating people right has become part of my nature because of my upbringing, and it's nice to have it come naturally. It would be too much work if you had to think about it every time or only did it for your own benefit.

If my baseball career were over next week, I'd be working. I've accumulated a lot of money and a lot of things, and I suppose I could coast for a good while if I chose to. But I'd go crazy not working. I enjoy manual labor. I enjoy working cattle. I get a lot of satisfaction out of doing a good job, whether it's mowing a yard, raking leaves, doing a flower bed, or building a fence. I look out at my property and see the fence I put up, and it makes me feel good that I dug the postholes and did the final paint job. I enjoy building things, and I don't like doing shoddy work. I don't like spending my time on something that isn't what it should have been or isn't going to last. I don't want to have to go back and redo it. Seems like a lot of folks want a shortcut; they don't want to have to do anything.

The bottom line is that even though I sometimes smile about whatever image a writer wants to create for me, I realized early on that I just had to be myself. I can't be worried about what people think of me or what they expect or want me to be. I have to be

Nolan Ryan and answer for myself. You don't need such a good memory that way, trying to be somebody different for every person or every situation. That was instilled in me by my parents.

My dad had an inner confidence, and he was a stabilizing force in our family. That was in my mind when I got to New York to play for the Mets. I really wasn't that far out of high school and hadn't had much experience in the world, but all of a sudden, because of my fastball, I was being compared to Bob Feller and Sandy Koufax. I started out thinking I had to go out there and show them what a good arm I had. I might strike out six or seven the first time through the lineup, but the hitters would realize I was wild and didn't have a breaking ball. Then they would get selective, and I wouldn't make it through the lineup a second time.

I realized I was playing right into their hands just because somebody had said something about me and I was trying to live up to it. I wasn't trying to be Nolan Ryan. I was trying to be Feller or Koufax, and nobody can do that.

I used to get upset when people called me a .500 pitcher because I've lost nearly as many games as I've won. That doesn't bother me anymore, because I know that anybody who says that doesn't know much about baseball or about pitching. I know what kind of a pitcher I am. I know what's gone on in my career. I know what I have to do to be effective. They don't. That's why I try to teach my kids to consider the source whenever they're criticized. Don't be influenced by what people say about you. Don't let it bother you to where you're distracted.

That's a hard lesson because everybody likes to be liked. You like to do right and be popular, but you have to look at the big picture and decide whether it's worth it to bend to peer pressure. When our oldest son, Reid, was pitching in high school, one night the guys on the other bench were razzing him pretty good. "Jose Canseco's gonna hit a grand slam off your old man!" they said, and other stuff like that. Ruth was ready to come out of the stands and pop every one of them.

Finally Reid just walked over and said nicely, "I'm proud of my dad. What do y'all's dads do?"

He was serious and interested in them and was trying to take the spotlight off himself and off me. They were speechless. Probably half of them didn't even have dads living at home and the others either weren't proud of their dads or didn't want to say what they did. Whatever, it worked. They quit razzing Reid.

I'm a big believer in listening to people. If you really listen, they'll tell you about themselves without even realizing it. People usually talk about what's on their mind, and what's on their mind is usually themselves. Within just a few minutes of meeting someone new, if you just listen you'll hear something about them that they consider real important. It might be where they work or used to work, or something they've accomplished, or where they graduated from. Most people know enough to just work it into the conversation so it doesn't sound like bragging, but if you listen, you'll hear it. Listen to salesmen too, because the thing they avoid talking about is probably some important negative part of whatever they're trying to sell you. Ask them about it and if they still talk around it, you can be sure.

The more people get to know me, the more frugal they know I am. If they don't know me, all they may've heard is that I make millions or am worth millions or own banks, and they figure I'm an easy mark. That would make the people around Alvin smile. When I go into a store, I don't want some salesperson trying to push something off on me. I want them available if I have questions, but I want to look at the product and make up my own mind. I do very little shopping because of that, and when I do, I usually know what I want and go in and get it. All these one-day specials are just sales gimmicks. They write books on how to do that.

I'm not real popular with the realtors around here either. If anybody thinks money's no object with me, he learns quickly. When I put the ranch together in Gonzales, Texas, I made a lot of land purchases. The realtors get frustrated with someone who doesn't buy on the spur of the moment, and I sure don't. I really think things through and spend a lot of time on it. One thing my dad told me a long time ago and I've tried to instill in my kids is that if something's real important to you and you think you want to do it, sleep on it. If you get up the next morning and you still feel strongly about it, then it might be the right thing. But if your attitude's changed, you need to give it more thought.

I admit I've lost out on some deals that could have been lucrative, but then there have been an awful lot of deals that I passed on—and thank goodness I did. I'm a believer in gut feelings. I pay a lot of attention to how I feel inside, and very few times have I acted on that and been wrong. If I sleep on it and still have that gut feeling in the morning, I'm usually ready to deal. When I miss out on something because of my methodical approach, I just figure it wasn't right and that it's not the last deal that's going to come along. If somebody tries to pressure me into a quick decision, they're going the wrong way with me. It won't work. Anybody making a commission on something I buy is going to earn every dime.

I don't try to buy below market value, but I do try to be realistic and not pay additional fees. If there's a lot of fat in the deal, I can usually find it and cut it out. Otherwise you're just throwing money away. I shop for things, and a lot of times when I make an offer, I don't lowball just to start the bidding. I'll say, "Look, I'm going to make you an offer of what I can pay and what I feel like the value is, and if you want to accept that, fine. But I don't want you to think I'm going to keep coming up, because I'm not." I want an honest, clean deal without all the games and long, drawn-out motions. If it works, great, and if they can't accept the offer, that's okay too. Let's not waste each other's time. A lot of times people don't believe you when you walk away from a deal, and when it dawns on them that you were serious and they call you, it's too late. If you're going to walk away, be prepared to stay away.

A lot of people with something to sell find out I'm interested and think that since I've got money they can really hook me. My income gets plastered all over the media. It was even on the front page of *USA Today*, so everybody knows that the Rangers paid me $1.4 million in 1990, $3.3 million in 1991, and $4.2 million in 1992. When we started looking into buying a couple of banks, we studied a lot of different deals and talked to a lot of people. Then when it came down to negotiating, I thought, *Wait a minute! Is this the same guy and the same deal?* Once they had attracted our interest by talking price and conditions, they changed their tune. We walked away from a lot of deals that suddenly changed when we got to the bargaining table.

I have my attorney with me—see, I really do like some of them—but I do the negotiating myself. When they start bringing in new contingencies and change the terms, it's time to walk. No matter what my income has ever been, I've tried not to lose sight of the value of the dollar and what it takes to earn a living in the normal world.

That's where most professional athletes fall short, because they don't have these concepts. A lot of them have never worked outside their sport and don't understand what it is to get up and go to work before daylight and work all day and come home after sundown. Some working people don't enjoy the light of day for a week. Too many baseball players are not prepared to work when they leave the game. It's such a shock and rude awakening that a lot of them refuse to make the transition back into the real world. They know there's no money like what they've been making if they try to stay in the game as a coach, so they'd rather go home and live off what little they've saved, and they wind up with lots of personal problems because their pride gets in the way. They don't want to have to really work for a living. I'd rather do business with real working people.

That's why I bought the Express Bank in Danbury, fifteen miles south of Alvin, in 1990 and a new branch in Alvin last year. My goal is that these banks have a down-home feel. All the big banks are going conglomerate and trying to be bigger. We just want to prosper by seeing our customers prosper. When I was growing up, customers knew their banker by name. That's the way it should be. I paid

$600,000 for the Danbury bank and it has grown from assets of under $10 million to more than $14 million. The Alvin branch gives us about $20 million more in assets. I've got more tied up in three ranches, so with that and baseball and endorsements, I'm busier than I ever wanted to be.

Sometimes it seems like Nolan Ryan is something besides me. But I know all this is temporary. There are days when doing all this business without the baseball looks pretty attractive. But I know it was the baseball that made it happen in the first place, and as long as the fame is paying off right now, I'll ride this wave.

Once I take the uniform off for good, the commercial requests will taper off. When you're on top it's demanding, but when you become a used-to-be, it has to slow down. I hope. Ruth worries that I'll have an image like Joe DiMaggio, who still can't go out in public without being mobbed. That would be prison. It'll sure be good to just do a couple of things well rather than try to do more. I could never be a full-time banker, though. I would get cabin fever being inside all day.

I still get people sending me investment stuff all the time, wanting me to get in on a great deal. But if these are such great deals, why don't these people get a loan and cut the deal themselves? I've got enough deals to worry about with my own banks. I was on the board of an Alvin bank in the 1980s when there were more than nineteen thousand banks in the state of Texas. Almost half of them have closed or been merged since then. There's a lesson there that we've got to learn. We can't risk bad loans. I won't lend money to someone for a store unless I know it's going to be profitable. If we had to foreclose, would anybody buy it? I have to ask that question every time we consider a loan. We have to be better business people when times are bad. The government won't be bailing us out.

I've taken big financial risks, and I've lost money. In the 1980s I lost a million on tax shelters. I've seen land drop 40 percent in value. I invested in oil when it was selling at more than $25 a barrel and saw it drop to under $10. There was a while there when I couldn't believe how many things went bad. I was in a limited partnership on some apartment buildings that were foreclosed when the economy fell. And I sold a ranch to buyers who went bankrupt and I had to repossess it. I learned the hard way that it's not how much money you make that counts. It's how much you keep.

The other part of my nature that doesn't exactly fit with my image is that I can be an emotional person. I try to control that quite a bit, especially when I do something special on the field, like reach a milestone record or pitch a no-hitter. I've never liked showing people up by displaying it, but emotionally I can be moved. What might be emotional for me wouldn't look the same on somebody else. Everyone shows emotion in different ways. Tommy Lasorda and Tug McGraw and those types of guys always make it clear what they're feeling. That's great and entertaining, but it's not me. I feel like I shouldn't get too high when things are going well or too down when things are going bad. I try to stay on an even keel and keep off the emotional roller coaster.

I can still get choked up watching my children accomplish something. It might be a little thing, like just seeing their joy. It also moves me when my teammates share in something I've accomplished. If it's a big deal for them to have been involved in one of the no-hitters, that means a lot to me.

Patriotic stuff moves me too. When the U.S. hockey team beat the Russians in the Olympics in 1980, I was as choked up as anybody who saw that. I take great pride in our country, no matter what I feel about how things are going at the time. When someone loses that love and emotion for his country, he can become a miserable person. I don't want that to happen to me.

Probably the biggest difference between my image and my real nature is how I am on the mound. If you believed everything you read about me, you'd figure I was a slow-talking, slow-walking, soft-spoken guy who just does his job in a detached way and gets on with his life. Part of that is true. I want to give an honest day's work for the enormous dollars they pay athletes these days, but actually I'm a totally different person on the mound than I am on the street.

The casual country gentleman, if that's what I could be called, wouldn't get anybody out in the big leagues. At that level you have to be single-minded, focused, and tough. I mean really tough. You've got to go after the hitters, take every advantage you can, work on their weak spots, and want to beat them. There's no playing around out there, no experimenting just because you've got a few effective pitches. Anybody who's ever been on a big league mound knows that you're always one pitch from failure.

When I'm on that mound, I don't even look the same. I don't feel or act the same. I'm there to do a job and to get people out, and if that means pitching inside, I pitch inside. If that means setting up a guy outside and then busting one in close, that's what I do. I spend a good bit of my life staying in shape and preparing for every start, and nobody's going to distract me or get my focus off my job. There's plenty of time after the game to be the other Nolan Ryan.

# 3

## The Other
## Nolan Ryan

*T*he baseball field is the only place I'm so fiercely competitive. I mean I can be stubborn and single-minded, and I'm kind of wary of people I don't know. I'll look at a deal every which way and can get pretty cold if I think you're trying to take me. But that focus on the task, that almost meanness about challenging the hitter, that's only on the mound.

If I go out to play tennis or basketball or any of that, I'm not that way. I was when I was in high school and competing, but now when I go out to enjoy a sport, sure I play to win, but I find it offensive if people get too excited about it. I'm out there for the enjoyment and the exercise and the socializing. We all do our best and we usually keep score, but the outcome doesn't mean a thing to me. If you make it obvious it means a lot to you, I might be busy next time you want to play.

Off the field I don't mind trying to live up to the image most people have of me. I get amused when people think I could succeed at pitching as a nice guy. There's nothing nice guy about it. I would never intentionally hit somebody, but boy I'll go after you and make you earn your hits. If anybody thinks I'm gonna shrug and say "Aw, shucks" if I start getting hit, they're crazy. My whole life's been fixed on power pitching. That's what got me in the game and that's what's kept me there.

Nobody would want to be that way off the field, and nobody could stand me if I was. Every once in a while you get a guy who thinks he needs to have his game face on and his attitude focused all the time. He's mean on the field and off the field. People usually just roll their eyes at a guy like that. It's not necessary. To me there's nothing inconsistent about being one way in the game and another way in real life. Imagine what kind of a dad I'd be if I was the same with my kids as I was with big league hitters. I want my kids to have memories of their growing up years as good as I have of mine, and that means my being easy to get along with.

I can be strict and firm, and I expect the kids to do their part. But I think they also can tell how much I love them and want them to enjoy life. They've grown up with a dad who's a big leaguer, so it's been a way of life for them. It's been exciting for them, I know, but I'm sure at times they wished I was more available. During the season I'm gone half the time, and during the off-season I'm sometimes busier than ever, depending upon my schedule. They understand some of the benefits that come with my being in demand, and they've gotten to do a lot of traveling because I always take them with me during the summer.

I've made a point of carrying them with me ever since they were big enough to go. Truth is, they're one of the reasons I'm still playing. Every year for the past several years I've thought about whether it's time to retire. You keep thinking you'll know because you've lost something on your fastball or your aches and pains are worse than ever, but with me it's mostly just been wondering if I've had enough. But the family wanted me to continue. They weren't ready for me to retire. So since I didn't have to, I kept on.

Kids of sports stars can have problems. They are either real proud of their dad or they're a little embarrassed about it and get teased. Sometimes they live and die with how their dad does on the field. If the team is losing or I'm losing, they'll hear about it at school. But mostly I know they're proud and they like having a dad who does something that most people don't do.

We've tried to stress with our kids that they should develop their own interests and their own personalities and their own identities. That's a tough battle at times, because no matter what they do athletically, they're going to get compared to their dad. Reid is a pitcher who was good enough in high school to go on and pitch in college. He may or may not play pro ball, but you gotta know everybody who watches him and knows who he is asks the same big question and compares him to me. I mean, do they really expect a kid to throw like I do? Experts tell me only 7 percent of all the pitchers in the majors throw as hard as I do. It's not fair to say Reid doesn't have my fastball. It'd be an amazing coincidence if he did. I wish they'd just let him pitch and play and enjoy the game. He was good enough that he could have played college basketball if he'd wanted to, but even then people would compare how he was as a basketball player to how I am as a baseball player. Silliness, really. Let him be himself.

The only time it really bothered him though was when some guys razzed him. He'd come home and say, "Why do people have to be that way? Why do they have to be mean and ugly like that?" But that comes with the territory, and you have to take the bad with the good. If nothing else, that teaches him a lot about human nature and people in general. You can't let it affect how you treat people. I figure, if nothing else, it'll show him the value of being a basically quiet and well-mannered person.

Reese, our younger boy, is a real responsible kid too. While Reid's mind was always on sports and he didn't like working around the ranch, Reese enjoys making spending money by doing chores. He'll always check to see what needs to be done first and how I want it done. I'd like all the kids to just do chores for the fun and accomplishment of it, but I guess that's too much to ask in this day and age.

One day last summer Reese was working at home alone and accidentally let one of the dogs in and didn't know it. When he came in later, he discovered the dog had torn up the drapes and gnawed on the door trying to get out. On his own, Reese called the interior decorator and got her out there to tell him what needed to be done, and he paid for it out of his own money. Ruth was pretty upset with him at first, but we were both impressed when he took that responsibility and wanted to make it right.

One of the toughest things about raising modern kids, especially when you really don't have to worry about money, is teaching them the value of a dollar. That came sort of naturally to me because we never had much extra when I was growing up, but it would be hard for me to convince my kids I can't afford something. One thing I can't afford, though, is to give them whatever they want. I know what that can do to a person, and it's not good. They'd start thinking that's how life is. What kind of adults would I be turning out if they get the idea that someone's going to be financing them all the way? I want my sons and my daughter to make their own ways.

There were things we were glad to see Reid discover when he went off to college. He played ball in Alaska for a season and then he went to school. For the first couple of years he wrote Ruth pretty regularly telling her how much he appreciated all she had done for him and how much he learned from the things I used to tell him. He thought I was crazy when I said them because a lot of what I say goes against current trends. You sit your kids down and try to tell them things and they look at you like you're from another planet. Then they get out in the real world and find out how things are, and they're amazed at what you know.

Our house is always open, and we want our kids' friends to feel welcome. Most of all that made Reid appreciate us as parents and the home life and stability he had. I know that'll happen to Reese and Wendy too, but they'll probably have to leave home to discover it. That's sure the way it happened with me. Nobody ever seems to learn lessons the easy way. At least not kids.

Like any other child of my generation, I didn't know how great my life was because I didn't know there was anything special about it. There are probably nicer places to grow up than hot and humid and mosquito-infested Alvin, Texas, but for some reason I came back here and will likely die here. A lot of it has to do with the memories from my childhood that, like I say, got better as I traveled and found out what I had.

Every spring we used to build a baseball diamond in a vacant lot not far from where I lived. The neighborhood kids would get their lawn mowers and trim up an infield, lay out the bases, and build a backstop. In the summertime there was always a baseball game, and all we'd do is play ball. It was horribly hot and humid, but we didn't care until sometimes in the middle of the day when it was so hot you couldn't stand it out in the sun. Then we'd lie around in the shade until it cooled down a few degrees and we could get back at it.

That's one thing you hardly see anymore, kids playing ball basically from sunup until sundown. You know, even if you didn't have good mechanics or any coaching, playing hour after hour after hour in the sun for the enjoyment was also good for your game. You got used to the ball. Your brain recorded angles and bounces and hops and even sounds. There's something about hitting a hundred different times in a day-long game, about throwing and fielding and running. You've got to wonder if today's kid could play that much.

There was no air conditioning in our houses back then and there was sure nothing on television. Our mothers wanted us out of the house, and we were glad to get out. We had gloves and bats and baseballs and that field we'd made ourselves. We didn't need anything else.

When I first broke into big league baseball most of the guys were my age or older of course, so they had all played ball like that. You'd start as soon as you had enough guys, while it was cool and there might even be dew on the grass. By mid-morning everybody was there. You'd break for lunch and to get out of the sun for awhile, but pretty soon everybody would be back at it. We never quit on our own. It was almost like that was against the rules. One by one we'd hear our moms or dads holler. You couldn't pretend not to hear them for long. The last several at bats were dangerous because we tried to squeeze in just one more time before it was too dark to see the ball.

It wasn't unusual to play ball seven or eight hours every day. You learn an awful lot that way. And when you got old enough for Little League and had your eye on those uniforms and especially the caps—which we all wore proudly to school to show that we were part of a team—you still played all day and then went to practice at four in the afternoon.

We couldn't get enough baseball. Sometimes I still feel that way. Maybe that's why I'm still in the game at forty-five. Somebody's hollering my name and telling me it's time for supper or that it's too dark and I've been playing too long. But c'mon. There's time for one more pitch. Just one more. Please?

# 4

## From Little League
## to the Bigs

*T*he attraction of Little League for me was that it was the first opportunity I had to play organized team sports. It was a big deal to get a uniform and take pride in your team, win or lose, and know that adults even took an interest in the games. Kids didn't have all the t-shirts with sports logos on them you see everywhere today, and you didn't see kids walking around in big league replica uniforms. So Little League was the only place you could pretend to be a big leaguer and really look the part.

Now baseball wasn't just a pick-up game in a vacant lot anymore. We had real bases and chalk lines and batter's boxes, a pitching rubber and a plate, coaches, the whole thing. The best part about our Little League was that, because of everybody's schedule and the climate, they put up lights and we played all our games at night. All of us kids fantasized about making the All-Star team and going to Williamsport, Pennsylvania for the Little League World Series. Of course only a few teams in the whole country ever made it that far each year, but that was our dream. They didn't televise it in those days, but you read about it in the paper, and it was what everybody talked about.

I made the All-Star team, but I wasn't the best player and we didn't get far in the postseason tournaments. Still I have to say that those were some of the best days of my life. I loved the excitement and the drama of it. It was great to be part of something with your friends and to learn and have fun. There's something about baseball that reached a certain part of my nature. You could be yourself and you could be competitive, but everything was structured and measured and controlled. It was fair. We were all pretty much the same age, and when we walked out between those foul lines, everybody was playing by the same rules and within the same boundaries.

I couldn't get enough of it, and I'm still proving that. Some people would call me the Peter Pan of baseball, never wanting to grow up. I sometimes see a picture of myself on the mound, maybe tipping my cap, and see a face that belongs on a coach and a hairline that belongs on somebody long out of the game, and it even surprises me. When I'm out there doing what I do best, I know it will take me longer to recover physically and it means more and harder workouts to stay in shape. But when I check my defense, stare in for that sign, consider the situation, and make a decision on a pitch, I'm thinking of nothing but that moment. I might as well be twelve years old, big ol' floppy glove on one hand and a ball too big for my hand in the other. I keep my eyes on that target and go into my own unique windup, and when I let fly the pitch, my age doesn't mean a thing.

If I have to come charging in to cover the plate or get behind third to backup a throw or angle over and beat a runner to the bag and take a toss from the first baseman, I'm ready. My uniform shirt has said New York, California, Houston, and Texas. Mets, Angels, Astros, and Rangers. But when I'm in the middle of a game it might as well say Alvin All-Stars, and those form-fitting uniform pants might as well be the billowy flannels, tucked just so under the knees, that I wore as a kid.

Big league baseball is a business, a serious, tough, competitive, and even dangerous thing that can't be done lightly. But the professional who really loves the game never loses sight of the fun and the challenge and the joy of it. The travel gets old, the season gets long, and the body suffers. But once the game starts you never want it to end.

In Little League I wasn't the kid who dominated the league or anything like that. I pitched and played the infield, but there were a lot of other good players. Once I got into high school and people saw how hard I could throw a ball, I became better known. I always hit third or fourth in the lineup, and I hit .700 in the 1965 state tournament, but it was my pitching that set me apart. I was 20–4 as a senior and was All-State. Since I was also a basketball player, I won the Outstanding Athlete Award at Alvin High. What was even more important, though I didn't realize it at the time, I had been discovered by a big league scout.

At first I had no idea what that might mean. Anybody likes to be thought of as a major league prospect, but I was just trying to grow up. I thought maybe if I could make the pros somehow I might be able to afford college without being such a burden on my dad. Otherwise, I had been a pretty typical high school kid, trying to take shortcuts and get out of what my parents wanted me to do. I wanted to satisfy them, but I wanted to get my job done and get out of it as quickly as possible. I hardly ever got away with that. It always came back to haunt me.

In Texas back then, because kids worked on the farms and ranches, you could get your driver's license at age fourteen, which I did. Because we had that *Houston Post* distributorship, I was often out in the middle of the night driving around, and I had to learn to deal with the responsibility of that freedom.

A lot of my friends found it exciting to be able to go down and help me roll papers on the weekend and be able to run around town after midnight. We weren't above stealing hubcaps and doing other mischief like that, even though we knew better. We justified it by not trying to profit from it by reselling them or anything. Some of the guys put the fancy ones on their own cars because they couldn't afford them otherwise, but I never could have placed unexplained "new" hubcaps on my car without my dad's knowing. A few close calls just added to the excitement. Mostly we were bored country kids who got a rush by trying to get away with something.

We never got caught, and it's a good thing. I would have been punished severely. I'd have been spanked, yes, even at that age, and grounded a good long time. I'm so glad my dad never knew about the time my friends and I stole some donuts at 4:00 in the morning. I felt more fear of getting caught than guilt, which is normal for a kid I guess. I knew I'd get punished and have to apologize and make it right—which kept me from doing it again even after the fear wore off. That was the end of my life of crime.

By the time I got close to the end of my high school years, all I could think about was getting away from home. Thinking I knew everything and having no clue to what the world was really all about, I thought my parents held tight rein on me and wouldn't let me do a lot of things. It would only be later, when I was off on my own, that I would realize how much they meant to me and how thankful I was for what they did for me and the opportunities they gave me.

What they gave me was sure not material things. When school started each year we'd go to the store and I'd get two pairs of jeans, three or four shirts, and a pair of shoes. That was my wardrobe until Christmas, when I'd get a few more things. My mother would wash and iron my dirty jeans so I'd have a clean pair every day. I don't ever remember feeling deprived just because some of the other kids' dads owned car dealerships or big businesses and gave them cars and motor scooters and stuff.

I didn't feel the peer pressure kids do nowadays. When I take Wendy to school these days I'm amazed to see how kids are dressed. They have the latest styles and fashions, and I'm thinking, How do these people afford those clothes? Both parents work because they don't want their kids to feel deprived of anything.

My parents did the same thing, but not for the same reasons. With four girls and two boys, my dad and mother believed she couldn't afford to be away from home to work. That's why dad had two jobs. That's just the way things were done in those days. As long as the father could bring in enough income to make that work, that's how it was. It wound up basically killing my dad, but that was his commitment to his family.

My mother's job was thankless, but she found personal rewards in doing for her kids. I always tell our kids that if there's one person they should respect in this world, it's their mother, because she makes the biggest sacrifice of anybody. There's nothing more tender or selfless than a mother's love, and that's why I take my hat off to all of them. I feel sorry for single mothers that have to work to support their families. They are really under a burden. They are dedicated to doing what they have to do, and because there are so many of them in the work force, we have come to depend on them as part of the backbone of our country. I just hope their kids become healthy adults in spite of having only one parent, and that one working most of the day.

My parents came to as many of my ball games as they could when I was in high school. They were there the day in the spring of my senior year when we were playing Deer Park for the district championship to see who would go to the state playoffs. By then I was pretty well known for my fastball, but I was wild. It worked to my advantage that day. I hit the first kid up squarely in the helmet and split it. I hit the next guy in the arm and broke it. The third kid went and begged his coach not to make him hit. That coach assaulted him verbally in front of everybody and shamed him into standing in there.

I had them after that. If I didn't walk them, I struck them out because they were up there at the edge of the batter's box on their toes, ready to bail out. They were so far from the plate that the inside corner was outside to them. I had no strategy and no finesse. I just kept winging them in there, trying to get as close to the plate as possible. They'd forgotten about trying to win the district. They just wanted to go home without any more injuries.

I'd been scouted for quite a while, but believe it or not, I didn't give the majors much thought. I saw the Astros play in Houston a few times, and the big leaguers looked so strong and polished that I knew I wasn't anywhere near their class. I was tall and skinny and wild, and even though everybody always talked about how hard I threw, I had no idea I could make a career out of that. I might have been impressed if I had been picked high in the draft that summer, but 294 high school and college players were picked before I was taken in the tenth round. I'd had a bad game when Red Murff, a scout for the Mets, had brought his boss, Bing Devine, especially to watch me. Getting to the majors hadn't been that big a deal to me anyway, but I figured my chance was gone after that.

I had no idea that of all the hundreds of kids drafted out of high school every summer, only one in a hundred winds up making a living in the majors. All I knew was that they thought almost three hundred kids had a better chance than I did to start with. I didn't really understand the draft and all that went with it, but I was pretty sure I didn't have what it took to make it. The worst part was I really didn't know if I had the desire. I know that sounds crazy, and maybe it was just a way of protecting myself from disappointment, but you have to understand, I wasn't one of those kids with a dream, imagining myself in the pros. I was so far removed from the big leagues that I had no clue.

When the Mets finally came to try to sign me I honestly didn't know what I should do. I didn't want to waste my time in a profession where so many people were already considered better. I had been thinking about college for years and didn't know if I should do that, get a job, or try baseball. The Mets probably thought I was playing hard to get, but I was just thinking it through. Somehow, even at that age, I was determined to make a careful choice. By the third meeting the Mets were offering a $20,000 signing bonus and $500 a month. My dad wasn't making much more than that every month as a longtime employee of American Oil. And the bonus alone would set me up for college if things didn't work out in baseball. Dad felt like it was an offer I couldn't turn down. A lot has been made of the pressure put on me by other people, but my dad's opinion and my own were the only ones I really cared about. And that's why I signed with the Mets on June 26, 1965.

That summer, seventy players came through in waves to play at one time or another for the Mets' rookie league team in Marion, Virginia. I was one lonely eighteen-year-old. Everybody I knew and loved was left at home when I took my first plane ride to get to Marion. By the time I got there, they had already started their season, and I had to wait until they cut someone before they had a uniform for me. Problem was, the guy they cut was a little second baseman who'd had his pants shortened to fit him just right. Here I was, six-foot-two and skinny, walking around in pants way too short. It was all I could do to keep from showing bare leg between the bottoms of my pants and the tops of my socks.

I was so homesick, especially for Ruth, that the only thing that saved me was her dad's agreeing to bring her to visit me. That gave me something to look forward to. Maybe everybody else was looking forward to the big leagues, but I was only there because I had signed a contract, and I had only signed the contract because my dad recommended I sign it. The only real ambition I had was to see my girlfriend.

# 5

## Growing Up in the Majors

$S$eeing Ruth was the highlight of that summer for me, but I also struck out 115 hitters in 78 innings. The Mets saw something they liked in my fastball and had me come to the winter instructional league in Florida. Only the top twenty prospects in the organization were invited, so I knew something was happening.

At minor league spring training the next spring I met Tom Seaver for the first time. Now there was a guy who had a goal and was focused on it. I was just there trying to have fun and make a living with a gigantic fastball. He wanted to be an excellent, thinking pitcher. I was amazed just to hear him talk about it. I was thrilled for him when he made the Hall of Fame in 1992 by the biggest vote ever. He and I have been friends since those early days with the Mets.

Pitching in the instructional league and in spring training put me in contact with big league pitching coaches and more help and advice than I knew existed. I know it helped, but at first all it did was show me how much I didn't know. I had no idea there was so much to the game, let alone to pitching. I had a long, long way to go.

Whatever I learned paid off quick. While Tom Seaver was sent right into triple A, I was shipped to Greenville, South Carolina to play class A ball. Though I was just nineteen years old and still wild, the hitters in that league were overmatched by my speed, and I had the best statistical year of my career. I was 17–2, with nine complete games, five shutouts, and 272 strikeouts in 183 innings. I also walked 127 batters, but the night my parents and youngest sister and Ruth came to see me pitch against Gastonia, I was on. In a seven-inning game I got nineteen of the twenty-one outs on strikes.

Late in the year I was sent to Williamsport, Pennsylvania, for about ten days in AA ball. I had never made Williamsport as a Little Leaguer, but here I was passing through as a pro. I knew I still had a lot to learn as a pitcher, but my success in Greenville had made me feel better about myself. I wasn't so homesick, and I was maturing and learning to be a little more independent. Though I was 0–2 in Williamsport in three games, I struck out thirty-five in nineteen innings (walking twelve), and had an 0.95 ERA.

I was set to pitch four innings in my last start and then catch a plane to join the Mets in the big leagues. At the end of those four innings I had a no-hitter going and my manager, Bill Virdon, asked if I wanted to stay and go for it. I couldn't see how a no-hitter in the minors could compare with making the majors, so I told him I'd just as soon get going. He wished me the best. In just over a year I had pitched in three leagues and was heading to the majors before I was twenty years old.

I got into a couple of games with the Mets, started one, and got hit around pretty good. I found out it was no picnic pitching to the best hitters in the world. The next year I served in the military for six months, then injured my arm in the minors and wondered if I'd ever pitch again. In four games for two minor league teams I didn't do much of anything. But Ruth and I got married in June, which was more important than whatever happened to me in baseball.

In the winter instructional league my arm came back around and I did well in spring training. Tom Seaver had been Rookie of the Year in the National League for the Mets in 1967, and the press made a big deal about the other fastballing righthander in the organization: me. It was flattering to be compared to Bob Feller and Sandy Koufax, but it was also pressure. I wasn't really a pitcher. I was just a hard thrower. Whitey Herzog told somebody that he just knew I'd be brought along before I was ready because I had such a good arm. At twenty-one years of age I was a big leaguer, and though the next four years in New York were rocky and I'd lose more games than I won, I never looked back.

I was frustrated as a Met. Because of my military duty I kept missing opportunities to pitch, and the Mets didn't seem to care about making up for it. I was wild and getting wilder, had a lot to learn, and wasn't learning it. I needed to be on a team that needed me. The Mets had great pitching and would win that amazing 1969 World Series while I was there, but I was hardly part of it. I wanted out and let it be known. Ruth wasn't happy in New York either. After four years I knew I hadn't progressed much, and I didn't see much of a future in baseball if I stayed with the Mets. I had the feeling that my manager, Gil Hodges, didn't like me, but as I look back on it I was probably wrong. I was just thinking like a kid. His style and personality were such that he was quiet and stern and not much of a communicator, and anyway, I was not one of the mainstays of his staff.

It wasn't the Mets' fault. I was in the bullpen most of the time, but they didn't use me in relief much because of my lack of control. And I had control problems because I wasn't pitching often enough to be effective. So it was one of those no-win situations that was only going to be solved if I went where I was needed. The Mets were trying to win championships, and they couldn't afford the luxury of bringing along this kid with the big gun.

It didn't help my state of mind that my dad died during that time. He'd always been a heavy smoker, but he even smoked in the night because of that newspaper distributorship of his. I hardly ever remember him not smoking. Because of all the health problems cigarettes brought him, I never had the desire to smoke. Seeing what he went through and what a horrible way that is to die squelched any temptation to think there was anything good about smoking. Because of how young I was and how much my father meant to me, it was traumatic to watch him go through that and to lose him. Being the last of his six kids, I felt the loss in a bad way and it was a real hard period for me.

I'd been home to see him when we were in Houston to play the Astros. I visited him in the hospital for three days, and when I left I felt he'd deteriorated to where it wouldn't be long before he died. One of my sisters called me in New York a few nights later to tell me he'd passed away. I headed straight home.

It wasn't a surprise, but you're never really prepared for that. I kind of crawled into a shell and wanted to be left to my own thoughts. I was relieved that he was not suffering anymore, but other than his smoking I had respected his judgment and counted on it a lot. I enjoyed being around him because he was more than my father; I also considered him a friend.

I had Ruth and I had baseball, but a lot of times I felt like I should pick up the phone and call my dad about something before I remembered he was gone. There was a void in my life and I had to learn to deal with that. To this day I've never heard anybody speak poorly of him. He understood that the paper route was a service-oriented business, and he expected us to deliver those papers where people wanted them and when they wanted them. If anybody called and said that they didn't receive their paper or that their paper was wet, we had to take them one right then. He didn't take any shortcuts, and he darn sure didn't expect us to. I came to respect that constant attention to basic values.

The next year I got to pitch more, but I completed only three of twenty-six starts and wound up 10–14. I had 137 strikeouts in 152 innings, but I also walked 116. Everybody knew I had the ability, but I was still a long way from being a consistently effective pitcher. I could blow the ball past just about anybody, but nobody knew if I could really pitch.

When Ruth and I left New York at the end of the season, I told her I was sure we wouldn't be back. She was pregnant with our first child, and Reid was born that November, two weeks before the baseball winter meetings. That's when a lot of deals are made, and I told Ruth that if the Mets were going to trade me, it would happen then. We were thrilled with the new life in our home, and I was excited that I might be getting a whole new opportunity the next season.

When the Mets called and told me I was on my way to sunny California, I immediately thought of the Dodgers. I was a National Leaguer and had hoped to maybe go to the Astros so I'd be a half-hour away from Alvin. But I wasn't going to Houston or Los Angeles. I had been traded to the California Angels in Anaheim. I went there along with three other players for veteran Jim Fregosi, who was to be the answer to the Mets' third base problem. It hurt me to read that Gil Hodges approved the deal not only because he wanted Fregosi—which made sense—but also because he thought I was the starting pitcher he would miss the least.

I may not have been an effective big league pitcher yet, but I sure wanted to make him regret that trade—or at least that comment. Though I still had a lot to learn about pitching, I was a willing student and was eager to do my best for my new team in 1972, even if it was in the American League.

In those days a lot of us players had to work during the off-season to make ends meet. It's hard to believe now, in light of today's salaries, but I was raised from $24,000 a year with the Mets to $27,000 for the Angels. I began an eight-year career with California that was really something. I would be in double figures in wins and losses every year, having only two losing seasons. Five out of the next six years I would strike out more than three hundred hitters each season, leading the American League seven out of eight years.

In my first year alone I was 19–16 starting thirty-nine games and finishing twenty with an ERA of 2.28, nine shutouts, and 329 strikeouts in 284 innings. I had seventeen games in which I struck out ten or more hitters, including two fourteens, a fifteen, two sixteens, and a seventeen. On July 9, pitching against Boston, I struck out sixteen, including eight in a row for an American League record. The next season my salary would be doubled to $54,000. It seemed like a lot of money back then.

Something much more important happened in 1972 than that: I finally turned around and had one of my best years as a pitcher. I discovered the weight room at Anaheim Stadium. It hadn't been installed for the baseball players, because back then it was believed that weight training made you musclebound. It must have been there for a soccer team or something. Anyway I started slipping in there and working out, being careful not to overdo it and letting my body tell me how it was responding. In my own way I learned how to work different areas of my body for balance and flexibility, taking a day off now and then to recover.

I've since worked with a lot of strength and conditioning coaches, and Tom House (pitching coach for the Rangers) and I even wrote a book called *Nolan Ryan's Pitcher's Bible*. In it I talk about everything from mechanics to conditioning to diet. It's really everything I've learned in my own conditioning program and in working with such good coaches and trainers over the years.

Things have changed for me as I have gotten older. I've had to vary my workouts to make up for longer recovery times. And as I've worked through injuries or pain, I've worked around some muscles and concentrated on others. Thanks may be due to some genetics that have allowed me to age more slowly than most, but there's no secret to what it takes to stay in shape at this age. And that's hours and hours of workouts, usually every day.

If that sounds boring or not worth the effort, you feel the same way that most big leaguers feel. I can't swear to it, but it may be one of the reasons most of them leave the game in their thirties. I feel many effects of age. My back bothers me at times. I get stiffer quicker and need to loosen up and stretch longer. I can run only so much and so hard and so long. But I still put myself through the paces of a long, hard workout nearly every day, because it's worth it to me.

I enjoy feeling good and strong and hard, especially at my age. I can't guarantee that a pitcher's fastball will still be with him twenty-five years in the big leagues if he does my workout, but something's working for me. I have to work harder and smarter every year, but the key is deciding to keep with it. Sure it would be easier to skip it. But at my age I would probably get soft or fat and, for sure, I would be out of shape.

A lot of people are amazed to see me on an exercise bicycle immediately after a game while my arm is being iced. Do I need exercise after I've thrown a complete game? No. I need to get started on my preparation for the next start. I'm cleansing my muscles of lactic acid, getting an aerobic benefit that pitching can't give me, and staying on course with my training.

I can't run three days in a row like I used to because I get too sore or too stiff, but I still have to run two or three times a week. Nothing takes the place of running. During the off-season I get a lot of road work in, just logging the miles. During the season I do sprint work if I'm healthy and my Achilles tendon isn't bothering me.

On days when I work out for four or five hours, I try to break it up and not do it all at once. I get more out of it that way. I do it in two- to two-and-a-half-hour increments and feel like I'm making progress. The morning after a start I get into my weight room by nine or ten o'clock and start an hour and a half of weight lifting in a complete program for upper and lower body. The first day I'll do four and a half to five hours, then the next day maybe two and a half to three. The third day I'll repeat the first day's workout and throw three-quarter speed off the mound for twenty minutes, just working on mechanics. The day before a start I'll back off the work schedule and give my body a recovery day.

There's no doubt in my mind that if it hadn't been for that weight room, I would have been out of the game many years ago. Not only has it helped me prevent injury, but it's also kept me strong so I could continue to hold up over the long grind. I'm a firm believer that you're only as strong as your weakest link, so I'm careful not to do just upper body and leg work, but also abdominal training. I don't want to break down in any area.

The first three years after discovering that weight room, I pitched a thousand innings, but I always felt there was more I could do to stay strong. I didn't want to be like a lot of the guys I saw in the Met clubhouse the first time I walked in there. They were in their thirties, but some looked like old guys, paunchy and out of shape. Many of the pitchers were all fifteen to twenty pounds overweight and it affected their effectiveness. I decided that if there was any way to keep that from happening, I was going to do it. The universal gym I found in Anaheim was a trial-and-error tool that really paid off.

It may have been only coincidental, but the next two seasons would be the best of my career. If you look at my stats in the Appendix, you'll see that my records in 1973 and 1974 were almost identical. I pitched nearly the same number of games and innings, and most of my other numbers were close too. I was a power pitcher with a lot of wins, a record number of strikeouts, and an ERA of under three. In both seasons, the only times I did it in twenty-four full big league seasons, I pitched more than three hundred innings.

On May 15, 1973, I pitched my first no-hitter, shutting out Kansas City on the road, 3–0. Exactly two months later I pitched another no-hitter, beating Detroit 6–0 and striking out seventeen. I had struck out sixteen in the first seven innings and probably should have gotten the single game strikeout record, but we batted around in the top of the eighth and I stiffened while sitting on the bench.

Having pitched two no-hitters in two months and having such overpowering stuff made people wonder if I could pitch two no-hitters in a row. It had been done only once in big league history, in 1938 by Johnny Vander Meer. I thought I had a better shot at striking out twenty in a game than pulling off something like that. But I almost did it. In my next start against Baltimore I took a no-hitter into the eighth before Mark Belanger, a .200 hitter, blooped a single. Not only did I lose the no-hitter, but in extra innings I also lost the game, 3–1.

In 1973 I struck out ten or more hitters in a game twenty-three different times, breaking Sandy Koufax's record of twenty-one in 1965. Besides the seventeen-strikeout no-hitter, I struck out sixteen in the last game of the season to break Sandy Koufax's single season record of 382 by one K. I had become only the third pitcher in history to strike out three hundred hitters in two straight seasons.

All I had needed was a chance to pitch regularly. I could hardly wait for the 1974 season.

# 6
---
# Wearing Out
a Welcome

*R*uth and I came back to Alvin after each season, but we enjoyed our lives in California. It was fun to play for an owner like Gene Autry who was personable and friendly and loved the game. The Angels increased my salary to $100,000, which was big money in those days, and some people thought I was the best pitcher in baseball. At age twenty-seven, I felt like I was on top of the world.

The 1974 season was almost identical to the one before. In fact, I almost pitched two no-hitters again. I struck out ten or more hitters in a game thirteen times, three times striking out fifteen and three times nineteen. Only five pitchers in this century have struck out nineteen hitters in a game, and I'm the only one who's done it more than once. Three of my four times came in that one season.

In early August I took a no-hitter into the ninth inning in Chicago against the White Sox, but Dick Allen beat out an infield roller to break it up. In my last start of the year, September 28, 1974, I no-hit Minnesota, putting me one behind Sandy Koufax's career record of four no-hitters.

After the game my manager, Dick Williams, was interviewed, and he said something amazingly prophetic. "He's twenty-eight now," he said, which wouldn't be true until January. "If he wants to, conceivably he could pitch for seven more years." Well, that wasn't the prophetic part, because in 1992 I started my eighteenth season since then. But get what he says next. The announcer asked him, "So, more no-hitters?" And Williams said, "Every time he goes out I can see a potential no-hitter. I can see Nolan Ryan spinning three, four, or five more no-hitters, and that is unheard of in the history of professional baseball."

The announcer asked him, "So, do we put him up there with Walter Johnson and Cy Young?"

Dick said, "If he can conquer the habit of walking a man in a ball game, there's no telling how great a pitcher he can be."

That win was the twenty-second of the season for my highest total ever. I had no way of knowing it would be my last twenty-win season, and if you had told me I would still be pitching today and have more than three hundred wins, I'd have thought you were crazy.

I also remember the 1974 season for two other reasons: I recorded the fastest pitch ever scientifically timed, 100.9 miles per hour, and I accidentally hit a batter in the head with a fastball. Doug Griffin of Boston was knocked out, and I was afraid I had killed him. When I called his home to check on him later, his little girl told me her Mommy was at the hospital with her Daddy. That got to me, and it was quite a while before I felt confident pitching inside again. Griffin missed fifty-one games. I don't know what I would have done if he had been permanently injured.

In three seasons I had pitched over a thousand innings, struck out more than a thousand, and won sixty-two games. In 1975 I suffered several minor but nagging injuries and my production was down in almost every category, but I was still a power pitcher, striking out almost one hitter per inning.

Though I won six of my first seven decisions, I'd had two groin pulls and bone chips in my pitching elbow. The highlight came in my twelfth start, pitching a no-hitter against Baltimore at home, even with throbbing pain. I'm glad it was in Anaheim, because Ruth was there. She had never seen me pitch a no-hitter live. In a *Time* magazine article on me that week, Oriole manager Earl Weaver had been quoted, "Ryan could pitch a no-hitter every time he goes to the mound."

Besides my three no-hitters up to that point, ten times as an Angel alone I had not allowed a hit before the seventh inning. You never set out to throw no-hitters, but you sure start thinking about them late in the game. And when one slips away you rehash every pitch, thinking about the might-have-beens. I've had nineteen games in my career where I allowed one hit or less, and when I think how close I came to no-hitters in all those one-hitters, it makes me wonder where the no-hit record might be but for one pitch or one bad break.

Anyway, in that June 1, 1975 game against the Orioles, I struck out Bobby Grich on a changeup to end the game and tie Sandy Koufax's career no-hitters record. So much was made about the record that most people lost sight of the progress I'd made, not as a fireballer but as a thinking pitcher. My temptation a few seasons before would have been to challenge Grich with my best fastball. But of course that was what he and everybody else in the ballpark was expecting. Maybe I would have gotten him, maybe I wouldn't have. But if I get that changeup over the plate, he doesn't have a chance. He told the press later that I had fooled him good. So much for being a one-pitch pitcher.

A huge crowd turned out for my next start, hoping for back-to-back no-hitters and a record-breaking career fifth. I took a no-hitter into the sixth with two outs before Hank Aaron broke it up with a single. I still won a two-hit shutout, giving me five shutouts with a record of 10–3. Then the bone chips in the elbow caught up with me and my season fell apart. By the time I finally agreed to have the chips surgically removed in August, I had pitched less than two hundred innings and my record was 14–12. At one point I lost eight straight games. I had gone from being a dominating power pitcher to one the hitters couldn't wait to face.

I was amazed at how quickly the writers started speculating on what was wrong. I was accused of everything from laziness to giving up. Instead of defending myself I quit talking to the press, and that only made them come after me harder. By now I was in the middle of a two-year deal at $125,000 a year, and people expected nothing less than perfection. That's all I wanted too, but when your body's not cooperating, there's not much you can do.

Reese's birth in January 1976 was the highlight of that off-season. My arm felt good, after having been immobilized through the end of the season, so I hoped to come back strong. I wound up leading the league in shutouts and struck out 327 hitters in 284 innings. I pitched four three-hitters in the second half of the season.

Our daughter Wendy was born the following spring (1977), and I celebrated by signing a three-year deal with the Angels (at $300,000 a year). I then had a year similar to '73 and '74. I won nineteen, led the American League in strikeouts for the fifth time in six years, and was named American League Pitcher of the Year by the *Sporting News*.

The following season, 1978, was disappointing for me. I turned thirty-one and felt the effects of my body adjusting to getting older. I missed several starts and wound up 10–13, my worst year since my last one with the Mets. Still, I led the American League in strikeouts and pitched three shutouts and fourteen complete games. No one knew that I wasn't even halfway through my career yet, because already I was one of the old men in baseball and the ranking veteran on the Angels. No one else was still around from the 1972 team. In seven years I had pitched forty-one games in which I had allowed three hits or less, and I was already eighth on the all-time list for career strikeouts.

Just before my thirty-second birthday I let Angels general manager Buzzie Bavasi know that I wanted a contract extension. I asked for a three-year deal at $400,000 a year, plus $200,000 for signing—a total of $1.4 million for three years. I heard back that he would not discuss my request till the end of the '79 season.

That would be another good season for me. I was 16–14 with seventeen complete games, five shutouts, and an average of a strikeout an inning for 223 innings to lead the league again. I also took the Yankees into the ninth inning on no hits before Reggie Jackson singled on July 13. He ruined my chance to break Koufax's no-hit record, but there would be more opportunities.

It was amazing that I could concentrate on pitching at all that season. Early in the year Reid, then seven, had been hit by a car and suffered severe internal injuries, including losing a kidney and his spleen. With two younger children at home, Ruth needed me. I went on road trips only the day before I was scheduled to pitch. It was a disrupted time when the things that really matter come into focus. That was one long season, much of the summer spent in the hospital with Reid.

I sensed that my time with the Angels was coming to an end. I had felt like Bavasi didn't care as much for me as Gene Autry did, but I sure wasn't going to run to the owner about my problems with management. I had always done my own negotiating, but now I hired Dick Moss, who had been legal counsel for the players' association, because I knew I might be getting into free agency if the Angels didn't get serious about re-signing me. I didn't want to disrupt my family and my life by moving on, but it seemed to me the Angels were dragging their feet. At one point during the season, Bavasi asked Moss what it would take to sign me. Dick told him $500,000 a year for two years and $700,000 for a third year. Later Buzzie was quoted as saying that I had demanded a million dollars a year and that all he would have had to do to replace me was to pick up two pitchers with 7–6 records.

That really hurt. I thought I deserved more than comments like that. I had given everything I had to the organization, and I felt good about my relationship with the fans. The only person I was upset with was Buzzie. Some people think everything can be forgiven with a big pile of money, but I couldn't imagine the Angels coming up with any amount that would have made up for his making me feel so unwelcome. At the end of the season we sold our house and moved back to Alvin. It had been a long, hard, bitter year with a lot of hurtful things said, and it felt good for Ruth and me and the kids to be back home.

I was hoping to find a team willing to pay me around $600,000–$650,000 a year, but Dick Moss thought I could get more. When more than twelve teams drafted me I thought he might be right. Yankees owner George Steinbrenner contacted Dick about my signing with the Yankees. Dick said that it would take a million a year, and George said that that would not be a problem. But I didn't even want to consider moving back to New York. Still, we had that offer to fall back on.

At one point I was called by an old friend from the Angels who wanted to know what it would take to get me to stay. I basically told him it would take Buzzie Bavasi's leaving. I didn't want to play for the man or be associated with him. In all fairness I have to say that later Buzzie admitted that letting me go was a big mistake.

When I found out that Houston had drafted me and wanted to talk to Dick about signing me, I told him to try hard to get it done. What could be better than playing for a team a half-hour away? I didn't want to get into a bidding war, as fun and exciting and ego-inflating as that might have been. Who knows what the numbers might have gotten up to? Dick told the Astros that if they could match the Yankees' offer, he was sure I would play for them. They did and I did. At a million a year for three years, I figured I would have financial security and be ready to settle in and finish out my career at home.

# 7

## Astro-nomical Problems

*I* moved into a new decade with a new team, the one I had dreamed of playing for since I was a kid. Now my friends and relatives could see me pitch in person if they wanted to.

The Astros had been bought by a man named John McMullen in 1979, and when he made me the highest paid player in team sports up to that point, he bought himself some trouble. Many executives in the game criticized McMullen for reaching the million-dollar plateau. McMullen wasn't stingy, I'll give him that. He paid a lot for several players. Nowadays a million dollars a year doesn't sound like much, when you think of the guys making five times that and more. But you can imagine the heat I took for being the first to break the million-dollar barrier.

Even in Alvin people were concerned about it. They'd been awful proud of their local boy going off and becoming a big league pitching star. They were thrilled when I came back home and would be pitching just up the road. But a million dollars? For throwing a baseball? Something wasn't right. How could anybody be worth that? You've heard all the arguments, how little we pay teachers and how little we pay the president of the United States, how anybody making that kind of money will lose his incentive and won't ever work hard again.

The biggest problem for me was that people expected a guy being paid like that to be a better pitcher than he was. I had always done the best I could and felt I worked as hard as anybody in the game. I took care of my body, lived a clean life, had good habits, and worked out constantly. I didn't let myself go over the winter and then have to overdo it to get in shape during spring training. I did my part, pitched my innings, and stayed out of trouble. I was a strikeout pitcher, a low-hit pitcher, a workhorse with a lot of innings. I was a dependable starter who was a threat to throw a no-hitter. I was an all-star-caliber player, and I could usually win you a bunch of games a year. But if people thought that now that I was making a million dollars I ought to all of a sudden be perfect and unbeatable and win twenty-five games a year, I had a problem.

I felt conspicuous in Alvin where everybody seemed ill at ease around me. I guess they kept expecting me to splurge and buy a yacht or a mansion or a foreign sports car. It took a long time for them to see that my income was a private matter with me. The only reason I ever talked about it was because it was plastered all over the newspapers and people asked me about it. I was embarrassed over it, but I wasn't about to turn it down, and I doubt anybody I knew would have either.

I wanted to get the season started and see other players pass me up in salary. I knew that in a few years that million dollars would not loom so large, but it was hard to convince anybody of that back then. The people in Alvin would soon realize that I was still Nolan Ryan, local guy. The money wouldn't change me. The people in Houston who expected me to be a better pitcher than I was, well, I didn't know what to do about that. All I could say was that they should look at my record, see that I'd been averaging fifteen wins the last five years, despite lots of injuries and playing for a team that was not usually a big offensive threat. I didn't want to blame my record on anybody or put down my teammates; I just wanted people to be realistic about their expectations. I mean, when did it become a terrible thing for a guy to pitch more than two hundred innings in a season and win in double figures? That's what I felt capable of doing, and if John McMullen thought that was worth $3 million over three years, that's what I had to offer.

I know part of the money had to do with the market. He knew other teams were prepared to come to the table with offers like that and maybe more. But they all knew what they'd be getting too. Most pitchers in my category, fastballers with lots of innings behind them, were looking at the twilights of their careers at my age. I'm sure the Astros thought it would be great if I could go out with three decent years and maybe one or two more if I was healthy. That's even the way I was thinking.

I tried to stay quiet about the money because of how uncomfortable it seemed to make everybody, but down deep I was overwhelmed myself with how much I was making. From one season to the next I more than tripled my salary. I wanted to buy a ranch and acquire a few things I'd always dreamed of having, but none of it was going to be showy. That wouldn't have looked good and it wasn't me anyway. I didn't want to be any less frugal with a million dollars than I had been with $7,000 when I joined the Mets as a teenager.

My new tax bracket was 50 percent, so I started looking hard at how I could protect myself from handing that much over to the government. I was very conservative and felt like I had a reasonable investment game plan until we had a player strike in 1981. Then I would be in trouble.

Meanwhile there were some immediate benefits to coming to the Astros, besides the money. Dr. A. Eugene Coleman, a professor of human performance at the University of Houston, was the Astros' instructor of strength and conditioning. He had done a lot of research and worked with NASA's astronauts. I have to say that meeting up with him was a turning point in my career. Up to then I had been pretty much self-taught and self-motivated. I had done okay, but now here was a man who really knew what he was talking about. He was like an oasis in the desert. The Astros had more sophisticated Nautilus machines and plenty of them, and Gene walked me through how to use them for my entire body. He showed me what part of my workout was a waste of time and what I could add to enhance my routine. I was off and running, and some would say I have been obsessed with conditioning ever since. I was really into it before, but now with the confidence that everything I was doing had a purpose and would show a benefit, I immersed myself in it.

It took me a while to get used to the National League. The strike zone was different, and back spasms didn't help my conditioning. I got a rocky start and wound up 11–10, but we won the National League West in a one-game playoff over the Dodgers. They had swept us in the final three-game series to tie. We wound up losing in the playoffs to Philadelphia. Despite my mediocre start, I did pitch 234 innings, strike out 200, and pitch a couple of shutouts.

I started out much better in 1981, but that was the year of the players' strike that lasted fifty-two days. It was a depressing, frustrating time that nearly turned the fans off to the game. The league and the players had lost something like $100 million. I might as well have. If a person with my kind of income can have a cash-flow problem, I had one. I listened to some advisers about getting into some very speculative tax shelters. I was uncomfortable with them from the day I bought in until the day I paid heavily to get out.

What had happened was that I had made a large land purchase and—not anticipating being on strike for six weeks—planned to pay my taxes at the end of the year. Those six strike weeks meant no income out of what was normally a six-month pay-out period, so a huge chunk of income was gone. At the end of the year I didn't have the cash to cover my tax obligation, so instead of just going down to the bank and borrowing the money to pay the taxes and then paying off the note the next year, I listened to people who thought I could get out of the taxes through sheltered investments.

Some were oil investments. Some were cargo containers for ships. One was a thoroughbred breeding program. They solved my tax problem temporarily, and when the investments matured I was supposed to have enough cash to do everything I needed to do.

The oil investments soured when they struck only gas.

The cargo deal was eventually disallowed by the IRS.

And the horse market fell to where my thoroughbreds were worth forty cents on the dollar.

It was a good thing I knew how to pitch and was still healthy. I had nothing to show for the investments and still had the tax obligation. It was a tough pill, but I was fortunate to be able to play long enough to overcome those mistakes. A lot of baseball players who got into that situation were soon out of baseball and wound up having to declare bankruptcy.

I was never keen on investments just for their tax consequences. An investment should stand on its own two feet (or four in the case of the horses), and if it didn't make sense from an investment standpoint without the tax angle, I never should have made the moves. I have since paid off my land purchases and our home, and now I have assets free and clear that are important to me regardless of their value in a fluctuating economy. We enjoy what we have, and we can keep it in the family. But that was a hard lesson.

Now as a banker I hate the bankruptcy laws even more than I used to. All they provide is a giant loophole allowing people to run up a lot of debt and then throw up their hands and say, "Time out. King's X. I'm sorry, but I can't pay you and the law's going to protect me." That's not right. It's not fair to the creditors. The laws today are so slanted toward thieves that honest people aren't protected. They're designed to reward failure. It's like we want to do everything for the people that aren't successful. We pity them, but they brought it on themselves.

It's just like the savings and loan fiasco. I'm not sure most taxpayers understand that we're having to pay to let the same people who were the stewards of the S&Ls steal and run rampant. I mean, no one's even being prosecuted or forced to return money in any substantial amount. And then the Resolution Trust Corporation, which took all the properties that were foreclosed, began discounting them all and trying to move them, but there's something crazy going on. They're letting the same people who were in the S&L business come back and buy the loans they originally made on these properties and go out and resell them to other investors. They may double the loan and double their money. The whole thing is complex, and it's run by bureaucrats and is a total mess.

Some say we're not in a recession, but I don't believe that. I go out and talk to people about their businesses and try to stay in touch with the working person through my banks. I don't want to be just a figurehead banker. The people I work with are people I grew up with, and we care about the economy and the people it affects in our area. People who take advantage of all the loopholes are not honest. I look at it from a moral viewpoint. I don't care how much money there is to make, if it's not morally right, I'm not going to do it.

A lot of people say, "Hey, that's just business, and business is business." I've had people say that to me. That's one of the problems with our country. Our moral attitude has deteriorated to the point that it is affecting everything. People say that there are no absolutes and that everything's relative. I say it's wrong; they say it's business. That's a shaky foundation for the future.

Well, back to baseball. The Dodgers had been leading our division before the strike, and it was decided that a new shortened season would begin right after the strike and the winners of the two halves would play for the pennants. That gave us new life, and we went after that second half in a big way.

On Saturday, September 26, 1981, I pitched against the Dodgers in Houston in a big game against their superstar rookie Fernando Valenzuela. We were fighting it out for first place in the second half, so the game was televised nationally. Ruth, my mother, and a lot of our friends were there. I started a little slow, walking three batters in the first three innings, but not giving up any hits. Twice during that season I had lost no-hitters in the seventh, and I was starting to think I no longer had the stamina to get that fifth no-hitter. I hadn't had one since I was twenty-eight years old, and now I was thirty-four. People may think that once you've pitched four, it's only a matter of time before another one comes along. Only thing is, they don't just come along. Everything has to be right. You have to be on. You have to get some breaks. There are usually a couple of key defensive plays. And there's always a little luck too.

What I began to notice, especially in long, tough games, was how difficult those last three innings were. It wasn't about just hanging on. To stay on top of hitters who've had a couple or three plate appearances to study you, you have to have some extra pop, something special. You have to get stronger as the game goes on, and that goes against logic.

Against the Dodgers I went into the ninth inning with a 5–0 lead and had retired sixteen hitters in a row. I added Reggie Smith, Ken Landreaux, and Dusty Baker in the ninth, and I had set the career no-hit record. I was glad my teammates were so excited about it. They carried me off the field and really seemed thrilled to have been part of history. One of the first phone calls I took after the game was from

Gene Autry. I always appreciated that he had no hard feelings for my leaving California. We remained friends and he was always gracious about my achievements.

Best of all, we were still in the pennant race. We wanted another shot at the Dodgers to see if we could get into the playoffs and the World Series.

# 8

## No Longer at Home in the Dome

We wound up winning the second half of the strike-shortened 1981 season and facing the Dodgers in a five-game playoff for the Western Division championship. I was the winning pitcher, 3–1, in the first game, again against Fernando, and we won the second too. But we were snake bit by the Dodgers. I guess we couldn't forget that they had won three straight at the end of the 1980 season to force us into that one-game playoff, and somehow we let them do that again. Only this time, it was three straight losses and we were out. We had come so close.

What a season that had been. There was a lot of dissension and uncertainty because of the strike, and worst of all it seemed we had offended the people who made the game possible—the fans. Some of us wondered if they would ever support us like they used to. But people are forgiving, even when they don't understand you. The truth is, they love the game more than any individual player.

I had had a good season, short as it was. I led the National League in earned run average with a 1.69, and I had gone 11–5. The next year, 1982, even though the Astros were out of the pennant race early, I went 16–12, started thirty-five games, completed ten, had three shutouts, pitched a one-hitter and a two-hitter, and struck out 245 in 250 innings. I wound up the year fifteen short of Walter Johnson's career strikeout record.

Because of minor injuries and illness, I pitched only eighteen innings in spring training in 1983 and didn't break Johnson's record until my fourth start of the year, in Montreal. For some reason that record meant as much to me as my five no-hitters. I had accomplished it in twenty-five hundred fewer innings than Johnson. I had no idea if I would keep the record, because two or three others were within striking distance (pardon the pun). Of course by now I've outlasted them all and most people think I've put the record far out of reach at more than five thousand.

Something that really disappointed me was that our owner, Mr. McMullen, was neither at the game nor called to congratulate me. By the time I got to that game, I only needed five strikeouts. The record came in the eighth inning, and I got a huge ovation from the crowd, but neither my owner nor the commissioner of baseball was there, and I never did hear from McMullen. I even heard from Gene Autry, but not from my own team's owner. The press sure made a big deal out of the record, but I never did figure out why it didn't seem that important to the man who was paying me all that money to do just what I had done.

I had been in Houston for three seasons, and that was long enough to see that things weren't quite right. I sure couldn't complain about my salary, but most people realize that big leaguers would play ball for nothing if they had to. They need to be treated with respect and dignity, and it's the little things that count the most. I'm sure it sounds petty and maybe amazing when you hear that multimillion-dollar athletes complain about not enough soap in the shower room or not enough food on the snack table. Maybe we get upset about our wives not getting invited on certain trips or that some other little thing has gone wrong. But those things are signals to players of whether they're appreciated as people. Sure, the money is great, but we all know the owners hate to pay the way they do and that that's all part of the business. The little personal things make a man feel as if someone cares about him. They cost so little and mean so much that you wonder why someone doesn't pay attention to them.

I won't apologize for how much of myself I gave to Houston during my nine years there. I worked hard and produced, and I was willing to give whatever it took to be as effective as possible. But it didn't seem to me the ball club was promoted the right way to the community. The owner didn't do what he really needed to do to make people feel welcome at the ballpark, to get all the employees happy and cheerful and greeting the paying customers. Basically I guess he was not a happy man, and that filtered down through the organization. It seemed he resented one of the limited partners, a man named Don Sanders, who was a local guy and very popular with us players. Don spent a lot of time in the clubhouse and had us over to his place, and I think John McMullen was jealous of his popularity. Don was a baseball fan and brought his kids around. He was one of the big sponsors of my golf tournament, and we became friends and often went out together. He even came on some road trips. Eventually McMullen barred outsiders from the clubhouse, including, if you can believe this, Sanders and the other limited partners. I think McMullen envied Sanders' friendships with the players, but John couldn't become friends with us when we only saw him two or three times a year. He was an absentee owner and still is, as far as I know.

McMullen didn't promote me the way he might have either, and I don't say that because I wanted the ego strokes of being played up as a star. We had plenty of stars. But when a guy is setting records or achieving outstanding numbers, it seems you'd just naturally start publicizing that to build interest so that more people would come out the next time the guy pitches. That's just good business.

But I didn't jump when McMullen said jump. I never attended his golf outings after the season, mostly because of time pressures and because, even though I host my own tournament for charity every year, I'm not really an avid golfer. John's deal was up at Pine Valley and involved four or five days in October. That's not my idea of a good time or the right use of family time. I'm sure he saw my absence as an independent attitude. He never told me that, but it filtered down.

Another thing I could never figure out about McMullen was that after Enos Cabell was traded away from Houston, John started talking about him as if he and John had been close friends. I knew Enos was about as opposite from John as a guy could be, and I felt that Enos used John's friendship to benefit Enos. John had gone to the Naval Academy, was educated in Europe, earned a doctorate, retired from the Navy, and owned a ship-building business. Enos was from Los Angeles and had a drug problem when he was in Pittsburgh, but somehow he and John had become buddies?

McMullen even told me that after Enos was traded to the Dodgers he would invite John out for dinner when he came to town. "None of you guys ever did that," he said. I didn't know a player was supposed to call the owner and invite him out to eat. I'm sure he felt I didn't appreciate him bringing me to Houston, but I did. I'd be crazy not to be glad about getting back home and making that kind of money. But maybe he took as much heat as I did over the size of the deal and eventually regretted it, I don't know.

I was my own person, and I had to decide if something was worthwhile or not. I felt like his attitude was that we were employees, he owned us and expected us to exhibit the attitudes and traits of employees. I'm a loyal person to the organization, but I also felt there was another principle involved. There's a limit to a man's obligation. I was paid to win ball games, and I didn't shirk at all when it came to things that contributed to that.

I know I have to be loyal and make a commitment because I'm accepting a salary. I always want to give an honest and fair effort, but it's also important that the ball club take that same attitude toward the players. Do they respect us and appreciate us, or are we supposed to act like servants? A lot of times ballplayers don't hold up their end of the obligation. They don't consistently work out or stay in shape or take care of themselves with proper diet and rest and conditioning. But a lot of times the ball clubs take an approach that's detrimental too, even to those of us who do give our all to the team.

When it feels like it's front office against the clubhouse and clubhouse against the front office, there's always friction. And those clubs don't win. The only time I ever saw a team win in spite of disagreements between the players and the owner was in the early '70s when the Oakland A's won three

World Series in a row, even though it seemed they couldn't stand Charlie Finley, their owner. Those guys didn't seem to care for each other either, but they sure put all that behind them when they went onto the field.

The Astros were going south. We fell in the standings, and our attendance dropped off. The team had mediocre years and sometimes drew crowds that rattled around in that big dome. We had a couple of games where we drew less than four thousand. That's demoralizing, and it's ridiculous. You can't tell me there isn't a way to drum up more interest than that, even in a team that's going badly. Look what the Mets did when they started out. That was one bad team, but they were beloved and drew huge crowds. And look how the Cubs have done over the years. They've had some good teams in the last couple of decades, but they haven't won a pennant in nearly fifty years, yet they keep drawing the fans. They're doing something right in their community, and they know how to promote.

In 1985, just before the All-Star break, I was closing in on four thousand strikeouts. You would think a team would know how to build support for something like that. I was nearly five hundred past the old record and would be the first in history to reach four thousand, but the Astros didn't even have a team photographer in the dome that night. Danny Heep of the Mets, a former teammate on the Astros, became my four thousandth K, and the only picture taken of it was by a friend of some of the players. He sold many a copy of that picture.

At the All-Star game Pete Rose and I were chosen to throw out the first pitches because he had reached four thousand hits and I had reached four thousand strikeouts. That was a real honor, but I have to say it felt strange to be recognized nationally by baseball itself when in Houston the event sort of came and went unnoticed. It wasn't like the record was something that crept up on the team. Everybody else seemed to know it was on the horizon.

Experts predicted the struggling Astros would lose a hundred games in 1986, but they didn't know Mike Scott would win the Cy Young Award for us. They didn't know power-hitting first baseman Glenn Davis would have an All-Star year and hit thirty-one homers. They didn't know Kevin Bass would be outstanding at the plate. And they sure didn't expect an aging pitcher like me to return to form, go 12–8, start thirty games, and strike out 194 in 178 innings. We won the division going away but lost a heartbreaking championship series to the hated Mets. I had been on the disabled list twice, but I came back strong both times.

I was not happy with our new general manager, Dick Wagner, who once put me on the DL without even consulting me. I was in my twentieth big league season and was closing in on my fortieth birthday, and he thought he knew what was best for me. Even though I was 5–1 in my last ten starts with a 2.31 ERA, winning my last four decisions to reach 253 career wins (sixth among active pitchers at the time), I was in for a shock in 1987.

I started the season without pain and threw about 135 pitches per game for a couple of games. Then I got the news that Wagner had told my manager, Hal Lanier, that I was to come out of a game after 115 pitches, no questions asked. I was mad and fought the decision, but nothing changed. It didn't make any difference that I was no longer pitching with pain, and it wouldn't have made any difference if I had had a no-hitter going, I guess. Once I pitched my limit, I was gone. I lost a lot of decisions when the club lost the lead. Ironically, my strikeouts were up, my walks were down, and I had Cy Young-type statistics except for my horrible won-lost record. The limit was expanded to 125 pitches late in the season, but I wound up 8–16. I had led the league in ERA (2.76) and strikeouts (270).

It was almost funny to be under a pitch limit and still lead the league in K's for the first time in eight years and ring up my highest total in ten seasons. I had walked only eighty-seven hitters and suddenly I was known as a control pitcher. Maybe Dick Wagner would like to take credit for extending my career, but somehow I think I could have completed a lot of games without hurting myself. I mean, I was a forty-year-old strikeout king with a fastball that could still get into the high nineties. I had broken a big league record by averaging 11.48 strikeouts per nine innings.

I was still making the same money I had signed for going into the 1980 season, and that was fine with me. Many players had passed me up salarywise, but I felt there were a lot of benefits to pitching close to home and seeing my family grow up. Maybe I was worth twice as much or more on the free-agent market, but it wouldn't have been worth it to me to uproot. I knew I had to kiss the hope of another no-hitter good-bye because of that crazy pitch limit, but I figured another no-hitter at my age was an impossible dream anyway. It had been six years between numbers four and five, and I was about to go into my seventh season since *then.* It was miraculous enough that I could still throw hard.

Dick Wagner was fired after the season, to be replaced as general manager by Bill Wood. I knew there would be little change in how the club was run because McMullen was still the owner. There were a lot of advantages to playing in Houston. My million-dollar-a-year contract had been renewed every season, and I looked forward to 1988 as maybe my last year in baseball. It wasn't, but it would be my last in Houston.

# 9

## Moving On

*I*n 1988 I got out from under the pitch limit and led the National League in strikeouts. I also pitched two complete games in a row without a walk, the first time I had ever done that. I only allowed four earned runs over my last forty-one innings and felt as strong as I had in years. Early in the season, April 27, I took Philadelphia into the ninth with a no-hitter before Mike Schmidt broke it up with a one-out single. It was the third straight time I had a ninth inning no-hitter broken up with one out.

Frankly I couldn't believe I had flirted with a no-hitter for that long. I'd gone a lot of innings without allowing hits before, but to go into the ninth again was like going back in time. That was the first time I had gone into the ninth with a no-hitter since my fifth in September 1981.

I also finished 1988 with 4,775 strikeouts, so unless I had a serious injury I had a decent shot at hitting five thousand in 1989. All I needed to do was to get close to 1988's K production. I would have thought that alone would have been enough reason for the Astros to want to keep me happy and keep me around. But my contract had expired and I waited to see what they wanted to do about extending it. I would have been perfectly content to go another year at slightly more than a million dollars. Again, no raise for nine years was not an issue with me because of the benefits that outweighed everything else.

I had never been a free agent or taken a hard stand because it was so convenient for me to be able to maintain one household the whole year round. Now I was at a point where I figured I had one more season in me, and I assumed that was what the Astros thought too.

It had been a long time since I had been the highest paid player in the game, but I didn't get wrapped up in those kinds of numbers. My situation was unique, but there were storm clouds. I still wasn't jumping when McMullen said jump, and I sensed the attitude of management toward the players had gotten worse.

It seemed like the club didn't want kids around. For several years, when Al Rosen was the GM, the players' kids had a lot of freedom, but now they were not allowed in the clubhouse before or after the game. They weren't ever allowed on the field, and most of them had gotten to the age where they didn't want to go to the Astrodome and sit around in the stands waiting for the game to start. There were few benefits to being a player's kid anymore. There had never been favoritism to my kids versus anybody else's. They were all in it together and everybody suffered. I always said it was kinda like prison. We were allowed family visits for an hour on Sundays and that was it. I don't care how much you're paying a ballplayer, when you treat him and his family like that, you're sending a loud message.

My kids didn't even want to come around on Sundays because they felt they weren't wanted, and they were right. The rest of the staff at the Astrodome felt the same way. You could tell that people just weren't having any fun at their jobs, and that always shows. Everybody from the ushers to the concessions people to the front office staff seemed to be looking over their shoulders, trying to stay out of trouble. That's no way to build a family or have team spirit.

A few days after the end of the season Bill Wood asked me to come in and talk about my contract for the next year. They didn't have an option, so I had wondered what was going to happen. I told my agent, Dick Moss, that I would just go in alone and see what was up. Dick and I talked about what I should try to accomplish and my attitude was I would see what the club position was and bring him in when it got down to details.

"Nolan," Bill said in his office, "we want to offer you a contract for '89, and we'd like you to consider taking a 20 percent cut from your present level." I stared at him, expressionless and speechless. He couldn't be serious. "You've had a remarkable career and accomplished a lot, but at 12–11 and with your performance not quite what it's been, well, we can maybe put in a few incentives so that if you return to form you can make about what you're making now."

"Bill," I said, "I finished strong and everybody knows it. There's no doubt I can still pitch effectively. I've always been honest and fair with this club, and if I get into a position where I don't think I'm worth what I'm making, I'll let you know."

I could tell from the look on Bill's face that *he* was letting *me* know. I quickly realized what was going on. I had been so grateful for the situation for the last several years and had said how pleased I was that I had such a good setup, that they thought I would never leave. Here's a middle-aged man finishing out a lucrative career, pitching virtually in his own backyard, so he'll take a cut in pay without a word. What they hadn't thought of was that I wasn't just hanging on. I was pitching as well as I ever had. I may have lost a couple of miles an hour off my fastball, but Gene Coleman had told me himself that only 7 percent of the pitchers in the big leagues could throw a ball ninety miles an hour. I was still throwing a lot harder than that.

If I had felt like my body was falling apart and that I would be lucky to last another season, I wouldn't have stayed just to milk another year out of them. That would have been dishonest and unfair. I would have retired and not taken their money under false pretenses. To think I would agree to a cut was an insult. The more I sat there, the worse I felt. Here was an organization, crying about keeping costs down and insulting their players to do it. They figured if they could get me to take a cut that would take the wind out of the sails of anyone else who came in with demands. I hadn't even made a demand. I figured they'd offer me the same deal I'd had, and I would have been inclined to take it.

I tried to stress to Bill that the Angels had made the same mistake. Buzzie Bavasi thought I would stay because of my friendship with Gene Autry, but there comes a time when a man can't be party to someone else's trying to prove a point. If the Astros were trying to keep salaries down by starting with me, well, that only fit in with all the other ways they were treating employees. I could see the direction things were going, and I knew nothing was going to get better. The club had developed a petty, negative attitude about everything. Maybe a $200,000 cut in pay shouldn't be considered petty, but it was indicative of their attitude about everything. Insulting one of your starting pitchers is no way to go about making yourself a contender and a winner.

I knew it wasn't Bill Wood's fault. It was McMullen's move, and Bill was only doing what he was told. Still I told Bill, "I won't accept that. There's no way I could agree. You know I'm going to have to test the market and see what's out there." Leaving Bill's office that day, I knew that Houston was no longer the type of an organization I wanted to be associated with. I'm sure he and even McMullen were thinking, *Sure, go ahead and go through the motions of free agency. Play the game and see what happens.*

Baseball had a system then where all the clubs could call in and find out what the current offers were to free agents, so there would be no secrets. The Astros had to be thinking there wouldn't be much interest in what they thought was an overpriced, overage pitcher. I was convinced they were certain I'd be back to accept their deal. If nothing else had materialized, I really don't know what I would have done. I like to think I'd have had too much pride to take a cut at that stage of my career. It came down to principle. What would that have said about my self-image, especially after I had stayed at the same salary for almost a decade?

I had come to Houston to finish my career. I had even had an interest in staying involved with the organization after my career was over. Now I could see it all sliding away. Nobody takes a 20 percent cut. Who was the last guy you ever heard of who stood still for that? It was absurd, but the Astros took that position and sat on it for quite a while.

I called Dick Moss at his office in Los Angeles and told him what Wood had said. He was more incensed than I was. I have a tendency to low-key those kinds of things. My attitude was that now that we knew where they stood, we could go about our business. Dick was insulted for me and quickly prepared to file for free agency. "You're going to be amazed what we can do," he said.

As soon as word got around that I was testing the market, we heard from the Angels. Gene Autry had wanted me back for years, and now he saw his chance. He made it clear that money would be no object. He would pay what he had to and beat any other offer. Meanwhile the Astros were still trying to get together with me, but they weren't budging from their insulting offer. They just wanted to get it done and announce it so they could move on. They didn't imagine that I would be the one moving on.

I knew something would break at the winter baseball meetings in Atlanta, and, frankly, Ruth and I thought we would be going back to California. That wouldn't have been all that bad, because it's nice to feel wanted, and Gene Autry was a good person to work for. Though they had never won a World Series, the Angels organization had a winning attitude. I didn't like the idea of moving my family halfway across the country for the better part of a year, but I didn't see any other choice. If I'd done what I wanted to, I'd have stayed with the Astros. But with the Angels' offer on the table, the Astros would have had to more than double theirs to match the Angels. It would have taken an awfully huge number to get me to say that bygones would be bygones after the way I felt I had been treated.

The kids got excited about the possibility of living in southern California, but to tell you the truth, if they had said they'd rather I retire and spend more time with them, I would have. I knew I had at least another year in me, but I'd had a lot of great years and would have been happy to quit. It wouldn't have been easy and I would have missed baseball, but what my family wants is more important to me than any personal goals. The kids loved the life baseball offered us, though, and they didn't want me to give it up. I wasn't wild about moving, but I became willing.

It was no easy decision, because my mother, who lived alone nearby, was getting up in age and I felt responsible for her. I took it upon myself to make sure everything was right with her and I took care of any needs she had. Though she was not as mobile as she used to be, she did make it to a lot of my home games because we were so close. She had trouble with her feet, but Ruth could drive her right up to one of the entrances to the Astrodome. Being indoors at a constant temperature was a big help to her. She didn't have to do a lot of walking and was in comfortable surroundings. I knew this move of mine would mean the end of that too.

She was proud of me, but whenever reporters asked her about that she was quick to say she had six kids and was proud of every one of them. She was a special lady. I would see her at least once and usually twice a week when I was home, just to sit and spend an hour or so with her. We'd often take her to lunch and get caught up on things. Our kids had a special relationship with her because when they were sick she wanted them at her place where she would wait on them hand and foot. If they ever got sick at school, they'd call her first and wind up over there. We had planned a big Thanksgiving 1988 bash at the ranch with my sisters, my brother, my mother, and about thirty other relatives.

The Astros heard that other teams might be interested in me, so Bill Wood called and said McMullen wanted a meeting on Wednesday before Thanksgiving. John was going to be in Houston. I told him the timing was bad and that I just couldn't come to Houston with our plans to be at the ranch. Later Bill called back and insisted that we all get together. I told him I didn't think it was that urgent and that the only reason John wanted it then was for his own convenience. Bill called me again and said McMullen would come to the ranch to make it easier for me. We figured out where he could fly into and where we could meet and all that, but the more I thought about it the more irritated I was. I called Bill about a week before Thanksgiving and told him I just didn't want to have them coming to the ranch with all my relatives there because it was a family and a social thing and I didn't want to have to contend with business at that time.

Later Bill would say that I had missed meetings and lied to him, but it just wasn't true. The only thing I had done wrong was to temporarily agree to the meeting in the first place. Finally deciding to refuse to have it at that time and at that place was the right thing to do. I wasn't bargaining, negotiating, or playing hard to get. I wasn't even making them pay for their insulting offer, which they still weren't budging from. It was just bad timing, and I should never have even considered it to begin with.

As the winter meetings approached (they would be the first week of December), I realized that this was a time I should be enjoying. But agonizing over leaving the Astros, maybe moving, not knowing what to do or how to sort it out really got to me. It was a pressure-filled time for me and Ruth and the family, and I just wanted to make a decision and get it over with. It should be a real emotional high to be pursued by four major league teams (San Francisco and Texas had indicated some interest in addition to California and Houston), but I was much too realistic to think I should get too excited.

We had a good time at Thanksgiving until my sister and my mother were pulling out of the ranch and had a bad auto accident. My mother was buckled in, but the impact bruised her chest and ribs and even her heart. She was admitted into the hospital in Alvin, but for about a week she didn't seem to be getting any better. I called the doctor and said, "Look, I want you to meet me at the hospital, because I've been here every day and I can see that something's wrong. Her condition is getting worse, and we've got to do something about it."

He came right out, and when I repeated that I wasn't happy with what I was seeing, he examined her and said, "I think you're right." He transferred her to Methodist Hospital in Houston where specialists took over. I had just returned home about eleven o'clock that night when the heart specialist called to tell me he had found an accumulation of fluid around her heart. He wanted permission to do an MRI and then immediate surgery if necessary. I told him to go ahead. The doctor had told me the procedure wasn't painful, but it would take about forty-five minutes. I've had an MRI, and I knew if Mother was not claustrophobic going in, she sure would be coming out.

By the time I got there, Mother was in what I call the torture chamber, where the image reader is close to your face, and she was giving the staff fits.

Fortunately they didn't find what they thought they were going to find, and she didn't need surgery. She came out of the hospital after several weeks, having had just about every test you can have. She got a clean bill of health, though she had been slowed down a good bit and took a while recovering completely.

She had always feared cancer, because my dad had died of that, so all the tests put her mind at ease. She was still a very independent person and insisted on going back to live in the house she raised me in, driving her own car, and taking care of herself.

One day while I was in Houston visiting with her doctor about some tests, Bill Wood called and asked for a one o'clock meeting at the dome. I figured I could do that, but then I got hung up at the hospital. I called him to apologize and say that I was just not going to be able to make it. He sounded as if he understood and said it was fine, but I found out later that he had already scheduled a press conference for 1:30. He had planned to tell me that the Astros were not going to offer me arbitration, so I could either take their offer or leave it. If I left it and if I didn't sign with them by January 22, the rules wouldn't allow me to come back to them until the middle of May. They were so sure I would buckle under that pressure that they were ready to announce my signing, or my losing out on arbitration, that same day.

It was a power play I had foiled without even knowing it.

Right about that time the Texas Rangers' general manager, Tom Grieve, contacted Dick Moss. Tom told me later that he was just testing the waters because he believed, like everyone else in baseball, that Houston was just doing some creative negotiating and would never let me get away. "There are no guarantees," Dick told him.

When I heard the Rangers had asked about me, it changed the picture completely. Ruth and I had been sure we were headed back to the Angels and a nice offer from Gene Autry. But that big league data bank everybody had access to was going to keep even Gene's offer as low as possible, because all he had to do was beat the next best offer by a hundred thousand dollars. That was just like collusion and doesn't exist anymore, but everybody was checking the data bank back then.

Ruth and I decided that if Texas was really interested, we had to be too. It wasn't as close and convenient as Houston, but we wouldn't have to move, we wouldn't have to buy or rent in California, and we wouldn't have to switch the kids' schools. I told Dick to keep Texas warm. He was to simply tell Grieve, "Nolan has a great deal of interest in Texas."

The Rangers were an up-and-coming club with a lot of potential, but their attendance was declining and they had had some rough years. Grieve said he knew that if they could actually sign someone like me, people would know they were serious about winning. He thought it was a long shot, but he and manager Bobby Valentine got excited about the possibilities.

The Giants, the Rangers, and the Angels were talking salary figures in the $1.5–1.8 million range. I was looking for one year, but some were offering two, which was even better. The Angels would have gone $1.8 million for one year, plus incentives. The Astros finally saw the handwriting on the wall and backed away from insisting on my taking a cut. Now they were back up to my original million-a-year base with another $300,000 or so in incentives. I could have told them right then that they weren't even close, but I didn't. They would have to be at least in the same range as the other offers, and then we'd see how much difference their location and its convenience meant to me.

Dick Moss had also heard from the Japanese, and that started me thinking. I only wanted a one-year deal, and for the right price—as long as I was likely going to have to uproot my family anyway—I might be tempted to pitch overseas. I would take the whole family. It would be for only about seven months, and it would be a good educational experience for them. I told Dick to tell the Japanese that for the right offer, I'd make the commitment.

*Lynn Nolan Ryan Jr., eight years old.*

*Lynn Nolan Ryan, Jr.,
16 years old.*

*Nolan and Ruth dating in 1966.*

*Nolan and Ruth on first Nolan Ryan Day in Alvin, Texas 1969.*

*The Ryan Family: seated, Mr. and Mrs. Lynn Nolan Ryan, Sr. Standing from left: Judy, Bob, Nolan, Lynda, Jean, and Mary Lou.*

*Nolan and Ruth,*
*Alvin, Texas, 1973.*

*Nolan Ryan,*
*California Angels, 1977.*

*Nolan and Ruth with first baby, Reid, in 1972.*

*Ruth, Reid, Reese and Wendy Ryan, June 1991.*

*Nolan Ryan, rancher.*

*Nolan on his south Texas ranch.*

*Nolan Ryan, banker.*

*Nolan Ryan, pitching for the Texas Rangers.*

*Nolan with Angels coach, Jimmie Reese,*
*for whom their second son was named.*

*Nolan Ryan,*
*Houston Astros.*

*Nolan Ryan,*
*Texas Rangers, after 7th*
*no-hitter, May 1, 1991*
*against Toronto.*

*Nolan Ryan, Texas Rangers.*

*Nolan Ryan,*
*Texas Rangers.*

*Nolan Ryan, Texas Rangers, 300th victory, July 31,*
*1990 at Milwaukee.*

*Then-Vice President Bush
throwing out the opening
pitch in the Astrodome,
August 28, 1988.*

*Nolan with President George Bush, a friendship that began during Nolan's career with the Houston Astros.*

*Nolan and Ruth Ryan with President George Bush and First Lady Barbara Bush at the White House, January 1991.*

*From left: Nolan, Ruth, Reese,*
*Wendy, and Reid Ryan,*
*New Year's Eve, 1991.*

*Nolan and*
*Muhammad Ali.*

*Nolan on the set for an Advil commercial shot.*

*Nolan, working out. (Sports Illustrated)*

*Nolan Ryan.*

# 10

## Another New Start

$S$everal representatives from Japanese teams were in the United States to go to the winter meetings in Atlanta, so Dick arranged for the team that showed interest in me—the Tokyo Swallows—to come to Alvin and meet the family and talk details. Dick and I picked them up at the airport, and we had quite a meeting over a Texas-style meal Ruth prepared at our home. The Swallows' general manager spoke no English, so their U.S. representative interpreted.

The kids were real uptight about this, because Japan sounded like another planet to them, and they didn't want to have anything to do with it. The Swallows' U.S. representative seemed to be able to tell the kids were skeptical, so he tried to sell them.

"You know you'd be going to an international school with kids from other countries," he said. "I went to that school and there are lots of students whose parents work in the embassies. You might be sitting next to an American on one side and a Russian on the other."

Reese said, "Russians! I'm not going to school with any Russians!"

The kids asked him about Sumo wrestlers and Ninjas and stuff like that. Meanwhile, Dick and I told the Swallows that their offer of $2 million for one season was half where it needed to be. We told the GM that if he could see his way clear to offer $4 million, I would make the commitment right then and we wouldn't negotiate with the U.S. teams.

While their representative translated very seriously to the GM, we watched their faces for clues. It didn't appear to be a major problem, though they both looked thoughtful. Finally the GM spoke quickly and the rep translated.

"In all honesty, the money is not an issue." For a split second, I thought I was going to Japan. "We'd be willing to pay that, but we do have a problem. We have an understanding with the commissioner of baseball that if a U.S. major league club is interested in a free agent, we're not allowed to offer more than the U.S. club."

Dick and I looked at each other. That was collusion pure and simple and on an international scale. We knew then we were dead in the water. No U.S. club was going to give me $4 million, and if they did, I would have taken it. There was no sense going halfway around the world for the same money I could make here.

We thanked them for coming and making the effort, but they didn't give up. They told me they could match the top offer and virtually guarantee that I would make up the difference in endorsements in Japan.

"Guaranteed?" Dick said.

"Well, if he does well. If he gets hurt or gets off to a bad start, no."

That was no guarantee, and I wouldn't have expected one. Still, I had found the meeting interesting and appreciated their regard for me.

When Dick and I flew to Atlanta a few days later, I was still in agony. I was leaning toward the

Texas Rangers, but I worried about pitching out-
doors in the heat and humidity at my age. The dome
had been perfect for me. Pitching half my games in
perfect weather with a big outfield is a pitcher's
dream. The other difficult part was that I had personal friendships on every team that was interested.
On the one hand, there's a wonderful feeling in
knowing that big league baseball franchises are bidding for your services. But, on the other, I couldn't
imagine turning any of them down. Mr. Autry had
already gone on record that he would top any offer,
so if I didn't go with the Angels, I would be settling
for less than I could have made. And how do you tell
someone you don't want the highest figure?

No matter where I went, unless the Astros surprised us with a huge new deal, I was going to be
uprooted from the ball club I had been on for so
many years, have to get used to a new bunch of guys
and coaches and fans, and get comfortable in a new
clubhouse and on a new mound. I'd been treated so
well by the fans in Houston that I was distraught
over leaving them, and I knew they wouldn't understand. It was going to look like I was just leaving for
the money. In a way I was, of course, but it was only
because the money represented something. It represented how the Astro ownership felt about me. They
hadn't tried to cut my pay just as a bargaining ploy.
They were serious. They meant it, and they expected
me to take it. But if I was going only for the money, I
would have gone to the Angels. Then the fans could
have criticized me all they wanted, and they would
have been justified.

The decision dominated Ruth's and my
thoughts day and night for weeks, especially the two
weeks before going to Atlanta. Between us we had

pretty much decided that all things being equal, we would lean toward the Rangers for the sake of the family. The Astros could still surprise us and turn our heads, but we just didn't see that happening. Too much had transpired. You never know what's going to happen, though, in the heat of battle, so though Ruth thought she knew what I'd do, she wouldn't have been surprised if I'd called with some other deal out of the blue. People who haven't been through it don't realize that this type of a decision is as unsettling for a big leaguer as it is for any man making a major career move.

Dick and I checked into a room in Atlanta and contacted the four interested clubs. I felt I owed it to all of them to make my decision there so they could know what to do about their other trading needs. Lots of dominoes are in place when you sign an expensive player, and if that money is freed up, there are a lot of other things you can do. The Rangers, for instance, had a lot of pitching needs, so what I did would determine what else they had to do at the meetings.

I asked Dick to start with the Astros, because this was going to be a process of elimination. In my mind they were basically already out of the picture, but officially I was still with them and willing to stay if things could be worked out. From strictly a convenience standpoint, that would have been even better than going with the Rangers. But first they were going to have to substantially increase their offer. If we could have worked something out, I would have immediately told the other clubs so they wouldn't have been misled. I made it clear to everyone from the beginning that it wasn't just about running up the numbers and that I wasn't trying to play games.

I wanted square dealings, and while both Dick and I were rightly upset about the fact that each knew what the others were offering, we wanted to be aboveboard anyway.

Bill Wood and John McMullen came to our room, and I told them that even though I wasn't happy with how they'd treated me recently, I wasn't one to hold a grudge and was willing to listen to a serious offer. Then and only then did they significantly raise their offer, but it was still a long way from where the other clubs were. I could tell they thought I'd still want to stay. They were banking on it.

I told them they were too far from what I could get somewhere else. John McMullen said, "Nolan, the Houston Astro organization has an obligation to Mike Scott. We can't pay you more than we're paying him, and he's already under contract. We're not willing to go back and renegotiate with him because of what we do with you."

It sounded to me like they had guaranteed Mike he'd be the highest paid player on the team, which was fine. What another guy can get for himself is none of my concern, unless it keeps me from being where I feel I need to be. If Mike Scott made twice as much as me, that would have been all right, as long as I felt I got what I was deserving. I said, "John, if that's your offer, I'm going to tell you now that we're not going to sign with you and that we will sign within the next day or two with another organization."

I also told him I appreciated him bringing me to Houston and that I'd had a great time there. There were no hard feelings on my part, and though the ing me get away by saying that I had misled them

Astros later started answering the criticism for letting me get away by saying that I had misled them and missed meetings, that day in Atlanta I thought we were okay on a personal basis. I only wish that when a guy makes a mistake he would admit it and not try to cover himself by spreading stories about the other person.

We followed with a meeting with the Giants. Al Rosen and his assistant offered pretty much the same deal as the Angels and the Rangers had talked about, but they made it two years guaranteed. That was a good effort and a generous approach, and I appreciated it. Dick and I asked a lot of questions, and we felt good about their interest, but I think they left knowing I was leaning toward either staying closer to home or taking the Angels up on their offer to top any other deal. I didn't tell them no on the spot, but I felt sure they knew.

Then we asked the Rangers to come over. General Manager Tom Grieve, Manager Bobby Valentine (who had been a younger teammate of mine with the Angels), and Mike Stone (the president of the club at the time) visited us and formalized their best offer. It was right in there with the Giants offer, but rather than two years guaranteed, it called for one year and an option on a second. I told them that if I signed I wouldn't have a problem with the option clause, although privately I doubted I would pitch more than one more year. In a way I liked the option idea better than a guarantee, because then I wouldn't feel obligated. This way, if I was going well and felt good, they would want me back and I wouldn't feel like I was holding a gun to their heads.

136

We talked quite a while, and I raised all my questions about climatizing and changing clubs and all that. They were sympathetic and encouraging, but they didn't try to fool me. I also appreciated that they didn't glad-hand me and try to hard-sell me. They had enough respect for me to know that I would make up my own mind and make as rational a decision as I could. I don't think I hid my discomfort. This was not as enjoyable a process as it might have been for a young man with no clue as to the complications.

I don't know how those guys felt when they left our room. I had made it pretty clear that I wanted to stay in Texas, and I think they knew Houston wasn't knocking the door down. But I'm also sure they still thought it was a long shot because of my doubts about the weather. They also knew, of course, like everybody else did, that Gene Autry did not want to be denied. If it was about money, they knew nobody had a chance against the Angels.

As the Rangers left us, we told them we'd get back to them. I didn't tell them my mind was pretty much made up.

Since the Angels were the first club to show an interest in me that fall and Gene Autry had always been a great owner and a good friend, I felt I owed it to him and to protocol to meet with him and his people in his suite. He was there with his man Mike Port, and we sat around talking about his club for the longest time. They said nothing about their offer, but unless they doubled it or something, it wasn't going to be a surprise to us. I was thinking how hard it was going to be to tell him that I was leaning toward Texas.

137

Gene's wife Jackie came in and greeted me warmly, then said something that made my decision as final as it could be. She said, "Nolan you just have to sign with the Angels and win us a World Series."

I know she meant well, and that's the kind of confidence that makes a lot of athletes feel wanted and needed. But I also knew the Angel organization. They were farther from a World Series than one strikeout pitcher who might win them a dozen or fifteen games. I mean, in one way I was flattered to know that she thought I could make the difference, but I also knew she was wrong. If they'd had the hitting and the other starters and the bullpen, she might have been right. They weren't bad, but they weren't in a position where I was the one missing ingredient. I knew then that even if they could have turned my head with a great offer, I would be a disappointment to them if we did anything but win the World Series.

They didn't finalize their offer during the time we spoke. Mike asked if he could speak with the Autrys alone and then come and make a final proposal in our room. We agreed and went to wait for him. The offer was a good one, clearly the best of the bunch, but by then I felt more confident of my decision. I didn't have much more peace about it, and there were still a lot of unknowns, but I had decided. When he finally left our room, without our answer, it was about one o'clock in the morning.

Dick wanted me to go to California. He thought it would be great to return there, to take the great offer, and to finish my career with a bang. He pushed as hard as was appropriate, but I explained that Ruth and I really wanted to stay in Texas. "Neither of the

California deals would be right, 'cause it's not gonna work for the family."

He said, "You've got to do what you've got to do."

The next morning, after a final talk with Ruth on the phone, I told Dick I'd decided on Texas and we invited them over.

"Money was not the determining factor," I told Stone, Grieve, and Valentine. "I'm a die-hard Texan, so if we can hammer out a few details, I want to stay in Texas." I told them some of my conditions, and they met alone in the other room. When they came out we shook hands and we had a deal. They acted happy, but I only found out later that when they left, Bobby jumped and clicked his heels.

We had already made clear to the Astros that they were out of the picture. I called Al Rosen and told him I appreciated the Giants' interest in me but that I had just signed with the Rangers. He was great. He said he understood and wished me the best.

I tried to get hold of Gene, but he was in a meeting. The Rangers wanted to announce the signing. I didn't want Gene to find out that way, but I had a plane to catch. We told Mike Port what the deal was, and he agreed to pass it on. Dick said he would also get to Gene and explain, and I talked to Gene later on the phone too. He was fine. In fact, he was not as disappointed as I thought he might me. I'm sure in his mind he had made an honest effort, and it didn't work out. He understood my reasoning and accepted it. I'd really like to see Gene get his World Series. Lord knows nobody has pumped more money and effort into a situation and gotten less out of it.

I was glad the decision had been made, but I still had a lot of apprehension about going up to play in Arlington. I was switching leagues again and would have to learn the new strike zone and all the hitters, not to mention my teammates and the fans. Would they accept me or resent me? Would they expect too much? Would they think, like Mrs. Autry did, that I was going to win them a World Series?

I wanted to tell people not to expect miracles. They might look forward to my five-thousand-strikeout milestone and maybe fifteen or so wins, but I didn't want them to expect me to be an even better pitcher than I was. I figured I had a good year left in me. I would be forty-two years old by the time the season started, and I would give it all I had, just like I always do. I couldn't give them more than that, and I hoped I wouldn't disappoint them.

# 11

## Texas Heat

$T$he previous season, 1988, the Rangers had finished sixth in their division and lost ninety-one games. Their attendance had dropped by nearly two hundred thousand. I knew nothing would be more exciting than if I had a good year and the club started to win. If we could set attendance records, people would talk about 1989 for years. Flirting with a couple of no-hitters the year before had me wondering if I might be able to do something really special, but I started slowly, injuring a hamstring in spring training and being able to go only one inning before a record crowd. I was able to throw about ten minutes just warming up on the sidelines a couple of weeks later, but then I went seven innings against the Astros. I knew then I was ready.

I started the regular season with a no-decision at home, then pitched against the Brewers on a cold April night in Milwaukee. My fastball was alive, so I stayed with it and I shut down the first twenty batters. I didn't allow a hit until Terry Francona hit an opposite field single in the eighth. I wound up striking out fifteen.

April 23, on another cold night in Toronto, I went into the ninth inning without allowing a hit for the ninth time in my career. Nelson Liriano broke it up with a one-out triple. It was the fourth time I'd lost a no-hitter with one out in the last inning. That was my fifteenth game allowing fewer than two hits, breaking Bob Feller's record.

People were amazed all over baseball and all over the country. What was this old man doing teasing them with almost-no-hitters as he had done years and years ago? People who didn't know better probably thought old Nolan Ryan had discovered a knuckle ball or some junk to hang on for so long. Nobody expected me to still be blowing away hitters.

In June I pitched a one-hitter in Seattle against the Mariners. Later that month I had a no-hitter until two were out in the eighth and Brook Jacoby of Cleveland doubled. That was the longest any Ranger had gone without giving up a hit at Arlington Stadium. I was 9–3 and cooking.

Every time I just missed another no-hitter it disappointed me more. I knew enough not to get excited about them until one actually happened, because so much can go wrong in those last three innings. But to come so close . . . Everybody thought it was just a matter of time, but I felt that every no-hitter that slipped away might be my last chance.

I went back to pitch against the Angels in Anaheim in July, my first time there in ten years. I was really moved by a long standing ovation that was one of the highlights of my career. I pitched a three-hit shutout, then pitched in the All-Star game there five days later and became the oldest pitcher to win that classic.

On August 10, at Arlington, I took Detroit into the ninth without a hit. Dave Bergman got a single off me with, you guessed it, one out, and I had my fifth ninth-inning no-hitter broken up.

On August 22, with a pitch clocked at ninety-six miles an hour, I struck out Rickey Henderson for the five thousandth K of my career. People had come from all over to see the milestone, and I had ignored the 101-degree heat. What made it so special was that when I got to within one strikeout, it seemed everybody in the sellout crowd flashed their cameras on every pitch. The tension rose and fell with each call. I was also impressed that George W. Bush, our managing general partner, was there for the occasion, along with A. Bart Giamatti, then commissioner of baseball.

A month later, in my last start of the year, I took a no-hitter into the eighth before giving up a single to Brian Downing. That made five times in one year, at forty-two years old, that I had taken a legitimate shot at a no-hitter. Earlier in my career I would have told myself I'd have a lot more opportunities, but now every time I missed one I knew it could easily be my last chance. I tried not to let myself dream about how exciting it would be to add one more no-hitter to my record, especially at my age.

I had had a fantasy year, far surpassing all my expectations. My sixteen wins were the most I'd had since 1982, and I became the oldest pitcher to ever strike out more than three hundred in a season, leading the league for the third year in a row. Striking out 301 in just 239 innings was also a record, and that was the most strikeouts in the American League since I had struck out 310 in 1977. Hitters batted .187 against me for the season.

Every game seemed like a bonus to me, but I felt so good that I accepted the Rangers' option and signed on for 1990. I signed that deal pretty certain it would be my last, but I've learned to just take them one at a time now. That would be the only season I would go into actually shooting for a statistic. I was eleven games short of three hundred career wins. A lot of the records I didn't really care about, but I did want to win three hundred. Only nineteen pitchers in the history of baseball had ever won that many.

The 1989 season had been one of the most enjoyable of my career. I was as surprised as anybody with my popularity and the attention I received, but the Rangers were the first organization to put me out front and promote me like that. They acted like they truly appreciated my being there, and so I've tried to accommodate them in every way possible. I somehow became more of a phenomenon in Arlington than I had been in Houston, because the Astro organization never would have pushed me or appreciated me the way the Rangers have.

I like the attitude at Arlington from the owners to the people who work the stadium. The whole organization is relaxed and having fun. Just like John McMullen's tension filtered down to everybody on the staff, the looseness in Arlington infects everybody too. The pride in the organization shows, and our whole family has enjoyed the situation.

My teammates have accepted me warmly, and I try to treat them right. I care about what goes on with them, and even though I'm old enough to be a father to some of them and certainly old enough to be their coach, I try to be just a teammate. I don't expect preferential treatment from management, even though a certain amount of it comes naturally because of my years. But players notice whether you demand that and how you react to it, and I think they know by now that the team comes first with me.

In January 1990, just before my forty-third birthday, I had to go to Dallas on a deal affecting my ranch. On the way that morning, I called to check on my mother as I often did, but I got no answer. During the winter I called her every day, and during the season at least twice a week. When I got back to the Houston airport that night, Ruth called me in the truck.

"I have some bad news, Nolan," she said. "Your mother passed away this morning."

I was stunned. My sister, a counselor at the high school in Alvin, had also called Mother in the morning without getting an answer, so she went over to check on her. The car was there, the dog had been let out into the yard, and the coffee had been made. But when my sister got back to the bedroom she discovered our mother on the bed. The bed was made, and Mother was dressed, so all we can guess is that she had gotten up and had done some of her chores, then laid back down when she didn't feel good.

I had worried ever since her accident whether she was okay there by herself, and I had thought about when she should move in with us or what other arrangements we might be able to make. She was such a big part of our lives that her death was really a shock, and dealing with the loss was a long process. All of a sudden I realized I had no living parent. I missed my dad a tremendous amount when he passed away. Now there are times when I still catch myself thinking about calling to check on my mother.

Just like when my dad died, I didn't want someone to talk to or someone to console me. I just wanted to be left alone to my thoughts. I like to deal with things on my own terms. I had to resolve in my mind to put the experience in its place and learn from it. I went through some regrets about having been busy and seeing so little of her, which is natural. But you can never do as much as you'd like for your loved ones. I always felt I could have done more. I just had to come to grips with it and know I did the best I could. Time is a healer, but we all sure miss her. The kids really felt it after having been so close to her. I didn't think I could do any more growing up and maturing at my age, but that was a sobering, learning experience.

That made me feel a little older when the season started, but I didn't have any less enthusiasm for what I was doing. In the opener against Toronto I had a no-hitter for five innings when Bobby Valentine took me out. He was criticized for it, but not by me. He said, "We're playing a season, not the Super Bowl." In my fourth start, I struck out sixteen White Sox in a one-hitter, giving up a second-inning single to Ron Kittle.

My back started bothering me after that. Here I was 4–0 but having muscle spasms. I had to leave my next two starts early and then went on the disabled list. Everybody was sure it was the beginning of the end for me, and I wasn't so sure myself.

On June 11, for my second start after coming off the disabled list, I was in Oakland on a chilly Monday night to face the Athletics, the defending World Series champions. It's tough enough facing a lineup like that without having to do it on the road. My back was still sore, but I knew early in the game that I had good stuff. I didn't allow a base runner until the third, when I walked Walt Weiss. We had already scored three runs by then, two on a homer by Julio Franco in the first and one on a solo homer by my catcher, John Russell, in the second. Ironically,

John had never caught for me before. In fact, he had been cut by the Braves in spring training and had just joined the Rangers less than a month before.

Franco hit another two-run homer in the fifth to give us a 5–0 lead, and I didn't allow another base runner until the bottom of the sixth, when I walked Mike Gallego with one out. Between pitches I had to bend and stretch on the mound to keep my back loose. And between innings, Reese (then fourteen years old), who had come along as one of our bat boys, massaged my back.

In the ninth, with one out, I went to a 2–2 count on Rickey Henderson, who was batting .342 at the time. He hit a slow roller to Jeff Huson at short, but Jeff charged the ball and threw him out. Jeff shook a fist at me, and I said, "Nice play." You could see how excited he was. It was written all over him. Then I got Willie Randolph on a fly to Ruben Sierra and, believe it or not, I had been perfect since the second walk in the sixth. I had struck out fourteen and walked only those two for my sixth no-hitter. I was mobbed, but John Russell was the first to get to me. He told me later he had never seen a look in a pitcher's eyes like he had seen in mine that night.

I was as shocked as anybody, and the news sure swept the country. The best part about it for me was how excited my teammates had been to be a part of it. I don't show much emotion, but that moved me. I became the oldest pitcher in history to throw a no-hitter. Obviously I wasn't counting, but they tell me I was forty-three years, four months, and twelve days old. I was also the only pitcher to throw no-hitters in three different decades. To me it wouldn't have been half as amazing if I wasn't basically the same kind of pitcher I had always been.

Someday somebody might match my no-hit record and even pitch no-hitters decades apart, but it is hard to imagine someone throwing fastballs and striking people out in what should be the twilight of his career.

It was my first no-hitter since September 26, 1981, the longest time between no-hitters ever. More amazing to me, it was seventeen years after my first one. The only drawback was that I wished it had happened in Arlington where those fans had been so wonderful to me.

On July 20, still hurting, I won my 299th game, my tenth win that season in fifteen starts. My next start was against the Yankees in Arlington, and I wanted more than anything to reach a milestone there for those fans. They came from all over, the way the media did. I just wanted it to be over so I could get back to a little more sane routine. There's nothing like being hounded everywhere you go by people asking any question they can think of.

The ballpark was sold out and it had the atmosphere of a playoff game. I thought I was ready for win number three hundred. Deion Sanders led off the game with a triple off me. I was wild in the strike zone and couldn't get untracked. The Yankees scored seven runs, but Bobby kept me in the game because we were scoring too, and he thought maybe I could hang on and win it. But I never got into a groove where I had any consistency, and it just kept getting worse and worse. I wound up with a no-decision, but it was one of my poorer outings of the year. I was really disappointed, feeling I had let down all those people.

I finally got my three hundredth win eleven days after number 299. It was a thrill, but it came on the road, in Milwaukee. I went seven and two-thirds innings in an 11–3 win, only wishing again that I could do something meaningful at Arlington Stadium. Those fans had made my last two years so special that I felt I owed it to them.

# 12
## Never Enough

*I*f I had ever felt unappreciated in my life, the attention I got after that sixth no-hitter made up for all of it. Everybody knows I'm pretty much a quiet guy, not looking for the spotlight, but I also get satisfaction out of what I've accomplished. Some folks are surprised to learn that with my daily workouts and what I have to do in the clubhouse and the training room and for the media, I spend seven or eight hours a day at the ballpark. It's amazing, but people who don't follow the game closely think there's something fluky that lets me keep pitching at my age. Fact is, and Tom House has been preaching this for years, anybody can be effective into his forties if he trains his body the right way. I'm not saying the fastball will stay with a man for twenty-five years, but I'd be the wrong one to say it wouldn't, too.

I'd been getting a lot of press coverage for being the oldest man in the game, showing up for spring training again, leading a much-improved Rangers team, and all that. Every time I flirted with a no-hitter, people in the press wrote glowing stories and shook their heads, wondering if I could actually pitch another one at my age. I can't speak for them, but I'd guess none of them would have put any money on it. I wouldn't either. As I've said, it gets harder and harder as the game gets longer, and of course I had everything working against me. But when that sixth no-hitter was over, the attention from the fans multiplied.

People would be amazed to see how much stuff I have to sign every day. First of all, I get between three hundred and four hundred letters a day, almost every one of them requesting an autograph, a card, or a picture. A lot of them come with those items ready to be signed. You can see what happens if I'm on the road and fall behind by a week or two. I'm not the kind of a person who would have other people fake my autograph or use one of those signing machines. I'm also not the type of a person who just gets in a scribbling mode and dashes off a scrawl on everything that passes under my nose. I admit it only takes a few seconds for each autograph, but I do each carefully and as legibly as possible. Some of these are on baseballs that will be sold as authentically autographed, and as I get paid for doing that and people pay their own money for them, I want them to look nice.

Every spare minute I've had for the last couple of years has been spent sitting somewhere with box after box of dozens of baseballs, stacks of color photos, and other memorabilia I have to sign. Whether I'm being interviewed, chatting with friends, or even talking on the phone, I've usually got a pen in one hand and a ball or something in the other. I sign hundreds and hundreds and hundreds of items every single day, and I'm still so far behind that I hate to even think about it.

It sounds terrible, because I do appreciate all the love and interest from the fans, but it's a never-ending deal. If you asked Ruth and me what we hate about our career in baseball, it would be the volume of mail and demands for autographs. There are good things and bad things, pluses and minuses, and this is the big minus that nobody understands.

I guess the reason they don't understand is that unless you've had to deal with it, it looks pretty glamorous. I mean, who wouldn't want to be known and loved and recognized by everybody? You're worshiped and people just want to be able to say that you took a second to sign your name on their baseball or card. Before you have that kind of recognition, you're jealous of anybody who has it. It's a sign that you've achieved something, that you've arrived, that you're somebody.

But then, when it happens, you realize what a monster it can be. I know how that sounds, and I know people are thinking, *Man, you make millions of dollars playing a game and you can't sign a few autographs for the people who made you what you are? If it weren't for the fans, there'd be no money in baseball.*

Well, that's true. But the autograph game has changed. I can usually tell when a kid just wants his moment with a big leaguer, and I try to give it to him. He's in awe, he's thrilled, and he wants to say he talked with Nolan Ryan. Great. I'll do it and give him a smile and shake his hand and even sign whatever he wants. But I can also tell these guys, and some of them are kids, who are only buying and selling autographs. That's why I don't criticize some of the ballplayers who charge for their autographs at card shows, and that's why I don't feel bad about taking money to sign stuff that will be retailed. If I knew nobody was making money off my signature, I wouldn't mind signing all this stuff if time allowed me to. But when I know what it does to my schedule and my family life, I wish I could tell for sure how many of the requests come

from legitimate fans and how many come from autograph brokers.

A lot of the people I play with get a box or two
of letters in a whole season, and they just let them sit.
At the end of the year they take them over to the gar-
bage can and dump them. There are days when I
wish those were all I had to deal with. I guarantee I
wouldn't throw away even one. I've had to hire a
full-time secretary just to handle the mail and the requests for appearances. I know. You might think,
*Nice problem.* The day may come when all this is gone
and I'll miss it and wonder if anybody remembers ol'
Nolan Ryan. I may walk down the street and feel
neglected and unappreciated. I don't know. Right
now that sounds pretty good.

When I was in high school I saw a couple of
Houston Colt .45s at the ballpark. One was a backup
catcher and the other was a pinch hitter. My buddies
and I hardly recognized their names, but we were
saying, "Man, if I could make fifteen thousand a year
for just sittin' on the bench, I'd be happy as a lark."
But when you get in the game, your competitive
spirit won't let that be true. You don't want to take
money for doing nothing. You want to excel, to
achieve. That's the same attitude that got you to the
big leagues in the first place. Like anything else, it
looks different when you're on the outside looking
in. Today kids look at us and say, "I'd sign autographs twenty-four hours a day for that kind of
money." Maybe you would. Maybe you'd toss them
all at the end of the season. I can't bring myself to do
that, but sometimes it seems like I'm signing my
name twenty-four hours a day.

People think the traveling life of a big leaguer is
glamorous too. Once you've experienced it for a

while, believe me your attitude changes. I don't know of anything in life that you have to do on regular basis as part of your job that isn't a lot different from how you once imagined it would be. For me, every new town I arrive in means another crush of media and fans. Again, I know, I sound ungrateful. And people who spend their whole lives in anonymity are thinking, *Send me some of that attention.* Believe me, if I could I would. It doesn't make me mad or bitter; it just wears me down.

See, I know I'm not worthy of being worshiped. Yeah, it's great to be appreciated. But somehow being able to still do with a baseball what I did twenty years ago has turned me into something else—an industry. I know who I am. I'm a country kid from Texas with the ability to throw a ball and the dedication to keep myself in shape. I love the cheers and the applause and I'm grateful people come out to watch me pitch. I even appreciate that people like to see me in person and talk to me and get an autograph. But I'm just a man. I'm no better than anybody else, even if I have an unusual and marketable talent. I'd rather sit and chat with you and hear about you and your family and your work than to pretend that I'm some royal being who can thrill you with a handshake or a signature.

I know I should be flattered and thrilled with all the attention, but if you think about it you can understand that too much adulation can make a man feel guilty. He knows he doesn't deserve all that, and if he starts thinking he does, he's going to be impossible to live with.

I have to say that, by and large, most of the people who ask for my autograph are wonderful, considerate fans. But it only takes a few of the rude ones to ruin your day. Some people are so self-centered that all they're concerned about is what they want and not whether they're imposing on me or the rest of the fans who are being patient. When people are rude and pushy it's an irritant, but I feel better about myself if I don't display my true feelings. When I do that I feel guilty and know I could have done a better job in that situation. I should never let people cause me to behave in a manner I don't consider acceptable. Just because somebody else is rude doesn't entitle me to be abrupt or discourteous in return. I try not to let myself be brought down to their level. That's not easy, because I'm not the best at disguising my feelings.

Some days it's easier than others, depending on what's been going on. I try not to get into positions where I'm going to be tied up for long periods. That can really ruin my day. There are appropriate ways to approach someone for an autograph. For instance, if Ruth and I are out for lunch, people should wait until we're through eating. I've had people butt right into a conversation. I've had someone interrupt me right when I'm putting a bite of food in my mouth. Some will just toss something in front of you to sign, right onto your plate.

On the other hand, some people will wait outside for us, sometimes as long as thirty minutes, and then politely ask for an autograph. I'm always happy to comply. If it means that much to them, it means a lot to me too. It's very important to me also that they acknowledge Ruth. She doesn't want star treatment, but it can wear on you when people walk over you or look through you to get to someone else. She's my wife. She's not an obstacle.

When I'm in a hurry, I just tell people, but I still try to sign unless they have a whole bunch of items. That can be the most irritating, when you sign a card or something and then they start producing every other thing that can fit an autograph.

One of the worst experiences I had was at the Astrodome in the late 1980s when I was leaving a game. I pulled out of the players' protected parking area past some barriers where the fans waited for autographs. I rolled down my window to sign for a few people as I rolled by, and there were maybe twenty people there. On some nights, when there were hundreds, security wouldn't be able to control them, so I couldn't stop. I never would have gotten out of there, and people would have been mashed up around my truck. But with just those twenty or so, I stopped.

A couple of young men in the crowd, both very drunk, shoved their programs in my face and demanded I sign them. It was all I could do to remain calm, they were so rude, but I gritted my teeth and signed. While I was signing for one, the other guy reached into the cab of my truck, right across my body, and grabbed for one of the baseball caps on the seat. "Hey, lemme have one of them caps," he said.

I was about to explode, and I don't know what would have happened if I'd broken his arm. Luckily a Houston police officer was standing there and saw what happened. He wrapped a forearm around that guy's neck and liked to tear him out of his shoes dragging him away from my truck. I was really grateful, because that could have gotten ugly.

Sometimes the worst offenders are kids around junior high age. If a crowd has a bunch of them in it, I know I'll get some obnoxious comments or actions.

Usually I figure if I'm out of sight, I'm out of mind, so I try to avoid big crowds. I don't try to walk past and ignore them, because that looks terrible. They know you can see and hear them, and you look rude. So I go out different exits and slip away. That way they might go home and complain that they didn't see me, but they won't tell everybody that I ignored them. I could go out there and sign a couple of hundred autographs a night, and there would be another two hundred who would complain that I didn't sign theirs.

The Rangers ball club got a letter last summer from a woman in Colorado who complained that she and her husband drove all the way to Arlington Stadium and yelled at me on the field and I wouldn't even look up so their son could take a picture. Well, I had no clue. When I go out before a ball game and do my running, first of all I try to do it early so there aren't a lot of fans. But at Arlington they have a policy of having the gates open for all but thirty minutes, so there are always lots of people in the stands. Well, I have my own policy that once I start my running I don't stop and do autographs, because if I stop and sign for one, then I have to sign for others. Before I know it, I don't get my workout done.

Part of my workout is sprinting out and walking back several times, and if I hear someone yelling for a picture I might look and wave. But I cannot go to the stands and start signing. If someone catches my eye and asks me point blank, I tell them nicely, "I'm sorry, I've got to get my work in." Most people accept that, but some will say, "Oh, come on, you can do one for this kid. He's your biggest fan." Then I try to explain that if I sign his, what will the kid next to him say? I can't discriminate. But for a woman to say I ignored her son who wanted to take a picture, that was too much. My name is shouted hundreds of times a night at the stadium. I'd sure never ignore an individual on purpose.

The more popular I have become, the more creative I need to be to avoid people without offending them. The last thing I want to be is rude, but there's only so much you can do for people and still do what you have to do for the ball club. I try to figure when is the best time to work out, where's the best place to park, all that. But people learn your routines and they know my vehicles. They know that if I pitch one night I'll get to the ballpark at nine the next morning to work out, so many will be waiting.

With them standing there expecting me to sign, out of guilt, I stop and do it. I tell them that I will sign for everybody, but only one item each. The only problem is, two and a half hours later when I come out, there are many of the original thirty people and maybe twenty more. One day I told them, "Look, I don't have time. I'm going to stop and sign one time, one item for each, so you might as well tell people that if I sign on the way in, I'm not signing on the way out."

But then that made them mad. I looked like a difficult guy. So I started driving in a different way and parking way out by the center field entrance instead of the players' parking area. I had to walk all the way across the field to the clubhouse, but I avoided upsetting the fans.

Well, one guy caught on to what I was doing. He said he was a schoolteacher and that he always had me sign something so he could reward his students for excelling in reading and stuff. Frankly I didn't believe him. Maybe that wasn't fair, but he sure had a lot of stuff, and he was always there. The day I parked in the parking lot he still found me. I got in the car and he flagged me down. I rolled down the window and told him I had an appointment and I only had time to sign one thing.

"You seem irritated with me," he said.

"Well, why do you think I parked all the way out here?"

"I don't know."

"Because I don't have time to stop and sign for everybody, and you're here every day expecting me to sign. I think that's enough."

He was offended and I never saw him again. I don't know. I felt bad about doing it, but he was really being presumptuous and infringing on my time. I knew it needed to be said, but it's so against my nature to be confrontive that I felt guilty about it for a couple of days.

I'm a real believer that you can't make everybody happy and not everybody is going to like you. I don't have problems with the fact that there are media and baseball people who like me and those who don't—I understand that. But there's something about the relationship with the fans, trying to accommodate them and keep them happy, that has given me a lot of trouble personally, inside.

If I knew they were getting my autograph because they respected me and it was a keepsake, that would be one thing. But for many it's not a hobby; it's a business. Still, I try to give twenty to thirty minutes every day during the season to sign autographs for the fans, and I carve out at least another thirty minutes a day for the media, and some days it may be as much as an hour and a half. That adds up to a lot of time, but it's never enough to satisfy everybody.

When I was a young player I didn't even dream about these kinds of demands. I never had any idea there would be days like this. Still, what I wanted to give the fans was not myself, my whole schedule, my family, my life. I wanted to give them something to really remember, something special they could talk about the rest of their lives. I wanted it to be more than an autograph, more than a picture, more than a glimpse of me in person.

I wanted to do something at Arlington Stadium for the people who had treated me so nice. It should be something that came from all the work and dedication I'd given to the sport. The five thousandth strikeout had been at home before a sellout crowd in 1989, but my sixth no-hitter and my three hundredth win had been on the road in 1990. With the back problems I'd had, I couldn't guarantee I'd be the same pitcher in '91, but it wouldn't be for lack of trying.

Two days after the sixth no-hitter I had been examined in Los Angeles by Dr. Lewis Yocum, the Angels' orthopedist and an old friend. He said I had a stress fracture and prescribed medication and exercises. It was still tight the rest of the season, but I didn't miss another start. It was a big help to understand what I was dealing with. I could pitch with the pain without injuring my back any worse. The last six weeks of the season I quit throwing off the mound on my off days and that seemed to give my back enough time to quiet down between starts. I could only hope that 1991 would be another great year. I was through predicting whether or not it would be my last.

# 13
## Something Special

*T*hings looked great for the Rangers for the 1991 season. We looked to have good hitting and a lot of pitching—at least until the first four games. I lost the opener to Milwaukee and then we lost three more straight. It was a good thing we won six of our next seven or we would have been in a real tailspin. By the time I started my fourth game, we were 6–6 and I was 2–1. I lost 5–2 to Cleveland on a Friday the thirteenth at Arlington, and I had thrown 133 pitches.

I was scheduled to pitch again the following Wednesday, May 1, with only four days' rest. I hadn't been that successful in '90 with less than five days' rest, but I was ready to give it a try. By game time we were 8–8 and needed to get on a winning track. We would be at home against the Toronto Blue Jays, one of the best hitting teams in the majors.

Ruth almost always comes to my home games, but if she can't she watches them on television. The only one she missed when I was with the Angels was when she was moving us back to Texas and I was making my last start in 1974. She still hasn't forgiven herself for missing that no-hitter.

So, when she found out, late in the afternoon, that the Toronto game wasn't going to be televised, she called one of my ranching partners, Jim Stinson, and asked if she could watch it at his place, because he has a satellite dish. "He's not pitchin' tonight," Jim told her. "He's pitchin' Friday in Detroit, right?"

"No," she said. "He's pitching tonight."

"Well, if I'd known that I'd have flown to the game. In fact, there's still time, Ruth. You wanna go?"

So Ruth flew into Arlington with Jim in his private plane. I was glad she was there. Harry Spilman, my old Astros teammate and now a neighbor who catches for me in January before spring training and whose wife Kim is my secretary, listened to the game on his car radio by driving all over the place. He thought it was going to be on television too. When I took a no-hitter into the seventh he called my kids, and they watched the end of it when ESPN cut away from the Detroit-Kansas City game to follow my progress.

I didn't expect to pitch well at all that night. I woke up with a sore back and took painkillers all day before leaving for the park. I went through extra stretching and exercises and even wore a heating pad during the scouting meeting where we go over the hitters. That wasn't the only thing wrong with me. While I was warming up I told Tom House, who was also forty-four years old at the time, "I don't know about you, but I feel old today. My back hurts, my finger hurts, my ankle hurts, everything hurts." Scar tissue tore open on the middle finger of my pitching hand in the bullpen, and I had one of my worst warmups ever. I didn't know it till later, but House told Bobby Valentine to keep an eye on me and not leave me in too long.

Before the game Bobby asked me how my back was. I told him that it was stiff. He said, "How will it be once you start pitching?" I said, "It'll be history." Adrenaline always takes over when I'm on the mound, and it did again, in the first inning.

With two out in the first, I lost Kelly Gruber on a full count and walked him. I was mad at myself, but settled down and got out of the inning by retiring Joe Carter. In the second I struck out the side on three curveballs. Steve Buechele, our third baseman, and shortstop Jeff Huson told each other as they came off the field that all we needed was one run that night if I had stuff like that. I had to admit my curve was really working, and I didn't have any trouble hitting my spots. The fastball was hopping too.

We scored our only three runs in the bottom of the third, two on a Ruben Sierra homer. After the Gruber walk in the first, I got eighteen straight hitters out before giving up another two-out, full-count walk in the seventh, this time to Joe Carter. Manny Lee had hit a blooper to center in the fifth, but Gary Pettis raced out from under his hat to catch it at his knees. He's one of the best. I'd thought that ball had a chance to drop in before Gary chased it down.

After the walk to Carter in the seventh, I retired the next seven hitters and the place went crazy. I had struck out sixteen, allowed only two base runners who never got past first, and had pitched my seventh no-hitter. Even I couldn't keep from grinning as the team raced out to the mound to congratulate me. I had been the oldest no-hit pitcher when my sixth came the year before. Who would have ever thought there'd be another one, especially in the condition I was in that day?

Ironically, my last out was a swinging strikeout of Blue Jay second baseman Roberto Alomar. His father, Sandy, had been my second baseman for the Angels in my first two no-hitters eighteen years before. In fact I remember little Roberto asking me to help him become a pitcher someday.

They tell me I threw 122 pitches, 83 for strikes, 62 of those fastballs. Of the sixteen strikeouts, all but the three in the second inning were swinging. The radar gun showed my fastest pitch at ninety-six miles per hour against Carter in the fourth, with an average of ninety-three miles per hour for the game. My last pitch, the one that got Alomar, was also at ninety-three miles per hour.

There's a lot of debate about which of my seven no-hitters was the best and in which one I had my best stuff. I'm not sure myself, but I know that the seventh was especially gratifying because it was at home before that Arlington crowd. My stuff was surprisingly good, considering all that was wrong with me that day. Somebody said my teammates were like spectators because I was that dominant, but I know better than that.

I had several other good outings before 1991 was over. On June 11, I shut out the White Sox on six hits, then I had a scare. I suffered such severe chest pains one morning early in July that I got myself to the hospital, worried about a heart attack. I was relieved to find it was only a pulled muscle near the sternum. A few days later, on July 7, just before the All-Star break, I retired the first eighteen hitters and took a no-hitter into the eighth inning against the Angels before Dave Winfield singled. Fifteen times during the season I allowed less than two runs and eleven times two or less hits.

I missed a lot of starts by being on the disabled list two different times, so my twenty-three starts and 173 innings were my fewest in twenty years in the majors. Still, fourteen different times I worked at least seven innings. I was frustrated with the down time, but starting June 6, I went 9–2 the rest of the way to finish at 12–6 with a 2.91 ERA. I was 5–1 in my last nine starts and 4–0 in my last seven, winning my last six decisions at home. I was pleased that I didn't allow a homer in my last nine games.

When the season was over I had 314 career victories and 5,511 strikeouts. I ranked third on the list of all-time leaders in starts with 733. On July 23 I set a record by making my 545th straight start since my last relief appearance. That record stood at 554 by the end of the season.

If my season had ended with the injuries instead of coming back with good closing appearances, I might have seriously considered hanging it up. But I seemed to return to form at the end, and I'm excited about the Rangers' future. They signed me for one more year (1992), with an option on 1993, which I decided to exercise. I also signed a ten-year personal services contract. That means that when my career is over I will give them one to two months a year for either promotional appearances or evaluating talent or whatever they need. I hope it won't involve much travel. I'm about all traveled out.

All that commercial stuff and the demands on my time that I complained about after my sixth no-hitter just multiplied with number seven. I've become as well known for Bic shavers and Advil as for my pitching, I think, but eventually that stuff will all come to an end. I've done enough of it by now that I'm starting to get more comfortable with it. I have a better idea what they want, and I'm learning to deliver with every take. No way I'm going to become an actor or anything like that, but I think I'm less stiff and self-conscious in front of the camera now than I used to be.

Like I've said, I know these opportunities won't always be here. It's the baseball that has made them possible, and since the extra income allows me to do things for my family I wouldn't have been able to otherwise, I carefully select the right ones and accept them. Some guys get on camera and think they've found a whole new career, but you don't see too many guys who are as good on the screen as they were on the field. I have no illusions about that. Even if somebody thought I was the hottest thing on television and could make a lucrative living off it, I wouldn't be interested. I'm on television because of baseball, and baseball is what I love.

There's something about the game that makes it the biggest challenge of my life. Of course it has dominated my life for so many years and naturally I've played it for so long that I understand the game now in ways I never did as a young player. Understanding the game and seeing its challenges are what made me come to love it.

At first I didn't have that burning desire to play and accomplish things. The pressure to do that was thrust on me because of my natural ability, and without much of a mind of my own at the time, I just followed. People thought I could pitch, so I pitched. They thought I should be a pro, so I went pro. They saw me as a power pitcher, so I threw as hard as I could.

I said earlier that Tom Seaver opened my eyes when I first met him, because he had a plan, a goal. He wanted to be great, to be one of the best. Before he ever pitched a big league inning he knew the history of the game and who held the records he would be shooting for. I didn't know who Walter Johnson was until Tom told me about his strikeout record. I was only in baseball because I had talent, and until I got focused I was really never an effective pitcher.

Now I've learned what to look for in a pitcher's record to be able to sense his effectiveness and his potential, and I'll tell you, it has little to do with his won-lost record. I've proved that more than once. The year I lost twice as many games as I won, I led the league in strikeouts and earned run average, so that ought to tell you something.

They show the stats of local minor league players in the Sunday paper. With a quick glance at their numbers, I can tell what kind of futures they have before them. Are they striking people out? Are they keeping runners off base? Are they staying away from walks and high earned run averages? How many hits are they giving up? What kind of innings are they pitching? Their hits, walks, and strikeout ratios give you a pretty good idea, especially if they have a good ERA.

Pitching has changed some since I broke into baseball. The split-finger fastball is the most dramatic new pitch. I've never thrown it in a game. With my curve I don't really need the splitter. It has changed some guys' careers though. Mike Scott won the Cy Young with it for Houston. Bruce Sutter became a dominant reliever with the Cubs and the Cardinals with that pitch. It seems to explode down in the strike zone after making the hitter think it's up where he can reach it. Few pitches make good hitters look worse.

The splitter has had more of an impact on baseball even than the spitter. Of course the spitter is illegal, but there are some guys who throw it. The thing is, not many can really control it, and if you can't control it, it doesn't help you a bit. It's the same thing with scuffing a ball. It makes it so hard to control that you don't see a lot of it going on. The benefits are exaggerated and the number of guys who know what to do with a scuffed or lubricated ball is getting smaller all the time.

When Mike Scott first learned the split-finger fastball from Roger Craig, a former pitcher and then manager, it gave Mike confidence. The more people became aware of his splitter and were afraid of it, the more effective his fastball was. You fool a guy with a bottoming-out splitter a couple of times and then bust a live fastball in there, he won't know whether to swing or sit down. That gives a pitcher just enough of a mental edge to make him more aggressive and confident.

I never felt I needed a split-finger with my repertoire. It can be a tough pitch to master, and it can be hard on your arm and hand if you don't do it just right. I did develop what's called a circle change, where you use your forefinger and thumb to form a circle and hold the ball in your palm. As you release the ball, you keep the thumb and forefinger touching (in fact, I curl the index finger almost down to the first bend in the thumb), causing the ball to slide out of your hand and off your remaining three fingers. Depending on the trajectory and the arm speed, the ball does all kinds of interesting things. Mostly, you can bring your arm down with the same speed as you would a fastball, but the pitch has less power behind it and becomes a wicked, moving changeup. I could never get consistent with any other kind of a changeup, but that has worked for me and made my fastball and my curve more effective. Still, the circle change is a tough pitch. I need to take enough velocity off it to fool a hitter, but if I get it up, it's my most hittable pitch and I can get hurt with it.

I've stayed away from sliders because I've never known of a pitcher who had both an outstanding curve and an outstanding slider. They tell me my curve is one of the better ones in the game, so people who say that I've succeeded for so long only because of my speed are wrong. Sandy Koufax had a great curve to offset his fastball. Walter Johnson and Bob Feller had the good curves. Tom Seaver, Steve Carlton, and Bob Gibson had excellent sliders. Most dominant-type pitchers do have a good breaking pitch too. But I didn't want to take away from my curve by throwing a slider. It seems to me a slider is harder on the arm.

I also believe—though this is just my opinion— that the slider shortens your career from a velocity standpoint. In other words, people who are successful with a slider seem to lose something off their fastball earlier in their career than they should. I don't know if the two go together or if pitchers just start relying on the slider more or what, but that's something I've noticed. And I've studied more than a few pitchers.

Back in my California Angel days I pitched in the ninety-seven- and ninety-eight-mile-per-hour range for a game. Now I'm at ninety-two/ninety-three, so I figure I've lost a couple of miles per hour off my fastball every ten years. That doesn't mean I still don't throw a good fastball, but it's not too often I throw one ninety-six or so. Early on I had an exceptional fastball. You get ahead of a guy with a pitch like that, he has to be ready to be quick or he'll strike out. Fool him with a curve, and there's no way he can hold up. If he does hold up and you get the pitch over, you've got him anyway.

I had such a live arm back then that people swore my curveball was coming in as fast as my fastball, but it wasn't. It was in the low eighties and now it's often in the seventies. The key to the breaking pitch is not how fast it is, but how much difference there is between it and the fastball. If a guy is throwing only eighty-five-mile-per-hour fastballs, his offspeed pitch can be pretty effective if it's a lot slower. And a guy throwing in the high nineties can surprise you with an offspeed pitch that's in the high eighties but is still faster than a lot of guys' fastballs.

The difference in the speed of my two primary pitches is eight to ten miles per hour. To get away with that, I have to keep the ball down. When you see me getting hit all over the yard or leaving a game early, it's because I've been unable to keep the ball low. That will be true with just about any pitcher, especially a power pitcher.

I'm not saying they were bad pitches, but I made a mistake as far as location. One thing I try to stress to young pitchers is that they shouldn't be upset when guys do hit their best stuff, because the advantage goes to the hitter when you fall behind him in the count. You've left yourself with fewer options. The guy pretty much knows what's coming, and if he can catch up to it, knowing you have to get it into the strike zone, he's got the edge.

He's seen your pitches, knows your location, and you have to take all that into consideration. When I give up home runs it's usually because I'm behind in the count 3–1 and can't get away with a breaking ball. Still, a pitcher has no one to blame but himself, because he's the one who got behind in the first place.

I'm not one of those pitchers who gets into a groove and feels like he can't be touched. I know when I've got good stuff, but I've also been successful when nothing seems to be working. And I've been hit well when I thought I was overpowering. Plus, even when I'm in the middle of a no-hitter late in the game and seem to be mowing people down, I know how quickly things can change. I never go for a strikeout unless I've got two strikes on a guy and we need to get him that way. I try to stay within my game and keep us out of trouble, worrying more about the win than the no-hitter. Yeah, if we're leading by several runs and I still haven't allowed a hit by the seventh or eighth, I think about the no-hitter. But I don't start overthrowing. I stick with what got me there and try not to make mistakes.

One thing I never do is get too careful. If there's one thing I wouldn't mind being remembered for it's that when I throw my fastball, no matter where in the game it is, I give the hitter my best stuff and go right at him. That takes a lot of work and concentration and confidence, but to me that's the only way a pitcher like me should pitch.

Because of adrenaline, my last pitch in a no-hitter might be close to my fastest pitch of the night, but I don't plan it that way. I'm careful not to over-throw, because if I hurt myself I'm out of the game anyway, maybe forever.

I was disappointed when I came so close to so many no-hitters in '89, but I had learned not to worry about them. You can't make them happen. Some-times the flukiest things break them up, and then you have to keep yourself together so you don't lose the game besides. If you get all rattled because some guy beats out an infield roller, you might let him steal second and see him score on a routine single. You've still pitched a great game, but not a smart one. If a no-hitter is going to happen, it'll happen. It's not automatic and you have to stay focused, but that's all you can do. A man can't control more than he can control, so I figure you should control what you can and let what happens happen.

Who hits me pretty well and consistently varies from year to year. I've had a lot of trouble lately with Mike Devereaux of Baltimore. I'm not sure why, but of course he's a good hitter and hits everybody well. Dave Valle of Seattle also hits about .400 off me, even though he hit only about .180 off the league last year. Once, somebody asked me who I had a lot of success against, and I said Sal Bando. I could hardly get him out at all after that.

I've had a lot of bad games, where I just didn't have it and got shelled early, but I always feel bad when I think the fans came to see me and didn't get their money's worth. I felt real bad about doing so poorly against the Yankees at Arlington going for my three hundredth win, but that wasn't the worst. In one home opener for the Astros in the mid-'80s, St. Louis knocked me out of the box in the second or third inning after six or so runs, and the young reliever we brought in couldn't do anything either. We wound up losing by what looked like a football score, and I felt terrible. Opening night should be just another game in a 162–game schedule, but I've never looked at it that way. It's always an honor to be chosen to pitch the opener and there's so much anticipation and excitement that you hate to lose, let alone get routed like that. Nobody remembers what happened a week later except you, but I want the fans to be glad they came out to the game.

# 14

## Opinions, Opinions

$A$ quarter of a century in big league baseball ought to give me the right to have a few opinions on the game. The only question is whether that gives me the right to express them. Well, you've for sure got a right to ignore 'em, so if you're not curious, just skip ahead. Otherwise, here are a few:

## Putting On a Game Face

I know a lot of players, especially pitchers, start getting their game face on a day ahead of when they're going to pitch. I don't. I get focused and prepared, but my work comes in the four or five days between starts. I find myself more jovial and relaxed than ever just before going out to warm up before a game. That's the time I feel best because I've worked hard and am confident that I'm prepared. If I'm not at my best and worried about something, then that's a different deal. But usually when I go out there to warm up, all the preparation is behind me and I have a job to do. Once I start to concentrate on that, then my game face goes on.

The actual pitching is a reward for everything I did on the off days to get ready. The win and the adulation are not as much a reward to me as the pitching itself—going out there and being able to be effective because of the preparation. So once I've started warming up, I'm all business. I've seen other pitchers joke around and talk to the hitters because

183

they're in control of their game and things are going right. I never do that, because I know things can change with one pitch, and I'm not going to leave the mound blaming it on losing my intensity.

That makes it pretty hard on me if I have a bad outing. The opportunity and the enjoyment of pitching are lost when I get knocked out early. The last time that happened I was so disgusted with myself that I went straight to the weight room and started lifting, preparing for my next start.

### The Strikeout Record

I'm not one to ever say that a record, especially one of mine, can't be broken. If I can set one, why can't someone else break it? But if I have one that's likely to stand longer than the rest, it's the career strikeout record. First of all, not many people are going to come along and be able to pitch five thousand innings. And not only will he have to log all those innings, he'll have to maintain a style that allows him to strike out at least a hitter per inning.

The way they use pitchers nowadays, with longer times off between starts and quicker use of relievers, not many pitchers are piling up those kinds of innings. For years with the Angels I pitched on a four-day rotation. Unless that becomes a tradition again, you won't see anyone with enough innings to threaten the strikeout record.

### A Pet Peeve

I have a problem with people in baseball who aren't baseball people. They make decisions about a pitcher, but they have never known what it is to stand on that mound when your arm's killing you or when you're not sure you can get a guy out and the game's riding on it. They don't know what it is to be in a slump and wonder if you're ever going to get out of it, or to know that everyone else thinks it's more than a slump and that you're on your way out of the game. They don't know what it is to be on the road when you have problems at home and are finding it tough to keep focused on your job. (Well, maybe they know that kind of frustration, but they're not contending with such a physically dangerous occupation as we are.)

More and more front office people are college grads—which is okay—but too many of them get their jobs through some sort of connection or relation. Maybe they were big fans, but that doesn't give them enough empathy with the players. I'm not saying every exec has to be a former ballplayer, but I hate to see it going totally the other way.

Worse are pitching coaches who've never pitched. That would be like me trying to become a hitting coach. I understand the principles and could teach to a point, but I don't really understand what goes on in a guy's mind—and that's a big part of this game.

### Racial Tension

When I was growing up I went to high school with Mexicans and whites; the blacks had their own schools. We never thought much about integration until it started happening after I graduated. My parents were not prejudiced, but I was not exposed to too many blacks, so race just wasn't an issue with me. The racial tension of the 1960s was something I saw on the news and didn't understand. At that time in Texas the Mexicans were probably as discriminated against as anyone, with many whites considering them inferior common laborers. It didn't take me long to see that that was wrong.

I never took the view that any racial group was inferior or should know and keep its place. I've played with and against many blacks over the years, and it gets to where I don't think we notice each other's color after a while. I've roomed with blacks and have had Latino and black friends I consider as close as any Anglos.

There is racism in the big leagues, just like there is anywhere. As long as you have people you'll have a few who don't think straight. Of course I've found that racism knows no color either. There are blacks and people of other races who are racist too. But there's not a whole lot of it in baseball anymore.

One thing I don't like is when someone gets criticized and blames it on racism. Too often, that's just a cop-out. There are always people going around looking for it, and when you're looking for something you can usually find it. I've played with people like that, and I've played with others who never give it a thought. A lot of it has to do with their backgrounds, their attitudes toward life in general, and whether they have a chip on their shoulder. Again, you learn a lot about people by just listening.

### The Designated Hitter

On this issue I have to say I prefer the National League. I think pitchers ought to have to hit and that it makes for a more interesting game. Of course, that comes from a guy with two home runs in a career and a lifetime batting average of .110!

The DH gives a pitcher an opportunity to win more ball games, get more decisions, and pitch more innings—which is what you get paid for—so you know I'm not being selfish in my opinion. The DH also gives a pitcher a little more offensive power, but then he has to face a better lineup too.

## My Own Hitting

I could have been a better hitter if I would have had someone to work with me and had the time to invest in it. Still, I never would have been a great hitter. People don't understand why pitchers don't put more time into batting practice, and I'm not sure myself. Maybe someday some organization will emphasize it, and their pitchers will start producing at the plate, and it will become popular. It's just one more part of the game to concern yourself with, but it really won't make you a better pitcher. So even though I prefer pitchers hitting, I don't mind not having to worry about it in the American League. When I was in the National League I never took batting practice except the day I pitched. Then I just basically used batting practice as a way to get loose and to get some bunting work in.

When I was younger I liked the hitting part of the game, but as I got older I realized how much effort goes into a guy staying on top of it enough to face big league pitching. I didn't get hung up with the ego aspect of it.

## Umpires

There are still too many incompetent umpires in the big leagues, but of course none of them are going to find out who I think they are. Baseball hasn't done a great job in two areas of umpiring: first, in making sure those guys are in shape, and second, in making sure that their personalities don't come into play on the field.

Seeing those guys overweight and out of shape is a bad image for baseball. I know they don't make the kind of money the players do, but still they have time to work out and they ought to do it. They ought to be mobile enough to get into position quickly and really see a play, even one in the alley. Did a guy catch the ball or trap it? Did it go over the fence or through it? Every play can affect the outcome of the game, so you want the fairest call possible.

I'm not saying they don't have tough jobs, because they do. And I know the pay is not the best, especially in the minors. But with as few umpiring jobs as there are and all the guys who'd love to have them, baseball ought to have tougher requirements and force those guys to stay in shape.

There are several umpires who do work out. We sometimes see them in the hotel weight rooms or even in some of the clubhouses. You feel that a guy takes a little pride in his appearance and his work when he does that.

Their travel schedules are worse than the players', but at least nowadays their schedules include some time off. Umpires have the winter off and have a lot of the benefits that the players have, but they will always have the worst travel schedules.

Television has brought out the worst in some of the personalities. It's okay when an ump wants to have fun and be a little dramatic or flashy when he makes a call, but when there's a disagreement and the umpire becomes the aggressor, like Joe West has done in the National League, something is wrong. West has been reprimanded several times, but he still antagonizes people and tries to intimidate them.

One area where I've fallen short over the years is in controlling my emotions on the mound. That will make some people laugh, because I have this image of being calm, cool, and collected, even when I pitch a no-hitter. But too often I let the umpires know when I think they have missed a call. I might glare at them or stomp around the mound between pitches, stuff like that. I don't mean to show them up, and sometimes I'll even apologize after the game. They usually understand. I wouldn't want to be shown up in a game either. It's just that I get so focused that it irritates me when I don't get a call and really believe it's wrong. Normally I won't talk to an umpire or expect him to talk to me unless I want an explanation for a balk call or a rule interpretation.

The only thing I ask of umpires is that they be consistent. There are some who are better ball-and-strike men than others, but I sure wouldn't ever put into print which was which. What a pitcher wants is a guy to establish his strike zone and not change it as the game goes on. If you're giving me the high strike early (which you rarely get in the National League), then give it to me in the eighth and ninth too. If you're not going to give me the low-and-away fastball off the corner, then don't give it to the other guy. I just want to know where I stand.

Just like pitchers, umpires have their good and bad days, and that can be frustrating. There's always a gray area where a call could go either way. Sometimes your veteran and star players get the edge there. If a hitter is known for having a great eye and he takes a close pitch, he might get the call. If he's a rookie and he takes a close pitch from me, I might get the call. The only way I can control the gray area is to make sure I haven't made an umpire mad or barked at him or showed him up. They don't like that, and I wouldn't either if I were back there. There can't be a tougher job anywhere. Every call you make makes one team happy and the other mad.

In the National League I'm convinced the strike zone has gotten smaller. You hardly ever see a strike called on a pitch above the waist. Some say the zone is below the thighs to the shins. I don't know how low it goes, but I know it's awfully small. The rule book says it's armpits to the top of the knees, but everybody knows you won't get a pitch that high called a strike and that you can get a lot of calls at the bottom of the knees.

I understand the commissioner wants the strike zone larger. That would sure get my vote.

I think umpires should all be under one jurisdiction. In other words, there shouldn't be American League and National League umpires. They should officiate in either league, and that would help their travel schedules even more. If a crew is in Houston and there's an open date when the Rangers are playing, they've got just a short hop. That would also help standardize the strike zones and a few other rule details. There would be fewer personality conflicts because you would see each crew less often.

### Interleague Play

There's nothing wrong with the alignment of the leagues, but because of tradition baseball is slow to make any changes. Each league is fighting for its identity, and that's why the umpiring is separate when it doesn't need to be and would be better off not. The separation of the leagues and divisions is not needed anymore. Football, basketball, and even the NCAA have shown that interleague play has increased interest.

If a team was having a real bad year, it would be good for their gate to have not just the great teams and stars from their own league come to town, but the best in all of baseball. It's not a burning desire of mine and I won't picket for it, but I don't think interleague play would hurt.

### The Best

I know this will get me into trouble with a lot of great, great stars, but the most talented player I ever played against was Willie Mays. Everybody knows he was a five-point player. A lot has been made of his ability to run, throw, field, hit for average, and hit with power. He didn't have a weakness in any facet of the game, and he found all kinds of ways to beat you. He was also enthusiastic and fun to watch. You could tell he loved the game and the fans.

Besides all that, Willie had longevity. He was the elite of the elite.

Today Barry Bonds of the Pirates may be the best player in the game, but when I left the National League I thought he was short on one ingredient: attitude. And I'm not sure that's changed. He has the most raw talent, but selfishness could keep him from being the best player in the game.

In our league I'd have to lean toward Ken Griffey, Jr. of Seattle. He and Bonds are something to watch, but it's interesting because they're from the new generation of ballplayers. I want to see what they make of their skills, what kind of drive they have, and whether they learn the game through the mastery of little things. I won't get into comparing my own teammates here, but I will later.

Cal Ripken of Baltimore is another outstanding player, but mostly because he's made so much of himself without having great natural talent. He's big and strong and has good eye-hand coordination, but he's not fast and may not have great range. Still, he's in the category of the special player and is one of the best in the game because he really knows how to play. Of course he hasn't missed a game in years, and there are advantages to that.

The best pitcher in the game today? Orel Hershiser of the Dodgers was before he got hurt. That scoreless-inning streak in '88 and his playoff and World Series work that year may never be matched. Dwight Gooden's awful tough for the Mets.

In the American League, and maybe all of baseball, Roger Clemens of the Red Sox has to be the best. It would be unfair for me to compare him with the best in the National League because I've been gone long enough, but of the people I see often, he's the best. He's a tough customer and he does all the things you want a front-liner to do. He doesn't walk many. He gives you the innings. He doesn't give up many hits. He's right there for you every time. If he has a bad game, he bounces back. That's a key. He's playing in a rough town, too. Boston fans are well educated and knowledgeable, and here's this Texas-raised boy (that may be why I'm partial to him) who says what he thinks, is fiery, taunts the hitters, and argues with the umpires. He's got to be good to back that up and still be accepted in a university town. He's one of the new breed of players.

# 15

## Today's Ballplayer

*B*aseball looks easy to the spectator. The rules aren't complicated, and lots of people have enough skill to fool around with the game. But when you listen to veteran big leaguers, not just us dinosaurs in our forties, you hear them talk about really learning the game. It's the little intricacies that make the difference between winning and losing. It can take years to learn it all, and growing up is part of the process.

Kids come into big league baseball with all this raw talent nowadays, and they've got bodies that won't quit. They've got speed, endurance, great arms, quickness, reflexes—everything but brains and attitude. For instance, ask a rookie pitcher how he's going to be judged, what's the ultimate rule? He'll tell you it's his won-loss record and whether he wins twenty games.

When he matures he'll know his job is to give his team a chance to win the ball game. The point is to keep the other guys off the bases or at least off the plate so your guys can get a lead. If I do that, I'm happy whether I get the win or somebody else does. I see less of that attitude in baseball today than I ever have. Hitters are less willing to sacrifice themselves to get the runner over. They're worried about how many hits they're going to get. They know that their earning power is based on statistics, but that's no way to win ball games. I've even seen hitters look at the manager in the dugout after getting a bunt sign as if to say that they couldn't believe it. That's sad.

Sometimes I try to counsel young relievers and get them thinking about what they'll do in different game situations. They look at me like they have no idea what I'm talking about. They'll say, "I'm gonna go in there and throw my curve," or "I'm gonna try to strike 'em out," as if that's what they get paid for and that's what got them here, so that's all they think about. That's how ball games are lost. They really don't understand, and a major part of baseball strategy has been lost.

In the old days there were a lot more players who spent several years in the minors really learning the game. By the time they got to the big leagues their talent may have still been in question, but they had a better idea of how to play. It was as if they had been to baseball college. Now if you've got the talent, someone assumes you can overcome your limited knowledge of strategy.

Some modern ballplayers think that they're entitled to their money just because they were born with talent. Some think they're entitled to be seated ahead of other people, to cut ahead in lines, to have somebody give them something for nothing just because of who they are. I don't understand that mentality. I don't care if you're a doctor, a lawyer, or an Indian chief, you should not be treated any differently than anybody else.

Some proprietors try to give me a free car wash or free parking or even a free meal in a restaurant. I know they're trying to be nice and generous, but first off, I don't need comps. I wish they'd park a laborer's car for free and give him a break. When it happens to me in a restaurant, I always insist on paying unless that creates a scene. I tell them, "I didn't come in here for a comp deal. You can't afford to be giving away free meals." I want to pay just like anybody else. If they want to do something nice, they should give to others in need. I'd rather they just come over and tell me they appreciate my stopping in and that they hope I enjoyed it and will come back.

If you're a starting pitcher in the majors and you stay healthy, you will make a lot of money in a short time. Where's the incentive? It's unbelievable. When I broke into the big leagues you had to excel if you even wanted to make a living. During my first three years with the Mets I didn't make a living, I survived.

The young guys on the Rangers pitching staff are a good group. They work hard and they're willing to condition their bodies. If I have one criticism it's that sometimes they lose sight of their goals. I want to ask them what it is exactly that they're trying to accomplish. When you're in the weight room, you shouldn't be just building muscle or staying in shape, although that's good. Anything that doesn't go into making you a better pitcher ought to be cut out of your regimen. Have a plan. Be committed. Get focused.

I'd love it if one rookie would come to me and say, "I've made the team and I want to do well. What do I need to do?"

I'd tell him it's a lot of work, but it's also fairly simple. Learn the game by studying it. Know what separates the average player from the good player. You'll see some players at this level who are just exceptionally gifted athletes. They're going to stand above everybody and there's nothing you can do about that. Then you've got guys who have just run-of-the-mill big league talent, which is no small thing. It already sets them apart from minor leaguers and tens of thousands of other guys who only dream of playing in the majors. Then you look at the Pete Roses and the Don Suttons and the Cal Ripkens and you ask yourself, how did these guys with run-of-the-mill talent or even less make themselves into outstanding Hall-of-Fame-type players? When you get a handle on that, you're on your way to doing well.

The answer is that it was their hearts and their drive and their intellects. They wanted to become the best ballplayers they could, so they put in extra work. They put in the time on fundamentals, played to their strengths, and worked on their weaknesses. They anticipated situations and made mental as well as physical commitments. Anybody can commit to physical exertion for a limited period. The man who can commit himself to mental discipline has to be alert constantly.

One thing that really disgusts me with the modern player is when he shows off. These guys who hit a home run and then stand in the box and flip their bat away like they're really something just make you want to put the first pitch in their ear the next time around. They might hit one out and then almost walk around the bases, pumping their fist or trying some other way to draw attention to themselves. You don't see me pumping my arms or pointing at guys when I strike them out. I've seen pitchers blow on their finger like it's a smoking pistol after a strikeout. That's bush league.

Sometimes a little emotion, if it's real and spontaneous, is refreshing. I smiled after my seventh no-hitter; I just couldn't help it. I was so happy it had come at Arlington Stadium and that everything worked well after how bad I felt before the game. But usually, even after an achievement like that, I don't do anything that rubs it in to the other team or makes it look like I think I'm hot stuff.

When Carlton Fisk hit that dramatic extra-inning home run in the World Series years ago, it was moving to see him waving and using body English to try to keep it from going foul. That was real. But how many times in all the years since have you seen Carlton do more than clap on the field?

When Kirk Gibson hit that game-winning homer in game one of the 1988 World Series, coming off the bench hardly able to walk, no one begrudged his little fist pumping celebration as he circled the bases. But that was for the situation, not for himself.

The young ballplayers do that all the time in normal games. It's become widespread, and it's horrible, but they think nothing of it. They grew up watching Rickey Henderson and Reggie Jackson and those guys doing it on ESPN and highlight shows, showing up the other team. And those are two guys with talent who didn't need to do that stuff.

Fisk wasn't admiring his homer. Gibson wasn't admiring his homer. They were pulling for their teams, trying to win, knowing how important their runs were. We had a guy come into Arlington with Seattle who was hitting under .200. I mean he was in a terrible slump and hadn't hit a homer for about six weeks. Well, he finally connects off one of our guys, and it's one of those shots that you know is gone when it hits the bat. He stands at home plate and flips his bat away like it was a weapon and he was Ted Williams or somebody. I was thinking, *What in the world is goin' on?*

That's when you wish Bob Gibson or Don Drysdale was pitching for you, because that guy would pay dearly for a stunt like that the next time up. The best revenge is success anyway, so even though I might not throw at a bat flipper, he'll sure be facing the best I've got to offer next time. With nobody out and nobody on I'll still go after him like we're tied in the bottom of an extra-inning World Series game with a man in scoring position. That's the way I pitched to Pete Rose when he was going for the National League career hit record. If Pete was going to break the record off me, he was going to earn it.

You won't see me ragging on a guy during a game either. Some guys are good at razzing and hollering. I don't think there's any profit in screaming at umpires from the bench either. It's a thankless job and every call is a judgment. If they're wrong, they're wrong, and you're not going to change that.

Mike Scott of the Astros was one of the most talented pitchers I ever played with as far as being big and strong and being able to throw. He knew what he was doing and was one of the premier big league pitchers during the last few years when I was with Houston.

When he was on the mound, he was a committed pitcher. He'd do whatever it took to win. But off the mound he was one of the laziest pitchers I have ever seen. He was blessed with natural strength and ability, and he took it as far as it would take him. He developed that split-finger fastball that made him almost unhittable in 1986 when he won the Cy Young Award and all that. He had people convinced he was scuffing the ball, which distracted them and made him even more effective, whether he was actually doing it or not. But he never did anything to enhance himself physically. Would never work. Nothing. Didn't run. Didn't lift. Had terrible eating habits. All he cared about was playing golf.

Now he has retired before his time due to an injury. Who am I to say the injury could have been prevented? I don't know. Just seems to me a guy who keeps himself in shape can either avoid a lot of serious injuries or bounce back from them. I always liked Mike, but I can't say it surprised me that his career didn't last as long as I felt it should have. When I used to tease him about not working out or about eating junk food, he'd say something like, "You think I want to be pitching 'til I'm forty? No way. I'll be out on the links."

Well, a fella's got the rest of his life for that. There's only so much golf you can play. While he's young and healthy, he should take advantage of the opportunities he has. And being in shape wouldn't have just allowed him to pitch longer. He would have been even better than he was, and when you're talking about Mike Scott being better, you're talking about an exciting thing. He was fabulous as it was. Just think of him being a complete pitcher; who knows what he might have accomplished?

Mike was a good-natured guy and could take my teasing. Sometimes we'd be sitting around harassing each other about habits and work and stuff, and he'd make fun of me for being a hick, working with cows and horses and all. I needled him about his inability to work and that he probably didn't know anything about animals or even a shovel or how to fix a flat tire. I said, "Mike, tell me, have you ever had a job?"

He looked at me funny, so I pressed him. I said, "Mike, I want you to tell me. Have you ever in your life had a real honest-to-goodness job?"

The other guys were hooting because they could see he was trying to think. "You haven't!" somebody said.

"I have a job," he muttered.

I said, "What's your job?"

"I play baseball."

"That's no job. You said it yourself. 'I *play*.' Have you ever had a *real* job, one where you had to get up in the morning and be somewhere at seven-thirty or eight o'clock? Where you had thirty minutes for lunch and didn't get off until five? Where you had to actually do something, and you got paid hourly?" Now we had an audience, so I kept pushing. "Have you ever had one of those?"

"Once," Mike said.

"Once? What was it?"

He told me that when he played in a college summer league they provided jobs for the guys because they couldn't pay them. They played for the local team at night and had jobs during the day.

"So what was *your* job?"

"I worked in a warehouse. I'd get there at nine and had to stay there 'til noon. Once in a while someone would call and have me put something in a box and tape it up and ship it out."

We were laughing. That was the only real job he had ever held in his life, and that's the case with a lot of ballplayers. They don't really know what it is to have to work. Because of that, they don't have a concept of what it means to be committed to your job or being in a situation where if you don't work you don't get paid, and if you don't get paid you don't make ends meet.

I'll never forget a player in the '70s who usually hit over .300 and was one of those elite, gifted athletes. He had a beautiful swing and could crush the ball, was a great base runner and a heads-up player. He made good money and was an All-Star, but he hardly ever took batting practice. Knowing how tough this game is and how hard it is to hit .300, you tell me: If a guy like that works hard, what happens? Could he have hit .400? Would he have been a Hall of Famer? There's no telling how great he could have been.

That lack of work ethic is why you see so many guys come in and out of baseball and make tremendous dollars for a short time and then wind up with very little. They take the same approach to their money that they took toward their jobs, and they don't plan for the future. If they are careful with the money they do receive, they can set *themselves* up for life, but most of them don't. There are a lot of real working people out there who won't make in a lifetime what some journeymen ballplayers make in a few years. But what have they got to show for it when they're out of the game?

Many of them end up declaring bankruptcy and leaving people holding the bag, then they say they got dealt a bad hand. The thing is, they had an opportunity and they didn't take advantage of it. All our lives we hear that old line about putting something away for a rainy day, but not too many ballplayers actually do it. They listen to the wrong people, the wrong financial advisers. They want to make a quick killing, a fast buck. They had no respect for their money so they spent it, thinking it would be a never-ending deal. They weren't prepared for the kinds of resources they got, and now they have to scratch for a living just like anybody else. You hate to see that happen.

I'm not the kind of a guy to give advice to the kids on the Rangers. I like this team, and occasionally I'll be asked for my opinion. But I low-key it. They have to learn on their own. They know I'm here and they can ask me anything: about baseball, money, life, whatever. I figure nobody listens to advice unless they ask for it, and a lot of the time they don't listen to that either.

I'm impressed that the Rangers ballplayers for the most part are hard workers and dedicated to conditioning. I do want to see them focus on what's really important, preparing to get every edge they can. The game is so competitive today and there is so much balance; that's why you see a last-place team beating a first-place team on a given night.

The Rangers had one of the best hitting clubs in the majors in 1991. Now if all the young guys can have the pride and commitment it takes to be excellent and not look at their careers as just a means to generate revenue, we might finally turn a corner and play up to the potential that's been here for the last few years. Arlington is ready for a winner, and I get asked all the time about whether the Rangers can really do it. Let me tell you about a few of the frontliners, and you decide.

# 16

---

## The 1993 Rangers

$O$bviously, the 1992 season was a large disappointment on a team basis and on an individual basis. We had high expectations and played pretty well for the first half of the season. But we wound up with injuries, the firing of Manager Bobby Valentine, and a late-season blockbuster trade that sent Ruben Sierra, Bobby Witt, and Jeff Russell to the Oakland A's for Jose Canseco. Any time you have great expectations that don't pan out, problems crop up.

On a personal level, I was disappointed that I didn't throw consistently. I was injured early in the year and found myself in a spot in the pitching rotation that didn't get a lot of run support. In fact, our run production in 1992 was considerably below what it was in 1991—682 compared to 829.

But 1993 is a new season, and I'm optimistic, so let me talk about our current ball club. My only hesitation is that things change so quickly. By the time you read this we could have traded away some of these players for someone who could make all the difference. But that's the hazard of writing about a profession like mine.

I also need to apologize in advance to the players I don't name here. I'm sticking with what I see as the basic starting lineup, but I know as well as anyone that it's the whole roster that makes a club a winner. As a pitcher it's great to be able to say that my team is one of the most potent offensive clubs in the league.

I feel we should be contenders. Of course, certain things have to happen. The pitching staff will need to be consistent. We're going to have to get a few innings from our starters and not overload the bull pen during each game. Offensively, we're going to have to match our performance in '91. We have the potential. If Julio Franco is healthy and has a good year and Rafael Palmeiro bounces back from a subpar year and Jose Canseco is healthy and returns to his classic form of the past few years, then we'll be a great offensive team.

When you look at the hitters on this team, you have to wonder how we could ever lose a game. But winning also takes good defense. That's been a problem for us. We made too many errors and too often didn't make the big play that would have kept us in the ball game.

At first base we have one of the best hitters in the league, Rafael Palmiero. In 1991, he and second baseman Julio Franco battled for the league batting title until the last few weeks when Rafael fell off to finish at .322 and Franco won it with a .341. In 1992, Palmeiro batted .268, but I believe he'll bounce back in '93. Palmeiro has a beautiful swing, a lot like Billy Williams had when he was with the Cubs and like Dave Justice has now with the Braves. You either have that swing or you don't; it's not something that can be taught.

Rafael is no Keith Hernandez or Ken Hrbek with the glove, but he's no Cecil Fielder either. He's got a great attitude and works hard at making himself a complete ballplayer, not just a hitter. He's matured and does a good job for being fairly new to the position. He came up as an outfielder with the Cubs, and they don't have a thing to show for trading him to us.

Julio Franco at second was injured most of 1992. If he returns to his '91 hitting form, it'll be impossible to keep him out of the lineup, but frankly he hurts us defensively. He makes a lot of errors, and I doubt that he's going to improve because his approach to ground balls lacks the fundamentals. He bends at his waist instead of his knees, and he fields the ball too far back. He makes outstanding plays once in a while because he's quick and fast and knows what he should do, but he hasn't got the correct approach to playing his position. He was an All-Star second baseman, but that's because of his hitting. It's the normal, routine plays that make you or break you, and even *Sports Illustrated* said, "There's no way the Rangers can win a championship with as poor a defensive player as Franco playing second base." *SI* was speculating that we'd trade Julio for pitching help, but we didn't. I don't know that it makes sense to trade away a batting champion, even if he's not the best fielder. There's been some talk about hiding him in the outfield, but I don't know if they'd really do that. I don't mean to put him down, but I think he likes to hit more than he likes to work at shoring up his defense—and he's quite a hitter. At the very least, the Rangers' acquisition of Billy Ripken offers some options too.

We could see Jeff Frye moved to second and Julio as our designated hitter. Jeff's experience from last year gives us a little depth at second base, especially if Julio's knee doesn't allow him to play second on a regular basis.

The Rangers solidified the shortstop position with the acquisition of Manny Lee, a seasoned, proven major league player. With Jeff Huson having rotorcuff surgery and not being available to us until after the All-Star break, Manny is a valuable asset.

At third base we have Dean Palmer. He's improved defensively and has incredible power. Dean hit .229 in 1992 with 26 home runs and 92 RBIs. If he makes consistent contact with the bat in '93, he'll hit more home runs and have more RBIs because of the power he puts on the bat.

In the outfield, I think the Rangers would like to move Juan Gonzalez to left field. Juan led the majors in home runs in 1992 with 43. He also had 109 RBIs. He's only twenty-three years old and is the youngest Ranger ever to hit 43 home runs in a season. I feel he can only get better offensively, and he'll help our ball club defensively by moving to left field.

David Hulse is probably penciled in for center field. He played well for us defensively in 1992 and hit well, too. It's a matter of him just getting on base, because we need a lead-off hitter and we don't really have one.

In right field we have Jose Canseco. If he's healthy, his bat will probably make Dean Palmer and Juan Gonzalez better hitters. He's also a good defensive player. Certainly, a healthy Canseco will have a very positive effect on the entire lineup.

That brings me to Ivan (Pudge) Rodriguez. Pudge joined our team in June 1991. He started 80 percent of our first hundred games in '91 and, except for the brief time he was injured, most of our games in 1992. He's only twenty-one and batted .260 in 1992 with 37 RBIs. He's going to be a great one and has the chance to be another Benito Santiago. My guess is he'll start most of our games in 1993. He's got another year's experience, which will make him a better receiver. He's made great progress in handling the pitchers. He's learning the league and the hitters and how to take charge. He can only get better.

As for our starting rotations, it's probably still up in the air as to who the five will be. Obviously, Kevin Brown has come into his own. He won twenty games in 1992. Charlie Leibrandt brings a lot of experience, and Craig Leifferts will probably fill a spot. Roger Pavlik pitched some last year. Todd Burns or one of the younger kids like Dan Smith are possibilities. We'll be going into camp with probably more depth in the pitching staff than we have ever had before, and we'll have a seasoned bull pen with the addition of Tom Henke. We have some left-handers, people who can either pitch out at the pen or as starters. I think the pitching staff has more flexibility and more experience than we've ever had before. It is just a matter of deciding who's going to try to fill what roles.

I should be able to contribute the way I have the past few years. If I can stay off the disabled list, I'll increase the number of innings I can pitch for the season. I probably won't have the biggest share of innings among the Rangers' pitchers. The club probably hopes that I can handle 175-200 innings, but I wouldn't mind shooting for 225 if I'm healthy.

So, as far as the '93 season is concerned, I think we could have a very exciting ball club. But it's going to be really hard to get a feel for how the club is going to come together until probably May or June because of our new manager, Kevin Kennedy, and the new coaches. Kevin comes highly recommended. He's been successful on a minor league level, so it's going to be a matter of him getting some experience. So much will depend on how his personnel perform. That's what it hinges on. There's so many new people on the playing field that I don't think it'll be something that just clicks right out of spring training. But if we get some breaks and stay healthy, the '93 Rangers can win. We've sure got the horses.

# 17

## As for Me

*T*his is going to be my last year as a major league ballplayer, and the Texas Rangers are the right kind of a ball club for me to finish my career with. There's a lot of offense, the possibility of some good pitching, I like the manager, and unless the ballpark were right up the road from Alvin, it couldn't be more convenient. Management's been good to me, and the fans are the greatest. There's something about how Texans take to one of their own. It's a real love affair between a guy who'd rather pitch before the home folks than anywhere else in the world.

In fact, one of the local sportswriters, who must have thought I might be getting too old or tired or feeble to keep up with the pace, speculated that maybe I should only pitch at home. Can you imagine? No road trips. No travel. No way that would work. I'd be all out of sync and rhythm and wouldn't pitch on a regular schedule.

It happened last year that I was on the disabled list a couple of times when the team was on the road, and I came off the list when they got home. Also, if I pitched the last game of a home stand, I might do my next day's workout in Arlington and not join the club on the road until the next day. I appreciate those kinds of privileges and think I've earned them, but I also think accommodating me a little like that is good for the club. If I'm healthy and in shape and rested, I do better.

---

I've so far surpassed any expectations I've ever had about longevity that I just take it a day at a time the way everybody else does. I know that an injury could stop me, and I also know that age is bound to catch up with me one of these days. But when? I shouldn't be able to do what I do now, so who's to say I can't still do it when I'm fifty?

I'd like to say this year is it, or next year for sure, but I've been saying that for a long time. I just don't want to say it anymore. I'll decide based on how I feel and whether I really believe I can help the club. If I don't think so or if they don't think so, I've got plenty to keep me busy.

The aging process is affecting me the way it does a lot of people, with aches and pains and stiffness, but for the most part it hasn't affected my pitching. I've given it every chance to catch up with me by throwing a lot more pitches than most, so I can only credit my staying power to genetics, mechanics, and conditioning.

One thing I'm glad of, and that is that I haven't lost my drive to pitch. That's a big part of my success. It would be real easy to sit back and enjoy all the records, and no one anywhere would begrudge me the pleasure. They'd say I've earned it and have nothing more to prove. But I've still got that competitive drive when I'm on the field. If I lost that, I'd quit real quick, because I'm convinced you can't survive at this level without it. You can lose a little of your physical power and compensate with drive, but without the drive it doesn't make any difference what kind of ability you have. You're not going to get far until you have a burning desire to excel.

Now after having said all that, I realize that this very well could be my last season, and it wouldn't surprise me a lot if it is. The wear and tear physically and mentally of trying to hold up under the demands makes me not want to think of the year after this. I have to walk away from it at some point.

In the summer of 1991 we signed a two-year extension that gives the club an option for the second year, 1993. I plan to play through that second year, but once I'm through as a player I'm committed to the ten-year personal services contract—which I'm more than happy to fulfill.

There are a lot of things we'd like to do as a family and that Ruth and I would like to do and haven't been able to because of all the travel. We'd like to see the country in the spring and summer when we're not on someone else's schedule. Think of it: my springs and summers have been booked solid for twenty-five years.

In some ways my schedule now is harder on Ruth than it's ever been. There are more demands on my time, more obligations to the public, all the commercial stuff—she'll be as happy as I am when that's all behind us. I've felt it necessary to take advantage of all the opportunities that have come to me with the attention from the three hundred wins and the five thousand strikeouts and the last two no-hitters. But the prospect of having a week to myself someday without having to plan for it months in advance, that looks pretty good.

You probably won't see me doing color work on television or anything like that. It isn't that I don't have anything to say or that I couldn't learn to be comfortable doing that. It's just that I have no desire to travel as part of a job. If I'm traveling, I want it to be with my wife and family, just going somewhere because we want to when we want to, not hurrying or worrying. I've always been a homebody. I like to be at home every night if I can. I like to sleep in my own bed. Life on the road, as I've said, is only glamorous to people who've never done it.

When the baseball life *is* finally over, it's going to be an adjustment for everybody in our family. One thing I'm sure of is that I will be through playing by the time Reese and Wendy are out of high school. I like the idea of being around here while they're still in school.

The only goal I ever really had was to be successful in whatever I was doing. There were things I wanted to acquire, and baseball has made that possible. I always wanted a ranch, and I still dream of putting together a spread that could run five or six hundred cows in one location. I'm in the process of putting that together, but I'll get serious about it when I free up some time. I've always been attracted to an area in south Texas where I can spend a lot of time doing what I want to do, operating a ranch on a day-to-day basis without being required to be there every minute.

I don't sit around reflecting on my career, and I probably never will. The reason I don't now is because I'm still in it. I don't want to live in the past. I get a lot of satisfaction out of what I have accomplished and knowing that it's brought joy to people, but when it's over, I'll just move on.

One thing I don't want to do is wait until I can't get the ball to the plate before I know it's time to hang it up. It's a bitter pill to swallow when you realize you can't get the job done any longer, and every player handles it differently. You see a lot of guys retire and live off the glow of that until it wears off, then they want to make a comeback. They watch television and they think they can hit the new pitchers or get out the new hitters. It's sad to see them try to come back. You'll never see me doing that. Once I decide it's over, it'll be over.

I can say I want to be prepared to deal with how much I'll miss the game, but I suppose it's like thinking you're prepared for a loved one's death. There's no doubt in my mind that I'll miss baseball a lot. You don't have something dominate your life this long and then walk away from it without regrets.

People are always asking me if I think about the Hall of Fame. I really don't, and I hope people know me well enough by now to know that I'm being truthful. The subject is brought up more and more each year as guys younger than me are being elected. People used to debate whether I'd make it. Now they pretty much assume I will. I don't think about it one way or the other. I believe you can only control what you can control, and since Hall of Famers are chosen by people voting, I'll leave it at that. If they think I'm deserving, I'll make it. If they don't, I won't.

I can live with that. Either way, I'll always be able to look in the mirror and know that the guy looking back gave the game and the fans and his ball club everything he had to give for as long as he could.

On Thursday, February 11, 1993, I announced that the 1993 season would be my final year in the major leagues. I feel like I have reached a point in my life when it is time to move on to other things. But I'm looking forward to going out with a good season for me and the Rangers in 1993.

# Appendix: Extra Innings

## Lynn Nolan (Nolan) Ryan, Jr.

Born: January 31, 1947  Height: 6'2"   Weight: 212
Bats: Right  Throws: Right
Birthplace/Residence:  Born in Refugio, TX...
  Raised and lives in Alvin, TX.
Major League Service:  24 years, 101 days
How Acquired:  Signed as a free agent, December 7, 1988.

### THE 1992 SEASON

Nolan placed 3rd on the staff in starts (27), complete games (2), and strikeouts (157) and was 41st in innings (157.1) and wins (5). He missed 6 starts due to injury and lasted less than 3 innings 3 other times due to weather and physical problems. As a result, his 5 wins were his fewest ever in a full season and his starts, innings, and strikeout totals were his smallest in a full season since 1971. Nolan recorded his 1st losing season since 1987 and finished as many as 4 games under .500 for only the 4th time ever. He recorded a 3.22 era in his last 23 starts but was only 5-8 in this span as the Rangers scored 2 or fewer runs 10 times.

Still, by season's end, he had increased his all-time major league leading strikeout total to 5668 while moving into 2nd place on the all-time list in games started (760) and ranking in the top 20 in 7 other pitching categories.

Nolan is 319-297 in 26 big league seasons. In 4 years with Texas, he is 46-34 with the best winning percentage (.575) and 3rd lowest era (3.30) in team history.

**Summary:** Had 2 streaks of 9 or more consecutive winless starts in 1992 after just 3 such spans in career entering the season...Was Texas opening night starter on Apr. 6 at Seattle and led in the 5th inning of no decision with a strained left calf and inflamed right Achilles (see injuries below…Was on d.l. from Apr. 7-30…In 1st 2 starts back, allowed 10 runs in 4.1 innings in loss to Chicago on Apr. 30 and no decision at Baltimore on May 5, increasing era to 11.42…Beginning May 9, was 0-2, 3.40 (17 er/45 ip) in next 8 starts, allowing 3 or fewer runs in all but one outing…At that point, was 0-3 in 11 starts in 1992 and winless in 13 straight starts since a victory on Sept. 25, 1991, the latter period matching the longest streak without a victory of his career (0-8 in 13 starts with Houston, June 22-Aug. 14, 1985)…Had never gone more than 4 starts at the beginning of a season without a win…Had no decision in 6 consecutive starts, May 5-June 1, the longest such span of his career.

Ended the drought with a win at Detroit on June 28 and was 5-0, 1.65 (8 er/43.2 ip) in 6 starts from June 28-July 26…Matched the longest winning streak of the season by a Ranger and was his 2nd longest with Texas (6 in 1990)… Last victory in that stretch was July 26 at Baltimore.

Went 0-6, 4.35 (29 er/60 ip) in his last 10 starts, just the 4th time has lost as many as 6 consecutive decisions in a season…Was 0-5, 7.16 (26 er/32.2 ip) in 6 August starts, his most defeats in a month since July 1987 (0-5)…Allowed 19 runs (18 er) in 13.2 innings in his last 3 August games and failed to last 5 innings in any of those starts, tying the longest such streak of his career…Was 0-1, 0.99 (3 er/27.1 ip) in his last 4 starts as Texas scored just 6 total runs with 2 shutouts.

**Tough Luck:** Left with a lead in a victory situation only to receive a no decision 6 times, the most of any season in his career…Since the start of 1972, has left with a lead in a position to win 39 times, only to receive a loss or no decision…Breakdown by club: California (6); Houston (19); Texas (14)…The Rangers scored zero or one run in 9 of 27 starts…Lost 4 times by shutout to give him 63 such losses in career, 2 behind all-time leader Walter Johnson.

**Injuries:** Strained his left calf and aggravated his right Achilles heal while running to cover 1st base in 5th inning on Apr. 6 at Seattle and was forced to leave the game... Was diagnosed as having acute tendinitis in the Achilles and was disabled from Apr. 7-30...On June 1 vs. New York, left with 2-0 count on game's 2nd batter with a strained left hamstring...Did not miss a turn but was hampered by problem again on June 12 at Oakland...Strained a muscle in his left side on Sept. 7 against Boston and was sidelined for 14 days before next start on Sept. 22.

**Miscellaneous:** Held opponents to .238 batting average, the lowest on the staff, .245 (72-294) vs. lefthanded batters and .231 (66-286) against righthanded batters...Opposition batted .225 (34-151) with men in scoring position...Of 9 homers allowed, 5 came in span of 4 starts, Aug. 11-27...Had gone 57.2 innings without allowing a long ball over 2 seasons before Cal Ripken went deep on May 5 at Baltimore...Allowed 7 runs 3 times, including consecutive starts, Aug. 21 & 27, matching his most as a Ranger (3 times total from 1989-91).

Threw only 10 pitches without a retiring a batter on June 1 against New York...Was just 2nd time in big league career that had happened, the other being a start on Sept. 28, 1971 against St. Louis...Was 2nd in the A.L. with 12 hit batters and tied for the club lead with 9 wild pitches...Was ejected for 1st time in major league career after hitting Oakland's Willie Wilson with a pitch on Aug. 6.

### 1992 AND MAJOR LEAGUE CAREER

**Honors:** Has received numerous honors and awards in his career...In 1990, received the 22nd annual Man of the Year Award from *The Sporting News*, Male Athlete of the Year honors from United Press International, and the United States Sports Academy/*USA Today* Pro Sportsman of the Year Award...Also finished 2nd to Joe Montana in the Associated Press 1990 Male Athlete of the Year voting...Won the American League's Joe Cronin Award for significant achievement in 1973 and 1989, the only 2-time recipient.

Among the Leaders: In addition to being the all-time strikeout leader, ranks among the lifetime major league leaders in walks (1st, 2755), wild pitches (1st, 274), games started (2nd, 760, 58 behind Cy Young), losses (3rd, 267), innings (6th, 5320.2), shutouts (T8th, 61), wins (12th, 319), era (18th, 3.17), and appearances (17th, 794)...Is 1st among active pitchers in wins, losses, era, starts, shutouts, innings, walks, and strikeouts, ranks 2nd in complete games (222, Bert Blyleven-242) and is 4th in appearances (Rich Gossage-927; Jeff Reardon-811; Charlie Hough-803)...Is 11th all-time in total runs allowed (2131)...Has allowed 8 grand slams, one shy of the major league career record shared by Ned Garver, Milt Pappas, and Jerry Reuss.

In the 1980s, finished 1st in strikeouts (2167) and was 8th in wins (122)...Was his 2nd consecutive decade with 2000+ strikeouts (2678 from 1970-79)...Is also the major's strikeout leader over the last 10 years (1983-92) at 2174 and ranks 3rd over the last 5 years (1988-92) at 1121...In addition, has majors' 5th lowest era (3.27) 1983-92...Holds outright or shares 52 Major League, American League, and National League records.

In addition to having the best winning percentage and 3rd lowest era in Rangers' history, also ranks among the club's all-time leaders in strikeouts (4th, 893), walks (5th, 313), shutouts (7th, 6), wins (9th, 46), and innings (10th, 773.2).

**Strikeouts:** His 157 strikeouts were fewest since 1981 (140) and smallest total in a full season since 1971 (137)... Fanned the 157 in 157.1 innings, ending a string of 6 straight seasons with at least one strikeout per inning... Was his 24th season with 100 or more strikeouts and the 23rd consecutive year, both extending his own major league marks...Snapped a string of 5 seasons with at least 200 strikeouts...Fanned Baltimore's Sam Horn for 5600th strikeout on July 16.

Has averaged 9.59 strikeouts per 9 innings in his career, joining Sandy Koufax (9.28) as only pitchers in history (1500 or more ip) to average a strikeout an inning...Has 2 of the top 3 ratios of all time (11.48 in 1987 and 11.32 in 1989) as well as 4 of the top 6...Is 1532 strikeouts ahead of 2nd place Steve Carlton on the all-time strikeout list, the largest percentage differential between 1st and 2nd in any major statistical category.

Had 10 or more strikeouts twice in 1992, his fewest since 1969: 13 on July 4 vs. Oakland (matching 2nd highest total in the A.L. in 1992) and 12 on Aug. 6 against Oakland...Is the oldest pitcher to ever fan as many as 10 batters in a game...Holds the Rangers' club record with 16 strikeouts on 2 occasions: Apr. 26, 1990 vs. Chicago and in his 7th no-hitter, May 1, 1991 against Toronto...Is the oldest pitcher to ever fan as many as 16 in a game, doing it 3 times since turning 40...Rube Waddell (16 in 1908 at age 32) is the only other pitcher in history since 1900 to accomplish that feat over age 30...Fanned 8 or more in 7 of 27 starts, just once in last 13 outings...Struck out game's 1st 5 hitters, May 9 vs. Milwaukee...Had just one strikeout in 4.1 innings on Aug. 21 at Cleveland, his fewest K's in a start of more than 2 innings since Apr. 19, 1985 vs. Atlanta (1 k/4.1 ip).

Has recorded 10 or more strikeouts in a game 215 times, a M.L. record (Koufax is 2nd with 98)...Has fanned 194 times, 3 of those in extra innings...His 19 strikeouts in a 9-inning game on Aug. 12, 1974 vs. Boston were an A.L. record until Roger Clemens' 20-strikeout performance in 1986...Fanned 10 or more a record 23 times in 1973 and set a Rangers' club record with 18 in 1989...Has 26 games of 15+ strikeouts, another M.L. mark...Struck out the side 6 times in 1992 and 331 in career.

His 6 seasons of 300 or more strikeouts and 15 years of 200 or more strikeouts are also records...Is the only Texas pitcher with more than one 200-strikeout campaign (3)...Fanned 383 with California in 1973, the most ever in modern history and owns 5 of the top 8 single season strikeout totals since 1900...Became the oldest pitcher by 11 years to fan 300 with a Rangers' club record 30 in 1989, the most in the A.L. since Ryan's 341 in 1977...Recorded 300 K's in fewest innings ever...Has fanned 203 at age 44 and 157 at age 45 with previous strikeout mark for pitcher, 44 or older, being 149 by the Yankees' Phil Niekro in 1985...Has fanned a total of 1167 different players (22 for 1st time in 1991), including 7 father and son combinations, 12 sets of brothers, and 21 members of Baseball's Hall of Fame.

Led the N.L. in strikeouts in 1987 and 1988 and has topped the A.L. on 9 occasions, 7 times in an 8-year span from 1972-79 and 1989-90...Became oldest player to ever lead the A.L. in a major statistical category with his strikeout crown at age 43 in 1990...His 11 overall strikeout titles is one shy of Walter Johnson's all-time mark...Is one of 3 pitchers to lead both leagues in strikeouts, joining Rube Waddell and Jim Bunning...Was the oldest pitcher to ever lead N.L. in strikeouts in 1987.

Wins: His 5 wins were fewest in a major league season (beginning 1968) with previous low being 6 in both 1968 and 1969...At 5-9, finished as many as 4 games under .500 for just the 4th time (7-11 in 1970; 10-14 in 1971; 8-16 in 1987)...Overall, has 66 wins since turning 40, 5th all-time behind Niekro (121), Jack Quinn (89), Cy Young (76), and Warren Spahn (75).

Is one of 9 pitchers in history to defeat all 26 major league teams, joining Doyle Alexander, Rich Gossage, Gaylord Perry, Scott Sanderson, Rick Sutcliffe, Don Sutton, Mike Torre, and Rick Wise...Accomplished that feat by defeating California in 1st lifetime appearance vs. the Angels on June 14, 1989...Is one of 5 ever with 100 or more wins in both leagues (Bunning, Jenkins, Perry, Young), and he and Young are the only pitchers to record 100 wins for teams in both leagues...His victory on July 26, 1992 at Oriole Park at Camden Yards gave him victories in 31 of the 35 major league ballparks in which he has pitched, the exceptions being Forbes Field in Pittsburgh, Kansas City's Municipal Stadium, the SkyDome in Toronto, and the new Comiskey Park in Chicago...Has defeated 218 different pitchers, beating Paul Splittorff a high of 7 times.

Has won 100 or more games in 20 of the last 22 seasons, including 16 consecutive years from 1971-86...His 20 10-win campaigns are 2nd most in history, one behind Sutton...Is a 2-time 20-game winner, 1973 (21) and 1974 (22) with the Angels...His 12 wins in 1991 marked the 6th time a pitcher 44 or older has won at least 12 games.

**Low-Hitters/Near No-Hitters:** His low-hit game in 1992 was the 31st 3-hitter of his career, July 4 vs. New York... Allowed just one hit in 1st 7 innings of that contest...On May 21 vs. Kansas City, allowed a 1st inning double, then held the Royals hitless in his final 6.1 innings of work, retiring the final 18 batters...Overall, allowed 5 or fewer hits in 14 of 27 starts.

Issued 7.89 hits per 9 innings in 1992...Had allowed just 5.31 hits per 9 innings in 1991, the 3rd best ratio in major league history behind own 5.26 mark with California in 1972 and Luis Tiant's 5.30 with Cleveland in 1968...His career ratio of 6.54 hits/9 innings is the lowest ever.

Has pitched a major league record 7 no-hitters, 3 more than Koufax...Has been the oldest pitcher to throw a no-hitter in each of last 2 gems...Has allowed one or fewer hits in a complete game 19 times, another record...His 12 one-hitters match Bob Feller for the most ever...Has hurled 2 no-hitters and 3 one-hitters in 4 years with Texas...Has issued 4 or fewer hits in a complete game on 96 occasions...Has also lost 5 no-hitters in the 9th inning...Opponents' career batting average is .203 (3869-19024).

**Shutouts:** Failed to record a complete game shutout in 1992 for 1st time since 1987 and 5th time in last 23 seasons (starting '70)...Does have 6 shutouts in 4 years with Texas after one total in previous seasons...Did not allow a run in 3 starts where pitched at least 6 innings, June 28 at Detroit (7 ip, win), Sept. 1 at Kansas City (6 ip, ND), and Sept. 22 vs. Minnesota (6 ip, ND)...Hurled 6.2 shutout innings on July 4 against New York before Danny Tartabull homered...Would have been the 3rd oldest pitcher to ever hurl a sho...Issued 3 or fewer runs in a game 21 times.

Had 2 or more sho for 13 straight seasons from 1972-84...His 9 shutouts in 1972 topped the league and matched the 2nd highest total in the A.L. over the last 28 years (beginning 1965)...Blanked 8 different opponents that year, and A.L. record and matching the major league mark...Also led the A.L. with 7 sho in 1976...Has 11 career cg 1-0 wins.

**Complete games:** Went the route twice for 2nd straight year in 1992, matching his fewest complete games in a season since 1987 and his 3rd lowest total in the last 23 years (starting '70)...His cgs were in a loss July 17 at California and the July 4 victory vs. New York...Worked 7 or more innings 11 times...Has 20 or more cgs in a year 5 times with a high of 26 in both 1973 an 1974...His longest consecutive complete game streak is 8 from May 15-June 15, 1973.

**Earned Run Average:** Compiled a 3.72 era in 1992, his highest since 1985 (3.80) and 2nd highest in the last 21 seasons (starting '72)...Has lowest career era among active players (3000 or more ip) (3.17), ahead of Blyleven (3.31) and has compiled era under 3.00 8 times...Led N.L. with career low 1.69 in 1981 and 2.76 in 1987...At 40 years, 8 months, was oldest to ever lead N.L. in era...His 2.91 figure in 1991 was the lowest for a Texas qualifying pitcher since 1983 and 7th best in team history.

**Walks:** His 69 walks in 1992 were his fewest since 1984 (69) and his ratio of 3.9 walks/9 innings was his 3rd best ever (3.26 in 1990 and 3.75 in 1991)...Did not issue a walk twice and had 2 or fewer 14 times...Season high was 7 on Aug. 16 vs. Detroit...Is 922 ahead of 2nd place Carlton on all-time walk list...Has led league in bb 8 times, most in history...Career highs are 204 in 1977 and 202 in 1974, the 2nd and 3rd highest single season totals all-time to Feller's 208 in 1938...Permitted career high 10 walks on Apr. 4, 1974 at Chicago White Sox.

**Home/Road:** In 1992, was 3-6, 3.40 in 15 starts at Arlington Stadium and 2-3, 4.18 in 12 games on the road...In 4 seasons with the Rangers, is 30-21, 3.38 (185 er/493.1 ip) in

73 Arlington starts and 16-13, 3.18 (99 er/280 ip) in 43 away games.

**Versus Opponents:** Since joining the Rangers, is 26-15 in 56 starts against the Eastern Division and 20-19 in 60 games vs. the West…Was 0-6 vs. the West in 1992 with last victory against that division coming in final 1991 decision, Sept. 25 vs. Seattle.

**Baltimore:** Was 24 in 3 starts and is 5-0, 2.29 (9 er/35.1 ip) in 6 starts the last 2 years since losing Sept. 7, 1989…Had been 0-9, 5.42 in previous 12 games…Before winning on Apr. 14, 1991, had not defeated the Orioles since Apr. 20, 1976 at Anaheim…Since pitching a no-hitter on June 1 1975 is still just 6-11 in 21 starts…Is 3-0, 1.89 (4 er/19 ip) in last 3 starts at Arlington…Win at Oriole Park at Camden Yards on July 26 marked 31st major league stadium in which he has recorded a victory…Finished 4-10 lifetime at Memorial Stadium, 1-7 in last 9 starts…His 4.05 era vs. the O's is highest against any big league club except Houston (5.59).

**Boston:** Lost only 1992 start and has faced the Red Sox just twice the last 2 years…Is 3-2, 2.61 (15 er/51.2 ip) in 7 starts against the Red Sox the last 4 years, going 3-1 in 4 starts at Arlington…Is 6-10 in 18 outings beginning 1975… At Fenway Park, is 0-2 in 4 starts since winning on May 6, 1977, is 1-5 in 8 games since a win on Apr. 30, 1974, and is 2-8 in 13 career outings…Has not pitched in Boston since July 2, 1990…Is 1-2, 2.78 (7 er/22.2 ip) in 3 lifetime starts against Roger Clemens, winning on April 30, 1989 at Arlington and losing on May 5, 1989 at Boston and Sept. 7, 1992 at Texas.

**California:** Was 0-2, 4.72 in 2 starts in 1992 after going 5-3, 1.76 in 8 outings from 1989-91…Has 5 complete games in 10 starts lifetime…Of 5 wins against the Angels, 4 have come over Chuck Finley with 1st career loss of Finley coming on Aug. 1…With Texas, is 2-2, 1.05 (4 er/34 ip) with 3 cgs at Anaheim Stadium…Also worked 2 scoreless innings in 1989 All-Star Game there…Is 85-58 lifetime at Anaheim.

**Chicago:** Is 7-4 in 18 starts against the White Sox since the start of 1978…In 4 years with Texas, is 4-0, 2.25 (14 er/ 56 ip) in 7 starts vs. the White Sox at Arlington Stadium…His 21 wins are 2nd highest versus any m.l. team.

**Cleveland:** Is 1-2, 6.41 (14 er/19.2 ip) in 3 starts the last 2 years and 3-3, 5.17 (27 er/47 ip) in 7 starts against the Indians since the start of 1989…At Cleveland Stadium, is 0-2, 12.10 (13 er/9.2 ip) in 2 starts with the Rangers and 0-4, 8.59 (21 er/22 ip) in 4 outings since last victory on Sept. 3, 1977.

**Detroit:** Had gone 5-0 in last 6 starts vs. the Tigers until loss on Aug. 16, 1992 at Arlington…Was his 1st defeat since Aug. 13, 1979 with California…Has a 2.36 era in 28 lifetime starts against the Tigers, matching his lowest vs. any team except California (2.26 in 10 games)…Has fanned 17 or more 3 times vs. Detroit.

**Kansas City:** Is 1-3, 5.03 (22 er/39.1 ip) in 8 starts vs. the Royals the last 3 years but is 5-3 in 13 outings since losing on Sept. 19, 1979…Has won more games (24) and pitched more innings (332.2) against the Royals than vs. any major league club…Has 24 complete games in 45 career starts.

**Milwaukee:** Had no decisions in 3 1992 starts and is 3-2, 2.63 (18 er/61.2 ip) in 9 starts since return to A.L.

**Minnesota:** Is 1-2 in 5 starts against the Twins the last 2 years…Was 4-0 in previous 7 games since a defeat on July 21, 1977…Has fanned 10 or more 19 times against the Twins, matching Oakland for career best.

**New York:** Was 1-0 in 2 starts in 1992 and is 8-0, 2.70 (28 er/93.1 ip) in last 13 games against the Yankees since losing on May 14, 1977…Is 3-0 in 6 career starts at Arlington…Lifetime at Yankee Stadium is 2-2 in just 5 starts.

**Oakland:** Is 0-2 in last 5 starts since hurling his 6th no-hitter on June 11, 1990 at Oakland…Is 1-5 in 9 starts against the A's since winning on Apr. 21, 1979…Since joining the Rangers, is 0-4 in 6 starts against the A's at Arlington Stadium.

**Seattle:** Is 3-0 in last 7 starts vs. the Mariners since a defeat on June 16, 1990 and is 5-2 in 12 games beginning 1989.

**Toronto:** Did not face the Blue Jays in 1992…With the Rangers is 3-4 in 8 starts despite a 2.35 era (15 er/57.1 ip).

**Opening Day:** At 45 years 12 months, was the 4th oldest pitcher to ever start an opener on Apr. 6, 1992 at Seattle, a no decision…Beat Toronto in 1990 opener to become 2nd oldest to ever win on opening day (Tommy John, 45 for the Yankees in 1989)…Is 5-31 3.83 (25 er/58.2 ip) in 9 lifetime openers for California (1973-'74-'75), Houston (1982-'85-'86), and Texas (1990-'91-'92).

**All-Star Games:** Has been named to 8 All-Star teams and appeared in 5 games…Pitched 2 scoreless relief innings to win the 1969 game at Anaheim, becoming the oldest pitcher to ever win an All-Star Game and the 2nd oldest to ever appear in one…Has worked 6 scoreless innings in last 3 All-Star appearances, all in relief…Had no decision in only start for A.L. in 1979 at Seattle…Joined Pete Rose in throwing out 1st pitch at 1985 game at Minnesota.

**Postseason:** Has 46 strikeouts in 4 League Championship Series, tying Jim Palmer for all-time lead…Won 3rd and deciding game of 1969 NLCS vs. Atlanta in relief, setting LCS record with 7 strikeouts in 7-inning stint…Saved game 4 of 1969 World Series vs. Baltimore…Started game one of 1979 ALCS against the Orioles and fanned 1st 4 batters faced, an LCS mark…Allowed 16 hilt in 2 starts vs. Philadelphia in 1980 LCS, an NLCS record for a 5-game series…Started twice in 1986 NLCS against New York, losing game 2 and allowing one run in 9 innings with no decision in the 5th game.

**Major League Service:** Made his major league debut with the Mets on Sept. 11, 1966…Leads active players with 25 years, 101 days of major league service…Is one of 22 players in history to appear in a game in 4 decades…Is the oldest player to ever appear in a game with the Rangers.

**Relief:** Enters 1993 with a record 581 consecutive starts since last relief outing on July 28, 1974 vs. Minnesota (earned win in 1.2 innings)…Set the major league mark for

consecutive starts without a relief appearance with his
545th straight start on July 23, 1991 vs. Boston, surpassing
Steve Carlton...Has appeared in 34 games in relief overall,
31 of those with New York from 1966-71.

**Fielding:** Had an .857 (3 e/21 tc) percentage in 1992, his
lowest since 1978...His miscue on June 6 was his 1st since
Sept. 24, 1989, snapping a string of 66 consecutive errorless
games...Allowed 26 stolen bases, tied for 6th most in the
A.L.

**Batting:** Set a Houston club record by going hitless in
42 consecutive at bats in 1988...Has 2 career homers, Apr.
12, 1980 off L.A.'s Sutton and May 1, 1987 against Charlie
Puleo at Atlanta...Tied for N.L. lead with 14 sacrifice hits
in 1985.

**Injuries:** Has been on the disabled list a total of 13 times
in his career...A list of Nolan's most serious injuries by
year prior to 1992:

**1991:** Was on the disabled list from May 14-29 with a
muscle strain in the back of his right shoulder and from
July 29-Aug. 19 with tightness in his right shoulder.

**1990:** Was disabled from May 18-June 6 due to a stress
fracture in his lower back...Was bothered for much of the
year by that problem.

**1986:** Was bothered all season by a sore right elbow...
Was disabled from June 2-24 and from July 28-Aug. 12
with a sprained medial collateral ligament.

**1984:** Was on d.l. twice, June 2-16 with blisters on right
hand and June 18-July 3 with pulled left calf muscle...Was
sidelined for season on Sept. 20 with pulled left hamstring.

**1983:** Was on d.l. from March 25-Apr. 17 with an in-
flammation of prostate gland and from May 3-June 6 with
pulled left hamstring.

**1978:** Was disabled from June 14-July 5 with pulled left
hamstring...Also sidelined from July 6-Aug 20 with a rib
separation on his left side.

**1975:** Injured his right elbow on Aug. 24 and missed the
rest of the year...Underwent surgery to remove 4 bone
chips from right elbow on Sept. 23.

**1968:** Was on d.l. from July 30-Aug 30 with blisters on right hand.

**1967:** Suffered right elbow injury pitching for Jacksonville on June 12...Spent rest of year on rehab with Mets and on d.l. from July 16-Aug. 30.

## PREVIOUS CAREER HIGHLIGHTS

**1991:** Was 3rd in the league in strikeouts (203), 5th in era (2.91), and 7th in winning percentage (.667)...Despite missing 36 days with injuries, led the staff in era, shutouts (2), and strikeouts and was 2nd in wins (12), starts (27), complete games (2), and innings (173)...Had A.L.'s best ratios for fewest hits (5.3), and baserunners (9.3) and most strikeouts (10.56) per 9 innings while yielding major league low .173 batting average...Pitched 7th career no-hitter against Toronto on May 1 at Arlington Stadium...Was named A.L.'s player of the week for Apr. 29-May 5 for that feat...Pitched against the University of Texas and his son, Reid, a freshman pitcher in an exhibition between the Rangers and Longhorns on Apr. 2 at Austin.

**1990:** Led the A.L. in strikeouts (232), tied for 6th in shutouts (2), and was 13th in era (3.44)...Ranked 2nd on the club in wins (13) and was 3rd in starts (30) and innings (204)...Pitched 6th career no-hitter on June 11 at Oakland and became 20th pitcher to win 300 games on July 31 at Milwaukee, the 4th oldest to ever accomplish that feat...Was 6-0 in span of 8 starts, June 22-July 31...Was selected as the A.L.'s Player of the Week, June 11-17 and July 30-Aug. 5.

**1989:** In his 1st season with the Rangers, led the majors in strikeouts (301) and ranked among the A.L. leaders in innings (8th, 239.1), era (12th, 3.20), and wins (T12th, 16)...Also led the staff in starts (32) and held opposition to major league low .187 batting average...Pitched a pair of one-hit complete games, Apr. 23 at Toronto and June 3 at Seattle and carried a total of 5 no-hitters into the 8th inning or later, losing 2 in the 9th...Fanned Oakland's Rickey Henderson for 5000th career strikeout on Aug. 22...Won his most games since 1982…Was the Rangers' Pitcher of the Year.

**Houston:** Was 106-94 with a 3.13 era in 282 starts with the Astros from 1980-88…Is the club's all-time strikeout leader (1866) and ranks in the top 6 in walks (2nd, 796), starts (3rd), innings (3rd, 1855), wins (5th), and era (6th).

Led the N.L. with 228 strikeouts in 1988, fewest for an N.L. leader since 1958…Allowed just 4 runs in final 41 innings before season ended on Sept. 19 due to left hamstring injury…In 1987, became the 1st player in history not to win the Cy Young Award after leading the league in strikeouts and era…Was the recipient of the N.L.'s Consort Control Award…Worked on a 100 and then a 125-pitch limit much of season because of elbow problems the previous year…Went 0-8 over 11 starts between wins on June 12 and Aug. 18…Despite injuries was 6th in N.L. in strikeouts in 1986.

Placed 3rd in the league in strikeouts in 1985 and captured 100th N.L. victory on June 12 vs. San Diego…Was also 3rd in N.L. in strikeouts in 1984 (197) despite 2 stints on disabled list…Broke Walter Johnson's major league strikeout record of 3508 on Apr. 27, 1983, fanning Montreal's Brad Mills…Won 16 games in 1982, his high with Houston, and ranked 3rd in the N.L. in strikeouts (245)…Was the Astros' Most Valuable Player in 1981, compiling the league's lowest era (1.69)…Allowed only 2 homers in 149 innings…Tossed a 2-hitter to defeat Los Angeles in game 1 of the Western Divisional Championship Series.

**California:** Had a 138-121 record with a 3.06 era in 291 games with the Angels from 1972-79…Is California's all-time leader in wins, starts (288), complete games (156), innings (2182), shutouts (40), and strikeouts (2416) and is 3rd in games…Holds or shares 20 club records…Was inducted into the Angels' Hall of Fame and had his number 30 retired in a pregame ceremony a Anaheim Stadium on June 16, 1992.

Led A.L. in strikeouts (223) and tied for lead in shutouts (5) in 1979…Bothered by injuries in 1978, winning an

Angel low 10 games but topped league with 260 strikeouts...Was 1st in strikeouts (341) and tied for top spot in complete games (22) in 1977...Was selected as A.L. Pitcher of the Year by *The Sporting News* and named to its All-Star team...Led league in strikeouts (327), shutouts (7). and losses (18) in 1976...Hampered by arm trouble in 1975 but recorded 4th no-hitter on June 1 vs Baltimore.

Won career high 22 games in 1974, tying club record, and also established team marks for starts (41) and innings (333)...Led league in innings and strikeouts (367)...Established major league record with 383 strikeouts in 1973, fanning Minnesota's Rich Reese on Sept. 27 to set mark...Set club record with 26 complete games and became only 5th pitcher in history to toss 2 no-hitters in one season...Led league in strikeouts (329) and shutouts (9) in 1st A.L. season in 1972...Tied major league and set A.L. record with 8 straight strikeouts on July 9.

**New York Mets:** Was 29-38 with a 3.8 era in 105 games (74 starts) with the Mets from 1966-71...Set a New York club record with 15 strikeouts on Apr. 18, 1970, a mark eclipsed 4 days later by Tom Seaver (19)...Recorded 1st official save in Mets history, Apr. 9, 1969 vs. Montreal...Missed most of the 1967 season with military obligations and elbow trouble...Pitched twice for Mets in relief in Sept. 1966, then won 1st major league game on Apr. 14, 1968 vs. Houston.

**Minors:** Was selected as the Western Carolinas Pitcher of the Year at Greenville in 1966, leading the league in wins (17) and strikeouts (272) and placing 4th in era (2.51)...Topped the Appalachian League in hit batsmen (8) in 1965.

Amateur Background: Played baseball and basketball at Alvin (TX) High School (graduated '65)...Also participated in Little League and Babe Ruth League programs.

**Personal:** Signed a 10-year personal services contract with the Rangers on July 18, 1991 that goes into effect upon retirement as an active player...Owns 4 cattle ranches and 2 banks in Texas and is very active in both businesses during the off-season...Is also very involved in charity work and sponsors the Nolan Ryan Scholarship Fund at Alvin Community College…Was the recipient of the 1992 Jim Sundberg Community Service Award…Was elected to the Texas Baseball Hall of Fame in 1987 and to the Peter J. McGovern Little League Museum Hall of Excellence in 1991…Has written 2 autobiographies, *Throwing Heat* in 1988 and *Miracle Man* in 1992…Also wrote *Kings of the Hill* in 1992 and co-authored *The Pitchers Bible* in 1991…Hobbies: hunting and fishing.

Nolan and his wife, Ruth, were married on June 26, 1967, and have 3 children: Robert Reid (11/21/71), Nolan Reese (1/21/76), and Wendy Lynn (3/22/77)…Reid is currently in his junior year at Texas Christian University and is on the baseball team.

## 300-GAME WINNERS

| | | |
|---|---|---|
| 511—Cy Young | 342—Tim Keefe | 311—Tom Seaver |
| 416—Walter Johnson | 329—Steve Carlton | 308—Hoss Radbourn |
| 373—Christy Mathewson | 327—John Clarkson | 307—Mickey Welch |
| 373—Grover Alexander | 324—Don Sutton | 305—Eddie Plank |
| 363—Warren Spahn | **319—NOLAN RYAN** | 300—Lefty Grove |
| 361—Kid Nichols | 318—Phil Niekro | 300—Early Wynn |
| 361—Pud Glavin | 314—Gaylord Perry | |

**RYAN'S ROUTINE:** Nolan Ryan follows a workout routine that begins after he finishes pitching a game. The sequence varies, depending on personal commitments.

*Post-game:* Ices right arm, 20-25 minutes…Rides Lifecycle, 30 minutes.

*Next morning:* Heavy weight work (50,000 to 55,000 pounds) for upper and lower body with medium dumbbells and weight machine.

*Afternoon after game:* Abdominal work, 15 varieties of lifts, crunches and sit ups, 40 minutes…Light dumbbell program, 20 minutes...Forward and backward 40-yard sprints, 15-20 minutes...Throws football and baseball, as tolerance allows...Rides Lifecycle or swims, 20 minutes (if stiff).

*Two days after game:* Duplicates first day routine except for weight work...Long toss with football, 10-15 minutes...Long toss one-hop drill with baseball, 10-15 minutes...Flat-ground work with fastball, working on fundamentals and skills at distance of 35 feet, 15 minutes.

*Three days after game:* Duplicates entire first day routine...Loosens up throwing football...Works off the bullpen mound at full speed, 10-15 minutes.

*Four days after game:* "Acute" rest day...Abbreviated heavy weights, light dumbbells, stretching, abdominal work and running as necessary.

*Pre-game:* Duplicates fourth day routine with weight work limited to 5,000-10,000 pounds...Throws football with catcher Mike Stanley...Three or four hard outfield sprints 20 minutes before game...Long toss with bullpen catcher, 4-5 minutes...Warm up in bullpen, 8-10 minutes...Returns to clubhouse, towels off...Takes the mound after the national anthem.

## CAREER STATS

| YEAR | CLUB | W-L | ERA | G | GS | CG | SHO | SV | IP | H | R | ER | BB | SO |
|------|------|-----|-----|---|----|----|-----|----|-----|---|---|----|----|----|
| 1965 | Marion-1 | 3-6 | 4.38 | 13 | 12 | 2 | 1 | 0 | 78.0 | 61 | 47 | 38 | 56 | 115 |
| 1966 | Greenville | *17.2 | 2.51 | *29 | 28 | 9 | 5 | 0 | 183.0 | 109 | 59 | 51 | *127 | *272 |
| | Williamsport | 0-2 | 0.95 | 3 | 3 | 0 | 0 | 0 | 19.0 | 9 | 6 | 2 | 12 | 35 |
| | New York (NL) | 0-1 | 15.00 | 2 | 1 | 0 | 0 | 0 | 3.0 | 5 | 5 | 5 | 3 | 6 |
| 1967 | Winter Haven-2 | 0-0 | 2.25 | 1 | 1 | 0 | 0 | 0 | 4.0 | 1 | 1 | 1 | 2 | 5 |
| | Jacksonville | 1-0 | 0.00 | 3 | 0 | 0 | 0 | 0 | 7.0 | 3 | 1 | 0 | 3 | 18 |
| 1968 | New York (NL) | 6-9 | 3.09 | 21 | 18 | 3 | 0 | 0 | 134.0 | 93 | 50 | 46 | 75 | 133 |
| 1969 | New York (NL)-3 | 6-3 | 3.54 | 25 | 10 | 2 | 0 | 1 | 89.0 | 60 | 38 | 35 | 53 | 92 |
| 1970 | New York (NL) | 7-11 | 3.41 | 27 | 19 | 5 | 2 | 1 | 132.0 | 86 | 59 | 50 | 97 | 125 |
| 1971 | New York (NL)-4 | 10-14 | 3.97 | 30 | 26 | 3 | 0 | 0 | 152.0 | 125 | 78 | 67 | 116 | 137 |
| 1972 | California | 19-16 | 2.28 | 39 | 39 | 20 | *9 | 0 | 284.0 | 166 | 80 | 72 | *157 | *329 |
| 1973 | California | 21-16 | 2.87 | 41 | 39 | 26 | 4 | 1 | 326.0 | 238 | 113 | 104 | *162 | *383 |
| 1974 | California | 22-16 | 2.89 | 42 | 41 | 26 | 3 | 0 | *333.0 | 221 | 127 | 107 | *202 | *367 |
| 1975 | California | 14-12 | 3.45 | 28 | 28 | 10 | 5 | 0 | 198.0 | 152 | 90 | 76 | 132 | 186 |
| 1976 | California | 17-*18 | 3.36 | 39 | 39 | 21 | *7 | 0 | 284.0 | 193 | 117 | 106 | *183 | *327 |
| 1977 | California | 19-16 | 2.77 | 37 | 37 | #22 | 4 | 0 | 299.0 | 198 | 110 | 92 | *204 | *341 |
| 1978 | California | 10-13 | 3.71 | 31 | 31 | 14 | 3 | 0 | 235.0 | 183 | 106 | 97 | *148 | *260 |
| 1979 | California-5 | 16-14 | 3.59 | 34 | 34 | 17 | #5 | 0 | 223.0 | 169 | 104 | 89 | 114 | *223 |
| 1980 | Houston | 11-10 | 3.35 | 35 | 35 | 4 | 2 | 0 | 234.0 | 205 | 100 | 87 | 98 | 200 |
| 1981 | Houston | 11-5 | *1.69 | 21 | 21 | 5 | 3 | 0 | 149.0 | 99 | 34 | 28 | 68 | 140 |
| 1982 | Houston | 16-12 | 3.16 | 35 | 35 | 10 | 3 | 0 | 250.1 | 196 | 100 | 88 | *109 | 245 |
| 1983 | Houston | 14-9 | 2.98 | 29 | 29 | 5 | 2 | 0 | 196.1 | 134 | 74 | 65 | 101 | 183 |
| 1984 | Houston | 12-11 | 3.04 | 30 | 30 | 5 | 2 | 0 | 183.2 | 143 | 78 | 62 | 69 | 197 |
| 1985 | Houston | 10-12 | 3.80 | 35 | 35 | 4 | 0 | 0 | 232.0 | 205 | 108 | 98 | 95 | 209 |
| 1986 | Houston | 12-8 | 3.34 | 30 | 30 | 1 | 0 | 0 | 178.0 | 119 | 72 | 66 | 82 | 194 |
| 1987 | Houston | 8-16 | *2.76 | 34 | 34 | 0 | 0 | 0 | 211.2 | 154 | 75 | 65 | 87 | *270 |
| 1988 | Houston-6 | 12-11 | 3.52 | 33 | 33 | 4 | 1 | 0 | 220.0 | 186 | 98 | 86 | 87 | *228 |
| 1989 | Texas | 16-10 | 3.20 | 32 | 32 | 6 | 2 | 0 | 239.1 | 162 | 96 | 85 | 98 | *301 |
| 1990 | Texas | 13-9 | 3.44 | 30 | 30 | 5 | 2 | 0 | 204.0 | 137 | 86 | 78 | 74 | *232 |
| 1991 | Texas | 12-6 | 2.91 | 27 | 27 | 2 | 2 | 0 | 170.0 | 102 | 58 | 55 | 72 | 203 |
| 1992 | Texas | 5-9 | 3.72 | 27 | 27 | 2 | 0 | 0 | 157.1 | 138 | 75 | 65 | 69 | 157 |
| A.L. Totals | | 184-155 | 3.13 | 407 | 404 | 171 | 46 | 1 | 2955.2 | 2059 | 1162 | 1027 | 1615 | 3309 |
| N.L. Totals | | 135-132 | 3.23 | 387 | 356 | 51 | 15 | 2 | 2365.0 | 1810 | 969 | 848 | 1140 | 2359 |
| M.L. Totals | | 314-278 | 3.15 | 767 | 733 | 220 | 61 | 3 | 5163.1 | 3731 | 2056 | 1810 | 2686 | 5511 |

| MAJOR LEAGUE | AVG | AB | H | HR | RBI |
|--------------|-----|----|---|----|----|
| Hitting Totals | .110 | 852 | 94 | 2 | 33 |

* - Led League    # - Tied for league lead

1-Selected by New York Mets organization in June '65 free agent draft (10th round, regular phase)...Signed by Red Murff on 6/26/65.

2-On military list, Jan. 3–May 13, '67.

3-On military list, Aug. 11–Sept. 1, '69

4-Acquired by California from New York Mets with pitcher Don Rose, Catcher Francisco Estrada, and outfielder Leroy Stanton in deal for infielder Jim Fregosi on 12/10/71.

5-Granted free agency on 11/1/79...Signed by Houston as a free agent on 11/19/79.

6-Granted free agency on 11/1/88...Signed by Texas as a free agent on 12/7/88.

# Appendix: Extra Innings

## DIVISIONAL SERIES RECORD

| YEAR | CLUB | W-L | ERA | G | GS | CG | SHO | SV | IP | H | R | ER | BB | SO |
|------|------|-----|-----|---|----|----|----|----|----|----|----|----|----|----|
| 1981 | Hou. vs. L.A. | 1-1 | 1.80 | 2 | 2 | 1 | 0 | 0 | 15.0 | 6 | 4 | 3 | 3 | 14 |

## CHAMPIONSHIP SERIES RECORD

| YEAR | CLUB | W-L | ERA | G | GS | CG | SHO | SV | IP | H | R | ER | BB | SO |
|------|------|-----|-----|---|----|----|----|----|----|----|----|----|----|----|
| 1969 | N.Y. vs. Atl. | 1-0 | 2.57 | 1 | 0 | 0 | 0 | 0 | 7.0 | 3 | 2 | 2 | 2 | 7 |
| 1979 | Cal. vs. Balt. | 0-0 | 1.29 | 1 | 1 | 0 | 0 | 0 | 7.0 | 4 | 3 | 1 | 3 | 8 |
| 1980 | Hou. vs. Phil. | 0-0 | 5.40 | 2 | 2 | 0 | 0 | 0 | 13.1 | 16 | 8 | 8 | 3 | 14 |
| 1986 | Hou. vs. N.Y. | 0-1 | 3.86 | 2 | 2 | 0 | 0 | 0 | 14.0 | 9 | 6 | 6 | 1 | 17 |
| L.C.S. Totals | | 1-1 | 3.70 | 6 | 5 | 0 | 0 | 0 | 41.1 | 32 | 19 | 17 | 9 | 46 |

## WORLD SERIES RECORD

| YEAR | CLUB | W-L | ERA | G | GS | CG | SHO | SV | IP | H | R | ER | BB | SO |
|------|------|-----|-----|---|----|----|----|----|----|----|----|----|----|----|
| 1969 | N.Y. vs. Balt. | 0-0 | 0.00 | 1 | 0 | 0 | 0 | 1 | 2.1 | 1 | 0 | 0 | 2 | 3 |

## ALL-STAR GAME RECORD

| YEAR | CLUB | W-L | ERA | G | GS | CG | SHO | SV | IP | H | R | ER | BB | SO |
|------|------|-----|-----|---|----|----|----|----|----|----|----|----|----|----|
| 1972 | A.L. Atl. | | Did Not Play | | | | | | | | | | | |
| 1973 | A.L. K.C. | 0-0 | 9.00 | 1 | 0 | 0 | 0 | 0 | 2.0 | 2 | 2 | 2 | 2 | 2 |
| 1975 | A.L. Mil. | | Did Not Play | | | | | | | | | | | |
| 1979 | A.L. Sea. | 0-0 | 13.50 | 1 | 1 | 0 | 0 | 0 | 2.0 | 5 | 3 | 3 | 1 | 2 |
| 1981 | N.L. Cle. | 0-0 | 0.00 | 1 | 0 | 0 | 0 | 0 | 1.0 | 0 | 0 | 0 | 0 | 1 |
| 1985 | N.L. Minn. | 0-0 | 0.00 | 1 | 0 | 0 | 0 | 0 | 3.0 | 2 | 0 | 0 | 2 | 2 |
| 1989 | A.L. Cal. | 1-0 | 0.00 | 1 | 0 | 0 | 0 | 0 | 2.0 | 1 | 0 | 0 | 0 | 3 |
| A.S.G. Totals | | 1-0 | 4.50 | 5 | 1 | 0 | 0 | 0 | 10.0 | 10 | 5 | 5 | 5 | 10 |

Named to 1977 A.L. squad to replace Frank Tanana, but declined

## 1992 AND CAREER PITCHING BREAKDOWN

| CLUB | 1992 | | | | | | CAREER | | | | | |
|------|------|-----|---|----|---|----|--------|-----|-----|------|-----|-----|
| | W-L-S | ERA | G | IP | H | ER | W-L-S | ERA | G | IP | H | ER |
| Baltimore | 2-0-0 | 3.38 | 3 | 16.0 | 9 | 6 | 10-16-0 | 4.05 | 31 | 202.1 | 156 | 91 |
| Boston | 0-1-0 | 2.16 | 1 | 8.1 | 6 | 2 | 9-15-0 | 3.43 | 29 | 212.2 | 157 | 81 |
| Cleveland | 1-1-0 | 7.15 | 2 | 11.1 | 14 | 9 | 13-13-0 | 3.75 | 28 | 201.2 | 160 | 84 |
| Detroit | 1-1-0 | 3.86 | 2 | 11.2 | 8 | 5 | 17-7-0 | 2.36 | 28 | 213.2 | 130 | 56 |
| Milwaukee | 0-0-0 | 2.41 | 3 | 18.2 | 18 | 5 | 12-10-0 | 2.96 | 28 | 210.0 | 146 | 69 |
| New York | 1-0-0 | 1.00 | 2 | 9.0 | 3 | 1 | 13-8-0 | 3.48 | 27 | 178.2 | 139 | 69 |
| Toronto | — | — | — | — | — | — | 7-6-0 | 2.36 | 16 | 126.0 | 79 | 33 |
| Vs. East | 5-3-0 | 3.36 | 13 | 75.0 | 58 | 28 | 81-75-0 | 3.23 | 187 | 1345.0 | 967 | 483 |

| California | 0-2-0 | 4.72 | 2 | 13.1 | 15 | 7 | 5-5-0 | 2.26 | 10 | 79.2 | 50 | 20 |
|---|---|---|---|---|---|---|---|---|---|---|---|---|
| Chicago | 0-1-0 | 8.68 | 2 | 9.1 | 11 | 9 | 21-16-1 | 3.37 | 46 | 323.1 | 221 | 121 |
| Kansas City | 0-1-0 | 4.08 | 3 | 17.2 | 12 | 8 | 24-14-0 | 2.65 | 45 | 332.2 | 233 | 98 |
| Minnesota | 0-1-0 | 2.50 | 3 | 18.0 | 16 | 5 | 20-10-0 | 2.70 | 37 | 290.1 | 201 | 87 |
| Oakland | 0-1-0 | 4.26 | 2 | 12.2 | 13 | 6 | 11-17-0 | 2.98 | 34 | 253.2 | 163 | 84 |
| Seattle | 0-0-0 | 1.59 | 2 | 11.1 | 13 | 2 | 11-5-0 | 3.35 | 22 | 156.0 | 99 | 58 |
| Texas | — | — | — | — | — | — | 11-13-0 | 3.92 | 26 | 174.1 | 125 | 76 |
| Vs. West | 0-6-0 | 4.04 | 14 | 82.1 | 80 | 37 | 103-80-1 | 3.04 | 220 | 1610.0 | 1092 | 544 |
| Pre A.S.G. | 3-3-0 | 3.76 | 14 | 76.2 | 67 | 32 | 177-145-2 | 3.18 | 433 | 2816.0 | 2144 | 994 |
| Post A.S.G. | 2-6-0 | 3.68 | 13 | 80.2 | 71 | 33 | 142-142-1 | 3.17 | 361 | 2503.2 | 1725 | 881 |
| Home | 3-6-0 | 3.40 | 15 | 92.2 | 73 | 35 | 185-134-2 | 2.75 | 419 | 2957.2 | 1980 | 905 |
| Road | 2-3-0 | 4.18 | 12 | 64.2 | 65 | 30 | 134-153-1 | 3.70 | 375 | 2362.0 | 1889 | 970 |
| Day | 2-0-0 | 2.17 | 5 | 29.0 | 26 | 7 | 84-68-1 | 3.37 | 215 | 1344.2 | 1021 | 503 |
| Night | 3-9-0 | 4.07 | 22 | 128.1 | 112 | 58 | 235-219-2 | 3.11 | 579 | 3975.0 | 2848 | 1372 |
| As Starter | 5-9-0 | 3.72 | 27 | 157.1 | 138 | 65 | 313-286-0 | 3.16 | 760 | 5259.2 | 3826 | 1848 |
| As Reliever | — | — | — | — | — | — | 6-1-3 | 4.05 | 34 | 60.0 | 43 | 27 |
| April | 0-1-0 | 10.60 | 2 | 6.2 | 10 | 8 | 50-35-1 | 3.24 | 108 | 699.2 | 491 | 252 |
| May | 0-0-0 | 3.21 | 5 | 28.0 | 21 | 10 | 57-47-1 | 3.06 | 134 | 933.2 | 643 | 317 |
| June | 1-2-0 | 3.46 | 5 | 26.0 | 26 | 10 | 52-45-0 | 3.15 | 130 | 883.2 | 666 | 309 |
| July | 4-0-0 | 1.96 | 5 | 36.2 | 23 | 8 | 50-66-0 | 3.48 | 140 | 945.1 | 715 | 366 |
| August | 0-5-0 | 7.16 | 6 | 32.2 | 36 | 26 | 49-53-0 | 3.26 | 135 | 911.1 | 684 | 330 |
| Sept./Oct. | 0-1-0 | 0.99 | 4 | 27.1 | 22 | 3 | 61-41-1 | 2.86 | 147 | 946.0 | 670 | 301 |

## A.L. CAREER BY PARK THRU 1992

| CLUB | W-L-S | ERA | G | IP | H | ER | CLUB | W-L-S | ERA | G | IP | H | ER |
|---|---|---|---|---|---|---|---|---|---|---|---|---|---|
| Bal.(M) | 4-10-0 | 4.21 | 15 | 98.1 | 75 | 46 | Cal. | 85-58-1 | 2.37 | 160 | 1267.0 | 792 | 334 |
| Bal.(CY) | 1-0-0 | 5.00 | 2 | 9.0 | 7 | 5 | Chi.(O) | 5-10-0 | 5.35 | 17 | 112.2 | 88 | 67 |
| Bos. | 2-8-0 | 4.92 | 13 | 78.2 | 75 | 43 | Chi.(N) | 0-1-0 | 8.59 | 2 | 7.1 | 6 | 7 |
| Cle. | 4-6-0 | 4.74 | 11 | 68.1 | 68 | 36 | K.C.(M) | 0-0-0 | 3.00 | 1 | 6.0 | 5 | 2 |
| Det. | 8-2-0 | 2.28 | 11 | 90.2 | 59 | 23 | K.C.(R) | 9-6-0 | 2.87 | 19 | 135.0 | 102 | 43 |
| Mil. | 4-5-0 | 3.43 | 12 | 89.1 | 77 | 34 | Min.(MS) | 8-5-0 | 3.27 | 14 | 118.1 | 89 | 43 |
| N.Y.(Y) | 2-2-0 | 5.87 | 6 | 30.2 | 35 | 20 | Min.(M) | 1-0-0 | 2.08 | 2 | 13.0 | 11 | 3 |
| N.Y.(Shea) | 1-2-0 | 3.66 | 3 | 19.2 | 18 | 8 | Oak. | 5-6-0 | 3.46 | 14 | 104.0 | 72 | 40 |
| Tor.(Ex) | 3-1-0 | 2.53 | 4 | 32.0 | 23 | 9 | Sea. | 7-3-0 | 3.01 | 12 | 83.2 | 48 | 28 |
| Tor.(Sky) | 0-1-0 | 2.92 | 2 | 12.1 | 7 | 4 | Tex. | 35-29-0 | 3.61 | 87 | 579.0 | 402 | 232 |

Bal.(M) = Memorial Stadium

Bal.(CY) = Camden Yards

N.Y.(Y) = Yankee Stadium

N.Y.(Shea) = Shea Stadium ('74-'75)

Tor.(Ex) = Exhibition Stadium

Tor.(Sky) = SkyDome

Chi.(O) = Old Comiskey Park

Chi.(N) = New Comiskey Park

K.C.(M) = Municipal Stadium

K.C.(R) = Royals Stadium

Min.(MS) = Metropolitan Stadium

Min.(M) = Metrodome

## CAREER LOW-HIT GAMES

**No Hitters (7):** May 15, 1973 at Kansas City (3-0); July 15, 1973 at Detroit (6-0); September 28, 1974 vs. Minnesota (4-0); June 1, 1975 vs. Baltimore (1-0); September 26, 1981 vs. Los Angeles (5-0); June 11, 1990 at Oakland (5-0); May 1, 1991 vs. Toronto (3-0).

**One Hitters (12):** April 18, 1970 vs Philadelphia (7-0); July 9, 1972 vs. Boston (3-0); August 29, 1973 vs. New York Yankees (5-0); June 27, 1974 vs. Texas (5-0); April 15, 1977 vs. Seattle (7-0); May 5, 1978 vs. Cleveland (5-0); July 13, 1979 vs. New York Yankees (6-1); August 11, 1982 at San Diego (3-0); August 3, 1983 at San Diego (1-0); April 23, 1989 at Toronto (4-1); June 3, 1989 at Seattle (6-1); April 26, 1990 vs. Chicago (1-0).

**Combined One Hitters (2):** June 19, 1980 vs. St. Louis, Ryan (7 ip) and Joe Sambito (2 ip) (2-0); July 22, 1986 vs. Montreal, Ryan (9.1 ip) and Dave Smith (0.2 ip) (1-0).

**Two Hitters (19):** (2 New York Mets; 13 California; 4 Houston), latest on August 31, 1982 at New York Mets.

**Three Hitters (30):** (5 New York Mets; 19 California; 3 Houston; 3 Texas), latest on Aug. 28, 1990 at California.

**Four Hitters (27):** (1 New York Mets; 21 California; 4 Houston; 1 Texas), latest on Sep. 24, 1990 vs. California.

## LONGEST WINNING STREAKS

**8 games:** April 27-July 13, 1983
**7 games, twice:** August 29-September 27, 1973; August 31-October 3, 1976
**6 games, 3 times:** July 16-August 31, 1982; May 6-June 17, 1984; June 22-July 31, 1990

## STRIKEOUT HIGHS

**19, 4 times:** June 14, 1974 vs. Boston; August 12, 1974 vs. Boston; August 20, 1974 vs. Detroit; June 8, 1977 vs. Toronto
**18, once:** September 10, 1976 at Chicago White Sox
**17, 3 times:** September 30, 1972 vs. Minnesota; July 15, 1973 at Detroit; August 18, 1976 at Detroit.
**16, 8 times:** latest on May 1, 1991 vs. Toronto
**15, 10 times:** latest on Aug. 17, 1990 vs. Chicago

## NOLAN RYAN'S MAJOR LEAGUE RECORDS

### STRIKEOUT RECORDS

1. Most Strikeouts, Major Leagues–5,668
2. Most Strikeouts, Season, Major and American League–383, California, 1973.
3. Most Strikeouts, Season, Major and American League, Right-handed Pitcher–383, California, 1973.
4. Most Years, 100 or More Strikeouts, Major Leagues–24, New York Mets, 1968, 1970, 1971; California 1972–79; Houston, 1980–88; Texas, 1989–92.
5. Most Consecutive Years, 100 or More Strikeouts–23, New York Mets, 1970–71; California, 1972–79; Houston, 1980–88; Texas, 1989–92.

6. Most Years, 200 or More Strikeouts, Major Leagues–15, California, 1972–79, except 1975; Houston, 1980, 1982, 1985, 1987, 1988; Texas, 1989–91.

7. Most Years, 200 or More Strikeouts, American League–10, California, 1972–79, except 1975; Texas, 1989–91.

8. Most Years, 300 or More Strikeouts, Major and American League–6, California, 1972, 1973, 1974, 1976, 1977; Texas, 1989.

9. Most Strikeouts, Losing Pitcher, Extra-Inning Game, Major and American League–19, California, August 20, 1974, 11 innings, lost 1–0.

10. Most Times, 15 or More Strikeouts, Major Leagues–26, New York Mets, 1970 (1), 1971 (1); California, 1972 (4), 1973 (2), 1974 (6), 1976 (3), 1977 (2), 1979 (1); Houston, 1987 (1); Texas, 1989 (1), 1990 (2), 1991 (1).

11. Most Times, 15 or More Strikeouts, Game, American League–23, California, 1972–79; Texas, 1989–91.

12. Most Times, 10 or More Strikeouts, Game, Major Leagues–215, 67 in National League, New York & Houston, 13 Years, 1966, 1968–71, 1980–88; 146 in American League, California & Texas, 11 Years, 1972–79, 1989–92.

13. Most Times, 10 or More Strikeouts, Game, American League–148, California & Texas, 11 Years, 1972–79, 1989–92.

14. Most Times, 10 or More Strikeouts, Game, Season–23, California, 1973.

15. Three Strikeouts, Inning, on Nine Pitched Balls*–New York Mets, April 19, 1968, 3rd inning; California, July 9, 1972, 2nd inning.

16. Most Consecutive Strikeouts, Game, American League–8*, California, July 9, 1972; California, July 15, 1973.

17. Most Strikeouts, Two Consecutive Games, Major and American League–32*, California, August 7 (13), August 12 (19), 1974, 17 innings.

18. Most Strikeouts, Three Consecutive Games, Major and American League–47, California, August 12 (19), August 16 (9), August 20 (19), 1974, 27.1 innings.

19. Oldest Pitcher, 10 or More Strikeouts, Game–45 yrs., 6 mos., 8 days, August 8, 1992 vs. Oakland.

## NO-HIT AND LOW-HIT GAME RECORDS

20. Most No-Hitters Pitched, Major Leagues–7, California, 1973 (2), 1974, 1975; Houston, 1981; Texas, 1990, 1991.

21. Most No-Hitters Pitched, American League–6, California, 1973 (2), 1974, 1975; Texas, 1990, 1991.

22. Most No-Hitters Pitched, Season–2*, California, May 15, & July 15, 1973.

23. Oldest Pitcher to Throw No-Hitter–44 yrs., 4 mos., 1 day, May 1, 1991 vs Toronto.

24. Most Teams, Throwing No-Hitter–3, California (4); Houston; Texas (2).

25. Most Different Decades, Throwing No-Hitter–3, 1970s, 1980s, 1990s.

26. Longest Span Between Throwing No-Hitters–8 yrs., 8 mos., 16 days, Sept. 26, 1981 until June 11, 1990.

27. Most Low-Hit (No-Hit and One-Hit) Games, Season, American League–3*, California, 1973.

28. Most Low-Hit (No-Hit and One-Hit) Games, Career, Major League–19.

29. Most One-Hit Games, Career, Major League–12*.

## BASE ON BALLS RECORDS

30. Most Bases on Balls, Major Leagues–2,755.

31. Most Years Leading Majors in Most Bases on Balls–8, California, 1972, 1973, 1974, 1976, 1977, 1978; Houston, 1980, 1982.

32. Most Years Leading American League in Most Bases on Balls–6, California, 1972, 1973, 1974, 1976, 1977, 1978.

## MISCELLANEOUS RECORDS

33. Most Clubs Shut Out (Won or Tied), Season, Major and American League–8*, California, 1972.
34. Most Years Leading Major Leagues in Most Wild Pitches–6*, California, 1972, 1977, 1978; Houston, 1981, 1986; Texas, 1989.
35. Most Years Leading Amercian League in Most Wild Pitches–4, California, 1972, 1977, 1978; Texas, 1989.
36. Most Wild Pitches, Major Leagues–274.
37. Most Years Leading American League in Most Errors, Pitcher–4*, California, 1975, 1976, 1977 (tied), 1978.
38. Highest Strikeout Average Per Nine Innings, Season–11.48, Houston, 1987, 270 Strikeouts, 211.2 Innings.
39. Highest Strikeout Average Per Nine Innings, Career–9.59, 26 Seasons, 1966, 1968–92, 5,668 Strikeouts, 5,320.2 Innings.
40. Lowest Hits Allowed Average Per Nine Innings, Season–5.26, California, 1972, 166 Hits, 284 Innings.
41. Lowest Hits Allowed Average Per Nine Innings, Career–8.54, 26 Seasons, 1966, 1968–92, 3,889 Hits, 5,320.2 Innings.
42. Most Consecutive Starts without a Relief Appearance–581, July 30, 1974–Sep. 27, 1992.
43. Most Different Seasons, Major Leagues–26*, New York Mets, 1968–71; California, 1972–79; Houston, 1980–88; Texas, 1989–92.

## CHAMPIONSHIP SERIES/ALL-STAR RECORDS

44. Most Hits Allowed, Five Game Series, National League–16, Houston, 1980.
45. Most Strikeouts, Total Series,–46*, New York Mets, 1969; California, 1979; Houston, 1980, 1986.
46. Most Strikeouts, Game Relief Pitcher–7, New York Mets, October 6, 1969, Pitched Seven Innings.
47. Most Consecutive Strikeouts, Game–4*, California, October 3, 1979.
48. Most Consecutive Strikeouts, Start of Game–4*, California, October 3, 1979.
49. Highest Fielding Percentage, Pitcher, With Most Chances Accepted, Five Game Series, National League–1.000*, Houston, 1980, Four Chances Accepted.
50. Most Assists, Pitcher, Five Game Series, National League–3*, Houston, 1980.
51. Most Chances Accepted, Pitcher, Five Game Series, National League–4*, Houston, 1980.
52. Oldest Pitcher to Win All-Star Game–42 yrs., 5 mos., 13 days, July 12, 1989 at California for A.L.

*Ties Record

# RYAN'S CAREER 319 VICTORIES

NO. ........ DATE ............. TEAM .................................. SCORE ........... LOSING PITCHER

## WITH NEW YORK METS

| NO. | DATE | TEAM | SCORE | LOSING PITCHER |
|---|---|---|---|---|
| 1 | 4/14/68 | Houston (A) | 4-2 | Larry Dierker |
| 2 | 5/2/68 | Philadelphia (H) | 3-0 | Woodie Fryman |
| 3 | 5/7/68 | St. Louis (A) | 4-1 | Nellie Briles |
| 4 | 5/14/68 | Cincinnati (H) | 3-2 | Milt Pappas |
| 5 | 6/7/68 | San Francisco (A) | 4-0 | Ray Sadecki |
| 6 | 6/23/68 | Los Angeles (H) | 5-4 | Bill Singer |
| 7 | 4/20/69 | *St. Louis (A) | 11-3 | Nellie Briles |
| 8 | 4/29/69 | *Montreal (A) | 2-0 | Mudcat Grant |
| 9 | 6/20/69 | St. Louis (H) | 4-3 | Bob Gibson |
| 10 | 8/5/69 | Cincinnati (A) | 10-1 | Jerry Arrigo |
| 11 | 9/7/69 | *Philadelphia (H) | 9-3 | Billy Champion |
| 12 | 9/10/69 | Montreal (H) | 7-1 | Howie Reed |
| 13 | 4/18/70 | Philadelphia (H) | 7-0 | Jim Bunning |
| 14 | 4/30/70 | San Francisco (A) | 4-1 | Mike McCormack |
| 15 | 5/24/70 | Chicago (H) | 3-1 | Joe Decker |
| 16 | 5/30/70 | Houston (H) | 4-3 | Larry Dierker |
| 17 | 6/24/70 | Chicago (A) | 6-1 | Archie Reynolds |
| 18 | 8/4/70 | Chicago (H) | 4-0 | Joe Decker |
| 19 | 9/22/70 | *Philadelphia (A) | 7-6 | Dick Selma |
| 20 | 4/23/71 | *Chicago (A) | 7-6 | Ron Tompkins |
| 21 | 4/29/71 | St. Louis (A) | 7-0 | Jerry Reuss |
| 22 | 5/4/71 | Chicago (H) | 2-1 | Milt Pappas |
| 23 | 5/11/71 | Houston (H) | 8-1 | Larry Dierker |
| 24 | 5/21/71 | Atlanta (H) | 6-2 | Pat Jarvis |
| 25 | 5/29/71 | San Diego (A) | 2-1 | Tom Phoebus |
| 26 | 6/25/71 | Montreal (A) | 4-1 | Claude Raymond |
| 27 | 6/30/71 | Pittsburgh (H) | 4-0 | Steve Blass |
| 28 | 8/7/71 | Atlanta (A) | 20-6 | Ron Reed |
| 29 | 9/23/71 | Chicago (A) | 5-4 | Juan Pizarro |

## WITH CALIFORNIA ANGELS

| NO. | DATE | TEAM | SCORE | LOSING PITCHER |
|---|---|---|---|---|
| 30 | 4/18/72 | Minnesota (H) | 2-0 | Jim Perry |
| 31 | 5/5/72 | Milwaukee (H) | 4-0 | Ken Brett |
| 32 | 5/26/72 | Kansas City (H) | 10-5 | Jim Rooker |
| 33 | 5/30/72 | Chicago (H) | 6-0 | Stan Bahnsen |
| 34 | 6/7/72 | Detroit (A) | 5-1 | Joe Niekro |
| 35 | 6/14/72 | Cleveland (H) | 4-3 | Milt Wilcox |
| 36 | 6/23/72 | Oakland (A) | 2-1 | Dave Hamilton |
| 37 | 6/27/72 | Minnesota (A) | 3-1 | Jim Perry |
| 38 | 7/1/72 | Oakland (H) | 5-3 | Dave Hamilton |
| 39 | 7/5/72 | Milwaukee (H) | 1-0 | Earl Stephenson |
| 40 | 7/9/72 | Boston (H) | 3-0 | Sonny Siebert |
| 41 | 7/27/72 | Texas (H) | 5-0 | Mike Paul |

| 42 | 8/22/72 | Baltimore (A) | 2-0 | Dave McNally |
| 43 | 8/27/72 | Cleveland (H) | 1-0 | Phil Hennigan |
| 44 | 8/31/72 | Detroit (A) | 4-0 | Woodie Fryman |
| 45 | 9/4/72 | Oakland (A) | 2-1 | Joe Horlen |
| 46 | 9/21/72 | Kansas City (H) | 4-2 | Roger Nelson |
| 47 | 9/25/72 | Texas (A) | 2-1 | Dick Bosman |
| 48 | 9/30/72 | Minnesota (H) | 3-2 | Dave Goltz |
| 49 | 4/6/73 | Kansas City (A) | 3-2 | Steve Busby |
| 50 | 4/11/73 | Minnesota (H) | 4-1 | Bill Hands |
| 51 | 4/18/73 | Minnesota (A) | 3-2 | Bert Blyleven |
| 52 | 5/2/73 | Detroit (A) | 5-3 | Lerrin LaGrow |
| 53 | 5/15/73 | Kansas City (A) | 3-0 | Bruce Dal Canton |
| 54 | 5/19/73 | Texas (H) | 9-1 | Rich Hand |
| 55 | 6/7/73 | Detroit (H) | 3-0 | Woodie Fryman |
| 56 | 6/16/73 | New York (H) | 5-2 | Pat Dobson |
| 57 | 6/25/73 | Kansas City (H) | 5-2 | Ken Wright |
| 58 | 7/7/73 | Cleveland (A) | 3-1 | Gaylord Perry |
| 59 | 7/15/73 | Detroit (A) | 6-0 | Jim Perry |
| 60 | 8/2/73 | Texas (H) | 3-2 | Sonny Siebert |
| 61 | 8/7/73 | Milwaukee (A) | 6-5 | Chris Short |
| 62 | 8/17/73 | Detroit (H) | 10-2 | Woodie Fryman |
| 63 | 8/29/73 | New York (H) | 5-0 | Doc Medich |
| 64 | 9/3/73 | Oakland (H) | 3-1 | John Odom |
| 65 | 9/11/73 | Chicago (H) | 3-1 | Wilbur Wood |
| 66 | 9/15/73 | Kansas City (H) | 3-1 | Gene Garber |
| 67 | 9/19/73 | Texas (A) | 6-2 | Pete Broberg |
| 68 | 9/23/73 | Minnesota (A) | 15-7 | Joe Decker |
| 69 | 9/27/73 | Minnesota (H) | 5-4 | Bill Campbell |
| 70 | 4/5/74 | Chicago (A) | 8-2 | Wilbur Wood |
| 71 | 4/12/74 | Chicago (H) | 15-1 | Terry Forster |
| 72 | 4/30/74 | Boston (A) | 16-6 | Reggie Cleveland |
| 73 | 5/10/74 | Kansas City (H) | 2-1 | Paul Splittorff |
| 74 | 5/19/74 | Minnesota (A) | 4-2 | Bert Blyleven |
| 75 | 5/23/74 | Kansas City (A) | 3-1 | Bruce Dal Canton |
| 76 | 6/1/74 | Detroit (H) | 4-1 | Joe Coleman |
| 77 | 6/18/74 | New York (H) | 3-0 | Dick Tidrow |
| 78 | 6/22/74 | Texas (A) | 7-4 | Jim Bibby |
| 79 | 6/27/74 | Texas (H) | 5-0 | Jackie Brown |
| 80 | 7/15/74 | Cleveland (A) | 4-2 | Steve Arlin |
| 81 | 7/20/74 | Baltimore (A) | 2-0 | Wayne Garland |
| 82 | 7/28/74 | *Minnesota (H) | 12-9 | Tom Burgmeier |
| 83 | 8/3/74 | Kansas City (A) | 4-3 | Paul Splittorff |
| 84 | 8/12/74 | Boston (H) | 4-2 | Roger Moret |
| 85 | 8/16/74 | Milwaukee (H) | 7-3 | Clyde Wright |
| 86 | 8/30/74 | Milwaukee (A) | 9-2 | Kevin Kobel |
| 87 | 9/7/74 | Chicago (H) | 3-1 | Jack Kucek |
| 88 | 9/11/74 | Kansas City (H) | 3-2 | Al Fitzmorris |
| 89 | 9/15/74 | Chicago (A) | 6-2 | Jack Kucek |
| 90 | 9/24/74 | Kansas City (A) | 9-3 | Paul Splittorff |
| 91 | 9/28/74 | Minnesota (H) | 4-0 | Joe Decker |
| 92 | 4/7/75 | Kansas City (H) | 3-2 | Steve Mingori |
| 93 | 4/11/75 | Chicago (H) | 5-0 | Claude Osteen |

| 94 | 4/15/75 | Minnesota (A) | 7-3 | Dave Goltz |
|---|---|---|---|---|
| 95 | 4/20/75 | Chicago (A) | 8-4 | Claude Osteen |
| 96 | 5/3/75 | Texas (A) | 4-2 | Jackie Brown |
| 97 | 5/8/75 | Oakland (A) | 5-0 | Dave Hamilton |
| 98 | 5/13/75 | New York (H) | 5-0 | Doc Medich |
| 99 | 5/18/75 | Baltimore (A) | 5-1 | Mike Torrez |
| 100 | 6/1/75 | Baltimore (H) | 1-0 | Ross Grimsley |
| 101 | 6/6/75 | Milwaukee (H) | 6-0 | Jim Slaton |
| 102 | 7/26/75 | Minnesota (H) | 5-0 | Vic Albury |
| 103 | 7/30/75 | Chicago (H) | 5-4 | Jim Kaat |
| 104 | 8/20/75 | Milwaukee (H) | 6-1 | Jim Slaton |
| 105 | 8/24/75 | New York (A) | 4-3 | Tippy Martinez |
| 106 | 4/15/76 | Kansas City (A) | 5-1 | Paul Splittorff |
| 107 | 4/20/76 | Baltimore (H) | 5-0 | Doyle Alexander |
| 108 | 5/1/76 | Cleveland (A) | 6-1 | Pat Dobson |
| 109 | 6/1/76 | Minnesota (A) | 6-4 | Pete Redfern |
| 110 | 6/15/76 | Milwaukee (H) | 1-0 | Jim Colburn |
| 111 | 6/19/76 | Boston (H) | 5-3 | Rick Wise |
| 112 | 7/7/76 | Cleveland (H) | 2-0 | Rick Waits |
| 113 | 7/30/76 | Chicago (H) | 3-0 | Ken Brett |
| 114 | 8/4/76 | Texas (A) | 9-6 | Nellie Briles |
| 115 | 8/18/76 | Detroit (A) | 5-4 | John Hiller |
| 116 | 8/31/76 | Detroit (H) | 6-3 | Vern Ruhle |
| 117 | 9/5/76 | Oakland (H) | 3-2 | Stan Bahnsen |
| 118 | 9/10/76 | Chicago (A) | 3-2 | Bart Johnson |
| 119 | 9/15/76 | Kansas City (H) | 2-1 | Doug Bird |
| 120 | 9/20/76 | Texas (H) | 1-0 | Bert Blyleven |
| 121 | 9/29/76 | Chicago (H) | 3-0 | Ken Brett |
| 122 | 10/3/76 | Oakland (A) | 1-0 | Mike Torrez |
| 123 | 4/7/77 | Seattle (A) | 2-0 | Enrique Romo |
| 124 | 4/15/77 | Seattle (H) | 7-0 | Glenn Abbott |
| 125 | 4/25/77 | Oakland (H) | 11-6 | Doc Medich |
| 126 | 5/6/77 | Boston (A) | 8-4 | Luis Tiant |
| 127 | 5/10/77 | Kansas City (A) | 6-1 | Paul Splittorff |
| 128 | 5/19/77 | Minnesota (H) | 5-3 | Dave Goltz |
| 129 | 5/24/77 | Detroit (A) | 2-1 | John Hiller |
| 130 | 5/29/77 | Toronto (A) | 3-2 | Dave Lemanczyk |
| 131 | 6/12/77 | Cleveland (H) | 11-4 | Pat Dobson |
| 132 | 6/29/77 | Kansas City (H) | 7-0 | Jim Colborn |
| 133 | 7/4/77 | Oakland (H) | 4-2 | Rick Langford |
| 134 | 7/12/77 | Minnesota (H) | 3-0 | Paul Thormodsgard |
| 135 | 7/16/77 | Seattle (H) | 5-4 | Enrique Romo |
| 136 | 7/25/77 | Seattle (A) | 4-3 | Dick Pole |
| 137 | 8/3/77 | New York (H) | 5-3 | Ron Guidry |
| 138 | 8/8/77 | Kansas City (A) | 6-4 | Andy Hassler |
| 139 | 8/13/77 | New York (A) | 6-5 | Sparky Lyle |
| 140 | 9/3/77 | Cleveland (A) | 3-2 | Wayne Garland |
| 141 | 9/8/77 | Chicago (H) | 2-0 | Francisco Barrios |
| 142 | 4/29/78 | Toronto (H) | 5-0 | Dave Lemanczyk |
| 143 | 5/5/78 | Cleveland (H) | 5-0 | Rick Wise |
| 144 | 5/23/78 | Chicago (H) | 5-4 | Jim Willoughby |
| 145 | 7/19/78 | Cleveland (H) | 3-0 | Rick Wise |

| | | | | |
|---|---|---|---|---|
| 146 | 7/23/78 | Detroit (A) | 4-3 | Jim Slaton |
| 147 | 8/11/78 | Seattle (A) | 3-1 | Byron McLaughlin |
| 148 | 9/10/78 | Kansas City (H) | 13-3 | Paul Splittorff |
| 149 | 9/19/78 | Minnesota (A) | 4-1 | Roger Erickson |
| 150 | 9/24/78 | Chicago (A) | 7-3 | Francisco Barrios |
| 151 | 10/1/78 | Chicago (A) | 5-4 | Francisco Barrios |
| 152 | 4/11/79 | Minnesota (H) | 11-2 | Dave Goltz |
| 153 | 4/17/79 | Minnesota (A) | 6-0 | Dave Goltz |
| 154 | 4/21/79 | Oakland (H) | 13-1 | Matt Keough |
| 155 | 5/2/79 | New York (H) | 1-0 | Ron Guidry |
| 156 | 5/20/79 | Chicago (A) | 4-0 | Ross Baumgarten |
| 157 | 5/30/79 | Seattle (A) | 3-2 | Shane Rawley |
| 158 | 6/9/79 | Detroit (H) | 9-1 | Dave Rozema |
| 159 | 6/14/79 | Toronto (A) | 10-2 | Phil Huffman |
| 160 | 6/18/79 | Texas (H) | 5-0 | Fergie Jenkins |
| 161 | 7/1/79 | Kansas City (A) | 14-2 | Paul Splittorff |
| 162 | 7/9/79 | Boston (H) | 6-0 | Mike Torrez |
| 163 | 7/13/79 | New York (H) | 6-1 | Luis Tiant |
| 164 | 8/18/79 | Toronto (H) | 7-5 | Tom Underwood |
| 165 | 9/3/79 | Chicago (H) | 6-5 | Ross Baumgarten |
| 166 | 9/7/79 | Milwaukee (H) | 6-3 | Bill Travers |
| 167 | 9/24/79 | Kansas City (H) | 4-3 | Larry Gura |

## WITH HOUSTON ASTROS

| | | | | |
|---|---|---|---|---|
| 168 | 4/22/80 | Cincinnati (H) | 8-0 | Frank Pastore |
| 169 | 5/18/80 | Philadelphia (H) | 3-0 | Randy Lerch |
| 170 | 5/28/80 | San Diego (H) | 1-0 | Rick Wise |
| 171 | 6/14/80 | Pittsburgh (A) | 7-3 | Don Robinson |
| 172 | 6/19/80 | St. Louis (H) | 2-0 | Bob Sykes |
| 173 | 8/4/80 | San Francisco (H) | 4-2 | Alan Hargesheimer |
| 174 | 8/14/80 | San Diego (A) | 2-1 | John Curtis |
| 175 | 8/19/80 | Pittsburgh (H) | 5-2 | John Candelaria |
| 176 | 8/24/80 | Chicago (H) | 2-1 | Bill Caudill |
| 177 | 9/25/80 | Atlanta (A) | 4-2 | Phil Niekro |
| 178 | 9/30/80 | Atlanta (H) | 7-3 | Doyle Alexander |
| 179 | 4/15/81 | Atlanta (A) | 2-0 | Tommy Boggs |
| 180 | 5/11/81 | Cincinnati (H) | 5-0 | Mike LaCross |
| 181 | 5/16/81 | Chicago (H) | 6-1 | Randy Martz |
| 182 | 5/26/81 | San Diego (H) | 1-0 | Juan Eichelberger |
| 183 | 6/5/81 | New York (H) | 3-0 | Randy Jones |
| 184 | 8/14/81 | San Diego (A) | 5-1 | Tim Lollar |
| 185 | 8/19/81 | Montreal (H) | 9-1 | Scott Sanderson |
| 186 | 9/4/81 | Montreal (A) | 5-0 | Bill Gullickson |
| 187 | 9/20/81 | San Francisco (A) | 7-3 | Gary Lavalle |
| 188 | 9/26/81 | Los Angeles (H) | 5-0 | Ted Power |
| 189 | 10/1/81 | Cincinnati (A) | 8-1 | Bruce Berenyi |
| 190 | 4/26/82 | St. Louis (A) | 6-2 | John Martin |
| 191 | 5/1/82 | Pittsburgh (A) | 6-3 | Paul Moskau |
| 192 | 5/11/82 | Pittsburgh (H) | 4-2 | Tom Griffin |
| 193 | 5/28/82 | New York (A) | 8-3 | Randy Jones |
| 194 | 6/2/82 | Montreal (A) | 6-4 | Scott Sanderson |

| 195 | 6/18/82 | San Diego (H) | 7-2 | Chris Welch |
|---|---|---|---|---|
| 196 | 6/28/82 | Atlanta (A) | 6-2 | Rick Mahler |
| 197 | 7/4/82 | Los Angeles (A) | 3-0 | Jerry Reuss |
| 198 | 7/16/82 | Pittsburgh (H) | 4-2 | Larry McWilliams |
| 199 | 7/21/82 | Chicago (A) | 2-1 | Allen Ripley |
| 200 | 7/27/82 | Cincinnati (H) | 3-2 | Charlie Leibrandt |
| 201 | 8/11/82 | San Diego (A) | 3-0 | Eric Show |
| 202 | 8/21/82 | Montreal (H) | 5-3 | Ray Burris |
| 203 | 8/31/82 | New York (A) | 4-0 | Ed Lynch |
| 204 | 9/15/82 | Atlanta (A) | 5-4 | Tommy Boggs |
| 205 | 9/26/82 | Cincinnati (A) | 4-0 | Bob Shirley |
| 206 | 4/17/83 | Montreal (H) | 6-3 | Bill Gullickson |
| 207 | 4/27/83 | Montreal (A) | 4-2 | Scott Sanderson |
| 208 | 5/2/83 | New York (A) | 3-2 | Mike Torrez |
| 209 | 6/12/83 | San Diego (H) | 2-0 | Eric Show |
| 210 | 6/17/83 | San Diego (A) | 4-1 | Eric Show |
| 211 | 6/28/83 | Atlanta (A) | 4-3 | Terry Forster |
| 212 | 7/2/83 | Los Angeles (H) | 3-1 | Joe Beckwith |
| 213 | 7/8/83 | New York (A) | 6-3 | Mike Torrez |
| 214 | 7/13/83 | Montreal (A) | 9-4 | Charlie Lea |
| 215 | 8/3/83 | San Diego (A) | 1-0 | Tim Lollar |
| 216 | 8/7/83 | San Francisco (A) | 2-1 | Greg Minton |
| 217 | 8/12/83 | San Francisco (H) | 5-2 | Renie Martin |
| 218 | 9/1/83 | Pittsburgh (H) | 3-0 | Cecilio Guante |
| 219 | 9/20/83 | Los Angeles (A) | 15-2 | Alejandro Pena |
| 220 | 4/4/84 | Montreal (H) | 8-2 | Bill Gullickson |
| 221 | 5/6/84 | New York (A) | 10-1 | Dwight Gooden |
| 222 | 5/11/84 | Chicago (H) | 3-1 | Dick Ruthven |
| 223 | 5/16/84 | Pittsburgh (A) | 1-0 | John Candelaria |
| 224 | 5/21/84 | St. Louis (A) | 3-2 | Bob Forsch |
| 225 | 5/26/84 | Pittsburgh (H) | 2-0 | Jose DeLeon |
| 226 | 6/17/84 | Los Angeles (H) | 1-0 | Bob Welch |
| 227 | 7/24/84 | San Francisco (A) | 10-3 | Mark Davis |
| 228 | 8/3/84 | San Diego (H) | 6-2 | Eric Show |
| 229 | 8/12/84 | Cincinnati (A) | 6-1 | Andy McGaffigan |
| 230 | 8/22/84 | Chicago (A) | 8-3 | Dick Ruthven |
| 231 | 9/5/84 | San Francisco (A) | 4-1 | Randy Lerch |
| 232 | 4/9/85 | Los Angeles (H) | 2-1 | Fernando Valenzuela |
| 233 | 4/14/85 | Philadelphia (H) | 5-3 | Steve Carlton |
| 234 | 5/18/85 | St. Louis (H) | 6-5 | Kurt Kepshire |
| 235 | 5/24/85 | Chicago (A) | 6-2 | Dick Ruthven |
| 236 | 5/29/85 | Pittsburgh (H) | 8-3 | Ray Krawczyk |
| 237 | 6/8/85 | San Francisco (H) | 4-1 | Bill Laskey |
| 238 | 6/12/85 | San Diego (H) | 3-2 | Eric Show |
| 239 | 6/17/85 | Atlanta (A) | 4-3 | Steve Shields |
| 240 | 8/28/85 | Chicago (H) | 3-0 | Jay Baller |
| 241 | 10/5/85 | San Diego (A) | 9-3 | Ed Wojna |
| 242 | 4/12/86 | Atlanta (H) | 4-3 | Rick Mahler |
| 243 | 4/16/86 | San Francisco (A) | 4-1 | Roger Mason |
| 244 | 4/25/86 | Cincinnati (H) | 3-1 | Tom Browning |
| 245 | 6/24/86 | Cincinnati (H) | 8-4 | Tom Browning |
| 246 | 7/8/86 | Montreal (A) | 4-1 | Jay Tibbs |

| 247 | 7/12/86 | Philadelphia (H) | 4-3 | Shane Rawley |
|---|---|---|---|---|
| 248 | 7/27/86 | Philadelphia (A) | 3-2 | Kevin Gross |
| 249 | 8/12/86 | Los Angeles (H) | 3-0 | Rick Honeycutt |
| 250 | 8/27/86 | Chicago (H) | 7-1 | Jamie Moyer |
| 251 | 9/8/86 | Cincinnati (H) | 3-1 | Chris Welsh |
| 252 | 9/24/86 | San Francisco (H) | 6-0 | Mike LaCoss |
| 253 | 10/3/86 | Atlanta (H) | 6-2 | Jim Acker |
| 254 | 4/8/87 | Los Angeles (H) | 7-3 | Matt Young |
| 255 | 5/1/87 | Atlanta (A) | 12-3 | Rick Mahler |
| 256 | 6/7/87 | San Francisco (H) | 3-0 | Atlee Hammaker |
| 257 | 6/12/87 | Los Angeles (A) | 5-1 | Bob Welch |
| 258 | 8/18/87 | St. Louis (H) | 4-0 | Danny Cox |
| 259 | 9/4/87 | Pittsburgh (H) | 5-1 | Mike Bielecki |
| 260 | 9/8/87 | San Francisco (H) | 4-2 | Atlee Hammaker |
| 261 | 9/14/87 | Los Angeles (A) | 8-1 | Shawn Hillegas |
| 262 | 4/12/88 | Atlanta (A) | 8-3 | Zane Smith |
| 263 | 4/17/88 | Cincinnati (H) | 5-3 | Danny Jackson |
| 264 | 5/13/88 | Chicago (H) | 8-2 | Jamie Moyer |
| 265 | 5/18/88 | Pittsburgh (H) | 4-2 | Doug Drabek |
| 266 | 5/29/88 | Chicago (A) | 7-1 | Jamie Moyer |
| 267 | 7/9/88 | New York (H) | 6-3 | Rick Aguilera |
| 268 | 7/21/88 | Philadelphia (H) | 2-0 | Mike Maddux |
| 269 | 7/27/88 | San Diego (A) | 4-1 | Ed Whitson |
| 270 | 8/15/88 | San Diego (H) | 7-3 | Andy Hawkins |
| 271 | 9/3/88 | St. Louis (H) | 10-1 | Larry McWilliams |
| 272 | 9/8/88 | Los Angeles (A) | 2-1 | John Tudor |
| 273 | 9/14/88 | Cincinnati (A) | 7-1 | Danny Jackson |

## WITH TEXAS RANGERS

| 274 | 4/12/89 | Milwaukee (A) | 8-1 | Bill Wegman |
|---|---|---|---|---|
| 275 | 4/23/89 | Toronto (A) | 4-1 | Todd Stottlemyre |
| 276 | 4/30/89 | Boston (H) | 2-1 | Roger Clemens |
| 277 | 5/11/89 | Kansas City (A) | 6-3 | Mark Gubicza |
| 278 | 5/23/89 | Kansas City (H) | 10-8 | Luis Aquino |
| 279 | 6/3/89 | Seattle (A) | 6-1 | Clint Zavaras |
| 280 | 6/8/89 | Chicago (H) | 11-7 | Eric King |
| 281 | 6/14/89 | California (H) | 5-1 | Chuck Finley |
| 282 | 6/25/89 | Cleveland (H) | 4-2 | Tom Candiotti |
| 283 | 7/6/89 | California (A) | 3-0 | Kirk McCaskill |
| 284 | 7/20/89 | New York (H) | 6-2 | Andy Hawkins |
| 285 | 7/30/89 | Milwaukee (H) | 9-3 | Don August |
| 286 | 8/10/89 | Detroit (H) | 4-1 | Doyle Alexander |
| 287 | 8/16/89 | Seattle (A) | 3-1 | Scott Bankhead |
| 288 | 9/2/89 | Kansas City (H) | 6-3 | Terry Leach |
| 289 | 9/30/89 | California (A) | 2-0 | Chuck Finley |
| 290 | 4/9/90 | Toronto (H) | 4-2 | Todd Stottlemyre |
| 291 | 4/14/90 | New York (A) | 8-4 | Andy Hawkins |
| 292 | 4/20/90 | New York (H) | 6-5 | Lee Guetterman |
| 293 | 4/26/90 | Chicago (A) | 1-0 | Melido Perez |
| 294 | 6/11/90 | Oakland (A) | 5-0 | Scott Sanderson |
| 295 | 6/22/90 | Seattle (H) | 5-2 | Matt Young |

| | | | | |
|---|---|---|---|---|
| 296 | 6/27/90 | Minnesota (A) | 9-2 | Kevin Tapani |
| 297 | 7/7/90 | Boston (H) | 7-4 | Mike Boddicker |
| 298 | 7/14/90 | Detroit (A) | 5-3 | Jeff Robinson |
| 299 | 7/20/90 | Detroit (H) | 5-3 | Steve Searcy |
| 300 | 7/31/90 | Milwaukee (A) | 11-3 | Chris Bosio |
| 301 | 8/22/90 | Seattle (H) | 5-4 | Bill Swift |
| 302 | 9/3/90 | Cleveland (H) | 6-2 | Mike Walker |
| 303 | 4/14/91 | Baltimore (H) | 15-3 | Jeff Robinson |
| 304 | 4/20/91 | Baltimore (A) | 1-0 | Jose Mesa |
| 305 | 5/1/91 | Toronto (H) | 3-0 | Jimmy Key |
| 306 | 6/11/91 | Chicago (H) | 2-0 | Alex Fernandez |
| 307 | 7/7/91 | California (H) | 7-0 | Chuck Finley |
| 308 | 7/23/91 | Boston (H) | 5-4 | Greg Harris |
| 309 | 7/28/91 | Detroit (H) | 10-6 | Frank Tanana |
| 310 | 8/19/91 | Baltimore (H) | 4-1 | Mike Mussina |
| 311 | 8/30/91 | Kansas City (H) | 6-2 | Mike Boddicker |
| 312 | 9/12/91 | Minnesota (H) | 4-3 | Jack Morris |
| 313 | 9/19/91 | California (H) | 10-3 | Chuck Finley |
| 314 | 9/25/91 | Seattle (A) | 7-1 | Rich Delucia |
| 315 | 6/26/92 | Detroit (A) | 8-4 | Mark Leiter |
| 316 | 7/4/92 | New York (H) | 4-1 | Scott Kamieniecki |
| 317 | 7/9/92 | Cleveland (H) | 14-4 | Scott Scudder |
| 318 | 7/16/92 | Baltimore (H) | 5-2 | Rick Sutcliffe |
| 319 | 7/26/92 | Baltimore (A) | 6-2 | Mike Mussina |

\* = relief appearance

# RYAN'S SEVEN CAREER NO-HITTERS

### NO-HITTER NUMBER 1
### MAY 15, 1973
### CALIFORNIA 3, KANSAS CITY 0

| CALIFORNIA | ab | r | h | bi | KANSAS CITY | ab | r | h | bi |
|---|---|---|---|---|---|---|---|---|---|
| Pinson lf | 5 | 1 | 2 | 0 | Patek ss | 4 | 0 | 0 | 0 |
| Alomar 2b | 4 | 0 | 0 | 0 | Hovley rf | 3 | 0 | 0 | 0 |
| Valentine cf | 4 | 0 | 1 | 0 | Otis cf | 4 | 0 | 0 | 0 |
| Robinson dh | 3 | 1 | 1 | 0 | Mayberry 1b | 3 | 0 | 0 | 0 |
| Oliver rf | 4 | 1 | 2 | 2 | Rojas 2b | 3 | 0 | 0 | 0 |
| Berry rf | 0 | 0 | 0 | 0 | Kirkpatr'k dh-c | 3 | 0 | 0 | 0 |
| Gallagher 3b | 4 | 0 | 2 | 1 | Pinella lf | 3 | 0 | 0 | 0 |
| Spencer 1b | 4 | 0 | 1 | 0 | Schaal 3b | 2 | 0 | 0 | 0 |
| Meoli ss | 4 | 0 | 1 | 0 | Taylor c | 1 | 0 | 0 | 0 |
| Torborg c | 4 | 0 | 1 | 0 | Hopkins ph | 1 | 0 | 0 | 0 |
| Ryan p | 0 | 0 | 0 | 0 | Dal Canton p | 0 | 0 | 0 | 0 |
|  |  |  |  |  | Garber p | 0 | 0 | 0 | 0 |
| Totals | 36 | 3 | 11 | 3 | Totals | 27 | 0 | 0 | 0 |

| | | | |
|---|---|---|---|
| **California** | 200 | 001 | 000 — 3 |
| **Kansas City** | 000 | 000 | 000 — 0 |

DP—Kansas City 1. LOB—California 8, Kansas City 3.
HR—Oliver (4). SB—Hovley. S—Alomar.

| California | IP | H | R | ER | BB | SO |
|---|---|---|---|---|---|---|
| Ryan (W 5—3) | 9 | 0 | 0 | 0 | 3 | 12 |
| **Kansas City** | | | | | | |
| Dal Canton (L 2—2) | 5 2/3 | 8 | 3 | 3 | 1 | 0 |
| Garber | 3 1/3 | 3 | 0 | 0 | 0 | 0 |

T—2:54. A—9,265.

Nolan Ryan chalked up the first of his major league record seven no-hitters for the California Angels as he stopped the Kansas City Royals for the first hitless game by an Angel righthander in the club's history. Ryan finished with 12 strikeouts as he recorded at least one whiff in every inning except the fifth. The only close call of the game came in the eighth inning when Royals pinch hitter Gail Hopkins hit a looping liner into left field which shortstop Rudy Meoli came up with on a running over-the-shoulder catch with his back to the plate. The Angels and Ryan got all the offensive support they needed from right-fielder Bob Oliver, two of the three RBI with a solo home run and a single.

Ryan and Torborg. Dal Canton, Garber (6) and Taylor, Kirkpatrick. WP—Ryan (5—3) LP—Dal Canton (2—2).

## NO-HITTER NUMBER 2
### JULY 15, 1973
### CALIFORNIA 6, DETROIT 0

| CALIFORNIA | ab | r | h | bi | DETROIT | ab | r | h | bi |
|---|---|---|---|---|---|---|---|---|---|
| Alomar 2b | 5 | 0 | 2 | 0 | Northrup lf | 4 | 0 | 0 | 0 |
| Pinson rf | 4 | 0 | 1 | 1 | M. Stanley cf | 3 | 0 | 0 | 0 |
| McCraw lf | 2 | 0 | 0 | 0 | G. Brown dh | 2 | 0 | 0 | 0 |
| Lienas ph | 1 | 0 | 1 | 2 | Cash 1b | 4 | 0 | 0 | 0 |
| Stanton lf | 0 | 1 | 0 | 0 | Sims c | 3 | 0 | 0 | 0 |
| Epstein 1b | 3 | 1 | 1 | 0 | McAuliffe 2b | 3 | 0 | 0 | 0 |
| Oliver dh | 3 | 1 | 1 | 1 | Sharon rf | 2 | 0 | 0 | 0 |
| Berry cf | 3 | 0 | 0 | 0 | A.Rodriguez 3b | 3 | 0 | 0 | 0 |
| Gallagher 3b | 4 | 0 | 2 | 2 | E.Brinkman ss | 3 | 0 | 0 | 0 |
| Meoli ss | 4 | 1 | 1 | 0 | J.Perry p | 0 | 0 | 0 | 0 |
| Kusnyer c | 3 | 2 | 1 | 0 | Scherman p | 0 | 0 | 0 | 0 |
| Ryan p | 0 | 0 | 0 | 0 | B.Miller p | 0 | 0 | 0 | 0 |
| | | | | | Farmer p | 0 | 0 | 0 | 0 |
| Totals | 32 | 6 | 9 | 6 | Totals | 27 | 0 | 0 | 0 |

| | | | | | | | |
|---|---|---|---|---|---|---|---|
| California | 0 0 1 | 0 0 0 | 0 5 0 — 6 |
| Detroit | 0 0 0 | 0 0 0 | 0 0 0 — 0 |

DP—Detroit 2, LOB—California 5, Detroit 4. 2B—Epstein, Meoli. SF—Pinson.

| California | IP | H | R | ER | BB | SO |
|---|---|---|---|---|---|---|
| Ryan (W 11—11) | 9 | 0 | 0 | 0 | 4 | 17 |
| **Detroit** | | | | | | |
| J.Perry (L 9—9) | 7 1/3 | 5 | 3 | 3 | 3 | 2 |
| Scherman | 1/3 | 0 | 0 | 0 | 0 | 0 |
| B.Miller | 0 | 2 | 3 | 3 | 1 | 0 |
| Farmer | 1 1/3 | 2 | 0 | 0 | 1 | 0 |

T—2:21.A—41,411.

The "easiest" no-hitter for Ryan in terms of scores as he turned in his second no-hitter of the 1973 campaign, again on the road, by stopping the Detroit Tigers 6–0. Ryan had 17 strikeouts for the game with 16 of them coming in the first seven innings. However, his arm stiffened up somewhat in the top of the eighth as the Angels batted around while scoring five runs to break open a close game. Ryan had to rely on no special defensive accomplishments to preserve the no-hitter as he became the fifth man in history to throw two no-hitters in a season.

Ryan and Kusnyer. J.Perry, Scherman (8), Miller (8), Farmer (8) and Sims. WP—Ryan (11—11). LP—J. Perry (9—9).

## NO-HITTER NUMBER 3
## SEPTEMBER 28, 1974
### CALIFORNIA 4, MINNESOTA 0

| MINNESOTA | ab | r | h | bi | CALIFORNIA | ab | r | h | bi |
|---|---|---|---|---|---|---|---|---|---|
| Brye cf | 2 | 0 | 0 | 0 | M.Nettles cf | 4 | 1 | 2 | 3 |
| Carew 2b | 2 | 0 | 0 | 0 | D.Doyle 2b | 4 | 0 | 1 | 0 |
| Braun 3b | 3 | 0 | 0 | 0 | Bochte 1b | 3 | 0 | 0 | 1 |
| Darwin rf | 4 | 0 | 0 | 0 | Lahoud dh | 4 | 0 | 1 | 0 |
| Oliva dh | 3 | 0 | 0 | 0 | Stanton rf | 4 | 0 | 1 | 0 |
| Hisle lf | 3 | 0 | 0 | 0 | Chalk 3b | 2 | 1 | 0 | 0 |
| Bourque 1b | 3 | 0 | 0 | 0 | Balaz lf | 2 | 1 | 1 | 0 |
| Killebrew ph | 0 | 0 | 0 | 0 | Meoli ss | 2 | 1 | 1 | 0 |
| Terrell pr | 0 | 0 | 0 | 0 | Egan c | 2 | 0 | 0 | 0 |
| Gomez ss | 2 | 0 | 0 | 0 | Ryan p | 0 | 0 | 0 | 0 |
| Soderholm ss | 2 | 0 | 0 | 0 | | | | | |
| Borgmann c | 3 | 0 | 0 | 0 | | | | | |
| Decker p | 0 | 0 | 0 | 0 | | | | | |
| Butler p | 0 | 0 | 0 | 0 | | | | | |
| Totals | 27 | 0 | 0 | 0 | Totals | 27 | 4 | 7 | 4 |

| | | | | | | | | |
|---|---|---|---|---|---|---|---|---|
| Minnesota | 0 0 0 | 0 0 0 | 0 0 0 — 0 |
| California | 0 0 2 | 2 0 0 | 0 0 x — 4 |

E—Braun. LOB—Minnesota 8, California 4. 2B—Meoli, Balaz. SB—M.Nettles. S—Egan. SF—Bochte.

| Minnesota | IP | H | R | ER | BB | SO |
|---|---|---|---|---|---|---|
| Decker (L 16—14) | 2 ²/₃ | 4 | 2 | 1 | 0 | 1 |
| Butler | 5 ¹/₃ | 3 | 2 | 2 | 3 | 8 |
| California | | | | | | |
| Ryan (W 22—16) | 9 | 0 | 0 | 0 | 8 | 15 |

T—2:22. A—10,872.

Nolan Ryan makes the most of his final start of the 1974 campaign by ringing up his third career no-hitter to raise his final record to 22–16 at the expense of Minnesota Twins, 4–0. Ryan started in splendid fashion as his first seven pitches were strikes and he struck out the side in both the first and second innings. He finished the game with 15 strikeouts, but also had to contend with no less than eight walks—seven of them in the first five innings. The Angels won it with two runs in both the third and fourth innings with centerfielder Morris Nettles driving home three of them.

Decker, Butler (3) and Borgmann. Ryan and Egan. WP—Ryan (22—16). LP—Decker (16—14).

## NO-HITTER NUMBER 4
### JUNE 1, 1975
### CALIFORNIA 1, BALTIMORE 0

| BALTIMORE | ab | r | h | bi | CALIFORNIA | ab | r | h | bi |
|---|---|---|---|---|---|---|---|---|---|
| Singleton rf | 4 | 0 | 0 | 0 | Remy 2b | 3 | 0 | 1 | 0 |
| Shopay cf | 3 | 0 | 0 | 0 | Rivers cf | 4 | 1 | 1 | 0 |
| Bumbry lf | 4 | 0 | 0 | 0 | Harper dh | 4 | 0 | 1 | 0 |
| Baylor dh | 2 | 0 | 0 | 0 | Chalk 3b | 3 | 0 | 2 | 1 |
| Davis dh | 2 | 0 | 0 | 0 | Llenas lf | 3 | 0 | 1 | 0 |
| Grich 2b | 2 | 0 | 0 | 0 | M.Nettles lf | 0 | 0 | 0 | 0 |
| May 1b | 3 | 0 | 0 | 0 | Stanton rf | 2 | 0 | 1 | 0 |
| Robinson 3b | 3 | 0 | 0 | 0 | Bochte 1b | 3 | 0 | 1 | 0 |
| Hendricks c | 3 | 0 | 0 | 0 | Rodriguez c | 3 | 0 | 0 | 0 |
| Belanger ss | 2 | 0 | 0 | 0 | Smith ss | 2 | 0 | 1 | 0 |
| Grimsley p | 0 | 0 | 0 | 0 | Ryan p | 0 | 0 | 0 | 0 |
| Garland p | 0 | 0 | 0 | 0 | | | | | |
| Totals | 28 | 0 | 0 | 0 | Totals | 27 | 1 | 9 | 1 |

```
Baltimore    000 000 000 — 0
California   001 000 00x — 1
```

E—Smith. DP—Baltimore 2. LOB—Baltimore 5, California 5. SB—Belanger. S—Stanton, Remy.

| Baltimore | IP | H | R | ER | BB | SO |
|---|---|---|---|---|---|---|
| Grimsley (L 1—7) | 3 1/3 | 8 | 1 | 1 | 0 | 1 |
| Garland | 4 2/3 | 1 | 0 | 0 | 1 | 1 |
| California | | | | | | |
| Ryan (W 9—3) | 9 | 0 | 0 | 0 | 4 | 9 |

T—2:01. A—18,492.

Nolan Ryan moved into a tie with Dodger great Sandy Koufax as he fired the fourth no-hitter of his career in nipping the Baltimore Orioles 1—0. Making his 12th start of the season, Ryan polished off the Orioles with nine strikeouts as he came up with his fourth no-hit effort in the period of 109 starts. The only offensive output in the game came in the bottom of the third when Angel third baseman Dave Chalk singled home Mickey Rivers.

Grimsley, Garland (4) and Hendricks. Ryan and Rodriguez. WP—Ryan (9—3). LP—Grimsley (1—7).

### NO-HITTER NUMBER 5
### SEPTEMBER 26, 1981
### HOUSTON 5, LOS ANGELES 0

| LOS ANGELES | ab | r | h | bi | HOUSTON | ab | r | h | bi |
|---|---|---|---|---|---|---|---|---|---|
| Lopes 2b | 3 | 0 | 0 | 0 | Puhl rf | 4 | 1 | 1 | 0 |
| Smith ph | 1 | 0 | 0 | 0 | Garner 2b | 4 | 0 | 2 | 1 |
| Landreaux cf | 3 | 0 | 0 | 0 | T.Scott cf | 5 | 1 | 0 | 0 |
| Baker lf | 4 | 0 | 0 | 0 | Cruz lf | 4 | 1 | 3 | 1 |
| Garvey 1b | 2 | 0 | 0 | 0 | Ashby c | 4 | 0 | 1 | 2 |
| Guerrero 3b | 3 | 0 | 0 | 0 | Howe 3b | 4 | 0 | 0 | 0 |
| Scioscia c | 3 | 0 | 0 | 0 | Spilman 1b | 2 | 0 | 0 | 0 |
| Roenicke rf | 3 | 0 | 0 | 0 | Pittman ph | 1 | 0 | 1 | 0 |
| Thomas ss | 2 | 0 | 0 | 0 | Walling 1b | 0 | 1 | 0 | 0 |
| Power p | 1 | 0 | 0 | 0 | Reynolds ss | 4 | 1 | 2 | 1 |
| Goltz p | 0 | 0 | 0 | 0 | Ryan p | 2 | 0 | 1 | 0 |
| Perconte ph | 1 | 0 | 0 | 0 | | | | | |
| Forster p | 0 | 0 | 0 | 0 | | | | | |
| Johnstone ph | 1 | 0 | 0 | 0 | | | | | |
| Stewart p | 0 | 0 | 0 | 0 | | | | | |
| Howe p | 0 | 0 | 0 | 0 | | | | | |
| Totals | 27 | 0 | 0 | 0 | Totals | 34 | 5 | 11 | 5 |

| | | | | |
|---|---|---|---|---|
| Los Angeles | 000 | 000 | 000 — 0 | |
| Houston | 002 | 000 | 03x — 5 | |

E—Thomas. LOB—Los Angeles 3, Houston 12. 2B—Cruz, Reynolds. 3B—Reynolds. SB—Garner, Garvey, Thomas, Cruz. S—Ryan.

| Los Angeles | IP | H | R | ER | BB | SO |
|---|---|---|---|---|---|---|
| Power (L 1—3) | 3 1/3 | 6 | 2 | 1 | 3 | 1 |
| Goltz | 2/3 | 0 | 0 | 0 | 0 | 0 |
| Forster | 3 | 2 | 0 | 0 | 1 | 2 |
| Stewart | 1/3 | 2 | 3 | 3 | 2 | 0 |
| Howe | 2/3 | 1 | 0 | 0 | 0 | 0 |
| **Houston** | | | | | | |
| Ryan (W 10—5) | 9 | 0 | 0 | 0 | 3 | 11 |

T—2:01. A—18,492.

History was made as Nolan Ryan became the first man in the history of the sport to pitch five no-hitters in his career as he notched a crucial 5—0 win over the Los Angeles Dodgers. Ryan wound up with 11 strikeouts (the 135th in his career fanned 10 or more men in a game) while walking only three. He threw a total of 129 pitches (52 balls, 77 strikes). Ryan stood at 10 strikeouts through the opening six innings, but set down only one more the rest of the way as he retired the final 19 batters in a row. Catcher Alan Ashby gave the Astros a 2—0 lead with a two-run single in the third and then Houston wrapped up the win with three more in the eighth.

Power, Goltz (4), Forster (5), Stewart (8), Howe (8) and Scioscia. Ryan and Ashby. WP—Ryan (10—5), LP—Power (1—3).

## NO-HITTER NUMBER 6
### JUNE 11, 1990
### TEXAS 5, OAKLAND 0

| TEXAS | ab | r | h | bi | OAKLAND | ab | r | h | bi |
|---|---|---|---|---|---|---|---|---|---|
| Pettis cf | 5 | 1 | 2 | 0 | R.Hend'son lf | 4 | 0 | 0 | 0 |
| Palmeiro 1b | 4 | 1 | 0 | 0 | Randolph 2b | 4 | 0 | 0 | 0 |
| Franco 2b | 4 | 2 | 2 | 4 | Jennings 1b | 3 | 0 | 0 | 0 |
| Sierra rf | 3 | 0 | 1 | 0 | Hassey dh | 3 | 0 | 0 | 0 |
| Baines dh | 4 | 0 | 1 | 0 | Jose rf | 3 | 0 | 0 | 0 |
| Incaviglia lf | 4 | 0 | 1 | 0 | D.Hend'son cf | 3 | 0 | 0 | 0 |
| JoRussell c | 3 | 1 | 1 | 1 | Quirk c | 2 | 0 | 0 | 0 |
| Buechele 3b | 4 | 0 | 0 | 0 | Lansford ph | 1 | 0 | 0 | 0 |
| Huson ss | 3 | 0 | 1 | 0 | Steinbach c | 0 | 0 | 0 | 0 |
| | | | | | Weiss ss | 2 | 0 | 0 | 0 |
| | | | | | Gallego 3b | 1 | 0 | 0 | 0 |
| | | | | | Phelps ph | 1 | 0 | 0 | 0 |
| Totals | 34 | 5 | 9 | 5 | Totals | 27 | 0 | 0 | 0 |

| | | | |
|---|---|---|---|
| Texas | 2 1 0 | 0 2 0 | 0 0 0 — 5 |
| Oakland | 0 0 0 | 0 0 0 | 0 0 0 — 0 |

LOB—Texas 6, Oakland 2. HR—Franco 2 (6), JoRussell (2). SB—Pettis (20), Sierra (5), Weiss (5).

| Texas | IP | H | R | ER | BB | SO |
|---|---|---|---|---|---|---|
| Ryan (W 5—3) | 9 | 0 | 0 | 0 | 2 | 14 |
| Oakland | | | | | | |
| Sanderson (L 7—3) | 6 | 8 | 5 | 5 | 2 | 3 |
| Norris | 2 | 1 | 0 | 0 | 2 | 3 |
| Nelson | 1 | 0 | 0 | 0 | 0 | 0 |

WP—Norris.
T—2:49. A—33,436.

Nolan Ryan accomplished several milestones with the sixth no-hitter of his major league career. At the age of 43 years, 4 months, 12 days, he became the oldest pitcher to ever throw a no-hitter while also becoming the first to reach that achievement in three different decades and with three different teams. Ryan was making just his second start since coming off the disabled list and was still bothered by the lower back trouble that had sidelined him for nearly three weeks. He allowed only two baserunners, walks to Walt Weiss in the third and Mike Gallego in the sixth, while fanning 14 and throwing 132 pitches. The Rangers offense was provided by a pair of 2-run homers by Julio Franco and a solo blast by John Russell, who was catching Ryan for the first time ever.

Ryan and Russell. Sanderson, Norris (7), Nelson (9) and Quirk, Steinbach (9). WP—Ryan (5—3), LP—Sanderson (7—3).

---

**NO-HITTER NUMBER 7**
**MAY 1, 1991**
**TEXAS 3, TORONTO 0**

| TORONTO | AB | R | H | BI | TEXAS | AB | R | H | BI |
|---|---|---|---|---|---|---|---|---|---|
| White cf | 4 | 0 | 0 | 0 | Pettis cf | 4 | 1 | 1 | 0 |
| R. Alomar 2b | 4 | 0 | 0 | 0 | Daugherty lf | 4 | 0 | 1 | 0 |
| Gruber 3b | 2 | 0 | 0 | 0 | Palmeiro 1b | 4 | 1 | 2 | 0 |
| Carter lf | 2 | 0 | 0 | 0 | Sierra rf | 4 | 1 | 1 | 2 |
| Olerud 1b | 3 | 0 | 0 | 0 | Franco 2b | 4 | 0 | 0 | 0 |
| Whiten rf | 3 | 0 | 0 | 0 | Gonzalez dh | 3 | 0 | 1 | 0 |
| G. Hill dh | 3 | 0 | 0 | 0 | Stanley c | 3 | 0 | 1 | 0 |
| Myers c | 3 | 0 | 0 | 0 | Buechele 3b | 4 | 0 | 1 | 0 |
| M. Lee ss | 3 | 0 | 0 | 0 | Huson ss | 2 | 0 | 0 | 0 |
| Totals | 27 | 0 | 0 | 0 | Totals | 32 | 3 | 8 | 2 |

| | | | | | |
|---|---|---|---|---|---|
| **Toronto** | 0 0 0 | 0 0 0 | 0 0 0 — 0 |
| **Texas** | 0 0 3 | 0 0 0 | 0 0 x — 3 |

E: Gruber (2), Myers (1), M. Lee (5), Palmeiro (1). LOB: Toronto 2, Texas 8, 2B: Gonzalez (3), Stanley (1), HR: Sierra (5). RBIs: Sierra 2 (15). SB: Pettis (8). CS: Gonzalez (1). S: Huson.

| Toronto | IP | H | R | ER | BB | SO |
|---|---|---|---|---|---|---|
| Key (L 4—1) | 6 | 5 | 3 | 3 | 1 | 5 |
| MacDonald | 1 | 2 | 0 | 0 | 0 | 2 |
| Fraser | 1 | 1 | 0 | 0 | 0 | 0 |
| **Texas** | **IP** | **H** | **R** | **ER** | **BB** | **SO** |
| Ryan (W 3—2) | 9 | 0 | 0 | 0 | 2 | 16 |

HBP: by Fraser (Gonzales).
Umpires: Home, Tschida; First, Coble; Second, Shulock; Third, Johnson.T:2.25. A: 33,439.

---

On Arlington Appreciation Night, Nolan Ryan gave 33,439 fans the thrill of a lifetime with perhaps the most dominating performance in any of his seven no-hitters. He retired 27 of 29 batters, issuing walks to Kelly Gruber in the first and Joe Carter in the seventh while tying his own club record of 16 strikeouts, his second most ever in a no-hitter. The closest that Toronto came to a hit was in the sixth inning on a shallow fly ball by Manuel Lee that Gary Pettis charged and caught at knee-level. He recorded at least one strikeout in every inning and fanned Roberto Alomar to end the game on his 122nd pitch. Ruben Sierra hit a two-run homer for the Rangers. It was the first no-hitter ever pitched by a Ranger at Arlington Stadium.

Key, MacDonald (7), Fraser (8) and Myers. Ryan and Stanley. WP—Ryan (3—2). LP—Key (4—1).

# RYAN'S CAREER 5,668 STIKEOUTS

| | | | |
|---|---|---|---|
| 1 ... 9/11/66 .. Pat Jarvis ............... Braves | 51 ... 5/14/68 .. Pete Rose ................. Reds |
| 2 ... 9/11/66 .. Eddie Mathews ...... Braves | 52 ... 5/14/68 .. Alex Johnson ............ Reds |
| 3 ... 9/11/66 .. Dennis Menke ........ Braves | 53 ... 5/14/68 .. Johnny Bench ............ Reds |
| 4 ... 9/18/66 .. Rusty Staub ............ Astros | 54 ... 5/14/68 .. Vada Pinson ............. Reds |
| 5 ... 9/18/66 .. Bob Aspromonte ..... Astros | 55 ... 5/14/68 .. Lee May ................... Reds |
| 6 ... 9/18/66 .. Bob Bruce ............... Astros | 56 ... 5/14/68 .. Leo Cardenas ........... Reds |
| 7 ... 4/14/68 .. Ron Davis ................ Astros | 57 ... 5/14/68 .. Mel Queen ................ Reds |
| 8 ... 4/14/68 .. Joe Morgan ............. Astros | 58 ... 5/14/68 .. Alex Johnson ............ Reds |
| 9 ... 4/14/68 .. Hal King .................. Astros | 59 ... 5/14/68 .. Tony Perez ............... Reds |
| 10 ... 4/14/68 .. Jim Wynn ............... Astros | 60 ... 5/14/68 .. Alex Johnson ............ Reds |
| 11 ... 4/14/68 .. Norm Miller ............ Astros | 61 ... 5/14/68 .. Vada Pinson ............. Reds |
| 12 ... 4/14/68 .. Hector Torres .......... Astros | 62 ... 5/14/68 .. Tony Perez ............... Reds |
| 13 ... 4/14/68 .. Ron Davis ............... Astros | 63 ... 5/14/68 .. Lee May ................... Reds |
| 14 ... 4/14/68 .. Rusty Staub ............ Astros | 64 ... 5/14/68 .. Johnny Bench ........... Reds |
| 15 ... 4/19/68 .. Wes Parker .......... Dodgers | 65 ... 5/19/68 .. Sonny Jackson ...... Braves |
| 16 ... 4/19/68 .. Zolio Versalles ..... Dodgers | 66 ... 5/19/68 .. Hank Aaron .......... Braves |
| 17 ... 4/19/68 .. Willie Davis .......... Dodgers | 67 ... 5/19/68 .. Ron Reed .............. Braves |
| 18 ... 4/19/68 .. Ron Fairly ............ Dodgers | 68 ... 5/19/68 .. Tito Francona ........ Braves |
| 19 ... 4/19/68 .. Claude Osteen .... Dodgers | 69 ... 5/19/68 .. Sonny Jackson ...... Braves |
| 20 ... 4/19/68 .. Wes Parker .......... Dodgers | 70 ... 5/19/68 .. Tito Francona ........ Braves |
| 21 ... 4/19/68 .. Zolio Versalles ..... Dodgers | 71 ... 5/19/68 .. Sandy Valdespino .. Braves |
| 22 ... 4/19/68 .. Ricky Colavito ...... Dodgers | 72 ... 5/24/68 .. Bob Tillman ........... Braves |
| 23 ... 4/19/68 .. Claude Osteen .... Dodgers | 73 ... 5/24/68 .. Felipe Alou ............ Braves |
| 24 ... 4/19/68 .. Jim Lefebvre ....... Dodgers | 74 ... 5/24/68 .. Joe Torre .............. Braves |
| 25 ... 4/19/68 .. Claude Osteen .... Dodgers | 75 ... 6/1/68 .... Lou Brock .......... Cardinals |
| 26 ... 4/27/68 .. Tony Perez ............... Reds | 76 ... 6/1/68 .... Roger Maris ....... Cardinals |
| 27 ... 4/27/68 .. Johnny Bench ........... Reds | 77 ... 6/1/68 .... Ray Washburn ... Cardinals |
| 28 ... 4/27/68 .. Leo Cardenas ........... Reds | 78 ... 6/1/68 .... Mike Shannon ... Cardinals |
| 29 ... 4/27/68 .. Mack Jones .............. Reds | 79 ... 6/1/68 .... Orlando Cepada  Cardinals |
| 30 ... 4/27/68 .. Vada Pinson ............. Reds | 80 ... 6/1/68 .... Bob Tolan .......... Cardinals |
| 31 ... 4/27/68 .. Milt Pappas .............. Reds | 81 ... 6/1/68 .... Dick Schofield .... Cardinals |
| 32 ... 4/27/68 .. Pete Rose ................. Reds | 82 ... 6/7/68 .... Frank Johnson ...... Giants |
| 33 ... 5/2/68 .... Cookie Rojas ........ Phillies | 83 ... 6/7/68 .... Dave Marshall ...... Giants |
| 34 ... 5/2/68 .... Johnny Callison ..... Phillies | 84 ... 6/7/68 .... Al Oliver .................. Giants |
| 35 ... 5/2/68 .... Tony Gonzalez ...... Phillies | 85 ... 6/7/68 .... Bob Barton ............. Giants |
| 36 ... 5/2/68 .... Bill White .............. Phillies | 86 ... 6/7/68 .... Frank Johnson ...... Giants |
| 37 ... 5/2/68 .... Tony Taylor ........... Phillies | 87 ... 6/7/68 .... Jim Davenport ....... Giants |
| 38 ... 5/2/68 .... Johnny Callison ..... Phillies | 88 ... 6/7/68 .... Jack Hiatt ................ Giants |
| 39 ... 5/2/68 .... Woodie Fryman ..... Phillies | 89 ... 6/12/68 .. Zolio Versalles ..... Dodgers |
| 40 ... 5/2/68 .... Johnny Callison ..... Phillies | 90 ... 6/12/68 .. Don Drysdale ....... Dodgers |
| 41 ... 5/2/68 .... Don Lock .............. Phillies | 91 ... 6/12/68 .. Wes Parker .......... Dodgers |
| 42 ... 5/2/68 .... Tony Taylor ........... Phillies | 92 ... 6/18/68 .. Dick Simpson ........ Astros |
| 43 ... 5/7/68 .... Lou Brock .......... Cardinals | 93 ... 6/18/68 .. Doug Rader ............ Astros |
| 44 ... 5/7/68 .... Bob Tolan .......... Cardinals | 94 ... 6/18/68 .. Bob Watson ............ Astros |
| 45 ... 5/7/68 .... Tim McCarver ..... Cardinals | 95 ... 6/18/68 .. Hector Torres ......... Astros |
| 46 ... 5/7/68 .... Nellie Briles ........ Cardinals | 96 ... 6/18/68 .. Dick Simpson ........ Astros |
| 47 ... 5/7/68 .... Mike Shannon .... Cardinals | 97 ... 6/18/68 .. Bob Watson ............ Astros |
| 48 ... 5/7/68 .... Dick Schofield .... Cardinals | 98 ... 6/18/68 .. Ron Brand .............. Astros |
| 49 ... 5/7/68 .... Dave Ricketts ..... Cardinals | 99 ... 6/18/68 .. Hector Torres ......... Astros |
| 50 ... 5/7/68 .... Johnny Edwards  Cardinals | 100 ... 6/18/68 .. Denny Lemaster ..... Astros |

| | | | |
|---|---|---|---|
| 101 ... 6/18/68 .. Ron Brand .............. Astros | 151 ... 4/29/69 .. Ty Cline .................. Expos |
| 102 ... 6/18/68 .. Dick Simpson .......... Astros | 152 ... 4/29/69 .. John Bateman ......... Expos |
| 103 ... 6/18/68 .. Denny Lemaster ..... Astros | 153 ... 4/29/69 .. Mack Jones ........... Expos |
| 104 ... 6/23/68 .. Paul Popovich      Dodgers | 154 ... 4/29/69 .. Coco Laboy ............. Expos |
| 105 ... 6/23/68 ... Jim Lefebvre ...... Dodgers | 155 ... 4/29/69 .. Gary Sutherland ...... Expos |
| 106 ... 6/23/68 .. Zolio Versalles ..... Dodgers | 156 ... 5/3/69 .... Ernie Banks ............. Cubs |
| 107 ... 6/23/68 .. Wes Parker .......... Dodgers | 157 ... 5/3/69 .... Don Young ................ Cubs |
| 108 ... 6/23/68 .. Zolio Versalles ..... Dodgers | 158 ... 5/3/69 .... Billy Williams ........... Cubs |
| 109 ... 6/23/68 .. Bill Singer ........... Dodgers | 159 ... 5/3/69 .... Willie Smith .............. Cubs |
| 110 ... 6/28/68 .. Bob Watson ............ Astros | 160 ... 6/11/69 .. Bobby Bonds .......... Giants |
| 111 ... 6/28/68 .. Larry Dierker .......... Astros | 161 ... 6/17/69 .. John Briggs ............ Phillies |
| 112 ... 6/28/68 .. Dick Simpson .......... Astros | 162 ... 6/17/69 .. Larry Hisle ............ Phillies |
| 113 ... 6/28/68 .. Rusty Staub ............ Astros | 163 ... 6/17/69 .. Terry Harmon ........ Phillies |
| 114 ... 6/28/68 .. Jim Wynn ............... Astros | 164 ... 6/17/69 .. Grant Jackson ....... Phillies |
| 115 ... 6/28/68 .. Dennis Menke ........ Astros | 165 ... 6/20/69 .. Curt Flood .......... Cardinals |
| 116 ... 7/3/68 .... Willie Stargell ........ Pirates | 166 ... 6/20/69 .. Mike Shannon .... Cardinals |
| 117 ... 7/3/68 ... Matty Alou ............. Pirates | 167 ... 6/20/69 .. Bob Gibson ........ Cardinals |
| 118 ... 7/3/68 .... Donn Clendenon .... Pirates | 168 ... 6/25/69 .. Larry Hisle ............ Phillies |
| 119 ... 7/3/68 .... Steve Blass ............ Pirates | 169 ... 6/25/69 .. John Briggs ............ Phillies |
| 120 ... 7/3/68 .... Donn Clendenon .... Pirates | 170 ... 6/25/69 .. Rick Joseph ........... Phillies |
| 121 ... 7/15/68 .. Cookie Rojas ......... Phillies | 171 ... 6/25/69 .. Gene Stone ........... Phillies |
| 122 ... 7/15/68 .. Roberto Pena ........ Phillies | 172 ... 6/25/69 .. Ron Stone ............. Phillies |
| 123 ... 7/15/68 .. John Briggs ............ Phillies | 173 ... 6/25/69 .. Lowell Palmer ........ Phillies |
| 124 ... 7/15/68 .. Cookie Rojas ......... Phillies | 174 ... 6/25/69 .. Larry Hisle ............ Phillies |
| 125 ... 7/15/68 .. Johnny Callison ..... Phillies | 175 ... 6/25/69 .. John Briggs ............ Phillies |
| 126 ... 7/15/68 .. Cookie Rojas ......... Phillies | 176 ... 6/25/69 .. Lowell Palmer ........ Phillies |
| 127 ... 7/15/68 .. Cookie Rojas ......... Phillies | 177 ... 6/25/69 .. Gene Stone ........... Phillies |
| 128 ... 7/24/68 .. Mike Lum ............... Braves | 178 ... 7/1/69 .... Joe Torre .......... Cardinals |
| 129 ... 7/24/68 .. Marty Martinez ....... Braves | 179 ... 7/1/69 .... Steve Huntz ....... Cardinals |
| 130 ... 7/29/68 .. Lou Brock ........... Cardinals | 180 ... 7/1/69 .... Steve Carlton ..... Cardinals |
| 131 ... 7/29/68 .. Curt Flood .......... Cardinals | 181 ... 7/1/69 .... Steve Carlton ..... Cardinals |
| 132 ... 7/29/68 .. Roger Maris ....... Cardinals | 182 ... 7/13/69 .. Kevin Collins ......... Expos |
| 133 ... 7/29/68 .. Orlando Cepada  Cardinals | 183 ... 7/13/69 .. Bob Bailey .............. Expos |
| 134 ... 7/29/68 .. Ray Washburn ... Cardinals | 184 ... 7/13/69 .. Kevin Collins ......... Expos |
| 135 ... 7/29/68 .. Ray Washburn ... Cardinals | 185 ... 7/27/69 .. Jerry Arrigo .............. Reds |
| 136 ... 7/29/68 .. Mike Shannon ... Cardinals | 186 ... 7/27/69 .. Tony Perez ............... Reds |
| 137 ... 9/3/68 .... Mike Lum ............... Braves | 187 ... 7/27/69 .. Lee May .................. Reds |
| 138 ... 9/3/68 .... Deron Johnson ...... Braves | 188 ... 7/27/69 .. Johnny Bench .......... Reds |
| 139 ... 9/10/68 .. Ron Santo ................ Cubs | 189 ... 7/30/69 .. Joe Morgan ............ Astros |
| 140 ... 4/9/69 .... Manny Mota ............ Expos | 190 ... 7/30/69 .. Norm Miller ............ Astros |
| 141 ... 4/9/69 .... Floyd Wicker ........... Expos | 191 ... 7/30/69 .. Curt Blefary ............ Astros |
| 142 ... 4/14/69 .. Deron Johnson ..... Phillies | 192 ... 7/30/69 .. Doug Rader ............ Astros |
| 143 ... 4/16/69 .. Fred Patek ............ Pirates | 193 ... 7/30/69 .. Jim Wynn ............... Astros |
| 144 ... 4/16/69 .. Bob Moose ............ Pirates | 194 ... 7/30/69 .. Norm Miller ............ Astros |
| 145 ... 4/20/69 .. Mike Shannon .... Cardinals | 195 ... 7/30/69 .. Curt Blefary ............ Astros |
| 146 ... 4/20/69 .. Nellie Briles ....... Cardinals | 196 ... 8/5/69 .... Lee May .................. Reds |
| 147 ... 4/20/69 .. Lou Brock ........... Cardinals | 197 ... 8/5/69 .... Pat Corrales ............. Reds |
| 148 ... 4/20/69 .. Joe Hague ........ Cardinals | 198 ... 8/5/69 .... Pete Rose ................ Reds |
| 149 ... 4/29/69 .. John Bateman ......... Expos | 199 ... 8/5/69 .... Bob Tolan ................ Reds |
| 150 ... 4/29/69 .. Don Bosch .............. Expos | 200 ... 8/5/69 .... Tony Perez ............... Reds |

**259**

| | | | |
|---|---|---|---|
| 201 | 8/5/69 | Jim Stewart | Reds |
| 202 | 8/5/69 | Johnny Bench | Reds |
| 203 | 9/3/69 | Andy Kosco | Dodgers |
| 204 | 9/3/69 | Ted Sizemore | Dodgers |
| 205 | 9/7/69 | Dave Watkins | Phillies |
| 206 | 9/7/69 | Cookie Rojas | Phillies |
| 207 | 9/7/69 | Tony Taylor | Phillies |
| 208 | 9/10/69 | Ty Cline | Expos |
| 209 | 9/10/69 | Angel Hermoso | Expos |
| 210 | 9/10/69 | Howie Reed | Expos |
| 211 | 9/10/69 | Ron Fairly | Expos |
| 212 | 9/10/69 | Ty Cline | Expos |
| 213 | 9/10/69 | Mack Jones | Expos |
| 214 | 9/10/69 | Coco Laboy | Expos |
| 215 | 9/10/69 | John Bateman | Expos |
| 216 | 9/10/69 | Jim Fairey | Expos |
| 217 | 9/10/69 | Rusty Staub | Expos |
| 218 | 9/10/69 | Coco Laboy | Expos |
| 219 | 9/14/69 | Willie Stargell | Pirates |
| 220 | 9/14/69 | Steve Blass | Pirates |
| 221 | 9/14/69 | Roberto Clemente | Pirates |
| 222 | 9/14/69 | Fred Patek | Pirates |
| 223 | 9/14/69 | Steve Blass | Pirates |
| 224 | 9/14/69 | Willie Stargell | Pirates |
| 225 | 9/14/69 | Roberto Clemente | Pirates |
| 226 | 9/19/69 | Willie Stargell | Pirates |
| 227 | 9/19/69 | Bob Veale | Pirates |
| 228 | 9/28/69 | John Briggs | Phillies |
| 229 | 9/28/69 | Ron Stone | Phillies |
| 230 | 9/28/69 | Johnny Callison | Phillies |
| 231 | 10/1/69 | Don Young | Cubs |
| 232 | 4/18/70 | John Briggs | Phillies |
| 233 | 4/18/70 | Deron Johnson | Phillies |
| 234 | 4/18/70 | Larry Hisle | Phillies |
| 235 | 4/18/70 | Ron Stone | Phillies |
| 236 | 4/18/70 | John Briggs | Phillies |
| 237 | 4/18/70 | Deron Johnson | Phillies |
| 238 | 4/18/70 | Tim McCarver | Phillies |
| 239 | 4/18/70 | Larry Bowa | Phillies |
| 240 | 4/18/70 | Jim Bunning | Phillies |
| 241 | 4/18/70 | John Briggs | Phillies |
| 242 | 4/18/70 | Tim McCarver | Phillies |
| 243 | 4/18/70 | Larry Hisle | Phillies |
| 244 | 4/18/70 | Ron Stone | Phillies |
| 245 | 4/18/70 | Larry Bowa | Phillies |
| 246 | 4/18/70 | Deron Johnson | Phillies |
| 247 | 4/24/70 | Maury Wills | Dodgers |
| 248 | 4/24/70 | Bill Buckner | Dodgers |
| 249 | 4/24/70 | Claude Osteen | Dodgers |
| 250 | 4/24/70 | Willie Crawford | Dodgers |
| 251 | 4/24/70 | Bill Grabarkewitz | Dodgers |
| 252 | 4/30/70 | Bobby Bonds | Giants |
| 253 | 4/30/70 | Dick Dietz | Giants |
| 254 | 4/30/70 | Bob Taylor | Giants |
| 255 | 4/30/70 | Bobby Bonds | Giants |
| 256 | 4/30/70 | Dick Dietz | Giants |
| 257 | 4/30/70 | Bob Taylor | Giants |
| 258 | 4/30/70 | Steve Whitaker | Giants |
| 259 | 4/30/70 | Dick Dietz | Giants |
| 260 | 5/5/70 | Von Joshua | Dodgers |
| 261 | 5/5/70 | Willie Crawford | Dodgers |
| 262 | 5/5/70 | Bill Grabarkewitz | Dodgers |
| 263 | 5/5/70 | Sandy Vance | Dodgers |
| 264 | 5/5/70 | Bill Grabarkewitz | Dodgers |
| 265 | 5/10/70 | Bob Burda | Giants |
| 266 | 5/10/70 | Juan Marichal | Giants |
| 267 | 5/24/70 | Billy Williams | Cubs |
| 268 | 5/24/70 | Ron Santo | Cubs |
| 269 | 5/24/70 | Jim Hickman | Cubs |
| 270 | 5/24/70 | Jack Hiatt | Cubs |
| 271 | 5/24/70 | Joe Decker | Cubs |
| 272 | 5/24/70 | Cleo James | Cubs |
| 273 | 5/24/70 | Jimmie Hall | Cubs |
| 274 | 5/24/70 | Willie Smith | Cubs |
| 275 | 5/30/70 | Jim Wynn | Astros |
| 276 | 5/30/70 | Norm Miller | Astros |
| 277 | 5/30/70 | Dennis enke | Astros |
| 278 | 5/30/70 | Joe Pepitone | Astros |
| 279 | 5/30/70 | Doug Rader | Astros |
| 280 | 5/30/70 | Jim Wynn | Astros |
| 281 | 5/30/70 | Dennis Menke | Astros |
| 282 | 5/30/70 | Joe Pepitone | Astros |
| 283 | 5/30/70 | Doug Rader | Astros |
| 284 | 5/30/70 | Johnny Edwards | Astros |
| 285 | 5/30/70 | Larry Dierker | Astros |
| 286 | 6/5/70 | Bernie Carbo | Reds |
| 287 | 6/5/70 | Bob Tolan | Reds |
| 288 | 6/5/70 | Lee May | Reds |
| 289 | 6/5/70 | Bernie Carbo | Reds |
| 290 | 6/5/70 | Dave Concepcion | Reds |
| 291 | 6/5/70 | Jim McGlothlin | Reds |
| 292 | 6/17/70 | Bernie Carbo | Reds |
| 293 | 6/24/70 | Willie Smith | Cubs |
| 294 | 6/24/70 | Willie Smith | Cubs |
| 295 | 7/14/70 | Ron Hunt | Giants |
| 296 | 7/14/70 | Ken Henderson | Giants |
| 297 | 7/14/70 | Jim Ray Hart | Giants |
| 298 | 7/14/70 | Frank Johnson | Giants |
| 299 | 7/14/70 | Rich Robertson | Giants |
| 300 | 7/14/70 | Bobby Bonds | Giants |

| 301 ... 7/14/70 | .. Rich Robertson | ....... Giants |
|---|---|---|
| 302 ... 7/22/70 | .. Clarence Gaston | .... Padres |
| 303 ... 8/4/70 | .... Ron Santo | ................. Cubs |
| 304 ... 8/4/70 | .... Joe Pepitone | ............ Cubs |
| 305 ... 8/4/70 | .... Johnny Callison | ........ Cubs |
| 306 ... 8/4/70 | .... Randy Hundley | ......... Cubs |
| 307 ... 8/4/70 | .... Joe Decker | ................ Cubs |
| 308 ... 8/4/70 | .... Jim Hickman | ............ Cubs |
| 309 ... 8/4/70 | .... Randy Hundley | ...... Cubs |
| 310 ... 8/4/70 | .... Joe Decker | ............... Cubs |
| 311 ... 8/4/70 | .... Ron Santo | ................. Cubs |
| 312 ... 8/4/70 | .... Jim Hickman | ............ Cubs |
| 313 ... 8/4/70 | .... Joe Pepitone | ............. Cubs |
| 314 ... 8/4/70 | .... Willie Smith | .............. Cubs |
| 315 ... 8/4/70 | .... Joe Pepitone | ............. Cubs |
| 316 ... 8/9/70 | .... Fred Patek | ............ Pirates |
| 317 ... 8/9/70 | .... Roberto Clemente | .. Pirates |
| 318 ... 8/9/70 | .... Manny Sanguillen | .. Pirates |
| 319 ... 8/9/70 | .... Fred Patek | ............ Pirates |
| 320 ... 8/9/70 | .... Roberto Clemente | .. Pirates |
| 321 ... 8/9/70 | .... Luke Walker | ........... Pirates |
| 322 ... 8/9/70 | .... Fred Patek | ............ Pirates |
| 323 ... 8/9/70 | .... Bob Robertson | ....... Pirates |
| 324 ... 8/9/70 | .... Manny Sanguillen | .. Pirates |
| 325 ... 8/9/70 | .... Luke Walker | ........... Pirates |
| 326 ... 8/14/70 | .. Felix Millan | ............. Braves |
| 327 ... 8/14/70 | .. Clete Boyer | ........... Braves |
| 328 ... 8/14/70 | .. Ron Reed | ................ Braves |
| 329 ... 8/25/70 | .. Mike Lum | ............... Braves |
| 330 ... 8/25/70 | .. Clete Boyer | ........... Braves |
| 331 ... 8/25/70 | .. Pat Jarvis | ............... Braves |
| 332 ... 8/30/70 | .. John Mayberry | ....... Astros |
| 333 ... 8/30/70 | .. Jesus Alou | .............. Astros |
| 334 ... 8/30/70 | .. Doug Rader | ............ Astros |
| 335 ... 9/4/70 | .... Jim Hickman | ............. Cubs |
| 336 ... 9/4/70 | .... Bill Hands | ................. Cubs |
| 337 ... 9/4/70 | .... Bill Hands | ................. Cubs |
| 338 ... 9/9/70 | .... Larry Bowa | ........... Phillies |
| 339 ... 9/9/70 | .... John Briggs | ........... Phillies |
| 340 ... 9/9/70 | .... Scott Reid | ............. Phillies |
| 341 ... 9/9/70 | .... Barry Lersch | .......... Phillies |
| 342 ... 9/9/70 | .... Denny Doyle | .......... Phillies |
| 343 ... 9/9/70 | .... John Briggs | ........... Phillies |
| 344 ... 9/9/70 | .... Don Money | ........... Phillies |
| 345 ... 9/9/70 | .... Scott Reid | ............. Phillies |
| 346 ... 9/9/70 | .... Tim McCarver | ........ Phillies |
| 347 ... 9/9/70 | .... Barry Lersch | .......... Phillies |
| 348 ... 9/9/70 | .... Larry Bowa | ........... Phillies |
| 349 ... 9/9/70 | .... Scott Reid | ............. Phillies |
| 350 ... 9/9/70 | .... Denny Doyle | .......... Phillies |
| 351 ... 9/14/70 | .. John Bateman | ......... Expos |
| 352 ... 9/27/70 | .. Dock Ellis | ............... Pirates |
| 353 ... 9/27/70 | .. Al Oliver | ................. Pirates |
| 354 ... 9/30/70 | .. Paul Popovich | ........... Cubs |
| 355 ... 9/30/70 | .. Don Kessinger | .......... Cubs |
| 356 ... 9/30/70 | .. Willie Smith | ............... Cubs |
| 357 ... 4/23/71 | .. Billy Williams | ............. Cubs |
| 358 ... 4/23/71 | .. Joe Pepitone | ............ Cubs |
| 359 ... 4/23/71 | .. Paul Popovich | .......... Cubs |
| 360 ... 4/29/71 | .. Lou Brock | ........... Cardinals |
| 361 ... 4/29/71 | .. Leron Lee | ........... Cardinals |
| 362 ... 4/29/71 | .. Jerry Reuss | ........... Cardinals |
| 363 ... 4/29/71 | .. Leron Lee | ........... Cardinals |
| 364 ... 4/29/71 | .. Jerry Reuss | ........... Cardinals |
| 365 ... 5/4/71 | .... Glen Beckert | ............. Cubs |
| 366 ... 5/4/71 | .... Ron Santo | ................. Cubs |
| 367 ... 5/4/71 | .... Johnny Callison | ........ Cubs |
| 368 ... 5/4/71 | .... Ernie Banks | ............. Cubs |
| 369 ... 5/4/71 | .... Joe Pepitone | ............. Cubs |
| 370 ... 5/4/71 | .... Billy Williams | ............. Cubs |
| 371 ... 5/4/71 | .... Ernie Banks | ............. Cubs |
| 372 ... 5/11/71 | .. Joe Morgan | ............. Astros |
| 373 ... 5/11/71 | .. Cesar Cedeno | ......... Astros |
| 374 ... 5/11/71 | .. Rich Chiles | ............. Astros |
| 375 ... 5/11/71 | .. Dennis Menke | ......... Astros |
| 376 ... 5/11/71 | .. Larry Dierker | ........... Astros |
| 377 ... 5/11/71 | .. Rich Chiles | ............. Astros |
| 378 ... 5/11/71 | .. Rich Chiles | ............. Astros |
| 379 ... 5/11/71 | .. Cesar Cedeno | ......... Astros |
| 380 ... 5/16/71 | .. Vic Davalillo | ........... Pirates |
| 381 ... 5/16/71 | .. Roberto Clemente | .. Pirates |
| 382 ... 5/16/71 | .. Gene Alley | ............. Pirates |
| 383 ... 5/16/71 | .. Roberto Clemente | .. Pirates |
| 384 ... 5/21/71 | .. Sonny Jackson | ........ Braves |
| 385 ... 5/21/71 | .. Marty Perez | ........... Braves |
| 386 ... 5/21/71 | .. Ralph Garr | ............. Braves |
| 387 ... 5/21/71 | .. Hank Aaron | ............. Braves |
| 388 ... 5/21/71 | .. Marty Perez | ........... Braves |
| 389 ... 5/21/71 | .. Pat Jarvis | ............... Braves |
| 390 ... 5/21/71 | .. Clete Boyer | ........... Braves |
| 391 ... 5/29/71 | .. Don Mason | ............ Padres |
| 392 ... 5/29/71 | .. Ollie Brown | ............ Padres |
| 393 ... 5/29/71 | .. Ed Spiezio | ............. Padres |
| 394 ... 5/29/71 | .. Fred Kendall | ............ Padres |
| 395 ... 5/29/71 | .. Tom Phoebus | ........ Padres |
| 396 ... 5/29/71 | .. Clarence Gaston | .... Padres |
| 397 ... 5/29/71 | .. Ivan Murrell | ............ Padres |
| 398 ... 5/29/71 | .. Tom Phoebus | ........ Padres |
| 399 ... 5/29/71 | .. Clarence Gaston | .... Padres |
| 400 ... 5/29/71 | .. Nate Colbert | ......... Padres |

| | | | |
|---|---|---|---|
| 401 ... 5/29/71 .. Ollie Brown ............. Padres | 451 ... 7/5/71 .... Bob Bailey ............... Expos |
| 402 ... 5/29/71 .. Ivan Murrell ............. Padres | 452 ... 7/5/71 .... Ron Fairly ............... Expos |
| 403 ... 5/29/71 .. Fred Kendall ............ Padres | 453 ... 7/5/71 .... Dave McDonald ..... Expos |
| 404 ... 5/29/71 .. Angel Bravo ............ Padres | 454 ... 7/5/71 .... John Strohmayer ..... Expos |
| 405 ... 5/29/71 .. Clarence Gaston .... Padres | 455 ... 7/11/71 .. Pete Rose ................. Reds |
| 406 ... 5/29/71 .. Ivan Murrell ............. Padres | 456 ... 7/11/71 .. Bernie Carbo ........... Reds |
| 407 ... 6/5/71 .... Maury Wills ......... Dodgers | 457 ... 7/16/71 .. Johnny Edwards ..... Astros |
| 408 ... 6/5/71 .... Duke Sims ........... Dodgers | 458 ... 7/16/71 .. Jack Billingham ....... Astros |
| 409 ... 6/5/71 .... Willie Davis ......... Dodgers | 459 ... 7/23/71 .. Roger Metzger ........ Astros |
| 410 ... 6/5/71 .... Von Joshua ......... Dodgers | 460 ... 7/29/71 .. Ted Simmons .... Cardinals |
| 411 ... 6/10/71 .. Enzo Hernandez .... Padres | 461 ... 7/29/71 .. Lou Brock ........... Cardinals |
| 412 ... 6/10/71 .. Clarence Gaston ... Padres | 462 ... 7/29/71 .. Jerry Reuss ....... Cardinals |
| 413 ... 6/10/71 .. Ed Spiezio ........... Padres | 463 ... 8/3/71 .... Tony Perez .............. Reds |
| 414 ... 6/10/71 .. Dave Campbell ...... Padres | 464 ... 8/3/71 .... Pat Corrales ........... Reds |
| 415 ... 6/15/71 .. Dick Allen ............ Dodgers | 465 ... 8/3/71 .... Wayne Simpson ....... Reds |
| 416 ... 6/15/71 .. Jim Lefebvre ....... Dodgers | 466 ... 8/7/71 .... Zolio Versalles ....... Braves |
| 417 ... 6/15/71 .. Tom Haller .......... Dodgers | 467 ... 8/7/71 .... Ron Reed ............. Braves |
| 418 ... 6/15/71 .. Al Downing .......... Dodgers | 468 ... 8/7/71 .... Mike Lum ............. Braves |
| 419 ... 6/15/71 .. Willie Crawford .... Dodgers | 469 ... 8/7/71 .... Ron Reed ............. Braves |
| 420 ... 6/15/71 .. Al Downing .......... Dodgers | 470 ... 8/7/71 .... Ron Reed ............. Braves |
| 421 ... 6/15/71 .. Willie Davis ......... Dodgers | 471 ... 8/7/71 .... Oscar Brown .......... Braves |
| 422 ... 6/15/71 .. Tom Haller .......... Dodgers | 472 ... 8/7/71 .... Ralph Garr ............. Braves |
| 423 ... 6/15/71 .. Maury Wills ......... Dodgers | 473 ... 8/12/71 .. Larry Stahl ............ Padres |
| 424 ... 6/20/71 .. Willie Montanez ..... Phillies | 474 ... 8/31/71 .. Ted Sizemore .... Cardinals |
| 425 ... 6/20/71 .. Oscar Gamble ....... Phillies | 475 ... 8/31/71 .. Ted Simmons .... Cardinals |
| 426 ... 6/20/71 .. Ron Stone ............. Phillies | 476 ... 8/31/71 .. Joe Hague ......... Cardinals |
| 427 ... 6/20/71 .. Deron Johnson ...... Phillies | 477 ... 8/31/71 .. Jose Cruz .......... Cardinals |
| 428 ... 6/20/71 .. Barry Lersch .......... Phillies | 478 ... 8/31/71 .. Jerry Reuss ....... Cardinals |
| 429 ... 6/20/71 .. Barry Lersch .......... Phillies | 479 ... 8/31/71 .. Lou Brock ........... Cardinals |
| 430 ... 6/20/71 .. Ron Stone ............. Phillies | 480 ... 8/31/71 .. Joe Torre ........... Cardinals |
| 431 ... 6/25/71 .. Ron Fairly ............... Expos | 481 ... 8/31/71 .. Jose Cruz .......... Cardinals |
| 432 ... 6/25/71 .. John Bateman ......... Expos | 482 ... 8/31/71 .. Dal Maxvill ......... Cardinals |
| 433 ... 6/25/71 .. Rusty Staub ............ Expos | 483 ... 8/31/71 .. Jerry Reuss ....... Cardinals |
| 434 ... 6/25/71 .. Ron Fairly ............... Expos | 484 ... 8/31/71 .. Lou Brock ........... Cardinals |
| 435 ... 6/25/71 .. John Bateman ......... Expos | 485 ... 8/31/71 .. Matty Alou ......... Cardinals |
| 436 ... 6/25/71 .. Jim Fairey ............... Expos | 486 ... 9/5/71 .... Deron Johnson ...... Phillies |
| 437 ... 6/25/71 .. Stan Swanson ......... Expos | 487 ... 9/5/71 .... Oscar Gamble ....... Phillies |
| 438 ... 6/25/71 .. John Bateman ......... Expos | 488 ... 9/14/71 .. John Strohmayer ..... Expos |
| 439 ... 6/25/71 .. Jim Gosger .............. Expos | 489 ... 9/23/71 .. Pat Bourque ............. Cubs |
| 440 ... 6/25/71 .. Stan Swanson ......... Expos | 490 ... 9/23/71 .. Gene Hiser ............... Cubs |
| 441 ... 6/30/71 .. Willie Stargell ....... Pirates | 491 ... 9/23/71 .. Frank Fernandez ...... Cubs |
| 442 ... 6/30/71 .. Al Oliver ................. Pirates | 492 ... 9/23/71 .. Gene Hiser ............... Cubs |
| 443 ... 6/30/71 .. Vic Davalillo ........... Pirates | 493 ... 9/23/71 .. Paul Popovich .......... Cubs |
| 444 ... 6/30/71 .. Willie Stargell ....... Pirates | 494 ... 4/18/72 .. Danny Thompson .... Twins |
| 445 ... 6/30/71 .. Al Oliver ................. Pirates | 495 ... 4/18/72 .. Rod Carew ............... Twins |
| 446 ... 6/30/71 .. Bob Robertson ....... Pirates | 496 ... 4/18/72 .. Charlie Manuel ........ Twins |
| 447 ... 6/30/71 .. Richie Hebner ........ Pirates | 497 ... 4/18/72 .. Jim Perry ................. Twins |
| 448 ... 6/30/71 .. Willie Stargell ....... Pirates | 498 ... 4/18/72 .. Danny Thompson .... Twins |
| 449 ... 6/30/71 .. Charlie Sands ........ Pirates | 499 ... 4/18/72 .. Rod Carew ............... Twins |
| 450 ... 7/5/71 .... Rich Hacker ............ Expos | 500 ... 4/18/72 .. Charlie Manuel ........ Twins |

| | | | |
|---|---|---|---|
| 501 ... 4/18/72 ... Rick Dempsey ......... Twins | | 551 ... 6/3/72 .... Lou Camilli ............. Indians |
| 502 ... 4/18/72 .. Steve Braun ............. Twins | | 552 ... 6/3/72 .... Alex Johnson ......... Indians |
| 503 ... 4/18/72 ... Rod Carew ............... Twins | | 553 ... 6/7/72 .... Mickey Stanley ........ Tigers |
| 504 ... 4/23/72 .. Hal King ............... Rangers | | 554 ... 6/7/72 .... Ed Brinkman ........... Tigers |
| 505 ... 4/23/72 ... Dave Nelson ........ Rangers | | 555 ... 6/7/72 .... Joe Niekro ............... Tigers |
| 506 ... 4/28/72 ... Don Buford ............. Orioles | | 556 ... 6/7/72 .... Gates Brown ........... Tigers |
| 507 ... 4/28/72 ... Boog Powell ........... Orioles | | 557 ... 6/7/72 .... Willie Horton ........... Tigers |
| 508 ... 4/28/72 ... Jim Palmer ............. Orioles | | 558 ... 6/11/72 .. Danny Cater ........ Red Sox |
| 509 ... 5/5/72 .... Davey May ........... Brewers | | 559 ... 6/14/72 .. Jack Brohammer ... Indians |
| 510 ... 5/5/72 .... Billy Conigliaro .... Brewers | | 560 ... 6/14/72 .. Eddie Leon ............ Indians |
| 511 ... 5/5/72 .... Darrell Porter ....... Brewers | | 561 ... 6/14/72 .. Jack Brohammer ... Indians |
| 512 ... 5/5/72 .... Ken Brett ............. Brewers | | 562 ... 6/14/72 .. Alex Johnson ......... Indians |
| 513 ... 5/5/72 .... Davey May ........... Brewers | | 563 ... 6/14/72 .. Chris Chambliss .... Indians |
| 514 ... 5/5/72 .... George Scott ........ Brewers | | 564 ... 6/14/72 .. Ray Fosse ............. Indians |
| 515 ... 5/5/72 .... Darrell Porter ....... Brewers | | 565 ... 6/14/72 .. Graig Nettles ......... Indians |
| 516 ... 5/5/72 .... Brock Davis .......... Brewers | | 566 ... 6/18/72 .. Dick McAuliffe ........ Tigers |
| 517 ... 5/5/72 .... Billy Conigliaro .... Brewers | | 567 ... 6/18/72 .. Bill Freehan ............ Tigers |
| 518 ... 5/5/72 .... Darrell Porter ....... Brewers | | 568 ... 6/18/72 .. Mickey Lolich .......... Tigers |
| 519 ... 5/5/72 .... Rick Auerbach ..... Brewers | | 569 ... 6/18/72 .. Aurelio Rodriguez ... Tigers |
| 520 ... 5/5/72 .... Bill Voss ............... Brewers | | 570 ... 6/18/72 .. Jim Northrup ........... Tigers |
| 521 ... 5/5/72 .... Davey May ........... Brewers | | 571 ... 6/18/72 .. Dick McAuliffe ........ Tigers |
| 522 ... 5/5/72 .... George Scott ........ Brewers | | 572 ... 6/18/72 .. Bill Freehan ............ Tigers |
| 523 ... 5/10/72 .. Reggie Smith ....... Red Sox | | 573 ... 6/18/72 .. Mickey Stanley ........ Tigers |
| 524 ... 5/10/72 .. Rick Miller ............ Red Sox | | 574 ... 6/18/72 .. Ed Brinkman ........... Tigers |
| 525 ... 5/10/72 .. Carlton Fisk ......... Red Sox | | 575 ... 6/23/72 .. Bert Campaneris .......... A's |
| 526 ... 5/10/72 .. Marty Pattin ......... Red Sox | | 576 ... 6/23/72 .. Mike Epstein .............. A's |
| 527 ... 5/10/72 .. Rick Miller ............ Red Sox | | 577 ... 6/23/72 .. Dave Duncan .............. A's |
| 528 ... 5/15/72 .. Angel Mangual ............ A's | | 578 ... 6/23/72 .. Angel Mangual ............ A's |
| 529 ... 5/15/72 .. Bert Campaneris .......... A's | | 579 ... 6/23/72 .. Tim Cullen .................... A's |
| 530 ... 5/15/72 .. Reggie Jackson ........... A's | | 580 ... 6/23/72 .. Dave Hamilton .............. A's |
| 531 ... 5/22/72 .. Reggie Jackson ........... A's | | 581 ... 6/23/72 .. Bert Campaneris .......... A's |
| 532 ... 5/22/72 .. Dave Duncan .............. A's | | 582 ... 6/23/72 .. Reggie Jackson ........... A's |
| 533 ... 5/22/72 .. Reggie Jackson ........... A's | | 583 ... 6/23/72 .. Angel Mangual ............ A's |
| 534 ... 5/22/72 .. Larry Brown .................. A's | | 584 ... 6/23/72 .. Mike Epstein .............. A's |
| 535 ... 5/22/72 .. Sal Bando .................... A's | | 585 ... 6/27/72 .. Cesar Tovar ............. Twins |
| 536 ... 5/22/72 .. Bert Campaneris .......... A's | | 586 ... 6/27/72 .. Rod Carew ............... Twins |
| 537 ... 5/26/72 .. Paul Schaal ............ Royals | | 587 ... 6/27/72 .. Jim Perry ................. Twins |
| 538 ... 5/26/72 .. Steve Hovley .......... Royals | | 588 ... 6/27/72 .. Charlie Manuel ........ Twins |
| 539 ... 5/30/72 .. Bill Melton ........ White Sox | | 589 ... 6/27/72 .. Cesar Tovar ............. Twins |
| 540 ... 5/30/72 .. Jay Johnstone .. White Sox | | 590 ... 6/27/72 .. Rod Carew ............... Twins |
| 541 ... 5/30/72 .. Stan Bahnsen .... White Sox | | 591 ... 6/27/72 .. Jim Nettles ................ Twins |
| 542 ... 5/30/72 .. Rich Morales ..... White Sox | | 592 ... 7/1/72 .... Joe Rudi ...................... A's |
| 543 ... 5/30/72 .. Walt Williams .... White Sox | | 593 ... 7/1/72 .... Reggie Jackson ........... A's |
| 544 ... 5/30/72 .. Pat Kelly .......... White Sox | | 594 ... 7/1/72 .... Dave Duncan .............. A's |
| 545 ... 5/30/72 .. Ed Herrmann .... White Sox | | 595 ... 7/1/72 .... Tim Cullen .................... A's |
| 546 ... 5/30/72 .. Rich Morales ..... White Sox | | 596 ... 7/1/72 .... Dave Hamilton .............. A's |
| 547 ... 5/30/72 .. Jorge Orta ........ White Sox | | 597 ... 7/1/72 .... Bert Campaneris .......... A's |
| 548 ... 5/30/72 .. Carlos May ........ White Sox | | 598 ... 7/1/72 .... Reggie Jackson ........... A's |
| 549 ... 6/3/72 .... Tom McCraw .......... Indians | | 599 ... 7/1/72 .... Sal Bando .................... A's |
| 550 ... 6/3/72 .... Eddie Leon ............ Indians | | 600 ... 7/1/72 .... Dave Duncan .............. A's |

| | | | |
|---|---|---|---|
| 601 ... 7/1/72 .... Tim Cullen .................... A's | 651 ... 7/27/72 ... Rich Billings ......... Rangers |
| 602 ... 7/1/72 .... Sal Bando .................... A's | 652 ... 7/27/72 ... Ted Ford .............. Rangers |
| 603 ... 7/1/72 .... Dave Duncan ............... A's | 653 ... 7/27/72 ... Jim Mason .......... Rangers |
| 604 ... 7/1/72 .... Bill Voss ....................... A's | 654 ... 7/27/72 ... Vic Harris ............ Rangers |
| 605 ... 7/1/72 .... Sal Bando .................... A's | 655 ... 7/27/72 ... Mike Paul ............. Rangers |
| 606 ... 7/1/72 .... Dave Duncan ............... A's | 656 ... 7/27/72 ... Ted Ford .............. Rangers |
| 607 ... 7/1/72 .... Adrian Garrett .............. A's | 657 ... 7/27/72 ... Jim Mason .......... Rangers |
| 608 ... 7/5/72 .... Earl Stephenson .. Brewers | 658 ... 7/27/72 ... Vic Harris ............ Rangers |
| 609 ... 7/5/72 .... John Briggs .......... Brewers | 659 ... 7/27/72 ... Dalton Jones ....... Rangers |
| 610 ... 7/5/72 .... Rick Auerbach ..... Brewers | 660 ... 7/27/72 ... Dave Nelson ........ Rangers |
| 611 ... 7/5/72 .... Earl Stephenson .. Brewers | 661 ... 7/27/72 ... Rich Billings ......... Rangers |
| 612 ... 7/5/72 .... John Briggs .......... Brewers | 662 ... 7/27/72 ... Jim Mason .......... Rangers |
| 613 ... 7/5/72 .... Earl Stephenson .. Brewers | 663 ... 7/27/72 ... Ted Ford .............. Rangers |
| 614 ... 7/5/72 .... Ellie Rodriguez ..... Brewers | 664 ... 7/31/72 ... Steve Hovley .......... Royals |
| 615 ... 7/5/72 .... Bob Heise ............ Brewers | 665 ... 7/31/72 ... Fred Patek ............. Royals |
| 616 ... 7/9/72 .... Doug Griffin ........ Red Sox | 666 ... 7/31/72 ... Roger Nelson ......... Royals |
| 617 ... 7/9/72 .... Reggie Smith ....... Red Sox | 667 ... 7/31/72 ... Cookie Rojas .......... Royals |
| 618 ... 7/9/72 .... Rico Petrocelli .... Red Sox | 668 ... 7/31/72 ... Ed Kirkpatrick ......... Royals |
| 619 ... 7/9/72 .... Carlton Fisk ......... Red Sox | 669 ... 7/31/72 ... Paul Schaal ........... Royals |
| 620 ... 7/9/72 .... Bob Burda ........... Red Sox | 670 ... 7/31/72 ... Roger Nelson ......... Royals |
| 621 ... 7/9/72 .... Juan Beniquez .... Red Sox | 671 ... 7/31/72 ... Steve Hovley .......... Royals |
| 622 ... 7/9/72 .... Sonny Siebert ...... Red Sox | 672 ... 7/31/72 ... Lou Piniella ............ Royals |
| 623 ... 7/9/72 .... Tommy Harper .... Red Sox | 673 ... 7/31/72 ... Paul Schaal ........... Royals |
| 624 ... 7/9/72 .... Doug Griffin ........ Red Sox | 674 ... 7/31/72 ... Roger Nelson ......... Royals |
| 625 ... 7/9/72 .... Carlton Fisk ......... Red Sox | 675 ... 8/4/72 .... Ed Kirkpatrick ......... Royals |
| 626 ... 7/9/72 .... Juan Beniquez .... Red Sox | 676 ... 8/4/72 .... John Mayberry ....... Royals |
| 627 ... 7/9/72 .... Sonny Siebert ...... Red Sox | 677 ... 8/4/72 .... Bruce DalCanton .... Royals |
| 628 ... 7/9/72 .... Carlton Fisk ......... Red Sox | 678 ... 8/4/72 .... Paul Schaal ........... Royals |
| 629 ... 7/9/72 .... Bob Burda ........... Red Sox | 679 ... 8/4/72 .... Fred Patek ............. Royals |
| 630 ... 7/9/72 .... Ben Oglivie .......... Red Sox | 680 ... 8/4/72 .... Bruce DalCanton .... Royals |
| 631 ... 7/9/72 .... Tommy Harper .... Red Sox | 681 ... 8/4/72 .... John Mayberry ....... Royals |
| 632 ... 7/14/72 .. Rick Auerbach ..... Brewers | 682 ... 8/4/72 .... Bruce DalCanton .... Royals |
| 633 ... 7/14/72 .. Ron Clark ............ Brewers | 683 ... 8/9/72 .... Pat Kelly .......... White Sox |
| 634 ... 7/14/72 .. John Felske ......... Brewers | 684 ... 8/9/72 .... Jay Johnstone .. White Sox |
| 635 ... 7/14/72 .. Jim Lonborg ......... Brewers | 685 ... 8/9/72 .... Carlos May ....... White Sox |
| 636 ... 7/14/72 .. John Felske ......... Brewers | 686 ... 8/9/72 .... Ed Spiezio ........ White Sox |
| 637 ... 7/14/72 .. George Scott ........ Brewers | 687 ... 8/9/72 .... Wilbur Wood ... White Sox |
| 638 ... 7/14/72 .. Dave May .............. Brewers | 688 ... 8/9/72 .... Ed Spiezio ........ White Sox |
| 639 ... 7/14/72 .. Dave May .............. Brewers | 689 ... 8/9/72 .... Mike Andrews ... White Sox |
| 640 ... 7/18/72 .. Rico Petrocelli ..... Red Sox | 690 ... 8/9/72 .... Luis Alvarado ...... White Sox |
| 641 ... 7/18/72 .. Carlton Fisk ......... Red Sox | 691 ... 8/9/72 .... Wilbur Wood ..... White Sox |
| 642 ... 7/18/72 .. Doug Griffin ........ Red Sox | 692 ... 8/13/72 .. Jim Nettles ............... Twins |
| 643 ... 7/18/72 .. Rico Petrocelli ..... Red Sox | 693 ... 8/13/72 .. Danny Thompson .... Twins |
| 644 ... 7/18/72 .. John Kennedy ..... Red Sox | 694 ... 8/13/72 .. Jim Nettles ............... Twins |
| 645 ... 7/18/72 .. Sonny Siebert ...... Red Sox | 695 ... 8/13/72 .. Harmon Killebrew .... Twins |
| 646 ... 7/18/72 .. Tommy Harper .... Red Sox | 696 ... 8/13/72 .. Danny Thompson .... Twins |
| 647 ... 7/22/72 .. Johnny Callison ... Yankees | 697 ... 8/13/72 .. Bobby Darwin .......... Twins |
| 648 ... 7/22/72 .. Roy White ............ Yankees | 698 ... 8/13/72 .. Glenn Borgmann ...... Twins |
| 649 ... 7/22/72 .. Bernie Allen .......... Yankees | 699 ... 8/13/72 .. Dick Woodson ......... Twins |
| 650 ... 7/27/72 .. Dave Nelson ........ Rangers | 700 ... 8/13/72 .. Jim Nettles ............... Twins |

| | | | |
|---|---|---|---|
| 701 ... 8/18/72 .. Gates Brown ........... Tigers | 751 ... 9/8/72 .... Carlos May ....... White Sox |
| 702 ... 8/18/72 .. Bill Freehan ............. Tigers | 752 ... 9/8/72 .... Pat Kelly ........... White Sox |
| 703 ... 8/18/72 .. Bill Freehan ............. Tigers | 753 ... 9/8/72 .... Rick Reichardt .. White Sox |
| 704 ... 8/18/72 .. Aurelio Rodriguez ... Tigers | 754 ... 9/12/72 .. Ted Ford .............. Rangers |
| 705 ... 8/18/72 .. Ed Brinkman ........... Tigers | 755 ... 9/12/72 .. Rich Billings ......... Rangers |
| 706 ... 8/22/72 .. Johnny Oates ........ Orioles | 756 ... 9/12/72 .. Bill Gogolewski ... Rangers |
| 707 ... 8/22/72 .. Tommy Davis ......... Orioles | 757 ... 9/12/72 .. Toby Harrah ......... Rangers |
| 708 ... 8/22/72 .. Don Baylor ............. Orioles | 758 ... 9/12/72 .. Larry Biittner ....... Rangers |
| 709 ... 8/22/72 .. Davey Johnson ...... Orioles | 759 ... 9/12/72 .. Rich Billings ......... Rangers |
| 710 .. 8/22/72 .. Johnny Oates ........ Orioles | 760 ... 9/12/72 .. Joe Lovitto ........... Rangers |
| 711 ... 8/22/72 .. Dave McNally ........ Orioles | 761 ... 9/12/72 .. Bill Fahey ............. Rangers |
| 712 ... 8/22/72 .. Tommy Davis ......... Orioles | 762 ... 9/12/72 .. Bill Gogolewski ... Rangers |
| 713 ... 8/22/72 .. Don Baylor ............. Orioles | 763 ... 9/12/72 .. Ted Ford .............. Rangers |
| 714 ... 8/22/72 .. Davey Johnson ...... Orioles | 764 ... 9/12/72 .. Joe Lovitto ........... Rangers |
| 715 ... 8/22/72 .. Boog Powell ........... Orioles | 765 ... 9/12/72 .. Bill Gogolewski ... Rangers |
| 716 ... 8/22/72 .. Davey Johnson ...... Orioles | 766 ... 9/12/72 .. Toby Harrah ......... Rangers |
| 717 ... 8/27/72 .. Chris Chambliss .... Indians | 767 ... 9/12/72 .. Dalton Jones ....... Rangers |
| 718 ... 8/27/72 .. Del Unser .............. Indians | 768 ... 9/12/72 .. Vic Harris ............ Rangers |
| 719 ... 8/27/72 .. Buddy Bell ............. Indians | 769 ... 9/16/72 .. Pat Kelly ........... White Sox |
| 720 ... 8/27/72 .. Jack Brohammer ... Indians | 770 ... 9/16/72 .. Dick Allen .......... White Sox |
| 721 ... 8/27/72 .. Chris Chambliss .... Indians | 771 ... 9/16/72 .. Rick Reichardt .. White Sox |
| 722 ... 8/27/72 .. Frank Duffy ............ Indians | 772 ... 9/16/72 .. Rich Morales ...... White Sox |
| 723 ... 8/27/72 .. Milt Wilcox ............. Indians | 773 ... 9/16/72 .. Rick Reichardt .. White Sox |
| 724 ... 8/27/72 .. Graig Nettles ......... Indians | 774 ... 9/16/72 .. Stan Bahnsen ... White Sox |
| 725 ... 8/27/72 .. Phil Hennigan ........ Indians | 775 ... 9/16/72 .. Ed Herrmann .... White Sox |
| 726 ... 8/27/72 .. Phil Hennigan ........ Indians | 776 ... 9/16/72 .. Stan Bahnsen .... White Sox |
| 727 ... 8/31/72 .. Aurelio Rodriguez ... Tigers | 777 ... 9/16/72 .. Carlos May ....... White Sox |
| 728 ... 8/31/72 .. Duke Sims .............. Tigers | 778 ... 9/16/72 .. Buddy Bradford . White Sox |
| 729 ... 8/31/72 .. Duke Sims .............. Tigers | 779 ... 9/16/72 .. Ed Spiezio ........ White Sox |
| 730 ... 8/31/72 .. Aurelio Rodriguez ... Tigers | 780 ... 9/21/72 .. Paul Schaal ........... Royals |
| 731 ... 8/31/72 .. Jim Northrup ........... Tigers | 781 ... 9/21/72 .. Steve Hovley .......... Royals |
| 732 ... 8/31/72 .. Norm Cash ............. Tigers | 782 ... 9/21/72 .. Lou Piniella ............ Royals |
| 733 ... 8/31/72 .. Aurelio Rodriguez ... Tigers | 783 ... 9/21/72 .. Roger Nelson ......... Royals |
| 734 ... 8/31/72 .. Jim Northrup ........... Tigers | 784 ... 9/25/72 .. Vic Harris ............ Rangers |
| 735 ... 8/31/72 .. Willie Horton ............ Tigers | 785 ... 9/25/72 .. Dick Bosman ....... Rangers |
| 736 ... 8/31/72 .. Norm Cash ............. Tigers | 786 ... 9/25/72 .. Jim Mason ........... Rangers |
| 737 ... 9/4/72 .... Dal Maxvill .................... A's | 787 ... 9/25/72 .. Tom Grieve .......... Rangers |
| 738 ... 9/4/72 .... Joe Horlen .................... A's | 788 ... 9/25/72 .. Dalton Jones ....... Rangers |
| 739 ... 9/4/72 .... Matty Alou .................... A's | 789 ... 9/25/72 .. Vic Harris ............ Rangers |
| 740 ... 9/4/72 .... Mike Epstein ................ A's | 790 ... 9/25/72 .. Dave Nelson ........ Rangers |
| 741 ... 9/4/72 .... Dave Duncan ................ A's | 791 ... 9/25/72 Y Ted Ford .............. Rangers |
| 742 ... 9/4/72 .... Reggie Jackson ............ A's | 792 ... 9/25/72 .. Tom Grieve .......... Rangers |
| 743 ... 9/4/72 .... Mike Hegan .................. A's | 793 ... 9/25/72 .. Ted Ford .............. Rangers |
| 744 ... 9/4/72 .... Don Mincher ................. A's | 794 ... 9/25/72 .. Dalton Jones ....... Rangers |
| 745 ... 9/4/72 .... Joe Rudi ...................... A's | 795 ... 9/25/72 .. Rich Billings ......... Rangers |
| 746 ... 9/4/72 .... Matty Alou .................... A's | 796 ... 9/30/72 .. Steve Braun ............ Twins |
| 747 ... 9/4/72 .... Gene Tenace ............... A's | 797 ... 9/30/72 .. Bobby Darwin .......... Twins |
| 748 ... 9/8/72 .... Carlos May ....... White Sox | 798 ... 9/30/72 .. Glenn Borgmann ..... Twins |
| 749 ... 9/8/72 .... Stan Bahnsen ... White Sox | 799 ... 9/30/72 .. Rick Renick ............. Twins |
| 750 ... 9/8/72 .... Dick Allen .......... White Sox | 800 ... 9/30/72 .. Dave Goltz .............. Twins |

| | | | |
|---|---|---|---|
| 801 ... 9/30/72 .. Danny Thompson .... Twins | 851 ... 4/18/73 .. Danny Thompson .... Twins |
| 802 ... 9/30/72 .. Bobby Darwin .......... Twins | 852 ... 4/18/73 .. George Mitterwald ... Twins |
| 803 ... 9/30/72 .. Steve Brye ............... Twins | 853 ... 4/18/73 .. Larry Hisle ............... Twins |
| 804 ... 9/30/72 .. Rick Renick .............. Twins | 854 ... 4/18/73 .. Harmon Killebrew .... Twins |
| 805 ... 9/30/72 .. Charlie Manuel ........ Twins | 855 ... 4/18/73 .. Tony Oliva ............... Twins |
| 806 ... 9/30/72 .. Danny Thompson .... Twins | 856 ... 4/18/73 .. Jim Holt .................... Twins |
| 807 ... 9/30/72 .. Steve Braun ............. Twins | 857 ... 4/18/73 .. Larry Hisle ............... Twins |
| 808 ... 9/30/72 .. Harmon Killebrew .... Twins | 858 ... 4/18/73 .. Rod Carew ............... Twins |
| 809 ... 9/30/72 .. Bobby Darwin .......... Twins | 859 ... 4/18/73 .. Bobby Darwin .......... Twins |
| 810 ... 9/30/72 .. Glenn Borgmann ..... Twins | 860 ... 4/22/73 .. Bert Campaneris .......... A's |
| 811 ... 9/30/72 .. Rick Renick .............. Twins | 861 ... 4/22/73 .. Bill North ...................... A's |
| 812 ... 9/30/72 .. Rick Renick .............. Twins | 862 ... 4/22/73 .. Gene Tenace ................ A's |
| 813 ... 10/4/72 .. Angel Mangual ............. A's | 863 ... 4/22/73 .. Bert Campaneris .......... A's |
| 814 ... 10/4/72 .. John Odom .................. A's | 864 ... 4/22/73 .. Joe Rudi ...................... A's |
| 815 ... 10/4/72 .. Ted Kubiak .................. A's | 865 ... 4/22/73 .. Sal Bando .................... A's |
| 816 ... 10/4/72 .. Angel Mangual ............. A's | 866 ... 4/22/73 .. Gene Tenace ................ A's |
| 817 ... 10/4/72 .. Dave Duncan ............... A's | 867 ... 4/22/73 .. Ray Fosse .................... A's |
| 818 ... 10/4/72 .. Angel Mangual ............. A's | 868 ... 4/22/73 .. Joe Rudi ...................... A's |
| 819 ... 10/4/72 .. Dal Maxvill ................... A's | 869 ... 4/27/73 .. Charlie Spikes ....... Indians |
| 820 ... 10/4/72 .. Ted Kubiak .................. A's | 870 ... 4/27/73 .. Ron Lolich ............. Indians |
| 821 ... 10/4/72 .. Matty Alou ................... A's | 871 ... 4/27/73 .. Dave Duncan ........ Indians |
| 822 ... 10/4/72 .. Larry Haney ................. A's | 872 ... 4/27/73 .. Leo Cardenas ....... Indians |
| 823 ... 4/6/73 .... Fred Patek .......... Royals | 873 ... 4/27/73 .. Jack Brohammer ... Indians |
| 824 ... 4/6/73 .... Amos Otis ............. Royals | 874 ... 4/27/73 .. Dave Duncan ........ Indians |
| 825 ... 4/6/73 .... Hal McRae ............. Royals | 875 ... 4/27/73 .. George Hendrick ... Indians |
| 826 ... 4/6/73 .... Paul Schaal .......... Royals | 876 ... 4/27/73 .. Leo Cardenas ....... Indians |
| 827 ... 4/6/73 .... Fred Patek .......... Royals | 877 ... 5/2/73 .... Mickey Stanley ........ Tigers |
| 828 ... 4/6/73 .... John Mayberry ....... Royals | 878 ... 5/2/73 .... Aurelio Rodriguez ... Tigers |
| 829 ... 4/6/73 .... Jerry May .............. Royals | 879 ... 5/2/73 .... Bill Freehan ............. Tigers |
| 830 ... 4/6/73 .... Amos Otis ............. Royals | 880 ... 5/2/73 .... Ed Brinkman ........... Tigers |
| 831 ... 4/6/73 .... Paul Schaal .......... Royals | 881 ... 5/2/73 .... Ed Brinkman ........... Tigers |
| 832 ... 4/6/73 .... Amos Otis ............. Royals | 882 ... 5/2/73 .... Bill Freehan ............. Tigers |
| 833 ... 4/6/73 .... John Mayberry ....... Royals | 883 ... 5/2/73 .... Ed Brinkman ........... Tigers |
| 834 ... 4/6/73 .... Hal McRae ............. Royals | 884 ... 5/6/73 .... Don Baylor ............ Orioles |
| 835 ... 4/11/73 .. Larry Hisle ............... Twins | 885 ... 5/6/73 .... Al Bumbry .............. Orioles |
| 836 ... 4/11/73 .. Phil Roof .................. Twins | 886 ... 5/6/73 .... Earl Williams .......... Orioles |
| 837 ... 4/11/73 .. Larry Hisle ............... Twins | 887 ... 5/6/73 .... Don Baylor ............ Orioles |
| 838 ... 4/11/73 .. Steve Braun ............. Twins | 888 ... 5/6/73 .... Brooks Robinson ... Orioles |
| 839 ... 4/11/73 .. Phil Roof .................. Twins | 889 ... 5/12/73 .. John Jeter ......... White Sox |
| 840 ... 4/11/73 .. Jim Holt .................... Twins | 890 ... 5/12/73 .. Dick Allen .......... White Sox |
| 841 ... 4/11/73 .. Steve Brye ............... Twins | 891 ... 5/12/73 .. Bill Melton ......... White Sox |
| 842 ... 4/11/73 .. Joe Lis ..................... Twins | 892 ... 5/12/73 .. Ken Henderson . White Sox |
| 843 ... 4/11/73 .. George Mitterwald ... Twins | 893 ... 5/15/73 .. Fred Patek ............ Royals |
| 844 ... 4/11/73 .. Jim Holt .................... Twins | 894 ... 5/15/73 .. Amos Otis ............. Royals |
| 845 ... 4/11/73 .. Larry Hisle ............... Twins | 895 ... 5/15/73 .. John Mayberry ....... Royals |
| 846 ... 4/18/73 .. Bobby Darwin .......... Twins | 896 ... 5/15/73 .. Lou Piniella ............ Royals |
| 847 ... 4/18/73 .. George Mitterwald ... Twins | 897 ... 5/15/73 .. Paul Schaal .......... Royals |
| 848 ... 4/18/73 .. Rod Carew ............... Twins | 898 ... 5/15/73 .. Fred Patek ............ Royals |
| 849 ... 4/18/73 .. Harmon Killebrew .... Twins | 899 ... 5/15/73 .. John Mayberry ....... Royals |
| 850 ... 4/18/73 .. Tony Oliva ............... Twins | 900 ... 5/15/73 .. Paul Schaal ........... Royals |

| | | | |
|---|---|---|---|
| 901 ... 5/15/73 .. Carl Taylor .............. Royals | 951 ... 6/7/73 .... Bill Freehan ............. Tigers |
| 902 ... 5/15/73 .. John Mayberry ....... Royals | 952 ... 6/7/73 .... Norm Cash .............. Tigers |
| 903 ... 5/15/73 .. Ed Kirkpatrick .......... Royals | 953 ... 6/12/73 .. Luis Aparicio ........ Red Sox |
| 904 ... 5/15/73 .. Steve Hovley ........... Royals | 954 ... 6/12/73 .. Rico Petrocelli ...... Red Sox |
| 905 ... 5/19/73 .. Dave Nelson ........ Rangers | 955 ... 6/12/73 .. John Kennedy ..... Red Sox |
| 906 ... 5/19/73 .. Joe Lovitto ........... Rangers | 956 ... 6/12/73 .. Rick Miller ............ Red Sox |
| 907 ... 5/19/73 .. Alex Johnson ....... Rangers | 957 ... 6/12/73 .. Carlton Fisk ......... Red Sox |
| 908 ... 5/19/73 .. Vic Harris ............. Rangers | 958 ... 6/12/73 .. Carl Yastrzemski . Red Sox |
| 909 ... 5/19/73 .. Dave Nelson ........ Rangers | 959 ... 6/12/73 .. Tommy Harper ...... Red Sox |
| 910 ... 5/19/73 .. Larry Biittner ........ Rangers | 960 ... 6/12/73 .. Carlton Fisk ......... Red Sox |
| 911 ... 5/19/73 .. Jim Mason ........... Rangers | 961 ... 6/12/73 .. Reggie Smith ....... Red Sox |
| 912 ... 5/19/73 .. Dave Nelson ........ Rangers | 962 ... 6/16/73 .. Roy White ........... Yankees |
| 913 ... 5/19/73 .. Alex Johnson ....... Rangers | 963 ... 6/16/73 .. Bobby Murcer ...... Yankees |
| 914 ... 5/19/73 .. Jeff Burroughs ..... Rangers | 964 ... 6/16/73 .. Jim Hart ............... Yankees |
| 915 ... 5/19/73 .. Dave Nelson ........ Rangers | 965 ... 6/16/73 .. Thurman Munson Yankees |
| 916 ... 5/19/73 .. Alex Johnson ....... Rangers | 966 ... 6/16/73 .. Gene Michael ...... Yankees |
| 917 ... 5/24/73 .. Bill Melton ......... White Sox | 967 ... 6/16/73 .. Roy White ........... Yankees |
| 918 ... 5/24/73 .. Rick Reichardt .. White Sox | 968 ... 6/16/73 .. Thurman Munson Yankees |
| 919 ... 5/24/73 .. Jorge Orta ......... White Sox | 969 ... 6/16/73 .. Horace Clarke ..... Yankees |
| 920 ... 5/24/73 .. Eddie Leon ....... White Sox | 970 ... 6/16/73 .. Thurman Munson Yankees |
| 921 ... 5/24/73 .. Ed Herrmann ...... White Sox | 971 ... 6/16/73 .. Roy White ........... Yankees |
| 922 ... 5/24/73 .. Jorge Orta ......... White Sox | 972 ... 6/20/73 .. Carlos May ....... White Sox |
| 923 ... 5/24/73 .. Ken Henderson . White Sox | 973 ... 6/20/73 .. Ed Herrmann .... White Sox |
| 924 ... 5/24/73 .. Bill Melton ......... White Sox | 974 ... 6/20/73 .. Dick Allen ......... White Sox |
| 925 ... 5/24/73 .. Carlos May ....... White Sox | 975 ... 6/20/73 .. Carlos May ....... White Sox |
| 926 ... 5/24/73 .. Jorge Orta ......... White Sox | 976 ... 6/20/73 .. Eddie Leon ....... White Sox |
| 927 ... 5/24/73 .. Eddie Leon ....... White Sox | 977 ... 6/20/73 .. Eddie Leon ....... White Sox |
| 928 ... 5/24/73 .. Pat Kelly .......... White Sox | 978 ... 6/25/73 .. Ed Kirkpatrick ......... Royals |
| 929 ... 5/24/73 .. Dick Allen ......... White Sox | 979 ... 6/25/73 .. Lou Piniella ............ Royals |
| 930 ... 5/29/73 .. Rick Miller ........... Red Sox | 980 ... 6/25/73 .. Fran Healy ............. Royals |
| 931 ... 5/29/73 .. Danny Cater ........ Red Sox | 981 ... 6/25/73 .. Steve Hovley .......... Royals |
| 932 ... 5/29/73 .. Reggie Smith ....... Red Sox | 982 ... 6/25/73 .. Frank White ............ Royals |
| 933 ... 5/29/73 .. John Kennedy ..... Red Sox | 983 ... 6/25/73 .. Ed Kirkpatrick ......... Royals |
| 934 ... 5/29/73 .. Danny Cater ........ Red Sox | 984 ... 6/25/73 .. Lou Piniella ............ Royals |
| 935 ... 5/29/73 .. John Kennedy ..... Red Sox | 985 ... 6/25/73 .. Paul Schaal ........... Royals |
| 936 ... 5/29/73 .. Rick Miller ........... Red Sox | 986 ... 6/25/73 .. Frank White ............ Royals |
| 937 ... 5/29/73 .. Carlton Fisk ......... Red Sox | 987 ... 6/29/73 .. Rod Carew .............. Twins |
| 938 ... 5/29/73 .. Orlando Cepeda .. Red Sox | 988 ... 6/29/73 .. Jerry Terrell ............ Twins |
| 939 ... 5/29/73 .. Rico Petrocelli .... Red Sox | 989 ... 6/29/73 .. Joe Lis .................... Twins |
| 940 ... 6/2/73 .... Roy White ........... Yankees | 990 ... 6/29/73 .. George Mitterwald ... Twins |
| 941 ... 6/2/73 .... Graig Nettles ....... Yankees | 991 ... 6/29/73 .. Steve Braun ............ Twins |
| 942 ... 6/2/73 .... Thurman Munson Yankees | 992 ... 6/29/73 .. Jim Holt .................... Twins |
| 943 ... 6/2/73 .... Horace Clarke ..... Yankees | 993 ... 6/29/73 .. Rod Carew ............... Twins |
| 944 ... 6/2/73 .... Gene Michael ...... Yankees | 994 ... 6/29/73 .. Bobby Darwin .......... Twins |
| 945 ... 6/2/73 .... Horace Clarke ..... Yankees | 995 ... 6/29/73 .. Larry Hisle ............... Twins |
| 946 ... 6/7/73 .... Duke Sims .............. Tigers | 996 ... 6/29/73 .. Joe Lis .................... Twins |
| 947 ... 6/7/73 .... Dick McAuliffe ......... Tigers | 997 ... 6/29/73 .. Rod Carew ............... Twins |
| 948 ... 6/7/73 .... Ed Brinkman ........... Tigers | 998 ... 6/29/73 .. Joe Lis .................... Twins |
| 949 ... 6/7/73 .... Aurelio Rodriguez ... Tigers | 999 ... 7/3/73 .... Bill North ...................... A's |
| 950 ... 6/7/73 .... Jim Northrup ........... Tigers | 1000 ... 7/3/73 .... Sal Bando .................... A's |

| | | | |
|---|---|---|---|
| 1001 ... 7/3/73 .... Reggie Jackson .......... A's | 1051 ... 7/19/73 .. Rich Coggins ......... Orioles |
| 1002 ... 7/3/73 .... Joe Rudi ...................... A's | 1052 ... 7/19/73 .. Earl Williams .......... Orioles |
| 1003 ... 7/3/73 .... Dick Green ................... A's | 1053 ... 7/19/73 .. Al Bumbry .............. Orioles |
| 1004 ... 7/3/73 .... Gene Tenace ............... A's | 1054 ... 7/19/73 .. Rich Coggins ......... Orioles |
| 1005 ... 7/3/73 .... Dick Green ................... A's | 1055 ... 7/19/73 .. Earl Williams .......... Orioles |
| 1006 ... 7/3/73 .... Reggie Jackson .......... A's | 1056 ... 7/26/73 .. Bill Sudakis .......... Rangers |
| 1007 ... 7/3/73 .... Burt Campaneris ......... A's | 1057 ... 7/26/73 .. Larry Biittner ........ Rangers |
| 1008 ... 7/3/73 .... Mike Hegan ................. A's | 1058 ... 7/26/73 .. Bill Sudakis .......... Rangers |
| 1009 ... 7/7/73 .... John Ellis .............. Indians | 1059 ... 7/29/73 .. Fred Patek ............ Royals |
| 1010 ... 7/7/73 .... John Lowenstein ... Indians | 1060 ... 7/29/73 .. Rich Reichardt ....... Royals |
| 1011 ... 7/7/73 .... Leo Cardenas ....... Indians | 1061 ... 7/29/73 .. Carl Taylor ............. Royals |
| 1012 ... 7/7/73 .... Charlie Spikes ....... Indians | 1062 ... 8/2/73 .... Alex Johnson ........ Rangers |
| 1013 ... 7/7/73 .... John Lowenstein ... Indians | 1063 ... 8/2/73 .... Jeff Burroughs ...... Rangers |
| 1014 ... 7/7/73 .... Chris Chambliss ... Indians | 1064 ... 8/2/73 .... Larry Biittner ........ Rangers |
| 1015 ... 7/11/73 .. Al Bumbry .............. Orioles | 1065 ... 8/2/73 .... Rich Billings ......... Rangers |
| 1016 ... 7/11/73 .. Brooks Robinson ... Orioles | 1066 ... 8/2/73 .... Jim Spencer ........ Rangers |
| 1017 ... 7/11/73 .. Boog Powell ........... Orioles | 1067 ... 8/2/73 .... Bill Sudakis ......... Rangers |
| 1018 ... 7/11/73 .. Earl Williams .......... Orioles | 1068 ... 8/2/73 .... Dave Nelson ........ Rangers |
| 1019 ... 7/11/73 .. Mark Belanger ....... Orioles | 1069 ... 8/2/73 .... Alex Johnson ........ Rangers |
| 1020 ... 7/11/73 .. Al Bumbry .............. Orioles | 1070 ... 8/2/73 .... Bill Sudakis ......... Rangers |
| 1021 ... 7/11/73 .. Boog Powell ........... Orioles | 1071 ... 8/2/73 .... Alex Johnson ....... Rangers |
| 1022 ... 7/11/73 .. Earl Williams .......... Orioles | 1072 ... 8/2/73 .... Jim Spencer ........ Rangers |
| 1023 ... 7/11/73 .. Bobby Grich ........... Orioles | 1073 ... 8/7/73 .... George Scott ........ Brewers |
| 1024 ... 7/11/73 .. Mark Belanger ....... Orioles | 1074 ... 8/7/73 .... George Scott ........ Brewers |
| 1025 ... 7/11/73 .. Al Bumbry .............. Orioles | 1075 ... 8/7/73 .... John Felske ......... Brewers |
| 1026 ... 7/15/73 .. Mickey Stanley ........ Tigers | 1076 ... 8/7/73 .... Ellie Rodriguez ..... Brewers |
| 1027 ... 7/15/73 .. Norm Cash .............. Tigers | 1077 ... 8/7/73 .... Tim Johnson ........ Brewers |
| 1028 ... 7/15/73 .. Duke Sims ............... Tigers | 1078 ... 8/7/73 .... Pedro Garcia ........ Brewers |
| 1029 ... 7/15/73 .. Dick McAuliffe ......... Tigers | 1079 ... 8/7/73 .... John Vukovich ..... Brewers |
| 1030 ... 7/15/73 .. Dick Sharon ............. Tigers | 1080 ... 8/7/73 .... John Briggs ......... Brewers |
| 1031 ... 7/15/73 .. Aurelio Rodriguez ... Tigers | 1081 ... 8/7/73 .... Bob Coluccio ........ Brewers |
| 1032 ... 7/15/73 .. Jim Northrup ........... Tigers | 1082 ... 8/7/73 .... John Felske ......... Brewers |
| 1033 ... 7/15/73 .. Gates Brown ............ Tigers | 1083 ... 8/7/73 .... George Scott ........ Brewers |
| 1034 ... 7/15/73 .. Norm Cash .............. Tigers | 1084 ... 8/7/73 .... John Felske ......... Brewers |
| 1035 ... 7/15/73 .. Duke Sims ............... Tigers | 1085 ... 8/7/73 .... Bob Coluccio ........ Brewers |
| 1036 ... 7/15/73 .. Dick McAuliffe ......... Tigers | 1086 ... 8/11/73 .. Mario Guerrero ..... Red Sox |
| 1037 ... 7/15/73 .. Aurelio Rodriguez ... Tigers | 1087 ... 8/11/73 .. Rico Petrocelli ..... Red Sox |
| 1038 ... 7/15/73 .. Mickey Stanley ........ Tigers | 1088 ... 8/11/73 .. Carlton Fisk ......... Red Sox |
| 1039 ... 7/15/73 .. Duke Sims ............... Tigers | 1089 ... 8/11/73 .. Ben Oglivie .......... Red Sox |
| 1040 ... 7/15/73 .. Dick McAuliffe ......... Tigers | 1090 ... 8/11/73 .. Orlando Cepada .. Red Sox |
| 1041 ... 7/15/73 .. Dick Sharon ............. Tigers | 1091 ... 8/11/73 .. Carlton Fisk ......... Red Sox |
| 1042 ... 7/15/73 .. Ed Brinkman ........... Tigers | 1092 ... 8/11/73 .. Ben Oglivie .......... Red Sox |
| 1043 ... 7/19/73 .. Al Bumbry .............. Orioles | 1093 ... 8/11/73 .. Tommy Harper .... Red Sox |
| 1044 ... 7/19/73 .. Boog Powell ........... Orioles | 1094 ... 8/11/73 .. Mario Guerrero ..... Red Sox |
| 1045 ... 7/19/73 .. Earl Williams .......... Orioles | 1095 ... 8/11/73 .. Carlton Fisk ......... Red Sox |
| 1046 ... 7/19/73 .. Terry Crowley ........ Orioles | 1096 ... 8/11/73 .. Rico Petrocelli ..... Red Sox |
| 1047 ... 7/19/73 .. Brooks Robinson ... Orioles | 1097 ... 8/11/73 .. Doug Griffin ......... Red Sox |
| 1048 ... 7/19/73 .. Al Bumbry .............. Orioles | 1098 ... 8/17/73 .. Gates Brown ........... Tigers |
| 1049 ... 7/19/73 .. Mark Belanger ....... Orioles | 1099 ... 8/17/73 .. Dick McAuliffe ......... Tigers |
| 1050 ... 7/19/73 .. Al Bumbry .............. Orioles | 1100 ... 8/17/73 .. Bill Freehan ............. Tigers |

| | | | |
|---|---|---|---|
| 1101 ... 8/17/73 .. Aurelio Rodriguez ... Tigers | 1151 ... 9/11/73 .. Sam Ewing ....... White Sox |
| 1102 ... 8/17/73 .. Norm Cash .............. Tigers | 1152 ... 9/11/73 .. Brian Downing .. White Sox |
| 1103 ... 8/17/73 .. Aurelio Rodriguez ... Tigers | 1153 ... 9/11/73 .. Carlos May ....... White Sox |
| 1104 ... 8/17/73 .. Ed Brinkman .......... Tigers | 1154 ... 9/11/73 .. Sam Ewing ....... White Sox |
| 1105 ... 8/17/73 .. Al Kaline .................. Tigers | 1155 ... 9/11/73 .. Sam Ewing ....... White Sox |
| 1106 ... 8/17/73 .. Bill Freehan ............. Tigers | 1156 ... 9/11/73 .. Luis Alvarado ... White Sox |
| 1107 ... 8/17/73 .. Ed Brinkman .......... Tigers | 1157 ... 9/11/73 .. Bill Sharp ......... White Sox |
| 1108 ... 8/17/73 .. Jim Northrup .......... Tigers | 1158 ... 9/11/73 .. Pat Kelly .......... White Sox |
| 1109 ... 8/17/73 .. Dick Sharon ........... Tigers | 1159 ... 9/11/73 .. Bucky Dent ...... White Sox |
| 1110 ... 8/17/73 .. Norm Cash .............. Tigers | 1160 ... 9/11/73 .. Sam Ewing ....... White Sox |
| 1111 ... 8/21/73 .. Bob Coluccio ....... Brewers | 1161 ... 9/15/73 .. Amos Otis .............. Royals |
| 1112 ... 8/21/73 .. Darrell Porter ....... Brewers | 1162 ... 9/15/73 .. Steve Hovley .......... Royals |
| 1113 ... 8/21/73 .. John Briggs .......... Brewers | 1163 ... 9/15/73 .. Amos Otis .............. Royals |
| 1114 ... 8/21/73 .. Tim Johnson ........ Brewers | 1164 ... 9/15/73 .. John Mayberry ....... Royals |
| 1115 ... 8/21/73 .. Pedro Garcia ....... Brewers | 1165 ... 9/15/73 .. Fred Patek ............. Royals |
| 1116 ... 8/21/73 .. Don Money .......... Brewers | 1166 ... 9/15/73 .. John Mayberry ....... Royals |
| 1117 ... 8/21/73 .. Darrell Porter ....... Brewers | 1167 ... 9/15/73 .. Hal McRae .............. Royals |
| 1118 ... 8/21/73 .. Davey May ............ Brewers | 1168 ... 9/15/73 .. Ed Kirkpatrick ........ Royals |
| 1119 ... 8/25/73 .. Rick Miller ........... Red Sox | 1169 ... 9/15/73 .. Fred Patek ............. Royals |
| 1120 ... 8/25/73 .. Mario Guerrero .... Red Sox | 1170 ... 9/15/73 .. Gail Hopkins ........... Royals |
| 1121 ... 8/25/73 .. Orlando Cepada .. Red Sox | 1171 ... 9/19/73 .. Jim Mason .......... Rangers |
| 1122 ... 8/25/73 .. Carlton Fisk ......... Red Sox | 1172 ... 9/19/73 .. Bill Sudakis ........ Rangers |
| 1123 ... 8/25/73 .. Ben Oglivie .......... Red Sox | 1173 ... 9/19/73 .. Jim Mason .......... Rangers |
| 1124 ... 8/25/73 .. Cecil Cooper ........ Red Sox | 1174 ... 9/19/73 .. Bill Sudakis ........ Rangers |
| 1125 ... 8/25/73 .. Doug Griffin ......... Red Sox | 1175 ... 9/19/73 .. Rich Billings ........ Rangers |
| 1126 ... 8/25/73 .. Mario Guerrero .... Red Sox | 1176 ... 9/19/73 .. Bill Sudakis ........ Rangers |
| 1127 ... 8/29/73 .. Ron Blomberg ..... Yankees | 1177 ... 9/19/73 .. Bill Madlock ........ Rangers |
| 1128 ... 8/29/73 .. Mike Hegan ......... Yankees | 1178 ... 9/23/73 .. Rod Carew ............. Twins |
| 1129 ... 8/29/73 .. Horace Clarke ..... Yankees | 1179 ... 9/23/73 .. Craig Kusick ........... Twins |
| 1130 ... 8/29/73 .. Thurman Munson Yankees | 1180 ... 9/23/73 .. Larry Hisle .............. Twins |
| 1131 ... 8/29/73 .. Bobby Murcer ...... Yankees | 1181 ... 9/23/73 .. Jerry Terrell ............. Twins |
| 1132 ... 8/29/73 .. Gene Michael ...... Yankees | 1182 ... 9/23/73 .. Jim Holt ................... Twins |
| 1133 ... 8/29/73 .. Graig Nettles ....... Yankees | 1183 ... 9/23/73 .. Jerry Terrell ............. Twins |
| 1134 ... 8/29/73 .. Mike Hegan ......... Yankees | 1184 ... 9/23/73 .. Glenn Borgmann ..... Twins |
| 1135 ... 8/29/73 .. Gene Michael ...... Yankees | 1185 ... 9/23/73 .. Larry Hisle .............. Twins |
| 1136 ... 8/29/73 .. Roy White ............ Yankees | 1186 ... 9/23/73 .. Jerry Terrell ............. Twins |
| 1137 ... 9/3/73 .... Bill North ...................... A's | 1187 ... 9/23/73 .. Steve Brye .............. Twins |
| 1138 ... 9/3/73 .... Bert Campaneris .......... A's | 1188 ... 9/23/73 .. Craig Kusick ........... Twins |
| 1139 ... 9/3/73 .... Sal Bando .................... A's | 1189 ... 9/23/73 .. Larry Hisle .............. Twins |
| 1140 ... 9/3/73 .... Reggie Jackson ........... A's | 1190 ... 9/27/73 .. Jim Holt ................... Twins |
| 1141 ... 9/3/73 .... Gene Tenace ................ A's | 1191 ... 9/27/73 .. George Mitterwald ... Twins |
| 1142 ... 9/3/73 .... Dick Green .................... A's | 1192 ... 9/27/73 .. Mike Adams ............. Twins |
| 1143 ... 9/3/73 .... Bill North ...................... A's | 1193 ... 9/27/73 .. Rod Carew ............... Twins |
| 1144 ... 9/3/73 .... Bert Campaneris .......... A's | 1194 ... 9/27/73 .. Tony Oliva ................ Twins |
| 1145 ... 9/3/73 .... Pat Bourque ................. A's | 1195 ... 9/27/73 .. Jim Holt ................... Twins |
| 1146 ... 9/3/73 .... Dick Green .................... A's | 1196 ... 9/27/73 .. Mike Adams ............. Twins |
| 1147 ... 9/3/73 .... Gene Tenace ................ A's | 1197 ... 9/27/73 .. Jerry Terrell ............. Twins |
| 1148 ... 9/3/73 .... Deron Johnson ............. A's | 1198 ... 9/27/73 .. Steve Brye .............. Twins |
| 1149 ... 9/11/73 .. Pat Kelly .......... White Sox | 1199 ... 9/27/73 .. Rod Carew ............... Twins |
| 1150 ... 9/11/73 .. Jorge Orta ......... White Sox | 1200 ... 9/27/73 .. Harmon Killebrew .... Twins |

| | | | |
|---|---|---|---|
| 1201 ... 9/27/73 .. Rod Carew .............. Twins | 1251 ... 4/30/74 .. Rick Miller ........... Red Sox |
| 1202 ... 9/27/73 .. Harmon Killebrew .... Twins | 1252 ... 4/30/74 .. Jaun Beniquez .... Red Sox |
| 1203 ... 9/27/73 ... George Mitterwald ... Twins | 1253 ... 4/30/74 ... Rico Petrocelli ..... Red Sox |
| 1204 ... 9/27/73 .. Steve Brye .............. Twins | 1254 ... 4/30/74 .. Dwight Evans ...... Red Sox |
| 1205 ... 9/27/73 .. Rich Reese .............. Twins | 1255 ... 4/30/74 .. Bob Montgomery . Red Sox |
| 1206 ... 4/5/74 .... Bill Melton ......... White Sox | 1256 ... 4/30/74 .. John Kennedy ..... Red Sox |
| 1207 ... 4/5/74 .... Jorge Orta ......... White Sox | 1257 ... 5/5/74 ... Ellie Hendricks ....... Orioles |
| 1208 ... 4/5/74 .... Pat Kelly .......... White Sox | 1258 ... 5/5/74 .... Al Bumbry .............. Orioles |
| 1209 ... 4/5/74 .... Dick Allen .......... White Sox | 1259 ... 5/5/74 .... Boog Powell ........... Orioles |
| 1210 ... 4/5/74 .... Carlos May ....... White Sox | 1260 ... 5/5/74 .... Ellie Hendricks ....... Orioles |
| 1211 ... 4/9/74 .... Toby Harrah ........ Rangers | 1261 ... 5/5/74 .... Al Bumbry .............. Orioles |
| 1212 ... 4/12/74 .. Ed Herrmann .... White Sox | 1262 ... 5/5/74 .... Boog Powell ........... Orioles |
| 1213 ... 4/12/74 .. Ron Santo ......... White Sox | 1263 ... 5/10/74 .. Fred Patek ............ Royals |
| 1214 ... 4/12/74 .. Ron Santo ......... White Sox | 1264 ... 5/10/74 .. Jim Wohlford ......... Royals |
| 1215 ... 4/12/74 .. Ken Henderson . White Sox | 1265 ... 5/10/74 .. Vada Pinson ........... Royals |
| 1216 ... 4/12/74 .. Bucky Dent ....... White Sox | 1266 ... 5/10/74 .. George Brett .......... Royals |
| 1217 ... 4/12/74 .. Carlos May ....... White Sox | 1267 ... 5/10/74 .. Jim Wohlford ......... Royals |
| 1218 ... 4/16/74 .. Steve Braun .......... Twins | 1268 ... 5/10/74 .. John Mayberry ....... Royals |
| 1219 ... 4/16/74 .. Sergio Ferrer .......... Twins | 1269 ... 5/10/74 .. Fran Healy ............ Royals |
| 1220 ... 4/16/74 .. Bobby Darwin .......... Twins | 1270 ... 5/10/74 .. George Brett .......... Royals |
| 1221 ... 4/16/74 .. Steve Braun .......... Twins | 1271 ... 5/10/74 .. Jim Wohlford ......... Royals |
| 1222 ... 4/16/74 .. Larry Hisle .............. Twins | 1272 ... 5/10/74 .. Hal McRae .............. Royals |
| 1223 ... 4/16/74 .. Rod Carew .............. Twins | 1273 ... 5/15/74 .. Mike Hargrove ..... Rangers |
| 1224 ... 4/16/74 .. Bobby Darwin .......... Twins | 1274 ... 5/15/74 .. Larry Brown ......... Rangers |
| 1225 ... 4/16/74 .. Larry Hisle .............. Twins | 1275 ... 5/15/74 .. Toby Harrah ........ Rangers |
| 1226 ... 4/16/74 .. Glenn Borgmann ..... Twins | 1276 ... 5/15/74 .. Mike Hargrove ..... Rangers |
| 1227 ... 4/16/74 .. Jerry Terrell .............. Twins | 1277 ... 5/15/74 .. Jim Sundberg ....... Rangers |
| 1228 ... 4/16/74 .. Jerry Terrell .............. Twins | 1278 ... 5/15/74 .. Jeff Burroughs ..... Rangers |
| 1229 ... 4/20/74 .. Bill North ...................... A's | 1279 ... 5/19/74 .. Larry Hisle .............. Twins |
| 1230 ... 4/20/74 .. Joe Rudi ...................... A's | 1280 ... 5/19/74 .. Tony Oliva .............. Twins |
| 1231 ... 4/20/74 .. Gene Tenace ............... A's | 1281 ... 5/19/74 .. Eric Soderholm ........ Twins |
| 1232 ... 4/20/74 .. Ted Kubiak ................... A's | 1282 ... 5/19/74 .. Glenn Borgmann ..... Twins |
| 1233 ... 4/20/74 .. Bill North ...................... A's | 1283 ... 5/19/74 .. Tony Oliva .............. Twins |
| 1234 ... 4/20/74 .. Sal Bando ...................... A's | 1284 ... 5/19/74 .. Harmon Killebrew .... Twins |
| 1235 ... 4/26/74 .. Oscar Gamble ....... Indians | 1285 ... 5/19/74 .. Bobby Darwin .......... Twins |
| 1236 ... 4/26/74 .. Dave Duncan ........ Indians | 1286 ... 5/19/74 .. Eric Soderholm ........ Twins |
| 1237 ... 4/26/74 .. Charlie Spikes ....... Indians | 1287 ... 5/19/74 .. Joe Lis ...................... Twins |
| 1238 ... 4/26/74 .. Leron Lee .............. Indians | 1288 ... 5/19/74 .. Larry Hisle .............. Twins |
| 1239 ... 4/26/74 .. Dave Duncan ........ Indians | 1289 ... 5/19/74 .. Jerry Terrell .............. Twins |
| 1240 ... 4/26/74 .. Oscar Gamble ....... Indians | 1290 ... 5/19/74 .. Jim Holt .................... Twins |
| 1241 ... 4/26/74 .. George Hendrick ... Indians | 1291 ... 5/23/74 .. John Mayberry ....... Royals |
| 1242 ... 4/30/74 .. Cecil Cooper ....... Red Sox | 1292 ... 5/23/74 .. Fred Patek ............ Royals |
| 1243 ... 4/30/74 .. Rico Petrocelli ..... Red Sox | 1293 ... 5/23/74 .. Jim Wohlford ......... Royals |
| 1244 ... 4/30/74 .. Rick Miller ........... Red Sox | 1294 ... 5/23/74 .. Amos Otis .............. Royals |
| 1245 ... 4/30/74 .. Cecil Cooper ....... Red Sox | 1295 ... 5/23/74 .. Richie Scheinblum . Royals |
| 1246 ... 4/30/74 .. Rico Petrocelli ..... Red Sox | 1296 ... 5/23/74 .. Fran Healy ............ Royals |
| 1247 ... 4/30/74 .. Cecil Cooper ...... Red Sox | 1297 ... 5/27/74 .. Davey May .......... Brewers |
| 1248 ... 4/30/74 .. Rico Petrocelli ..... Red Sox | 1298 ... 5/27/74 .. Bob Hansen ......... Brewers |
| 1249 ... 4/30/74 .. Dwight Evans ...... Red Sox | 1299 ... 5/27/74 .. John Briggs .......... Brewers |
| 1250 ... 4/30/74 .. Carlton Fisk ......... Red Sox | 1300 ... 5/27/74 .. Bob Hansen ......... Brewers |

| | | | |
|---|---|---|---|
| 1301 ... 5/27/74 .. Bob Coluccio ........ Brewers | 1351 ... 6/18/74 .. Jim Mason ........... Yankees |
| 1302 ... 5/27/74 .. George Scott ....... Brewers | 1352 ... 6/18/74 .. Graig Nettles ....... Yankees |
| 1303 ... 5/27/74 .. Bob Hansen ......... Brewers | 1353 ... 6/22/74 .. Dave Nelson ........ Rangers |
| 1304 ... 5/27/74 .. Don Money ........... Brewers | 1354 ... 6/22/74 .. Tom Grieve ......... Rangers |
| 1305 ... 6/1/74 .... Mickey Stanley ........ Tigers | 1355 ... 6/22/74 .. Jim Sundberg ...... Rangers |
| 1306 ... 6/1/74 .... Norm Cash .............. Tigers | 1356 ... 6/22/74 .. Alex Johnson ....... Rangers |
| 1307 ... 6/1/74 .... Aurelio Rodriguez ... Tigers | 1357 ... 6/22/74 .. Mike Hargrove ..... Rangers |
| 1308 ... 6/1/74 .... Gary Sutherland ...... Tigers | 1358 ... 6/22/74 .. Toby Harrah ........ Rangers |
| 1309 ... 6/1/74 .... Jim Northrup ........... Tigers | 1359 ... 6/22/74 .. Dave Nelson ........ Rangers |
| 1310 ... 6/1/74 .... Ben Oglivie ............. Tigers | 1360 ... 6/22/74 .. Alex Johnson ....... Rangers |
| 1311 ... 6/1/74 .... Jim Northrup ........... Tigers | 1361 ... 6/22/74 .. Tom Grieve ......... Rangers |
| 1312 ... 6/1/74 .... Norm Cash .............. Tigers | 1362 ... 6/22/74 .. Toby Harrah ........ Rangers |
| 1313 ... 6/1/74 .... Aurelio Rodriguez ... Tigers | 1363 ... 6/27/74 .. Dave Nelson ........ Rangers |
| 1314 ... 6/1/74 .... Ben Oglivie ............. Tigers | 1364 ... 6/27/74 .. Jim Spencer ........ Rangers |
| 1315 ... 6/1/74 .... Gates Brown ........... Tigers | 1365 ... 6/27/74 .. Lenny Randle ...... Rangers |
| 1316 ... 6/5/74 .... Darrell Porter ....... Brewers | 1366 ... 6/27/74 .. Toby Harrah ........ Rangers |
| 1317 ... 6/5/74 .... Rob Ellis .............. Brewers | 1367 ... 6/27/74 .. Jeff Burroughs ..... Rangers |
| 1318 ... 6/5/74 .... Robin Yount ........ Brewers | 1368 ... 6/27/74 .. Jim Spencer ........ Rangers |
| 1319 ... 6/5/74 .... Davey May ........... Brewers | 1369 ... 7/1/74 .... Bert Campaneris .......... A's |
| 1320 ... 6/5/74 .... Robin Yount ........ Brewers | 1370 ... 7/1/74 .... Angel Mangual ............. A's |
| 1321 ... 6/9/74 .... Al Kaline ................... Tigers | 1371 ... 7/1/74 .... Larry Haney ................ A's |
| 1322 ... 6/9/74 .... Willie Horton ............ Tigers | 1372 ... 7/1/74 .... Bill North ................... A's |
| 1323 ... 6/9/74 .... Bill Freehan ............. Tigers | 1373 ... 7/1/74 .... Angel Mangual ............. A's |
| 1324 ... 6/9/74 .... Gerry Moses ............ Tigers | 1374 ... 7/1/74 .... Bill North ................... A's |
| 1325 ... 6/9/74 .... Al Kaline ................... Tigers | 1375 ... 7/1/74 .... Bert Campaneris .......... A's |
| 1326 ... 6/9/74 .... Bill Freehan ............. Tigers | 1376 ... 7/1/74 .... Joe Rudi ...................... A's |
| 1327 ... 6/14/74 .. Cecil Cooper ....... Red Sox | 1377 ... 7/1/74 .... Larry Haney ................ A's |
| 1328 ... 6/14/74 .. Rick Miller ........... Red Sox | 1378 ... 7/1/74 .... Pat Bourque ................ A's |
| 1329 ... 6/14/74 .. Bernie Carbo ....... Red Sox | 1379 ... 7/5/74 .... John Ellis ............... Indians |
| 1330 ... 6/14/74 .. Terry Hughes ....... Red Sox | 1380 ... 7/5/74 .... Charlie Spikes ...... Indians |
| 1331 ... 6/14/74 .. Cecil Cooper ....... Red Sox | 1381 ... 7/5/74 .... Dave Duncan ........ Indians |
| 1332 ... 6/14/74 .. Rick Miller ........... Red Sox | 1382 ... 7/5/74 .... Charlie Spikes ....... Indians |
| 1333 ... 6/14/74 .. Dick McAuliffe ..... Red Sox | 1383 ... 7/5/74 .... Frank Duffy ........... Indians |
| 1334 ... 6/14/74 .. Mario Guerrero .... Red Sox | 1384 ... 7/5/74 .... John Lowenstein ... Indians |
| 1335 ... 6/14/74 .. Cecil Cooper ....... Red Sox | 1385 ... 7/5/74 .... John Ellis ............... Indians |
| 1336 ... 6/14/74 .. Rick Miller ........... Red Sox | 1386 ... 7/5/74 .... Charlie Spikes ....... Indians |
| 1337 ... 6/14/74 .. Bernie Carbo ....... Red Sox | 1387 ... 7/10/74 .. Al Bumbry .............. Orioles |
| 1338 ... 6/14/74 .. Rico Petrocelli ..... Red Sox | 1388 ... 7/10/74 .. Bobby Grich ........... Orioles |
| 1339 ... 6/14/74 .. Cecil Cooper ....... Red Sox | 1389 ... 7/10/74 .. Don Baylor ............. Orioles |
| 1340 ... 6/14/74 .. Bernie Carbo ....... Red Sox | 1390 ... 7/10/74 .. Ellie Hendricks ...... Orioles |
| 1341 ... 6/14/74 .. Cecil Cooper ....... Red Sox | 1391 ... 7/15/74 .. John Lowenstein ... Indians |
| 1342 ... 6/14/74 .. Dick McAuliffe ..... Red Sox | 1392 ... 7/15/74 .. Dave Duncan ........ Indians |
| 1343 ... 6/14/74 .. Carl Yastrzemski . Red Sox | 1393 ... 7/15/74 .. Charlie Spikes ....... Indians |
| 1344 ... 6/14/74 .. Rick Burleson ...... Red Sox | 1394 ... 7/15/74 .. John Lowenstein ... Indians |
| 1345 ... 6/14/74 .. Cecil Cooper ....... Red Sox | 1395 ... 7/15/74 .. John Ellis ............... Indians |
| 1346 ... 6/18/74 .. Elliott Maddox ..... Yankees | 1396 ... 7/15/74 .. Buddy Bell ............. Indians |
| 1347 ... 6/18/74 .. Bobby Murcer ...... Yankees | 1397 ... 7/15/74 .. Dave Duncan ........ Indians |
| 1348 ... 6/18/74 .. Jim Mason ........... Yankees | 1398 ... 7/15/74 .. Oscar Gamble ....... Indians |
| 1349 ... 6/18/74 .. Graig Nettles ....... Yankees | 1399 ... 7/20/74 .. Bobby Grich ........... Orioles |
| 1350 ... 6/18/74 .. Thurman Munson Yankees | 1400 ... 7/20/74 .. Brooks Robinson ... Orioles |

| | | | |
|---|---|---|---|
| 1401 ... 7/20/74 .. Rich Coggins ......... Orioles | 1451 ... 8/12/74 .. Doug Griffin ......... Red Sox |
| 1402 ... 7/20/74 .. Al Bumbry .............. Orioles | 1452 ... 8/12/74 .. Bob Montgomery . Red Sox |
| 1403 ... 7/20/74 .. Bobby Grich ........... Orioles | 1453 ... 8/12/74 .. Rico Petrocelli ..... Red Sox |
| 1404 ... 7/20/74 .. Boog Powell ........... Orioles | 1454 ... 8/12/74 .. Dwight Evans ...... Red Sox |
| 1405 ... 7/20/74 .. Ellie Hendricks ....... Orioles | 1455 ... 8/12/74 .. Rick Miller ........... Red Sox |
| 1406 ... 7/20/74 .. Al Bumbry .............. Orioles | 1456 ... 8/12/74 .. Bob Montgomery . Red Sox |
| 1407 ... 7/25/74 .. Tony Solaita .......... Royals | 1457 ... 8/12/74 .. Rico Petrocelli ..... Red Sox |
| 1408 ... 7/25/74 .. Vada Pinson .......... Royals | 1458 ... 8/12/74 .. Dwight Evans ...... Red Sox |
| 1409 ... 7/25/74 .. George Brett ......... Royals | 1459 ... 8/12/74 .. Rick Miller ........... Red Sox |
| 1410 ... 7/25/74 .. John Mayberry ....... Royals | 1460 ... 8/12/74 .. Bob Montgomery . Red Sox |
| 1411 ... 7/25/74 .. Vada Pinson .......... Royals | 1461 ... 8/12/74 .. Jaun Beniquez .... Red Sox |
| 1412 ... 7/25/74 .. Fred Patek ............. Royals | 1462 ... 8/12/74 .. Cecil Cooper ....... Red Sox |
| 1413 ... 7/25/74 .. Fred Patek ............. Royals | 1463 ... 8/12/74 .. Rico Petrocelli ..... Red Sox |
| 1414 ... 7/25/74 .. Fran Healy ............. Royals | 1464 ... 8/12/74 .. Rick Miller ........... Red Sox |
| 1415 ... 7/25/74 .. Amos Otis ............. Royals | 1465 ... 8/12/74 .. Bernie Carbo ....... Red Sox |
| 1416 ... 7/28/74 .. Steve Braun ............. Twins | 1466 ... 8/16/74 .. Don Money .......... Brewers |
| 1417 ... 7/30/74 .. Jorge Orta ......... White Sox | 1467 ... 8/16/74 .. John Briggs ......... Brewers |
| 1418 ... 7/30/74 .. Bill Sharp .......... White Sox | 1468 ... 8/16/74 .. Robin Yount ........ Brewers |
| 1419 ... 7/30/74 .. Ed Herrmann .... White Sox | 1469 ... 8/16/74 .. Pedro Garcia ....... Brewers |
| 1420 ... 7/30/74 .. Jorge Orta ......... White Sox | 1470 ... 8/16/74 .. Davey May .......... Brewers |
| 1421 ... 7/30/74 .. Ken Henderson . White Sox | 1471 ... 8/16/74 .. Don Money .......... Brewers |
| 1422 ... 7/30/74 .. Jorge Orta ......... White Sox | 1472 ... 8/16/74 .. John Briggs ......... Brewers |
| 1423 ... 7/30/74 .. Bill Sharp .......... White Sox | 1473 ... 8/16/74 .. Robin Yount ........ Brewers |
| 1424 ... 7/30/74 .. Dick Allen .......... White Sox | 1474 ... 8/16/74 .. John Briggs ......... Brewers |
| 1425 ... 8/3/74 .... Fred Patek ............. Royals | 1475 ... 8/20/74 .. Jim Nettles ............. Tigers |
| 1426 ... 8/3/74 .... Tony Solaita .......... Royals | 1476 ... 8/20/74 .. Aurelio Rodriguez ... Tigers |
| 1427 ... 8/3/74 .... Jim Wohlford ......... Royals | 1477 ... 8/20/74 .. Dick Sharon ............ Tigers |
| 1428 ... 8/3/74 .... George Brett ......... Royals | 1478 ... 8/20/74 .. Ron LeFlore ............ Tigers |
| 1429 ... 8/3/74 .... Fran Healy ............. Royals | 1479 ... 8/20/74 .. Tom Veryzer ............ Tigers |
| 1430 ... 8/3/74 .... Amos Otis ............. Royals | 1480 ... 8/20/74 .. Dick Sharon ............ Tigers |
| 1431 ... 8/3/74 .... Jim Wohlford ......... Royals | 1481 ... 8/20/74 .. Ron LeFlore ............ Tigers |
| 1432 ... 8/3/74 .... Cookie Rojas ......... Royals | 1482 ... 8/20/74 .. Bill Freehan ............ Tigers |
| 1433 ... 8/3/74 .... Fran Healy ............. Royals | 1483 ... 8/20/74 .. Jim Nettles ............. Tigers |
| 1434 ... 8/7/74 .... Pat Kelly ........... White Sox | 1484 ... 8/20/74 .. Aurelio Rodriguez ... Tigers |
| 1435 ... 8/7/74 .... Jorge Orta ......... White Sox | 1485 ... 8/20/74 .. Tom Veryzer ............ Tigers |
| 1436 ... 8/7/74 .... Dick Allen .......... White Sox | 1486 ... 8/20/74 .. Ron LeFlore ............ Tigers |
| 1437 ... 8/7/74 .... Ken Henderson . White Sox | 1487 ... 8/20/74 .. Gary Sutherland ...... Tigers |
| 1438 ... 8/7/74 .... Jorge Orta ......... White Sox | 1488 ... 8/20/74 .. Ben Oglivie ............. Tigers |
| 1439 ... 8/7/74 .... Dick Allen .......... White Sox | 1489 ... 8/20/74 .. Bill Freehan ............ Tigers |
| 1440 ... 8/7/74 .... Brian Downing .. White Sox | 1490 ... 8/20/74 .. Jim Nettles ............. Tigers |
| 1441 ... 8/7/74 .... Jorge Orta ......... White Sox | 1491 ... 8/20/74 .. Dick Sharon ............ Tigers |
| 1442 ... 8/7/74 .... Ken Henderson . White Sox | 1492 ... 8/20/74 .. Gene Lamont .......... Tigers |
| 1443 ... 8/7/74 .... Bill Melton ......... White Sox | 1493 ... 8/20/74 .. Ron LeFlore ............ Tigers |
| 1444 ... 8/7/74 .... Bill Sharp .......... White Sox | 1494 ... 8/25/74 .. Chris Chambliss .. Yankees |
| 1445 ... 8/7/74 .... Brian Downing .. White Sox | 1495 ... 8/25/74 .. Roy White .......... Yankees |
| 1446 ... 8/7/74 .... Jorge Orta ......... White Sox | 1496 ... 8/25/74 .. Elliott Maddox ..... Yankees |
| 1447 ... 8/12/74 .. Cecil Cooper ....... Red Sox | 1497 ... 8/25/74 .. Ron Blomberg ..... Yankees |
| 1448 ... 8/12/74 .. Rico Petrocelli ..... Red Sox | 1498 ... 8/25/74 .. Thurman Munson  Yankees |
| 1449 ... 8/12/74 .. Carl Yastrzemski . Red Sox | 1499 ... 8/25/74 .. Jim Mason .......... Yankees |
| 1450 ... 8/12/74 .. Dwight Evans ...... Red Sox | 1500 ... 8/25/74 .. Sandy Alomar ..... Yankees |

| | | | |
|---|---|---|---|
| 1501 ... 8/30/74 .. Tim Johnson ........ Brewers | 1551 ... 9/24/74 .. Tony Solaita ........... Royals |
| 1502 ... 8/30/74 .. George Scott ........ Brewers | 1552 ... 9/24/74 .. Amos Otis .............. Royals |
| 1503 ... 8/30/74 .. John Briggs ........ Brewers | 1553 ... 9/24/74 .. Tony Solaita ........... Royals |
| 1504 ... 8/30/74 .. Darrell Porter ....... Brewers | 1554 ... 9/24/74 .. Frank White ............ Royals |
| 1505 ... 8/30/74 .. Mike Hegan .......... Brewers | 1555 ... 9/24/74 .. Buck Martinez ........ Royals |
| 1506 . 8/30/74 .. Don Money .......... Brewers | 1556 ... 9/24/74 .. Vada Pinson .......... Royals |
| 1507 ... 8/30/74 .. John Briggs .......... Brewers | 1557 ... 9/24/74 .. Amos Otis ............. Royals |
| 1508 ... 8/30/74 .. Mike Hegan .......... Brewers | 1558 ... 9/28/74 .. Steve Brye .............. Twins |
| 1509 ... 8/30/74 .. Don Money .......... Brewers | 1559 ... 9/28/74 .. Rod Carew .............. Twins |
| 1510 ... 9/3/74 .... Gene Tenace ............... A's | 1560 ... 9/28/74 .. Bobby Darwin .......... Twins |
| 1511 ... 9/3/74 .... Gene Tenace ............... A's | 1561 ... 9/28/74 .. Larry Hisle .............. Twins |
| 1512 ... 9/7/74 .... Brian Downing .. White Sox | 1562 ... 9/28/74 .. Pat Bourque ............ Twins |
| 1513 ... 9/7/74 .... Lee Richard ...... White Sox | 1563 ... 9/28/74 .. Luis Gomez .............. Twins |
| 1514 ... 9/7/74 .... Brian Downing .. White Sox | 1564 ... 9/28/74 .. Bobby Darwin .......... Twins |
| 1515 ... 9/7/74 .... Pat Kelly .......... White Sox | 1565 ... 9/28/74 .. Pat Bourque ............ Twins |
| 1516 ... 9/7/74 .... Bill Sharp ......... White Sox | 1566 ... 9/28/74 .. Bobby Darwin .......... Twins |
| 1517 ... 9/7/74 .... Jorge Orta ........ White Sox | 1567 ... 9/28/74 .. Larry Hisle .............. Twins |
| 1518 ... 9/7/74 .... Ken Henderson . White Sox | 1568 ... 9/28/74 .. Pat Bourque ............ Twins |
| 1519 ... 9/7/74 .... Brian Downing .. White Sox | 1569 ... 9/28/74 .. Rod Carew .............. Twins |
| 1520 ... 9/7/74 .... Carlos May ....... White Sox | 1570 ... 9/28/74 .. Steve Braun ............. Twins |
| 1521 ... 9/11/74 .. Fred Patek ............. Royals | 1571 ... 9/28/74 .. Larry Hisle .............. Twins |
| 1522 ... 9/11/74 .. Jim Wohlford .......... Royals | 1572 ... 9/28/74 .. Eric Soderholm ........ Twins |
| 1523 ... 9/11/74 .. Frank White ............ Royals | 1573 ... 4/7/75 .... Fred Patek ............. Royals |
| 1524 ... 9/11/74 .. Vada Pinson .......... Royals | 1574 ... 4/7/75 .... Hal McRae .............. Royals |
| 1525 ... 9/11/74 .. Hal McRae ............. Royals | 1575 ... 4/7/75 .... Harmon Killebrew ... Royals |
| 1526 ... 9/11/74 .. Jim Wohlford .......... Royals | 1576 ... 4/7/75 .... John Mayberry ....... Royals |
| 1527 ... 9/11/74 .. Al Cowens .............. Royals | 1577 ... 4/7/75 .... Hal McRae .............. Royals |
| 1528 ... 9/11/74 .. Frank White ............ Royals | 1578 ... 4/7/75 .... Harmon Killebrew ... Royals |
| 1529 ... 9/11/74 .. Jim Wohlford .......... Royals | 1579 ... 4/7/75 .... Fred Patek ............. Royals |
| 1530 ... 9/11/74 .. Al Cowens .............. Royals | 1580 ... 4/7/75 .... Harmon Killebrew ... Royals |
| 1531 ... 9/11/74 .. Frank White ............ Royals | 1581 ... 4/7/75 .... George Brett .......... Royals |
| 1532 ... 9/11/74 .. Buck Martinez ........ Royals | 1582 ... 4/7/75 .... Cookie Rojas .......... Royals |
| 1533 ... 9/11/74 .. George Brett .......... Royals | 1583 ... 4/7/75 .... Hal McRae .............. Royals |
| 1534 ... 9/11/74 .. Tony Solaita ........... Royals | 1584 ... 4/7/75 .... Harmon Killebrew ... Royals |
| 1535 ... 9/11/74 .. Vada Pinson .......... Royals | 1585 ... 4/11/75 .. Jorge Orta ......... White Sox |
| 1536 ... 9/15/74 .. Ken Henderson . White Sox | 1586 ... 4/11/75 .. Deron Johnson . White Sox |
| 1537 ... 9/15/74 .. Lee Richard ...... White Sox | 1587 ... 4/11/75 .. Bucky Dent ....... White Sox |
| 1538 ... 9/15/74 .. Carlos May ....... White Sox | 1588 ... 4/11/75 .. Brian Downing .. White Sox |
| 1539 ... 9/15/74 .. Lee Richard ...... White Sox | 1589 ... 4/11/75 .. Nyls Nyman ...... White Sox |
| 1540 ... 9/15/74 .. Tony Muser ....... White Sox | 1590 ... 4/11/75 .. Ken Henderson . White Sox |
| 1541 ... 9/15/74 .. Ken Henderson . White Sox | 1591 ... 4/11/75 .. Deron Johnson . White Sox |
| 1542 ... 9/15/74 .. Bill Stein ........... White Sox | 1592 ... 4/11/75 .. Brian Downing .. White Sox |
| 1543 ... 9/20/74 .. Pat Bourque ............ Twins | 1593 ... 4/11/75 .. Bill Melton ........ White Sox |
| 1544 ... 9/20/74 .. Danny Thompson ..... Twins | 1594 ... 4/11/75 .. Ken Henderson . White Sox |
| 1545 ... 9/20/74 .. Glenn Borgmann ..... Twins | 1595 ... 4/15/75 .. Glenn Borgmann ..... Twins |
| 1546 ... 9/20/74 .. Steve Braun ............. Twins | 1596 ... 4/15/75 .. Bobby Darwin .......... Twins |
| 1547 ... 9/20/74 .. Rod Carew .............. Twins | 1597 ... 4/15/75 .. Glenn Borgmann ..... Twins |
| 1548 ... 9/20/74 .. Pat Bourque ............ Twins | 1598 ... 4/15/75 .. Bobby Darwin .......... Twins |
| 1549 ... 9/24/74 .. Al Cowens .............. Royals | 1599 ... 4/15/75 .. Steve Braun ............. Twins |
| 1550 ... 9/24/74 .. George Brett .......... Royals | 1600 ... 4/15/75 .. Lyman Bostock ........ Twins |

| | | | | | |
|---|---|---|---|---|---|
| 1601 ... 4/15/75 .. Larry Hisle ............... Twins | 1651 ... 5/23/75 .. Jim Rice .............. Red Sox |
| 1602 ... 4/20/75 .. Ken Henderson . White Sox | 1652 ... 5/23/75 .. Fred Lynn ............ Red Sox |
| 1603 ... 4/20/75 .. Pete Varney ...... White Sox | 1653 ... 5/23/75 .. Rico Petrocelli ... Red Sox |
| 1604 ... 4/20/75 .. Pete Varney ...... White Sox | 1654 ... 5/28/75 .. Buddy Bell .......... Indians |
| 1605 ... 4/20/75 .. Deron Johnson . White Sox | 1655 ... 5/28/75 .. Charlie Spikes ....... Indians |
| 1606 ... 4/20/75 .. Pat Kelly ........... White Sox | 1656 ... 5/28/75 .. Oscar Gamble ....... Indians |
| 1607 ... 4/20/75 .. Pat Kelly ........... White Sox | 1657 ... 5/28/75 .. Alan Ashby ............ Indians |
| 1608 ... 4/24/75 .. Willie Davis .......... Rangers | 1658 ... 5/28/75 .. George Hendrick ........ Indians |
| 1609 ... 4/24/75 .. Mike Hargrove ...... Rangers | 1659 ... 5/28/75 .. Boog Powell ........ Indians |
| 1610 ... 4/24/75 .. Roy Howell .......... Rangers | 1660 ... 6/1/75 .... Tom Shopay .......... Orioles |
| 1611 ... 4/24/75 .. Willie Davis .......... Rangers | 1661 ... 6/1/75 .... Al Bumbry .............. Orioles |
| 1612 ... 4/24/75 .. Jeff Burroughs ..... Rangers | 1662 ... 6/1/75 .... Lee May ................ Orioles |
| 1613 ... 4/24/75 .. Jim Sundberg ...... Rangers | 1663 ... 6/1/75 .... Ken Singleton ........ Orioles |
| 1614 ... 4/24/75 .. Cesar Tovar ......... Rangers | 1664 ... 6/1/75 .... Al Bumbry .............. Orioles |
| 1615 ... 4/24/75 .. Jeff Burroughs ..... Rangers | 1665 ... 6/1/75 .... Ken Singleton ...... Orioles |
| 1616 ... 5/3/75 .... Jeff Burroughs ..... Rangers | 1666 ... 6/1/75 .... Al Bumbry .............. Orioles |
| 1617 ... 5/3/75 .... Roy Howell .......... Rangers | 1667 ... 6/1/75 .... Mark Belanger ....... Orioles |
| 1618 ... 5/3/75 .... Willie Davis .......... Rangers | 1668 ... 6/1/75 .... Bobby Grich .......... Orioles |
| 1619 ... 5/3/75 .... Lenny Randle ........ Rangers | 1669 ... 6/6/75 .... Bill Sharp ............ Brewers |
| 1620 ... 5/3/75 .... Roy Smalley ........ Rangers | 1670 ... 6/6/75 .... George Scott ....... Brewers |
| 1621 ... 5/3/75 .... Cesar Tovar ......... Rangers | 1671 ... 6/6/75 .... Bill Sharp ............ Brewers |
| 1622 ... 5/3/75 .... Willie Davis .......... Rangers | 1672 ... 6/6/75 .... Kurt Bevacqua ..... Brewers |
| 1623 ... 5/3/75 .... Mike Hargrove ...... Rangers | 1673 ... 6/6/75 .... Robin Yount ....... Brewers |
| 1624 ... 5/3/75 .... Joe Lovitto .......... Rangers | 1674 ... 6/6/75 .... Sixto Lezcano ....... Brewers |
| 1625 ... 5/8/75 .... Bill North ................ A's | 1675 ... 6/10/75 ... Elliott Maddox ..... Yankees |
| 1626 ... 5/8/75 .... Bert Campaneris .......... A's | 1676 ... 6/10/75 ... Roy White ........... Yankees |
| 1627 ... 5/8/75 .... Joe Rudi ...................... A's | 1677 ... 6/10/75 .. Chris Chambliss .. Yankees |
| 1628 ... 5/8/75 .... Larry Haney .............. A's | 1678 ... 6/10/75 .. Ed Herrmann ....... Yankees |
| 1629 ... 5/8/75 .... Gene Tenace ............. A's | 1679 ... 6/10/75 .. Sandy Alomar ...... Yankees |
| 1630 ... 5/8/75 .... Claudell Washington .... A's | 1680 ... 6/14/75 .. Sixto Lezcano ,..... Brewers |
| 1631 ... 5/8/75 .... Joe Rudi ...................... A's | 1681 ... 6/14/75 .. Gorman Thomas .. Brewers |
| 1632 ... 5/8/75 .... Billy Williams ................ A's | 1682 ... 6/14/75 ..Robin Yount ......... Brewers |
| 1633 ... 5/8/75 .... Bill North ................ A's | 1683 ... 6/14/75 .. Tim Johnson ....... Brewers |
| 1634 ... 5/8/75 .... Charlie Sands .............. A's | 1684 ... 6/14/75 .. Gorman Thomas .. Brewers |
| 1635 ... 5/13/75 .. Graig Nettles ....... Yankees | 1685 ... 6/14/75 .. Sixto Lezcano ...... Brewers |
| 1636 ... 5/13/75 .. Sandy Alomar ..... Yankees | 1686 ... 6/14/75 .. George Scott ....... Brewers |
| 1637 ... 5/13/75 .. Bobby Bonds ....... Yankees | 1687 ... 6/14/75 .. Hank Aaron .......... Brewers |
| 1638 ... 5/13/75 .. Chris Chambliss .. Yankees | 1688 ... 6/14/75 .. Darrell Porter ....... Brewers |
| 1639 ... 5/13/75 .. Fred Stanley ....... Yankees | 1689 ... 6/14/75 .. Pedro Garcia ........ Brewers |
| 1640 ... 5/13/75 .. Elliott Maddox ..... Yankees | 1690 ... 6/14/75 .. Tim Johnson ........ Brewers |
| 1641 ... 5/13/75 .. Elliott Maddox ..... Yankees | 1691 ... 6/14/75 .. Robin Yount ........ Brewers |
| 1642 ... 5/18/75 .. Ken Singleton ........ Orioles | 1692 ... 6/18/75 .. George Brett .......... Royals |
| 1643 ... 5/18/75 .. Mark Belanger ...... Orioles | 1693 ... 6/18/75 .. Amos Otis .............. Royals |
| 1644 ... 5/18/75 .. Al Bumbry .............. Orioles | 1694 ... 6/29/75 .. Phil Garner .................. A's |
| 1645 ... 5/18/75 .. Dave Duncan ......... Orioles | 1695 ... 6/29/75 .. Gene Tenace ............. A's |
| 1646 ... 5/18/75 .. Al Bumbry .............. Orioles | 1696 ... 6/29/75 .. Claudell Washington .... A's |
| 1647 ... 5/23/75 .. Jim Rice .............. Red Sox | 1697 ... 6/29/75 .. Reggie Jackson ........... A's |
| 1648 ... 5/23/75 .. Dwight Evans ...... Red Sox | 1698 ... 7/3/75 .... Eric Soderholm ........ Twins |
| 1649 ... 5/23/75 .. Rico Petrocelli .... Red Sox | 1699 ... 7/3/75 .... Rod Carew ............... Twins |
| 1650 ... 5/23/75 .. Dwight Evans ...... Red Sox | 1700 ... 7/3/75 .... Jerry Terrell ............. Twins |

| | | | |
|---|---|---|---|
| 1701 ... 7/3/75 .... Lyman Bostock ........ Twins | 1751 ... 8/24/75 .. Thurman Munson Yankees |
| 1702 ... 7/3/75 .... Glenn Borgmann ..... Twins | 1752 ... 8/24/75 .. Graig Nettles ....... Yankees |
| 1703 ... 7/3/75 .... Dan Ford .................. Twins | 1753 ... 8/24/75 .. Walt Williams ...... Yankees |
| 1704 ... 7/3/75 .... Steve Braun .............. Twins | 1754 ... 8/24/75 .. Sandy Alomar ..... Yankees |
| 1705 ... 7/3/75 .... Tom Kelly ................Twins | 1755 ... 8/24/75 .. Thurman Munson Yankees |
| 1706 ... 7/8/75 .... Ken Singleton ........ Orioles | 1756 ... 8/24/75 .. Rich Coggins ...... Yankees |
| 1707 ... 7/8/75 .... Bobby Grich ........... Orioles | 1757 ... 8/24/75 .. Sandy Alomar ..... Yankees |
| 1708 ... 7/8/75 .... Ellie Hendricks ...... Orioles | 1758 ... 8/24/75 .. Ed Herrmann ....... Yankees |
| 1709 ... 7/8/75 .... Lee May ................. Orioles | 1759 ... 4/10/76 .. Gene Tenace ............... A's |
| 1710 ... 7/8/75 .... Paul Blair ............... Orioles | 1760 ... 4/10/76 .. Phil Garner .................... A's |
| 1711 ... 7/12/75 .... Duane Kuiper ........ Indians | 1761 ... 4/10/76 .. Claudell Washington .... A's |
| 1712 ... 7/12/75 .... Boog Powell .......... Indians | 1762 ... 4/10/76 .. Gene Tenace ............... A's |
| 1713 ... 7/12/75 .... Buddy Bell ............. Indians | 1763 ... 4/10/76 .. Claudell Washington .... A's |
| 1714 ... 7/12/75 .... John Lowenstein ... Indians | 1764 ... 4/10/76 .. Don Baylor .................... A's |
| 1715 ... 7/12/75 .. Rick Manning ........ Indians | 1765 ... 4/10/76 .. Sal Bando ...................... A's |
| 1716 ... 7/12/75 .... Buddy Bell ............. Indians | 1766 ... 4/15/76 .. Fran Healy ............. Royals |
| 1717 ... 7/18/75 .. Bobby Darwin ...... Brewers | 1767 ... 4/15/76 .. Amos Otis ............. Royals |
| 1718 ... 7/18/75 .. Charlie Moore ....... Brewers | 1768 ... 4/15/76 .. George Brett ......... Royals |
| 1719 ... 7/18/75 .. Bobby Darwin ...... Brewers | 1769 ... 4/15/76 .. Fran Healy ............. Royals |
| 1720 ... 7/18/75 .. Charlie Moore ....... Brewers | 1770 ... 4/15/76 .. Jim Wohlford .......... Royals |
| 1721 ... 7/18/75 .. Sixto Lezcano ...... Brewers | 1771 ... 4/15/76 .. Frank White ........... Royals |
| 1722 ... 7/18/75 .. Don Money ............ Brewers | 1772 ... 4/15/76 .. Amos Otis ............. Royals |
| 1723 ... 7/22/75 .. Don Baylor ............. Orioles | 1773 ... 4/15/76 .. Fran Healy ............. Royals |
| 1724 ... 7/22/75 .. Mark Belanger ....... Orioles | 1774 ... 4/15/76 .. Jamie Quirk ............ Royals |
| 1725 ... 7/26/75 .. John Briggs .............. Twins | 1775 ... 4/20/76 .. Royle Stillman ........ Orioles |
| 1726 ... 7/26/75 .. Dan Ford .................. Twins | 1776 ... 4/20/76 .. Brooks Robinson ... Orioles |
| 1727 ... 7/30/75 .. Jorge Orta ......... White Sox | 1777 ... 4/20/76 .. Al Bumbry ............. Orioles |
| 1728 ... 7/30/75 .. Carlos May ....... White Sox | 1778 ... 4/20/76 .. Royle Stillman ........ Orioles |
| 1729 ... 7/30/75 .. Ken Henderson . White Sox | 1779 ... 4/20/76 .. Mark Belanger ....... Orioles |
| 1730 ... 7/30/75 .. Bill Melton ......... White Sox | 1780 ... 4/20/76 .. Al Bumbry ............. Orioles |
| 1731 ... 7/30/75 .. Bucky Dent ........ White Sox | 1781 ... 4/20/76 .. Ellie Hendricks ....... Orioles |
| 1732 ... 8/3/75 .... Jeff Burroughs ..... Rangers | 1782 ... 4/20/76 .. Brooks Robinson .... Orioles |
| 1733 ... 8/3/75 .... Toby Harrah .......... Rangers | 1783 ... 4/20/76 .. Al Bumbry ............. Orioles |
| 1734 ... 8/3/75 .... Tom Grieve .......... Rangers | 1784 ... 4/20/76 .. Paul Blair ............... Orioles |
| 1735 ... 8/3/75 .... Roy Howell .......... Rangers | 1785 ... 4/20/76 .. Bobby Grich ........... Orioles |
| 1736 ... 8/3/75 .... Jim Sundberg ...... Rangers | 1786 ... 4/20/76 .. Ken Singleton ........ Orioles |
| 1737 ... 8/3/75 .... Dave Moates ....... Rangers | 1787 ... 4/27/76 .. Tommy Harper ....... Orioles |
| 1738 ... 8/3/75 .... Lenny Randle ....... Rangers | 1788 ... 4/27/76 .. Paul Blair ............... Orioles |
| 1739 ... 8/3/75 .... Tom Grieve .......... Rangers | 1789 ... 4/27/76 .. Andres Mora .......... Orioles |
| 1740 ... 8/3/75 .... Jim Sundberg ...... Rangers | 1790 ... 4/27/76 .. Doug DeCinces ..... Orioles |
| 1741 ... 8/8/75 .... Fred Stanley ........ Yankees | 1791 ... 4/27/76 .. Paul Blair ............... Orioles |
| 1742 ... 8/20/75 .. Bob Mitchell ......... Brewers | 1792 ... 4/27/76 .. Andres Mora .......... Orioles |
| 1743 ... 8/20/75 .. Bill Sharp ............. Brewers | 1793 ... 4/27/76 .. Ken Singleton ........ Orioles |
| 1744 ... 8/20/75 .. Kurt Bevacqua ..... Brewers | 1794 ... 4/27/76 .. Ellie Hendricks ....... Orioles |
| 1745 ... 8/20/75 .. Gorman Thomas .. Brewers | 1795 ... 4/27/76 .. Mark Belanger ....... Orioles |
| 1746 ... 8/20/75 .. Mike Hegan .......... Brewers | 1796 ... 4/27/76 .. Andres Mora .......... Orioles |
| 1747 ... 8/20/75 .. Kurt Bevacqua ..... Brewers | 1797 ... 4/27/76 .. Mark Belanger ....... Orioles |
| 1748 ... 8/20/75 .. Bob Mitchell ......... Brewers | 1798 ... 5/1/76 .... Duane Kuiper ........ Indians |
| 1749 ... 8/20/75 .. Gorman Thomas .. Brewers | 1799 ... 5/1/76 .... Charlie Spikes ....... Indians |
| 1750 ... 8/20/75 .. Bob Sheldon ........ Brewers | 1800 ... 5/1/76 .... Alan Ashby ............. Indians |

| | | | |
|---|---|---|---|
| 1801 ... 5/1/76 .... Buddy Bell ............. Indians | 1851 ... 6/6/76 .... Fred Lynn ............ Red Sox |
| 1802 ... 5/1/76 .... Rick Manning ......... Indians | 1852 ... 6/6/76 .... Rick Burleson ...... Red Sox |
| 1803 ... 5/1/76 .... Duane Kuiper ........ Indians | 1853 ... 6/6/76 .... Jim Rice .............. Red Sox |
| 1804 ... 5/5/76 .... Roy White ........... Yankees | 1854 ... 6/11/76 .. Alex Johnson .......... Tigers |
| 1805 ... 5/5/76 .... Lou Piniella ......... Yankees | 1855 ... 6/11/76 .. Jason Thompson .... Tigers |
| 1806 ... 5/5/76 .... Graig Nettles ....... Yankees | 1856 ... 6/11/76 .. Ben Oglivie .............. Tigers |
| 1807 ... 5/5/76 .... Jim Mason ........... Yankees | 1857 ... 6/11/76 .. Ron LeFlore ............. Tigers |
| 1808 ... 5/5/76 .... Roy White ........... Yankees | 1858 ... 6/11/76 .. Pedro Garcia ........... Tigers |
| 1809 ... 5/5/76 .... Lou Piniella ......... Yankees | 1859 ... 6/11/76 .. Alex Johnson .......... Tigers |
| 1810 ... 5/5/76 .... Graig Nettles ....... Yankees | 1860 ... 6/11/76 .. Chuck Scrivener ..... Tigers |
| 1811 ... 5/5/76 .... Willie Randolph ... Yankees | 1861 ... 6/11/76 .. Ron LeFlore ............. Tigers |
| 1812 ... 5/10/76 .. Bill North ...................... A's | 1862 ... 6/11/76 .. Alex Johnson .......... Tigers |
| 1813 ... 5/10/76 .. Sal Bando .................... A's | 1863 ... 6/15/76 .. George Scott ....... Brewers |
| 1814 ... 5/10/76 .. Billy Williams ................ A's | 1864 ... 6/15/76 .. Jim Rosario ......... Brewers |
| 1815 ... 5/10/76 .. Phil Garner ................... A's | 1865 ... 6/15/76 .. Gary Sutherland ... Brewers |
| 1816 ... 5/10/76 .. Joe Rudi ...................... A's | 1866 ... 6/15/76 .. Jim Rosario ......... Brewers |
| 1817 ... 5/10/76 .. Sal Bando ................... A's | 1867 ... 6/15/76 .. Bernie Carbo ........ Brewers |
| 1818 ... 5/10/76 .. Phil Garner ................... A's | 1868 ... 6/15/76 .. Robin Yount ......... Brewers |
| 1819 ... 5/10/76 .. Bill North ...................... A's | 1869 ... 6/15/76 .. Darrell Porter ....... Brewers |
| 1820 ... 5/10/76 .. Sal Bando ................... A's | 1870 ... 6/15/76 .. Hank Aaron ......... Brewers |
| 1821 ... 5/10/76 .. Billy Williams ................ A's | 1871 ... 6/15/76 .. Don Money ......... Brewers |
| 1822 ... 5/10/76 .. Phil Garner ................... A's | 1872 ... 6/19/76 .. Rick Miller ............ Red Sox |
| 1823 ... 5/10/76 .. Billy Williams ................ A's | 1873 ... 6/19/76 .. Rick Miller ............ Red Sox |
| 1824 ... 5/14/76 .. Lyman Bostock ........ Twins | 1874 ... 6/19/76 .. Dwight Evans ...... Red Sox |
| 1825 ... 5/14/76 .. Dan Ford .................. Twins | 1875 ... 6/19/76 .. Carl Yastrzemski . Red Sox |
| 1826 ... 5/14/76 .. Danny Thompson .... Twins | 1876 ... 6/19/76 .. Rico Petrocelli ..... Red Sox |
| 1827 ... 5/14/76 .. Rod Carew ............... Twins | 1877 ... 6/19/76 .. Dwight Evans ...... Red Sox |
| 1828 ... 5/14/76 .. Dan Ford .................. Twins | 1878 ... 6/19/76 .. Fred Lynn ............ Red Sox |
| 1829 ... 5/18/76 .. Rich Coggins .... White Sox | 1879 ... 6/19/76 .. Jim Rice .............. Red Sox |
| 1830 ... 5/18/76 .. Jorge Orta ......... White Sox | 1880 ... 6/19/76 .. Rico Petrocelli ..... Red Sox |
| 1831 ... 5/18/76 .. Jack Brohamer . White Sox | 1881 ... 6/19/76 .. Rick Miller ............ Red Sox |
| 1832 ... 5/18/76 .. Rich Coggins .... White Sox | 1882 ... 6/19/76 .. Dwight Evans ...... Red Sox |
| 1833 ... 5/18/76 .. Jim Spencer ...... White Sox | 1883 ... 6/19/76 .. Jim Rice .............. Red Sox |
| 1834 ... 5/18/76 .. Bill Stein ........... White Sox | 1884 ... 6/19/76 .. Carlton Fisk ......... Red Sox |
| 1835 ... 5/18/76 .. Jorge Orta ......... White Sox | 1885 ... 6/19/76 .. Rico Petrocelli ..... Red Sox |
| 1836 ... 5/18/76 .. Bill Stein ............ White Sox | 1886 ... 6/19/76 .. Rick Burleson ...... Red Sox |
| 1837 ... 5/18/76 .. Rich Coggins .... White Sox | 1887 ... 6/26/76 .. George Brett ......... Royals |
| 1838 ... 5/23/76 .. Jeff Burroughs ..... Rangers | 1888 ... 6/26/76 .. Fred Patek ............. Royals |
| 1839 ... 5/28/76 .. Fred Patek ............ Royals | 1889 ... 6/26/76 .. Frank White ........... Royals |
| 1840 ... 5/28/76 .. Amos Otis .............. Royals | 1890 ... 6/26/76 .. Amos Otis .............. Royals |
| 1841 ... 5/28/76 .. George Brett .......... Royals | 1891 ... 6/26/76 .. Tony Solaita ........... Royals |
| 1842 ... 5/28/76 .. Fred Patek ............. Royals | 1892 ... 6/26/76 .. Bob Stinson ........... Royals |
| 1843 ... 5/28/76 .. Amos Otis ............. Royals | 1893 ... 6/26/76 .. Frank White ........... Royals |
| 1844 ... 6/1/76 .... Tony Oliva .............. Twins | 1894 ... 6/26/76 .. Gerorge Brett ......... Royals |
| 1845 ... 6/1/76 .... Lyman Bostock ........ Twins | 1895 ... 7/3/76 .... Roy Smalley ............ Twins |
| 1846 ... 6/1/76 .... Craig Kusick ............ Twins | 1896 ... 7/3/76 .... Rod Carew ............... Twins |
| 1847 ... 6/1/76 .... Jerry Terrell ............. Twins | 1897 ... 7/3/76 .... Larry Hisle .............. Twins |
| 1848 ... 6/1/76 .... Dan Ford .................. Twins | 1898 ... 7/3/76 .... Bob Randall ............. Twins |
| 1849 ... 6/1/76 .... Lyman Bostock ........ Twins | 1899 ... 7/3/76 .... Roy Smalley ............ Twins |
| 1850 ... 6/1/76 .... Larry Hisle ................ Twins | 1900 ... 7/3/76 .... Lyman Bostock ........ Twins |

| | | | |
|---|---|---|---|
| 1901 ... 7/3/76 .... Larry Hisle ............... Twins | 1951 ... 7/30/76 .. Jerry Hairston ... White Sox |
| 1902 ... 7/3/76 .... Lyman Bostock ........ Twins | 1952 ... 7/30/76 .. Ralph Garr ........ White Sox |
| 1903 ... 7/7/76 .... George Hendrick ... Indians | 1953 ... 8/4/76 .... Tom Grieve .......... Rangers |
| 1004 ... 7/7/76 .... Buddy Boll ............. Indiane | 1954 ... 8/4/76 .... Lenny Randle ...... Rangers |
| 1005 ... 7/7/76 .... Larvell Blanks ........ Indians | 1955 ... 8/4/76 .... Juan Beniquez ..... Rangers |
| 1906 ... 7/7/76 .... Rico Carty .............. Indians | 1956 ... 8/4/76 .... Jeff Burroughs ..... Rangers |
| 1907 ... 7/7/76 .... Duane Kuiper ........ Indians | 1957 ... 8/4/76 .... Lenny Randle ...... Rangers |
| 1908 ... 7/7/76 .... Larvell Blanks ........ Indians | 1958 ... 8/8/76 .... Bill North ...................... A's |
| 1909 ... 7/7/76 .... Rick Manning ........ Indians | 1959 ... 8/8/76 .... Jeff Newman ................ A's |
| 1910 ... 7/7/76 .... George Hendrick ... Indians | 1960 ... 8/8/76 .... Bill North ...................... A's |
| 1911 ... 7/7/76 .... Orlando Gonzalez . Indians | 1961 ... 8/8/76 .... Bert Campaneris .......... A's |
| 1912 ... 7/7/76 .... Duane Kuiper ........ Indians | 1962 ... 8/8/76 .... Jeff Newman ................ A's |
| 1913 ... 7/11/76 .. Bobby Grich ........... Orioles | 1963 ... 8/8/76 .... Joe Rudi ...................... A's |
| 1914 ... 7/11/76 .. Lee May ................. Orioles | 1964 ... 8/8/76 .... Gene Tenace .............. A's |
| 1915 ... 7/11/76 .. Bobby Grich ........... Orioles | 1965 ... 8/8/76 .... Billy Williams ................ A's |
| 1916 ... 7/11/76 .. Ken Singleton ........ Orioles | 1966 ... 8/12/76 .. Denny Doyle ........ Red Sox |
| 1917 ... 7/11/76 .. Brooks Robinson ... Orioles | 1967 ... 8/12/76 .. Carl Yastrzemski . Red Sox |
| 1918 ... 7/11/76 .. Rick Dempsey ....... Orioles | 1968 ... 8/12/76 .. Jim Rice ............. Red Sox |
| 1919 ... 7/11/76 .. Tim Nordbrook ....... Orioles | 1969 ... 8/12/76 .. Cecil Cooper ....... Red Sox |
| 1920 ... 7/11/76 .. Ken Singleton ........ Orioles | 1970 ... 8/12/76 .. Carlton Fisk ......... Red Sox |
| 1921 ... 7/11/76 .. Rick Dempsey ....... Orioles | 1971 ... 8/12/76 .. Butch Hobson ...... Red Sox |
| 1922 ... 7/11/76 .. Tony Muser ........... Orioles | 1972 ... 8/12/76 .. Rick Burleson ...... Red Sox |
| 1923 ... 7/11/76 .. Brooks Robinson ... Orioles | 1973 ... 8/12/76 .. Jim Rice ............. Red Sox |
| 1924 ... 7/11/76 .. Paul Blair .............. Orioles | 1974 ... 8/12/76 .. Cecil Cooper ....... Red Sox |
| 1925 ... 7/16/76 .. Terry Crowley ........ Orioles | 1975 ... 8/18/76 .. Ron LeFlore ............ Tigers |
| 1926 ... 7/16/76 .. Dave Duncan ......... Orioles | 1976 ... 8/18/76 .. Willie Horton ........... Tigers |
| 1927 ... 7/16/76 .. Tony Muser ........... Orioles | 1977 ... 8/18/76 .. Jason Thompson .... Tigers |
| 1928 ... 7/16/76 .. Reggie Jackson ..... Orioles | 1978 ... 8/18/76 .. Aurelio Rodriguez ... Tigers |
| 1929 ... 7/16/76 .. Dave Duncan ......... Orioles | 1979 ... 8/18/76 .. Tom Veryzer ........... Tigers |
| 1930 ... 7/16/76 .. Ken Singleton ........ Orioles | 1980 ... 8/18/76 .. Willie Horton ........... Tigers |
| 1931 ... 7/16/76 .. Reggie Jackson ..... Orioles | 1981 ... 8/18/76 .. Jason Thompson .... Tigers |
| 1932 ... 7/16/76 .. Terry Crowley ........ Orioles | 1982 ... 8/18/76 .. Ron LeFlore ............ Tigers |
| 1933 ... 7/21/76 .. Rick Manning ........ Indians | 1983 ... 8/18/76 .. Rusty Staub ............ Tigers |
| 1934 ... 7/21/76 .. George Hendrick ... Indians | 1984 ... 8/18/76 .. Jason Thompson .... Tigers |
| 1935 ... 7/21/76 .. Rick Manning ........ Indians | 1985 ... 8/18/76 .. John Wockenfuss .... Tigers |
| 1936 ... 7/26/76 .. Tom Poquette ........ Royals | 1986 ... 8/18/76 .. Ben Oglivie .............. Tigers |
| 1937 ... 7/26/76 .. Jamie Quirk ........... Royals | 1987 ... 8/18/76 .. Ron LeFlore ............ Tigers |
| 1938 ... 7/26/76 .. Frank White ........... Royals | 1988 ... 8/18/76 .. Willie Horton ........... Tigers |
| 1939 ... 7/26/76 .. Tom Poquette ........ Royals | 1989 ... 8/18/76 .. Tom Veryzer ........... Tigers |
| 1940 ... 7/26/76 .. Jamie Quirk ........... Royals | 1990 ... 8/18/76 .. Ron LeFlore ............ Tigers |
| 1941 ... 7/26/76 .. Fred Patek ............. Royals | 1991 ... 8/18/76 .. Willie Horton ........... Tigers |
| 1942 ... 7/26/76 .. Frank White ........... Royals | 1992 ... 8/23/76 .. Denny Doyle ........ Red Sox |
| 1943 ... 7/30/76 .. Jim Spencer ...... White Sox | 1993 ... 8/23/76 .. Fred Lynn ............ Red Sox |
| 1944 ... 7/30/76 .. Jack Brohamer . White Sox | 1994 ... 8/23/76 .. Carl Yastrzemski . Red Sox |
| 1945 ... 7/30/76 .. Bucky Dent ...... White Sox | 1995 ... 8/23/76 .. Cecil Cooper ....... Red Sox |
| 1946 ... 7/30/76 .. Jim Essian ........ White Sox | 1996 ... 8/23/76 .. Denny Doyle ........ Red Sox |
| 1947 ... 7/30/76 .. Jerry Hairston ... White Sox | 1997 ... 8/23/76 .. Fred Lynn ............ Red Sox |
| 1948 ... 7/30/76 .. Jorge Orta ......... White Sox | 1998 ... 8/23/76 .. Cecil Cooper ....... Red Sox |
| 1949 ... 7/30/76 .. Bill Stein ........... White Sox | 1999 ... 8/28/76 .. Willie Randolph ... Yankees |
| 1950 ... 7/30/76 .. Jorge Orta ......... White Sox | 2000 ... 8/31/76 .. Ron LeFlore ............ Tigers |

| | | | |
|---|---|---|---|
| 2001 ... 8/31/76 .. Dan Meyer .............. Tigers | 2051 ... 9/25/76 .. Lyman Bostock ........ Twins |
| 2002 ... 8/31/76 .. Rusty Staub ............ Tigers | 2052 ... 9/25/76 .. Butch Wynegar ........ Twins |
| 2003 ... 8/31/76 .. Pedro Garcia ........... Tigers | 2053 ... 9/25/76 .. Larry Hisle ............... Twins |
| 2004 ... 8/31/76 .. Ron LeFlore ............. Tigers | 2054 ... 9/25/76 .. Mike Cubbage .......... Twins |
| 2005 ... 8/31/76 .. Ben Oglivie ............. Tigers | 2055 ... 9/25/76 .. Roy Smalley ........... Twins |
| 2006 ... 8/31/76 .. Jason Thompson .... Tigers | 2056 ... 9/25/76 .. Butch Wynegar ........ Twins |
| 2007 ... 8/31/76 .. Dan Meyer .............. Tigers | 2057 ... 9/25/76 .. Dan Ford .................. Twins |
| 2008 ... 8/31/76 .. Phil Mankowski ....... Tigers | 2058 ... 9/25/76 .. Bob Randall ............. Twins |
| 2009 ... 8/31/76 .. Ron LeFlore ............. Tigers | 2059 ... 9/25/76 .. Steve Braun ............. Twins |
| 2010 ... 8/31/76 .. Ron LeFlore ............. Tigers | 2060 ... 9/25/76 .. Roy Smalley ............ Twins |
| 2011 ... 9/5/76 .... Bill North ...................... A's | 2061 ... 9/29/76 .. Alan Bannister .. White Sox |
| 2012 ... 9/5/76 .... Claudell Washington .... A's | 2062 ... 9/29/76 .. Bill Stein ............ White Sox |
| 2013 ... 9/5/76 .... Joe Rudi .................... A's | 2063 ... 9/29/76 .. Alan Bannister .. White Sox |
| 2014 ... 9/5/76 .... Willie McCovey ............. A's | 2064 ... 9/29/76 .. Chet Lemon ...... White Sox |
| 2015 ... 9/5/76 .... Don Baylor .................. A's | 2065 ... 9/29/76 .. Jim Essian ....... White Sox |
| 2016 ... 9/5/76 .... Bert Campaneris .......... A's | 2066 ... 9/29/76 .. Ralph Garr ........ White Sox |
| 2017 ... 9/5/76 .... Claudell Washington .... A's | 2067 ... 9/29/76 .. Jorge Orta ......... White Sox |
| 2018 ... 9/5/76 .... Sal Bando .................. A's | 2068 ... 9/29/76 .. Chet Lemon ...... White Sox |
| 2019 ... 9/10/76 .. Bill Stein ............ White Sox | 2069 ... 9/29/76 .. Bucky Dent ....... White Sox |
| 2020 ... 9/10/76 .. Sam Ewing ....... White Sox | 2070 ... 9/29/76 .. Alan Bannister .. White Sox |
| 2021 ... 9/10/76 .. Chet Lemon ...... White Sox | 2071 ... 9/29/76 .. Jerry Hairston ... White Sox |
| 2022 ... 9/10/76 .. Bucky Dent ....... White Sox | 2072 ... 10/3/76 .. Dennis Walling ............. A's |
| 2023 ... 9/10/76 .. Jim Essian ....... White Sox | 2073 ... 10/3/76 .. Wayne Gross ............... A's |
| 2024 ... 9/10/76 .. Jim Spencer ...... White Sox | 2074 ... 10/3/76 .. Jim Holt ....................... A's |
| 2025 ... 9/10/76 .. Sam Ewing ....... White Sox | 2075 ... 10/3/76 .. Matt Alexander .......... A's |
| 2026 ... 9/10/76 .. Chet Lemon ...... White Sox | 2076 ... 10/3/76 .. Jeff Newman ................ A's |
| 2027 ... 9/10/76 .. Alan Bannister .. White Sox | 2077 ... 10/3/76 .. Ron Fairly ................... A's |
| 2028 ... 9/10/76 .. Ralph Garr ........ White Sox | 2078 ... 10/3/76 .. Ken McMullen .............. A's |
| 2029 ... 9/10/76 .. Bill Stein ............ White Sox | 2079 ... 10/3/76 .. Matt Alexander .......... A's |
| 2030 ... 9/10/76 .. Jorge Orta ......... White Sox | 2080 ... 10/3/76 .. Jeff Newman ................ A's |
| 2031 ... 9/10/76 .. Sam Ewing ....... White Sox | 2081 ... 10/3/76 .. Tommy Sandt ............... A's |
| 2032 ... 9/10/76 .. Ralph Garr ........ White Sox | 2082 ... 10/3/76 .. Dennis Walling ............. A's |
| 2033 ... 9/10/76 .. Bill Stein ............ White Sox | 2083 ... 10/3/76 .. Jim Holt ....................... A's |
| 2034 ... 9/10/76 .. Jim Spencer ...... White Sox | 2084 ... 10/3/76 .. Bill North ...................... A's |
| 2035 ... 9/10/76 .. Jorge Orta ......... White Sox | 2085 ... 10/3/76 .. Phil Garner .................. A's |
| 2036 ... 9/10/76 .. Sam Ewing ....... White Sox | 2086 ... 4/7/77 .... Dave Collins ........ Mariners |
| 2037 ... 9/15/76 .. Hal McRae ............. Royals | 2087 ... 4/7/77 .... Lee Stanton ......... Mariners |
| 2038 ... 9/15/76 .. Bob Stinson ........... Royals | 2088 ... 4/7/77 .... Craig Reynolds ... Mariners |
| 2039 ... 9/15/76 .. Fred Patek ............. Royals | 2089 ... 4/7/77 .... Dave Collins ........ Mariners |
| 2040 ... 9/15/76 .. Hal McRae ............. Royals | 2090 ... 4/7/77 .... Bill Stein .............. Mariners |
| 2041 ... 9/15/76 .. Al Cowens .............. Royals | 2091 ... 4/7/77 .... Lee Stanton ......... Mariners |
| 2042 ... 9/15/76 .. Frank White ............ Royals | 2092 ... 4/11/77 .. Rodney Scott ............... A's |
| 2043 ... 9/15/76 .. Hal McRae ............. Royals | 2093 ... 4/11/77 .. Tony Armas .................. A's |
| 2044 ... 9/15/76 .. Al Cowens .............. Royals | 2094 ... 4/11/77 .. Rodney Scott ............... A's |
| 2045 ... 9/15/76 .. Tom Poquette ......... Royals | 2095 ... 4/11/77 .. Mitchell Page ............... A's |
| 2046 ... 9/20/76 .. Lenny Randle ...... Rangers | 2096 ... 4/11/77 .. Wayne Gross ............... A's |
| 2047 ... 9/20/76 .. Jim Sundberg ...... Rangers | 2097 ... 4/11/77 .. Tony Armas .................. A's |
| 2048 ... 9/20/76 .. Jeff Burroughs ..... Rangers | 2098 ... 4/11/77 .. Rob Picciolo ................. A's |
| 2049 ... 9/20/76 .. Gene Clines ......... Rangers | 2099 ... 4/11/77 .. Bill North ...................... A's |
| 2050 ... 9/25/76 .. Rod Carew ............... Twins | 2100 ... 4/11/77 .. Rich McKinney ............. A's |

| | | | |
|---|---|---|---|
| 2101 ... 4/11/77 .. Jeff Newman ................ A's | 2151 ... 5/10/77 .. Fred Patek ............. Royals |
| 2102 ... 4/11/77 .. Wayne Gross .............. A's | 2152 ... 5/10/77 .. Darrell Porter .......... Royals |
| 2103 ... 4/15/77 .. Dave Collins ........ Mariners | 2153 ... 5/10/77 .. Amos Otis .............. Royals |
| 2104 ... 4/15/77 .. Bob Stinson ......... Mariners | 2154 ... 5/10/77 .. Pete Lacock ........... Royals |
| 2105 ... 4/15/77 .. Ruppert Jones ..... Mariners | 2155 ... 5/14/77 .. Reggie Jackson .. Yankees |
| 2106 ... 4/15/77 .. Dan Meyer ......... Mariners | 2156 ... 5/14/77 .. Chris Chambliss .. Yankees |
| 2107 ... 4/15/77 .. Carlos Lopez ...... Mariners | 2157 ... 5/14/77 .. Roy White .......... Yankees |
| 2108 ... 4/15/77 .. Carlos Lopez ....... Mariners | 2158 ... 5/14/77 .. Graig Nettles ....... Yankees |
| 2109 ... 4/15/77 .. Ruppert Jones ..... Mariners | 2159 ... 5/14/77 .. Carlos May .......... Yankees |
| 2110 ... 4/15/77 .. Bill Stein .............. Mariners | 2160 ... 5/14/77 .. Bucky Dent .......... Yankees |
| 2111 ... 4/20/77 .. Alan Bannister .. White Sox | 2161 ... 5/14/77 .. Reggie Jackson .. Yankees |
| 2112 ... 4/20/77 .. Tim Nordbrook .. White Sox | 2162 ... 5/14/77 .. Bucky Dent .......... Yankees |
| 2113 ... 4/20/77 .. Richie Zisk ........ White Sox | 2163 ... 5/19/77 .. Dan Ford ................. Twins |
| 2114 ... 4/20/77 .. Oscar Gamble .. White Sox | 2164 ... 5/19/77 .. Butch Wynegar ........ Twins |
| 2115 ... 4/20/77 .. Chet Lemon ..... White Sox | 2165 ... 5/19/77 .. Rod Carew .............. Twins |
| 2116 ... 4/20/77 .. Chet Lemon ..... White Sox | 2166 ... 5/19/77 .. Roy Smalley ............ Twins |
| 2117 ... 4/25/77 .. Dick Allen .................... A's | 2167 ... 5/19/77 .. Rod Carew .............. Twins |
| 2118 ... 4/25/77 .. Rob Picciolo ............... A's | 2168 ... 5/19/77 .. Lyman Bostock ........ Twins |
| 2119 ... 4/25/77 .. Rodney Scott ............... A's | 2169 ... 5/19/77 .. Rich Chiles ............. Twins |
| 2120 ... 4/25/77 .. Mitchell Page ............... A's | 2170 ... 5/19/77 .. Dan Ford ................. Twins |
| 2121 ... 4/30/77 .. Mark Belanger ....... Orioles | 2171 ... 5/19/77 .. Roy Smalley ............ Twins |
| 2122 ... 4/30/77 .. Ken Singleton ........ Orioles | 2172 ... 5/19/77 .. Lyman Bostock ........ Twins |
| 2123 ... 4/30/77 .. Larry Harlow ......... Orioles | 2173 ... 5/19/77 .. Larry Hisle .............. Twins |
| 2124 ... 4/30/77 .. Ken Singleton ........ Orioles | 2174 ... 5/19/77 .. Butch Wynegar ........ Twins |
| 2125 ... 4/30/77 .. Lee May ................. Orioles | 2175 ... 5/24/77 .. Tito Fuentes ............ Tigers |
| 2126 ... 4/30/77 .. Eddie Murray ......... Orioles | 2176 ... 5/24/77 .. Rusty Staub ............ Tigers |
| 2127 ... 4/30/77 .. Larry Harlow ......... Orioles | 2177 ... 5/24/77 .. Steve Kemp ............ Tigers |
| 2128 ... 4/30/77 .. Rick Dempsey ....... Orioles | 2178 ... 5/24/77 .. Mickey Stanley ....... Tigers |
| 2129 ... 4/30/77 .. Al Bumbry .............. Orioles | 2179 ... 5/24/77 .. Tito Fuentes ............ Tigers |
| 2130 ... 4/30/77 .. Mark Belanger ....... Orioles | 2180 ... 5/24/77 .. Steve Kemp ............ Tigers |
| 2131 ... 4/30/77 .. Al Bumbry .............. Orioles | 2181 ... 5/24/77 .. Tom Veryzer ........... Tigers |
| 2132 ... 4/30/77 .. Ken Singleton ........ Orioles | 2182 ... 5/24/77 .. Rusty Staub ............ Tigers |
| 2133 ... 4/30/77 .. Larry Harlow ......... Orioles | 2183 ... 5/24/77 .. Steve Kemp ............ Tigers |
| 2134 ... 5/6/77 .... Bernie Carbo ....... Red Sox | 2184 ... 5/24/77 .. Milt May ................... Tigers |
| 2135 ... 5/6/77 .... Denny Doyle ........ Red Sox | 2185 ... 5/24/77 .. Mickey Stanley ....... Tigers |
| 2136 ... 5/6/77 .... George Scott ....... Red Sox | 2186 ... 5/24/77 .. Ron LeFlore ........... Tigers |
| 2137 ... 5/6/77 .... Dwight Evans ...... Red Sox | 2187 ... 5/29/77 .. John Scott ......... Blue Jays |
| 2138 ... 5/6/77 .... Butch Hobson ...... Red Sox | 2188 ... 5/29/77 .. Alan Ashby ........ Blue Jays |
| 2139 ... 5/6/77 .... Steve Dillard ........ Red Sox | 2189 ... 5/29/77 .. Sam Ewing ........ Blue Jays |
| 2140 ... 5/6/77 .... Bernie Carbo ....... Red Sox | 2190 ... 5/29/77 .. Doug Ault .......... Blue Jays |
| 2141 ... 5/6/77 .... Jim Rice .............. Red Sox | 2191 ... 5/29/77 .. Hector Torres ..... Blue Jays |
| 2142 ... 5/6/77 .... Denny Doyle ........ Red Sox | 2192 ... 5/29/77 .. Otto Velez ......... Blue Jays |
| 2143 ... 5/6/77 .... Butch Hobson ...... Red Sox | 2193 ... 5/29/77 .. Sam Ewing ........ Blue Jays |
| 2144 ... 5/6/77 .... Bernie Carbo ....... Red Sox | 2194 ... 5/29/77 .. Doug Ault .......... Blue Jays |
| 2145 ... 5/6/77 .... Denny Doyle ........ Red Sox | 2195 ... 5/29/77 .. Hector Torres ..... Blue Jays |
| 2146 ... 5/6/77 .... Carlton Fisk ......... Red Sox | 2196 ... 5/29/77 .. Otto Velez .......... Blue Jays |
| 2147 ... 5/6/77 .... Dwight Evans ...... Red Sox | 2197 ... 5/29/77 .. Doug Ault .......... Blue Jays |
| 2148 ... 5/6/77 .... Jim Rice .............. Red Sox | 2198 ... 5/29/77 .. Ernie Whitt ........ Blue Jays |
| 2149 ... 5/10/77 .. Tom Poquette ........ Royals | 2199 ... 6/4/77 .... Ron LeFlore ........... Tigers |
| 2150 ... 5/10/77 .. Amos Otis .............. Royals | 2200 ... 6/4/77 .... Jason Thompson .... Tigers |

| | | |
|---|---|---|
| 2201 ... 6/4/77 .... Phil Mankowski ....... Tigers | 2251 ... 6/16/77 .. Rich Chiles .............. Twins |
| 2202 ... 6/4/77 .... Tom Veryzer ........... Tigers | 2252 ... 6/16/77 .. Roy Smalley ............ Twins |
| 2203 ... 6/4/77 .... Tito Fuentes ............. Tigers | 2253 ... 6/21/77 .. Jorge Orta ......... White Sox |
| 2204 ... 6/4/77 .... Tim Corcoran .......... Tigers | 2254 ... 6/21/77 .. Royle Stillman .. White Sox |
| 2205 ... 6/4/77 .... Jason Thompson .... Tigers | 2255 ... 6/21/77 .. Chet Lemon ...... White Sox |
| 2206 ... 6/4/77 .... Ben Oglivie .............. Tigers | 2256 ... 6/21/77 .. Oscar Gamble .. White Sox |
| 2207 ... 6/4/77 .... Tim Corcoran .......... Tigers | 2257 ... 6/21/77 .. Ralph Garr ....... White Sox |
| 2208 ... 6/4/77 .... Tom Veryzer ........... Tigers | 2258 ... 6/21/77 .. Alan Bannister .. White Sox |
| 2209 ... 6/4/77 .... Tito Fuentes ............. Tigers | 2259 ... 6/21/77 .. Jorge Orta ......... White Sox |
| 2210 ... 6/8/77 .... John Scott ........ Blue Jays | 2260 ... 6/21/77 .. Royle Stillman .. White Sox |
| 2211 ... 6/8/77 .... Otto Velez ........ Blue Jays | 2261 ... 6/21/77 .. Chet Lemon ...... White Sox |
| 2212 ... 6/8/77 .... Ron Fairly .......... Blue Jays | 2262 ... 6/25/77 .. Juan Beniquez ... Rangers |
| 2213 ... 6/8/77 .... Al Woods ............ Blue Jays | 2263 ... 6/25/77 .. Ken Henderson ... Rangers |
| 2214 ... 6/8/77 .... Alan Ashby ........ Blue Jays | 2264 ... 6/25/77 .. Bump Wills .......... Rangers |
| 2215 ... 6/8/77 .... Dave McKay ...... Blue Jays | 2265 ... 6/25/77 .. Jim Sundberg ...... Rangers |
| 2216 ... 6/8/77 .... Bob Bailor ......... Blue Jays | 2266 ... 6/25/77 .. Bert Campaneris . Rangers |
| 2217 ... 6/8/77 .... Roy Howell ........ Blue Jays | 2267 ... 6/25/77 .. C. Washington ..... Rangers |
| 2218 ... 6/8/77 .... Otto Velez ........ Blue Jays | 2268 ... 6/25/77 .. Ken Henderson ... Rangers |
| 2219 ... 6/8/77 .... Ron Fairly .......... Blue Jays | 2269 ... 6/25/77 .. Toby Harrah ........ Rangers |
| 2220 ... 6/8/77 .... Al Woods ............ Blue Jays | 2270 ... 6/25/77 .. Bump Wills .......... Rangers |
| 2221 ... 6/8/77 .... Alan Ashby ........ Blue Jays | 2271 ... 6/25/77 .. Jim Sundberg ...... Rangers |
| 2222 ... 6/8/77 .... Dave McKay ...... Blue Jays | 2272 ... 6/25/77 .. C. Washington ..... Rangers |
| 2223 ... 6/8/77 .... Otto Velez ........ Blue Jays | 2273 ... 6/25/77 .. Ken Henderson ... Rangers |
| 2224 ... 6/8/77 .... Al Woods ............ Blue Jays | 2274 ... 6/29/77 .. George Brett .......... Royals |
| 2225 ... 6/8/77 .... Roy Howell ........ Blue Jays | 2275 ... 6/29/77 .. Darrell Porter .......... Royals |
| 2226 ... 6/8/77 .... Otto Velez ........ Blue Jays | 2276 ... 6/29/77 .. Fred Patek ........... Royals |
| 2227 ... 6/8/77 .... Dave McKay ...... Blue Jays | 2277 ... 6/29/77 .. Tom Poquette ........ Royals |
| 2228 ... 6/8/77 .... Ernie Whitt ........ Blue Jays | 2278 ... 6/29/77 .. Darrell Porter .......... Royals |
| 2229 ... 6/12/77 .. Bruce Bochte ......... Indians | 2279 ... 6/29/77 .. Frank White ........... Royals |
| 2230 ... 6/12/77 .. Buddy Bell .............. Indians | 2280 ... 6/29/77 .. Tom Poquette ........ Royals |
| 2231 ... 6/12/77 .. John Lowenstein ... Indians | 2281 ... 6/29/77 .. John Mayberry ....... Royals |
| 2232 ... 6/12/77 .. Bruce Bochte ......... Indians | 2282 ... 6/29/77 .. Dave Nelson .......... Royals |
| 2233 ... 6/12/77 .. Frank Duffy ............. Indians | 2283 ... 6/29/77 .. Tom Poquette ........ Royals |
| 2234 ... 6/12/77 .. Duane Kuiper ........ Indians | 2284 ... 6/29/77 .. Hal McRae ............ Royals |
| 2235 ... 6/12/77 .. Paul Dade .............. Indians | 2285 ... 6/29/77 .. Darrell Porter .......... Royals |
| 2236 ... 6/12/77 .. Buddy Bell .............. Indians | 2286 ... 7/4/77 .... Matt Alexander ............. A's |
| 2237 ... 6/12/77 .. John Lowenstein ... Indians | 2287 ... 7/4/77 .... Tony Armas .................. A's |
| 2238 ... 6/12/77 .. Bill Melton ............. Indians | 2288 ... 7/4/77 .... Earl Williams ................. A's |
| 2239 ... 6/16/77 .. Roy Smalley ............ Twins | 2289 ... 7/4/77 .... Mike Jorgensen ............. A's |
| 2240 ... 6/16/77 .. Lyman Bostock ........ Twins | 2290 ... 7/4/77 .... Willie Crawford ............. A's |
| 2241 ... 6/16/77 .. Glenn Adams ........... Twins | 2291 ... 7/4/77 .... Mitchell Page ............... A's |
| 2242 ... 6/16/77 .. Rich Chiles .............. Twins | 2292 ... 7/4/77 .... Earl Williams ................. A's |
| 2243 ... 6/16/77 .. Butch Wynegar ........ Twins | 2293 ... 7/4/77 .... Mike Jorgensen ............. A's |
| 2244 ... 6/16/77 .. Rob Wilfong ............ Twins | 2294 ... 7/4/77 .... Tony Armas .................. A's |
| 2245 ... 6/16/77 .. Glenn Adams ........... Twins | 2295 ... 7/4/77 .... Marty Perez .................. A's |
| 2246 ... 6/16/77 .. Roy Smalley ............ Twins | 2296 ... 7/4/77 .... Wayne Gross ............... A's |
| 2247 ... 6/16/77 .. Butch Wynegar ........ Twins | 2297 ... 7/8/77 .... Mike Hargrove ..... Rangers |
| 2248 ... 6/16/77 .. Rob Wilfong ............ Twins | 2298 ... 7/8/77 .... Bump Wills .......... Rangers |
| 2249 ... 6/16/77 .. Rod Carew .............. Twins | 2299 ... 7/8/77 .... Willie Horton ........ Rangers |
| 2250 ... 6/16/77 .. Lyman Bostock ........ Twins | 2300 ... 7/12/77 .. Roy Smalley ............ Twins |

| | | |
|---|---|---|
| 2301 ... 7/12/77 .. Rod Carew .............. Twins | 2351 ... 8/13/77 .. Roy White .......... Yankees |
| 2302 ... 7/12/77 .. Roy Smalley ........... Twins | 2352 ... 8/13/77 .. Thurman Munson Yankees |
| 2303 ... 7/12/77 .. Rod Carew .............. Twins | 2353 ... 8/13/77 .. Reggie Jackson .. Yankees |
| 2304 ... 7/12/77 .. Roy Smalley ........... Twins | 2354 ... 8/13/77 .. Mickey Rivers ...... Yankees |
| 2305 ... 7/12/77 .. Rob Wilfong ............. Twins | 2355 ... 8/13/77 .. Thurman Munson Yankees |
| 2306 ... 7/12/77 .. Larry Hisle .............. Twins | 2356 ... 8/13/77 .. Reggie Jackson .. Yankees |
| 2307 ... 7/12/77 .. Glenn Adams .......... Twins | 2357 ... 8/19/77 .. Doug Ault .......... Blue Jays |
| 2308 ... 7/16/77 .. Dave Collins ....... Mariners | 2358 ... 8/19/77 .. Dave McKay ...... Blue Jays |
| 2309 ... 7/16/77 .. Dan Meyer .......... Mariners | 2359 ... 8/19/77 .. Ron Fairly .......... Blue Jays |
| 2310 ... 7/16/77 .. Lee Stanton ......... Mariners | 2360 ... 8/19/77 .. Doug Ault .......... Blue Jays |
| 2311 ... 7/16/77 .. Steve Braun ........ Mariners | 2361 ... 8/19/77 .. Dave McKay ...... Blue Jays |
| 2312 ... 7/16/77 .. Julio Cruz ........... Mariners | 2362 ... 8/19/77 .. Ron Fairly .......... Blue Jays |
| 2313 ... 7/16/77 .. Dave Collins ....... Mariners | 2363 ... 8/19/77 .. Sam Ewing ........ Blue Jays |
| 2314 ... 7/16/77 .. Dan Meyer .......... Mariners | 2364 ... 8/19/77 .. Al Woods .......... Blue Jays |
| 2315 ... 7/16/77 .. Lee Stanton ......... Mariners | 2365 ... 8/19/77 .. Doug Ault .......... Blue Jays |
| 2316 ... 7/16/77 .. Lee Stanton ......... Mariners | 2366 ... 8/19/77 .. Steve Staggs ..... Blue Jays |
| 2317 ... 7/16/77 .. Bill Stein ............. Mariners | 2367 ... 8/19/77 .. Roy Howell ........ Blue Jays |
| 2318 ... 7/16/77 .. Ruppert Jones ..... Mariners | 2368 ... 8/19/77 .. Doug Ault .......... Blue Jays |
| 2319 ... 7/16/77 .. Dan Meyer .......... Mariners | 2369 ... 8/19/77 .. Sam Ewing ........ Blue Jays |
| 2320 ... 7/21/77 .. Rod Carew .............. Twins | 2370 ... 8/24/77 .. Paul Dade .............. Indians |
| 2321 ... 7/21/77 .. Rob Wilfong ............. Twins | 2371 ... 8/24/77 .. Duane Kuiper ........ Indians |
| 2322 ... 7/21/77 .. Roy Smalley ........... Twins | 2372 ... 8/24/77 .. Bruce Bochte ........ Indians |
| 2323 ... 7/21/77 .. Rob Wilfong ............. Twins | 2373 ... 8/24/77 .. Larvell Blanks ....... Indians |
| 2324 ... 7/25/77 .. Julio Cruz ........... Mariners | 2374 ... 8/24/77 .. Andre Thornton .... Indians |
| 2325 ... 7/25/77 .. Dave Collins ....... Mariners | 2375 ... 8/24/77 .. Bruce Bochte ........ Indians |
| 2326 ... 7/25/77 .. Lee Stanton ......... Mariners | 2376 ... 8/24/77 .. Ray Fosse .............. Indians |
| 2327 ... 7/25/77 .. Ruppert Jones ..... Mariners | 2377 ... 8/24/77 .. Paul Dade .............. Indians |
| 2328 ... 7/25/77 .. Bill Stein ............. Mariners | 2378 ... 8/24/77 .. Larvell Blanks ....... Indians |
| 2329 ... 7/25/77 .. Lee Stanton ......... Mariners | 2379 ... 8/24/77 .. Ray Fosse .............. Indians |
| 2330 ... 7/25/77 .. Craig Reynolds ... Mariners | 2380 ... 8/29/77 .. Mark Belanger ...... Orioles |
| 2331 ... 7/25/77 .. Lee Stanton ......... Mariners | 2381 ... 8/29/77 .. Eddie Murray ......... Orioles |
| 2332 ... 7/25/77 .. Ruppert Jones ..... Mariners | 2382 ... 8/29/77 .. Pat Kelly .............. Orioles |
| 2333 ... 7/25/77 .. Dave Collins ....... Mariners | 2383 ... 8/29/77 .. Ken Singleton ........ Orioles |
| 2334 ... 7/30/77 .. Jim Rice .............. Red Sox | 2384 ... 8/29/77 .. Eddie Murray ......... Orioles |
| 2335 ... 7/30/77 .. George Scott ....... Red Sox | 2385 ... 8/29/77 .. Doug DeCinces ..... Orioles |
| 2336 ... 7/30/77 .. Rick Burleson ...... Red Sox | 2386 ... 8/29/77 .. Billy Smith .............. Orioles |
| 2337 ... 7/30/77 .. Fred Lynn ............ Red Sox | 2387 ... 8/29/77 .. Mark Belanger ...... Orioles |
| 2338 ... 7/30/77 .. Carlton Fisk ......... Red Sox | 2388 ... 8/29/77 .. Doug DeCinces ..... Orioles |
| 2339 ... 7/30/77 .. Denny Doyle ........ Red Sox | 2389 ... 8/29/77 .. Billy Smith .............. Orioles |
| 2340 ... 8/3/77 .... Bucky Dent ........ Yankees | 2390 ... 8/29/77 .. Doug DeCinces ..... Orioles |
| 2341 ... 8/3/77 .... Roy White .......... Yankees | 2391 ... 9/3/77 .... Andre Thornton ..... Indians |
| 2342 ... 8/3/77 .... Chris Chambliss .. Yankees | 2392 ... 9/3/77 .... Rico Carty .............. Indians |
| 2343 ... 8/8/77 .... Joe Lahoud ............ Royals | 2393 ... 9/3/77 .... Paul Dade .............. Indians |
| 2344 ... 8/8/77 .... Joe Lahoud ............ Royals | 2394 ... 9/3/77 .... Bruce Bochte ........ Indians |
| 2345 ... 8/8/77 .... Tom Poquette ........ Royals | 2395 ... 9/3/77 .... Larvell Blanks ........ Indians |
| 2346 ... 8/13/77 .. Willie Randolph ... Yankees | 2396 ... 9/3/77 .... Jim Norris .............. Indians |
| 2347 ... 8/13/77 .. Reggie Jackson .. Yankees | 2397 ... 9/3/77 .... Paul Dade .............. Indians |
| 2348 ... 8/13/77 .. Carlos May .......... Yankees | 2398 ... 9/8/77 .... Oscar Gamble .. White Sox |
| 2349 ... 8/13/77 .. George Zeber ....... Yankees | 2399 ... 9/8/77 .... Jim Essian ........ White Sox |
| 2350 ... 8/13/77 .. Mickey Klutts ....... Yankees | 2400 ... 9/8/77 .... Jorge Orta ........ White Sox |

**281**

| | | | |
|---|---|---|---|
| 2401 ... 9/8/77 .... Richie Zisk ........ White Sox | 2451 ... 4/13/78 .. Bob Randall ............. Twins |
| 2402 ... 9/8/77 .... Alan Bannister .. White Sox | 2452 ... 4/18/78 .. Bob Stinson ........ Mariners |
| 2403 ... 9/12/77 .. C. Washington ..... Rangers | 2453 ... 4/18/78 .. John Hale ........... Mariners |
| 2404 ... 9/12/77 .. Toby Harrah ........ Rangers | 2454 ... 4/18/78 .. John Hale ........... Mariners |
| 2405 ... 9/12/77 .. Tom Grieve ......... Rangers | 2455 ... 4/18/78 .. Julio Cruz ........... Mariners |
| 2406 ... 9/12/77 .. Mike Hargrove ..... Rangers | 2456 ... 4/18/78 .. Bob Stinson ........ Mariners |
| 2407 ... 9/12/77 .. C. Washington ..... Rangers | 2457 ... 4/18/78 .. Ruppert Jones .... Mariners |
| 2408 ... 9/12/77 .. Toby Harrah ........ Rangers | 2458 ... 4/18/78 .. Dan Meyer ......... Mariners |
| 2409 ... 9/12/77 .. Willie Horton ....... Rangers | 2459 ... 4/18/78 .: Lee Stanton ....... Mariners |
| 2410 ... 9/12/77 .. C. Washington ..... Rangers | 2460 ... 4/24/78 .. Ruppert Jones .... Mariners |
| 2411 ... 9/12/77 .. Mike Hargrove ..... Rangers | 2461 ... 4/24/78 .. Dan Meyer ......... Mariners |
| 2412 ... 9/19/77 .. C. Washington ..... Rangers | 2462 ... 4/24/78 .. John Hale ........... Mariners |
| 2413 ... 9/19/77 .. Dave May ........... Rangers | 2463 ... 4/24/78 .. Craig Reynolds ... Mariners |
| 2414 ... 9/19/77 .. Ken Henderson ... Rangers | 2464 ... 4/24/78 .. Julio Cruz ........... Mariners |
| 2415 ... 9/19/77 .. Jim Sundberg ...... Rangers | 2465 ... 4/24/78 .. Bob Stinson ........ Mariners |
| 2416 ... 9/19/77 .. Toby Harrah ........ Rangers | 2466 ... 4/24/78 .. Ruppert Jones ..... Mariners |
| 2417 ... 9/25/77 .. Clint Hurdle .......... Royals | 2467 ... 4/24/78 .. Bill Stein ............ Mariners |
| 2418 ... 9/25/77 .. Joe Lahoud ........... Royals | 2468 ... 4/24/78 .. Craig Reynolds ... Mariners |
| 2419 ... 9/25/77 .. Darrell Porter ......... Royals | 2469 ... 4/24/78 .. Julio Cruz ........... Mariners |
| 2420 ... 9/25/77 .. Bob Heise ............. Royals | 2470 ... 4/24/78 .. John Hale ........... Mariners |
| 2421 ... 9/25/77 .. Joe Lahoud ........... Royals | 2471 ... 4/24/78 .. Bob Stinson ........ Mariners |
| 2422 ... 9/25/77 .. Pete Lacock .......... Royals | 2472 ... 4/24/78 .. Lee Stanton ....... Mariners |
| 2423 ... 9/25/77 .. U.L. Washington .... Royals | 2473 ... 4/24/78 .. Bill Stein .............. Mariners |
| 2424 ... 9/25/77 .. Willie Wilson .......... Royals | 2474 ... 4/24/78 .. Craig Reynolds ... Mariners |
| 2425 ... 9/25/77 .. Dave Nelson .......... Royals | 2475 ... 4/29/78 .. Roy Howell ....... Blue Jays |
| 2426 ... 9/25/77 .. Clint Hurdle ........... Royals | 2476 ... 4/29/78 .. Luis Gomez ....... Blue Jays |
| 2427 ... 4/8/78 .... Miguel Dilone .......... A's | 2477 ... 4/29/78 .. Roy Howell ....... Blue Jays |
| 2428 ... 4/8/78 .... Tony Armas .................. A's | 2478 ... 4/29/78 .. Rick Cerone ....... Blue Jays |
| 2429 ... 4/8/78 .... Dave Revering .............. A's | 2479 ... 4/29/78 .. Garth Iorg ......... Blue Jays |
| 2430 ... 4/8/78 .... Jim Essian ................... A's | 2480 ... 4/29/78 .. Luis Gomez ....... Blue Jays |
| 2431 ... 4/8/78 .... Wayne Gross ............... A's | 2481 ... 4/29/78 .. Bob Bailor ......... Blue Jays |
| 2432 ... 4/8/78 .... Miguel Dilone .............. A's | 2482 ... 4/29/78 .. Tim Johnson ...... Blue Jays |
| 2433 ... 4/8/78 .... Gary Thomasson .......... A's | 2483 ... 4/29/78 .. Sam Ewing ........ Blue Jays |
| 2434 ... 4/8/78 .... Tony Armas .................. A's | 2484 ... 4/29/78 .. John Mayberry ... Blue Jays |
| 2435 ... 4/8/78 .... Dave Revering .............. A's | 2485 ... 4/29/78 .. Rick Cerone ...... Blue Jays |
| 2436 ... 4/8/78 .... Wayne Gross ............... A's | 2486 ... 5/5/78 .... Buddy Bell ............ Indians |
| 2437 ... 4/8/78 .... Steve Staggs ................ A's | 2487 ... 5/5/78 .... John Grubb ........... Indians |
| 2438 ... 4/8/78 .... Bill North ..................... A's | 2488 ... 5/5/78 .... Larvell Blanks ........ Indians |
| 2439 ... 4/8/78 .... Tony Armas .................. A's | 2489 ... 5/5/78 .... Paul Dade .............. Indians |
| 2440 ... 4/13/78 .. Willie Norwood ........ Twins | 2490 ... 5/5/78 .... Buddy Bell ............ Indians |
| 2441 ... 4/13/78 .. Glenn Adams .......... Twins | 2491 ... 5/5/78 .... Andre Thornton ..... Indians |
| 2442 ... 4/13/78 .. Butch Wynegar ........ Twins | 2492 ... 5/5/78 .... Larvell Blanks ........ Indians |
| 2443 ... 4/13/78 .. Dan Ford ................ Twins | 2493 ... 5/5/78 .... Paul Dade .............. Indians |
| 2444 ... 4/13/78 .. Bob Randall ............. Twins | 2494 ... 5/5/78 .... Rick Manning ......... Indians |
| 2445 ... 4/13/78 .. Glenn Adams ........... Twins | 2495 ... 5/5/78 .... John Grubb ........... Indians |
| 2446 ... 4/13/78 .. Mike Cubbage ........ Twins | 2496 ... 5/5/78 .... Larvell Blanks ........ Indians |
| 2447 ... 4/13/78 .. Roy Smalley ............ Twins | 2497 ... 5/5/78 .... Ron Pruitt ............. Indians |
| 2448 ... 4/13/78 .. Glenn Adams ........... Twins | 2498 ... 5/12/78 .. Willie Horton .......... Indians |
| 2449 ... 4/13/78 .. Dan Ford ................. Twins | 2499 ... 5/12/78 .. Ron Hassey ........... Indians |
| 2450 ... 4/13/78 .. Hosken Powell ......... Twins | 2500 ... 5/12/78 .. Buddy Bell ............. Indians |

| | | | | |
|---|---|---|---|---|
| 2501 | 5/12/78 | Andre Thornton | Indians |
| 2502 | 5/12/78 | Jim Norris | Indians |
| 2503 | 5/17/78 | Ron Blomberg | White Sox |
| 2504 | 5/17/78 | Bob Molinaro | White Sox |
| 2505 | 5/17/78 | Ralph Garr | White Sox |
| 2506 | 5/17/78 | Don Kessinger | White Sox |
| 2507 | 5/17/78 | Chet Lemon | White Sox |
| 2508 | 5/17/78 | Ron Blomberg | White Sox |
| 2509 | 5/23/78 | Jorge Orta | White Sox |
| 2510 | 5/23/78 | Ron Blomberg | White Sox |
| 2511 | 5/23/78 | Eric Soderholm | White Sox |
| 2512 | 5/23/78 | Bill Naharodny | White Sox |
| 2513 | 5/23/78 | Eric Soderholm | White Sox |
| 2514 | 5/23/78 | Eric Soderholm | White Sox |
| 2515 | 5/23/78 | Bill Naharodny | White Sox |
| 2516 | 5/28/78 | Cecil Cooper | Brewers |
| 2517 | 5/28/78 | Gorman Thomas | Brewers |
| 2518 | 5/28/78 | Ben Oglivie | Brewers |
| 2519 | 5/28/78 | Gorman Thomas | Brewers |
| 2520 | 5/28/78 | Don Money | Brewers |
| 2521 | 5/28/78 | Charlie Moore | Brewers |
| 2522 | 5/28/78 | Cecil Cooper | Brewers |
| 2523 | 5/28/78 | Sixto Lezcano | Brewers |
| 2524 | 6/2/78 | Jerry Remy | Red Sox |
| 2525 | 6/2/78 | Jerry Remy | Red Sox |
| 2526 | 6/2/78 | Carlton Fisk | Red Sox |
| 2527 | 6/2/78 | Rick Burleson | Red Sox |
| 2528 | 6/2/78 | Jim Rice | Red Sox |
| 2529 | 6/6/78 | Larry Harlow | Orioles |
| 2530 | 6/6/78 | Pat Kelly | Orioles |
| 2531 | 6/6/78 | Billy Smith | Orioles |
| 2532 | 6/10/78 | Reggie Jackson | Yankees |
| 2533 | 6/10/78 | Willie Randolph | Yankees |
| 2534 | 6/10/78 | Reggie Jackson | Yankees |
| 2535 | 6/10/78 | Graig Nettles | Yankees |
| 2536 | 6/10/78 | Mickey Rivers | Yankees |
| 2537 | 6/10/78 | Roy White | Yankees |
| 2538 | 6/10/78 | Willie Randolph | Yankees |
| 2539 | 6/10/78 | Mike Heath | Yankees |
| 2540 | 7/5/78 | Clint Hurdle | Royals |
| 2541 | 7/9/78 | John Hale | Mariners |
| 2542 | 7/9/78 | Tom Paciorek | Mariners |
| 2543 | 7/9/78 | Dan Meyer | Mariners |
| 2544 | 7/9/78 | Bill Stein | Mariners |
| 2545 | 7/9/78 | John Hale | Mariners |
| 2546 | 7/14/78 | Rick Bosetti | Blue Jays |
| 2547 | 7/14/78 | Roy Howell | Blue Jays |
| 2548 | 7/14/78 | John Mayberry | Blue Jays |
| 2549 | 7/14/78 | Dave McKay | Blue Jays |
| 2550 | 7/14/78 | Rick Cerone | Blue Jays |
| 2551 | 7/14/78 | Roy Howell | Blue Jays |
| 2552 | 7/14/78 | Rico Carty | Blue Jays |
| 2553 | 7/14/78 | John Mayberry | Blue Jays |
| 2554 | 7/14/78 | Dave McKay | Blue Jays |
| 2555 | 7/14/78 | Rick Bosetti | Blue Jays |
| 2556 | 7/14/78 | Dave McKay | Blue Jays |
| 2557 | 7/14/78 | Tommy Hutton | Blue Jays |
| 2558 | 7/14/78 | Dave McKay | Blue Jays |
| 2559 | 7/19/78 | John Grubb | Indians |
| 2560 | 7/19/78 | Andre Thornton | Indians |
| 2561 | 7/19/78 | Gary Alexander | Indians |
| 2562 | 7/19/78 | Gary Alexander | Indians |
| 2563 | 7/19/78 | Jim Norris | Indians |
| 2564 | 7/19/78 | Duane Kuiper | Indians |
| 2565 | 7/19/78 | Rick Manning | Indians |
| 2566 | 7/19/78 | John Grubb | Indians |
| 2567 | 7/19/78 | Andre Thornton | Indians |
| 2568 | 7/19/78 | Gary Alexander | Indians |
| 2569 | 7/23/78 | Phil Mankowski | Tigers |
| 2570 | 7/23/78 | Rusty Staub | Tigers |
| 2571 | 7/23/78 | Lance Parrish | Tigers |
| 2572 | 7/23/78 | Mark Wagner | Tigers |
| 2573 | 7/23/78 | Phil Mankowski | Tigers |
| 2574 | 7/23/78 | Steve Kemp | Tigers |
| 2575 | 7/23/78 | Lance Parrish | Tigers |
| 2576 | 7/23/78 | Tim Corcoran | Tigers |
| 2577 | 7/23/78 | Phil Mankowski | Tigers |
| 2578 | 7/23/78 | Steve Kemp | Tigers |
| 2579 | 7/23/78 | Lance Parrish | Tigers |
| 2580 | 7/27/78 | Ben Oglivie | Brewers |
| 2581 | 7/27/78 | Larry Hisle | Brewers |
| 2582 | 7/27/78 | Jim Gantner | Brewers |
| 2583 | 8/1/78 | Jeff Newman | A's |
| 2584 | 8/1/78 | Joe Wallis | A's |
| 2585 | 8/1/78 | Mitchell Page | A's |
| 2586 | 8/1/78 | Mike Edwards | A's |
| 2587 | 8/1/78 | Dave Revering | A's |
| 2588 | 8/1/78 | Joe Wallis | A's |
| 2589 | 8/1/78 | Willie Horton | A's |
| 2590 | 8/1/78 | Tony Armas | A's |
| 2591 | 8/6/78 | Hosken Powell | Twins |
| 2592 | 8/6/78 | Roy Smalley | Twins |
| 2593 | 8/6/78 | Mike Cubbage | Twins |
| 2594 | 8/6/78 | Mike Cubbage | Twins |
| 2595 | 8/6/78 | Glenn Adams | Twins |
| 2596 | 8/6/78 | Rich Chiles | Twins |
| 2597 | 8/6/78 | Hosken Powell | Twins |
| 2598 | 8/6/78 | Roy Smalley | Twins |
| 2599 | 8/6/78 | Dan Ford | Twins |
| 2600 | 8/6/78 | Butch Wynegar | Twins |

---

# Miracle Man

| 2601 | 8/11/78 | Julio Cruz | Mariners |
| 2602 | 8/11/78 | Ruppert Jones | Mariners |
| 2603 | 8/11/78 | John Hale | Mariners |
| 2604 | 8/11/78 | Bob Stinson | Mariners |
| 2605 | 8/11/78 | Leon Roberts | Mariners |
| 2606 | 8/11/78 | John Hale | Mariners |
| 2607 | 8/11/78 | Bob Stinson | Mariners |
| 2608 | 8/11/78 | Leon Roberts | Mariners |
| 2609 | 8/11/78 | Bob Stinson | Mariners |
| 2610 | 8/11/78 | Bob Robertson | Mariners |
| 2611 | 8/16/78 | Jerry Remy | Red Sox |
| 2612 | 8/16/78 | Jim Rice | Red Sox |
| 2613 | 8/16/78 | Fred Lynn | Red Sox |
| 2614 | 8/16/78 | Garry Hancock | Red Sox |
| 2615 | 8/16/78 | Dwight Evans | Red Sox |
| 2616 | 8/16/78 | Butch Hobson | Red Sox |
| 2617 | 8/16/78 | Rick Burleson | Red Sox |
| 2618 | 8/16/78 | Carlton Fisk | Red Sox |
| 2619 | 8/16/78 | Garry Hancock | Red Sox |
| 2620 | 8/16/78 | Dwight Evans | Red Sox |
| 2621 | 8/16/78 | Butch Hobson | Red Sox |
| 2622 | 8/16/78 | Carlton Fisk | Red Sox |
| 2623 | 8/16/78 | Jim Rice | Red Sox |
| 2624 | 8/20/78 | Billy Smith | Orioles |
| 2625 | 8/20/78 | Pat Kelly | Orioles |
| 2626 | 8/20/78 | Ken Singleton | Orioles |
| 2627 | 8/20/78 | Eddie Murray | Orioles |
| 2628 | 8/20/78 | Rick Dempsey | Orioles |
| 2629 | 8/20/78 | Billy Smith | Orioles |
| 2630 | 8/20/78 | Pat Kelly | Orioles |
| 2631 | 8/20/78 | Rick Dempsey | Orioles |
| 2632 | 9/6/78 | John Lowenstein | Rangers |
| 2633 | 9/6/78 | Bobby Bonds | Rangers |
| 2634 | 9/6/78 | Bump Wills | Rangers |
| 2635 | 9/6/78 | Juan Beniquez | Rangers |
| 2636 | 9/6/78 | Bump Wills | Rangers |
| 2637 | 9/6/78 | Richie Zisk | Rangers |
| 2638 | 9/6/78 | Jim Sundberg | Rangers |
| 2639 | 9/6/78 | Mike Hargrove | Rangers |
| 2640 | 9/6/78 | Bobby Bonds | Rangers |
| 2641 | 9/10/78 | Hal McRae | Royals |
| 2642 | 9/10/78 | Amos Otis | Royals |
| 2643 | 9/10/78 | U.L. Washington | Royals |
| 2644 | 9/10/78 | Tom Poquette | Royals |
| 2645 | 9/10/78 | Hal McRae | Royals |
| 2646 | 9/10/78 | Pete Lacock | Royals |
| 2647 | 9/10/78 | Amos Otis | Royals |
| 2648 | 9/10/78 | Hal McRae | Royals |
| 2649 | 9/10/78 | U.L. Washington | Royals |
| 2650 | 9/10/78 | Tom Poquette | Royals |
| 2651 | 9/10/78 | Pete Lacock | Royals |
| 2652 | 9/10/78 | Willie Wilson | Royals |
| 2653 | 9/15/78 | Al Cowens | Royals |
| 2654 | 9/15/78 | Fred Patek | Royals |
| 2655 | 9/15/78 | Pete Lacock | Royals |
| 2656 | 9/15/78 | Al Cowens | Royals |
| 2657 | 9/15/78 | Steve Braun | Royals |
| 2658 | 9/19/78 | Mike Cubbage | Twins |
| 2659 | 9/19/78 | Rod Carew | Twins |
| 2660 | 9/19/78 | Glenn Adams | Twins |
| 2661 | 9/19/78 | Dan Ford | Twins |
| 2662 | 9/19/78 | Rich Chiles | Twins |
| 2663 | 9/19/78 | Butch Wynegar | Twins |
| 2664 | 9/19/78 | Roy Smalley | Twins |
| 2665 | 9/19/78 | Rob Wilfong | Twins |
| 2666 | 9/19/78 | Dan Ford | Twins |
| 2667 | 9/19/78 | Dan Ford | Twins |
| 2668 | 9/24/78 | Chet Lemon | White Sox |
| 2669 | 9/24/78 | Lamar Johnson | White Sox |
| 2670 | 9/24/78 | Eric Soderholm | White Sox |
| 2671 | 9/24/78 | Mike Squires | White Sox |
| 2672 | 9/24/78 | Harry Chappas | White Sox |
| 2673 | 9/24/78 | Ralph Garr | White Sox |
| 2674 | 10/1/78 | Eric Soderholm | White Sox |
| 2675 | 10/1/78 | Greg Pryor | White Sox |
| 2676 | 10/1/78 | C.Washington | White Sox |
| 2677 | 10/1/78 | Eric Soderholm | White Sox |
| 2678 | 10/1/78 | Marv Foley | White Sox |
| 2679 | 10/1/78 | Harry Chappas | White Sox |
| 2680 | 10/1/78 | C. Washington | White Sox |
| 2681 | 10/1/78 | Eric Soderholm | White Sox |
| 2682 | 10/1/78 | Lamar Johnson | White Sox |
| 2683 | 10/1/78 | C. Washington | White Sox |
| 2684 | 10/1/78 | Mike Squires | White Sox |
| 2685 | 10/1/78 | Marv Foley | White Sox |
| 2686 | 10/1/78 | Ron Blomberg | White Sox |
| 2687 | 4/6/79 | Willie Horton | Mariners |
| 2688 | 4/11/79 | Butch Wynegar | Twins |
| 2689 | 4/11/79 | Rick Sofield | Twins |
| 2690 | 4/11/79 | Willie Norwood | Twins |
| 2691 | 4/11/79 | Roy Smalley | Twins |
| 2692 | 4/11/79 | Butch Wynegar | Twins |
| 2693 | 4/11/79 | Rob Wilfong | Twins |
| 2694 | 4/11/79 | Ron Jackson | Twins |
| 2695 | 4/11/79 | Willie Norwood | Twins |
| 2696 | 4/11/79 | Rob Wilfong | Twins |
| 2697 | 4/11/79 | Rick Sofield | Twins |
| 2698 | 4/17/79 | Mike Cubbage | Twins |
| 2699 | 4/17/79 | Rob Wilfong | Twins |
| 2700 | 4/17/79 | Ken Landreaux | Twins |

| | | | |
|---|---|---|---|
| 2701 ... 4/17/79 .. Rick Sofield .............. Twins | 2751 ... 5/25/79 .. Bill Nahorodny .. White Sox |
| 2702 ... 4/17/79 .. Mike Cubbage ......... Twins | 2752 ... 5/25/79 .. C. Washington .. White Sox |
| 2703 ... 4/17/79 .. Ken Landreaux ........ Twins | 2753 ... 5/30/79 .. Julio Cruz ........... Mariners |
| 2704 ... 4/17/79 .. Glenn Adams ........... Twins | 2754 ... 5/30/79 .. Willie Horton ........ Mariners |
| 2705 ... 4/17/79 .. Rick Sofield .............. Twins | 2755 ... 5/30/79 .. Dan Meyer .......... Mariners |
| 2706 ... 4/17/79 .. Roy Smalley ............ Twins | 2756 ... 5/30/79 .. Tom Paciorek ...... Mariners |
| 2707 ... 4/17/79 .. Glenn Adams ........... Twins | 2757 ... 5/30/79 .. Mario Mendoza ... Mariners |
| 2708 ... 4/21/79 .. Larry Murray ................. A's | 2758 ... 5/30/79 .. Willie Horton ........ Mariners |
| 2709 ... 4/21/79 .. Mitchell Page ............... A's | 2759 ... 5/30/79 .. Leon Roberts ...... Mariners |
| 2710 ... 4/21/79 .. Wayne Gross ................ A's | 2760 ... 5/30/79 .. Larry Milbourne ... Mariners |
| 2711 ... 4/21/79 .. Mickey Klutts ................ A's | 2761 ... 5/30/79 .. Julio Cruz ........... Mariners |
| 2712 ... 4/21/79 .. Jim Essian .................... A's | 2762 ... 5/30/79 .. Bruce Bochte ...... Mariners |
| 2713 ... 4/21/79 .. Larry Murray ................. A's | 2763 ... 5/30/79 .. Larry Cox ........... Mariners |
| 2714 ... 4/21/79 .. Dave Revering ............. A's | 2764 ... 5/30/79 .. Willie Horton ........ Mariners |
| 2715 ... 4/21/79 .. Mickey Klutts ................ A's | 2765 ... 6/9/79 .... Ron LeFlore ............ Tigers |
| 2716 ... 4/21/79 .. Mike Edwards .............. A's | 2766 ... 6/9/79 .... Lou Whitaker ......... Tigers |
| 2717 ... 4/21/79 .. Larry Murray ................. A's | 2767 ... 6/9/79 .... Alan Trammell ........ Tigers |
| 2718 ... 4/21/79 .. Jim Essian .................... A's | 2768 ... 6/9/79 .... Ron LeFlore ............ Tigers |
| 2719 ... 4/21/79 .. Larry Murray ................. A's | 2769 ... 6/9/79 .... Lou Whitaker ......... Tigers |
| 2720 ... 4/26/79 .. Eddie Murray ......... Orioles | 2770 ... 6/9/79 .... Lance Parrish ......... Tigers |
| 2721 ... 4/26/79 .. John Lowenstein .... Orioles | 2771 ... 6/9/79 .... Alan Trammell ........ Tigers |
| 2722 ... 5/2/79 .... Juan Beniquez ..... Yankees | 2772 ... 6/9/79 .... Ron LeFlore ............ Tigers |
| 2723 ... 5/2/79 .... Thurman Munson Yankees | 2773 ... 6/9/79 .... Steve Kemp ........... Tigers |
| 2724 ... 5/2/79 .... Reggie Jackson .. Yankees | 2774 ... 6/9/79 .... Jason Thompson .... Tigers |
| 2725 ... 5/2/79 .... Lou Piniella ......... Yankees | 2775 ... 6/9/79 .... Champ Summers .... Tigers |
| 2726 ... 5/2/79 .... Juan Beniquez .... Yankees | 2776 ... 6/9/79 .... Alan Trammell ........ Tigers |
| 2727 ... 5/2/79 .... Reggie Jackson .. Yankees | 2777 ... 6/9/79 .... Lou Whitaker ......... Tigers |
| 2728 ... 5/2/79 .... Graig Nettles ....... Yankees | 2778 ... 6/9/79 .... Steve Kemp ........... Tigers |
| 2729 ... 5/7/79 .... Dwight Evans ...... Red Sox | 2779 ... 6/9/79 .... Rusty Staub ........... Tigers |
| 2730 ... 5/15/79 .. Cecil Cooper ........ Brewers | 2780 ... 6/9/79 .... Jason Thompson .... Tigers |
| 2731 ... 5/15/79 .. Gorman Thomas .. Brewers | 2781 ... 6/14/79 .. Danny Ainge ...... Blue Jays |
| 2732 ... 5/15/79 .. Ben Oglivie .......... Brewers | 2782 ... 6/14/79 .. Al Woods ........... Blue Jays |
| 2733 ... 5/15/79 .. Gorman Thomas .. Brewers | 2783 ... 6/14/79 .. Alfredo Griffin .... Blue Jays |
| 2734 ... 5/15/79 .. Dick Davis ............ Brewers | 2784 ... 6/14/79 .. Bob Davis .......... Blue Jays |
| 2735 ... 5/15/79 .. Gorman Thomas .. Brewers | 2785 ... 6/14/79 .. Danny Ainge ...... Blue Jays |
| 2736 ... 5/15/79 .. Ben Oglivie .......... Brewers | 2786 ... 6/18/79 .. John Grubb .......... Rangers |
| 2737 ... 5/20/79 .. Ralph Garr ........ White Sox | 2787 ... 6/18/79 .. Oscar Gamble ...... Rangers |
| 2738 ... 5/20/79 .. Jorge Orta ........ White Sox | 2788 ... 6/18/79 .. Bump Wills .......... Rangers |
| 2739 ... 5/20/79 .. Marv Foley ........ White Sox | 2789 ... 6/18/79 .. Pat Putnam .......... Rangers |
| 2740 ... 5/20/79 .. C. Washington .. White Sox | 2790 ... 6/18/79 .. Nelson Norman ... Rangers |
| 2741 ... 5/20/79 .. Chet Lemon ...... White Sox | 2791 ... 6/18/79 .. Bump Wills .......... Rangers |
| 2742 ... 5/20/79 .. Eric Soderholm . White Sox | 2792 ... 6/18/79 .. John Grubb .......... Rangers |
| 2743 ... 5/20/79 .. Greg Pryor ........ White Sox | 2793 ... 6/18/79 .. Eric Soderholm ... Rangers |
| 2744 ... 5/20/79 .. C. Washington .. White Sox | 2794 ... 6/18/79 .. Bump Wills .......... Rangers |
| 2745 ... 5/20/79 .. Chet Lemon ...... White Sox | 2795 ... 6/18/79 .. John Grubb .......... Rangers |
| 2746 ... 5/20/79 .. Eric Soderholm . White Sox | 2796 ... 6/22/79 .. Al Cowens .............. Royals |
| 2747 ... 5/20/79 .. Joe Gates ......... White Sox | 2797 ... 6/22/79 .. Darrell Porter ......... Royals |
| 2748 ... 5/25/79 .. Chet Lemon ...... White Sox | 2798 ... 6/22/79 .. George Scott ......... Royals |
| 2749 ... 5/25/79 .. C. Washington .. White Sox | 2799 ... 6/22/79 .. Pete Lacock .......... Royals |
| 2750 ... 5/25/79 .. Chet Lemon ...... White Sox | 2800 ... 6/22/79 .. Al Cowens .............. Royals |

| # | Date | Player | Team |
|---|---|---|---|
| 2801 | 6/22/79 | Darrell Porter | Royals |
| 2802 | 6/22/79 | George Scott | Royals |
| 2803 | 6/22/79 | Willie Wilson | Royals |
| 2804 | 6/22/79 | George Scott | Royals |
| 2805 | 6/27/79 | Pat Putnam | Rangers |
| 2806 | 6/27/79 | Bump Wills | Rangers |
| 2807 | 6/27/79 | John Grubb | Rangers |
| 2808 | 6/27/79 | Dave Roberts | Rangers |
| 2809 | 6/27/79 | Bump Wills | Rangers |
| 2810 | 6/27/79 | Dave Roberts | Rangers |
| 2811 | 7/1/79 | Steve Braun | Royals |
| 2812 | 7/1/79 | Pete Lacock | Royals |
| 2813 | 7/1/79 | Frank White | Royals |
| 2814 | 7/1/79 | Fred Patek | Royals |
| 2815 | 7/1/79 | Darrell Porter | Royals |
| 2816 | 7/1/79 | Al Cowens | Royals |
| 2817 | 7/1/79 | Frank White | Royals |
| 2818 | 7/1/79 | Willie Wilson | Royals |
| 2819 | 7/1/79 | Frank White | Royals |
| 2820 | 7/1/79 | Pete Lacock | Royals |
| 2821 | 7/5/79 | Jeff Newman | A's |
| 2822 | 7/5/79 | Rickey Henderson | A's |
| 2823 | 7/5/79 | Tony Armas | A's |
| 2824 | 7/5/79 | Tony Armas | A's |
| 2825 | 7/5/79 | Larry Murray | A's |
| 2826 | 7/9/79 | Jim Rice | Red Sox |
| 2827 | 7/9/79 | Bob Watson | Red Sox |
| 2828 | 7/9/79 | Butch Hobson | Red Sox |
| 2829 | 7/9/79 | Bob Montgomery | Red Sox |
| 2830 | 7/9/79 | Rick Burleson | Red Sox |
| 2831 | 7/9/79 | Jim Rice | Red Sox |
| 2832 | 7/9/79 | Carl Yastrzemski | Red Sox |
| 2833 | 7/9/79 | Bob Watson | Red Sox |
| 2834 | 7/9/79 | Butch Hobson | Red Sox |
| 2835 | 7/9/79 | Bob Montgomery | Red Sox |
| 2836 | 7/9/79 | Jim Rice | Red Sox |
| 2837 | 7/9/79 | Bob Watson | Red Sox |
| 2838 | 7/13/79 | Graig Nettles | Yankees |
| 2839 | 7/13/79 | Lou Piniella | Yankees |
| 2840 | 7/13/79 | Bucky Dent | Yankees |
| 2841 | 7/13/79 | Bobby Murcer | Yankees |
| 2842 | 7/13/79 | Thurman Munson | Yankees |
| 2843 | 7/13/79 | Graig Nettles | Yankees |
| 2844 | 7/13/79 | Lou Piniella | Yankees |
| 2845 | 7/13/79 | Willie Randolph | Yankees |
| 2846 | 7/13/79 | Chris Chambliss | Yankees |
| 2847 | 7/21/79 | Mark Belanger | Orioles |
| 2848 | 7/21/79 | Pat Kelly | Orioles |
| 2849 | 7/21/79 | Ken Singleton | Orioles |
| 2850 | 7/21/79 | Ken Singleton | Orioles |
| 2851 | 7/21/79 | Doug DeCinces | Orioles |
| 2852 | 7/21/79 | Mark Belanger | Orioles |
| 2853 | 7/25/79 | Mickey Rivers | Yankees |
| 2854 | 7/25/79 | Willie Randolph | Yankees |
| 2855 | 8/13/79 | Lance Parrish | Tigers |
| 2856 | 8/13/79 | Steve Kemp | Tigers |
| 2857 | 8/18/79 | Joe Cannon | Blue Jays |
| 2858 | 8/18/79 | John Mayberry | Blue Jays |
| 2859 | 8/18/79 | Danny Ainge | Blue Jays |
| 2860 | 8/18/79 | Joe Cannon | Blue Jays |
| 2861 | 8/18/79 | Roy Howell | Blue Jays |
| 2862 | 8/18/79 | Danny Ainge | Blue Jays |
| 2863 | 8/18/79 | Alfredo Griffin | Blue Jays |
| 2864 | 8/22/79 | Ron Hassey | Indians |
| 2865 | 8/26/79 | Tony Solaita | Blue Jays |
| 2866 | 8/30/79 | Bobby Bonds | Indians |
| 2867 | 8/30/79 | Bobby Bonds | Indians |
| 2868 | 8/30/79 | Jim Norris | Indians |
| 2869 | 8/30/79 | Bobby Bonds | Indians |
| 2870 | 8/30/79 | Ron Hassey | Indians |
| 2871 | 9/3/79 | Thad Bosley | White Sox |
| 2872 | 9/3/79 | Chet Lemon | White Sox |
| 2873 | 9/3/79 | Chet Lemon | White Sox |
| 2874 | 9/7/79 | Gorman Thomas | Brewers |
| 2875 | 9/7/79 | Ben Oglivie | Brewers |
| 2876 | 9/7/79 | Ben Oglivie | Brewers |
| 2877 | 9/7/79 | Charlie Moore | Brewers |
| 2878 | 9/7/79 | Paul Molitor | Brewers |
| 2879 | 9/15/79 | Don Money | Brewers |
| 2880 | 9/15/79 | Gorman Thomas | Brewers |
| 2881 | 9/15/79 | Sixto Lezcano | Brewers |
| 2882 | 9/15/79 | Jim Gantner | Brewers |
| 2883 | 9/15/79 | Paul Molitor | Brewers |
| 2884 | 9/15/79 | Ben Oglivie | Brewers |
| 2885 | 9/15/79 | Charlie Moore | Brewers |
| 2886 | 9/15/79 | Paul Molitor | Brewers |
| 2887 | 9/15/79 | Jim Gantner | Brewers |
| 2888 | 9/15/79 | Cecil Cooper | Brewers |
| 2889 | 9/19/79 | U.L. Washington | Royals |
| 2890 | 9/19/79 | George Brett | Royals |
| 2891 | 9/19/79 | Amos Otis | Royals |
| 2892 | 9/19/79 | U.L. Washington | Royals |
| 2893 | 9/19/79 | Frank White | Royals |
| 2894 | 9/19/79 | U.L. Washington | Royals |
| 2895 | 9/19/79 | Amos Otis | Royals |
| 2896 | 9/19/79 | U.L. Washington | Royals |
| 2897 | 9/19/79 | Willie Wilson | Royals |
| 2898 | 9/24/79 | Hal McRae | Royals |
| 2899 | 9/24/79 | Darrell Porter | Royals |
| 2900 | 9/24/79 | Hal McRae | Royals |

| | | | |
|---|---|---|---|
| 2901 ... 9/24/79 .. Amos Otis .............. Royals | 2951 ... 5/18/80 .. Greg Luzinski ........ Phillies |
| 2902 ... 9/24/79 .. Al Cowens .............. Royals | 2952 ... 5/18/80 .. Garry Maddox ....... Phillies |
| 2903 ... 9/24/79 .. Frank White ............ Royals | 2953 ... 5/18/80 .. Randy Lerch .......... Phillies |
| 2904 ... 9/24/79 .. Willie Wilson ........... Royals | 2954 ... 5/18/80 .. Bake McBride ........ Phillies |
| 2905 ... 9/24/79 .. Al Cowens .............. Royals | 2955 ... 5/18/80 .. Greg Luzinski ........ Phillies |
| 2906 ... 9/28/79 .. Mickey Rivers ...... Rangers | 2956 ... 5/18/80 .. Mike Schmidt ........ Phillies |
| 2907 ... 9/28/79 .. Al Oliver ............... Rangers | 2957 ... 5/18/80 .. Bake McBride ........ Phillies |
| 2908 ... 9/28/79 .. Richie Zisk .......... Rangers | 2958 ... 5/18/80 .. Mike Schmidt ........ Phillies |
| 2909 ... 9/28/79 .. Bump Wills ........... Rangers | 2959 ... 5/18/80 .. Greg Luzinski ........ Phillies |
| 2910 ... 4/12/80 .. Ron Cey .............. Dodgers | 2960 ... 5/23/80 .. Steve Carlton ........ Phillies |
| 2911 ... 4/12/80 .. Davey Lopes ....... Dodgers | 2961 ... 5/28/80 .. Willie Montanez ..... Padres |
| 2912 ... 4/12/80 .. Reggie Smith ....... Dodgers | 2962 ... 5/28/80 .. Ozzie Smith .......... Padres |
| 2913 ... 4/17/80 .. Bill Russell .......... Dodgers | 2963 ... 5/28/80 .. Gene Tenace ......... Padres |
| 2914 ... 4/17/80 .. Don Sutton .......... Dodgers | 2964 ... 5/28/80 .. Rick Wise .............. Padres |
| 2915 ... 4/17/80 .. Dusty Baker ........ Dodgers | 2965 ... 5/28/80 .. Gene Tenace ......... Padres |
| 2916 ... 4/17/80 .. Derrel Thomas ..... Dodgers | 2966 ... 5/28/80 .. Von Joshua ........... Padres |
| 2917 ... 4/17/80 .. Reggie Smith ....... Dodgers | 2967 ... 5/28/80 .. Dave Winfield ........ Padres |
| 2918 ... 4/22/80 .. Ken Griffey ............... Reds | 2968 ... 6/2/80 .... Willie Montanez ..... Padres |
| 2919 ... 4/22/80 .. Dan Driessen ........... Reds | 2969 ... 6/2/80 .... Barry Evans .......... Padres |
| 2920 ... 4/22/80 .. Junior Kennedy ......... Reds | 2970 ... 6/2/80 .... Rick Wise .............. Padres |
| 2921 ... 4/22/80 .. Cesar Geronimo ....... Reds | 2971 ... 6/2/80 .... Eric Rasmussen .... Padres |
| 2922 ... 4/22/80 .. Junior Kennedy ......... Reds | 2972 ... 6/8/80 .... Bill North ................ Giants |
| 2923 ... 4/22/80 .. Cesar Geronimo ....... Reds | 2973 ... 6/8/80 .... Terry Whitfield ........ Giants |
| 2924 ... 4/22/80 .. Hector Cruz .............. Reds | 2974 ... 6/8/80 .... Rennie Stennett ...... Giants |
| 2925 ... 4/27/80 .. Mike Jorgensen ........ Mets | 2975 ... 6/8/80 .... Vida Blue .............. Giants |
| 2926 ... 4/27/80 .. Jose Cardenal ........... Mets | 2976 ... 6/8/80 .... Bill North ................ Giants |
| 2927 ... 4/27/80 .. Frank Taveras ........... Mets | 2977 ... 6/8/80 .... Terry Whitfield ........ Giants |
| 2928 ... 4/27/80 .. Ron Hodges .............. Mets | 2978 ... 6/8/80 .... Johnnie LeMaster ... Giants |
| 2929 ... 4/27/80 .. Ray Burris ................. Mets | 2979 ... 6/8/80 .... Bill North ................ Giants |
| 2930 ... 5/2/80 .... George Hendrick Cardinals | 2980 ... 6/8/80 .... Rich Murray ........... Giants |
| 2931 ... 5/2/80 .... Tony Scott ......... Cardinals | 2981 ... 6/8/80 .... Bill North ................ Giants |
| 2932 ... 5/2/80 .... Tony Scott .......... Cardinals | 2982 ... 6/14/80 .. Mike Easler ........... Pirates |
| 2933 ... 5/2/80 .... Bob Forsch ........ Cardinals | 2983 ... 6/14/80 .. Ed Ott .................... Pirates |
| 2934 ... 5/2/80 .... Ken Oberkfell ..... Cardinals | 2984 ... 6/14/80 .. Omar Moreno ......... Pirates |
| 2935 ... 5/2/80 .... Jim Kaat ............. Cardinals | 2985 ... 6/19/80 .. Ted Simmons ...... Cardinals |
| 2936 ... 5/7/80 .... Scott Sanderson ..... Expos | 2986 ... 6/19/80 .. George Hendrick Cardinals |
| 2937 ... 5/7/80 .... Ron LeFlore ............ Expos | 2987 ... 6/19/80 .. Leon Durham ...... Cardinals |
| 2938 ... 5/7/80 .... Ken Macha .............. Expos | 2988 ... 6/19/80 .. Tommy Herr ....... Cardinals |
| 2939 ... 5/7/80 .... Tony Bernazard ...... Expos | 2989 ... 6/19/80 .. Bob Sykes ......... Cardinals |
| 2940 ... 5/7/80 .... Scott Sanderson ..... Expos | 2990 ... 6/19/80 .. Bob Sykes ......... Cardinals |
| 2941 ... 5/13/80 .. Warren Cromartie ... Expos | 2991 ... 6/19/80 .. Terry Kennedy .... Cardinals |
| 2942 ... 5/13/80 .. Tony Bernazard ...... Expos | 2992 ... 6/24/80 .. Rudy Law ............ Dodgers |
| 2943 ... 5/13/80 .. Gary Carter ............. Expos | 2993 ... 6/24/80 .. Ron Cey .............. Dodgers |
| 2944 ... 5/13/80 .. Tony Bernazard ...... Expos | 2994 ... 6/24/80 .. Ron Cey .............. Dodgers |
| 2945 ... 5/13/80 .. Larry Parrish ........... Expos | 2995 ... 6/24/80 .. Davey Lopes ....... Dodgers |
| 2946 ... 5/13/80 .. Tony Bernazard ...... Expos | 2996 ... 6/24/80 .. Steve Howe ........ Dodgers |
| 2947 ... 5/13/80 .. Ron LeFlore ............ Expos | 2997 ... 6/29/80 .. Dave Concepcion ..... Reds |
| 2948 ... 5/13/80 .. Rodney Scott ......... Expos | 2998 ... 7/4/80 .... Ken Griffey ............... Reds |
| 2949 ... 5/13/80 .. Andre Dawson ........ Expos | 2999 ... 7/4/80 .... Dan Driessen ........... Reds |
| 2950 ... 5/18/80 .. Bake McBride ........ Phillies | 3000 ... 7/4/80 .... Cesar Geronimo ....... Reds |

| | | | |
|---|---|---|---|
| 3001 ... 7/4/80 .... Dave Concepcion ..... Reds | | 3051 ... 8/19/80 .. Omar Moreno ......... Pirates | |
| 3002 ... 7/4/80 .... Dave Collins .............. Reds | | 3052 ... 8/24/80 .. Ivan DeJesus ............ Cubs | |
| 3003 ... 7/4/80 .... Ray Knight ................ Reds | | 3053 ... 8/24/80 .. Scot Thompson ........ Cubs | |
| 3004 ... 7/10/80 .. Rudy Law ............ Dodgers | | 3054 ... 8/24/80 .. Mike Tyson ............... Cubs | |
| 3005 ... 7/10/80 .. Steve Yeager ....... Dodgers | | 3055 ... 8/24/80 .. Doug Capilla ............. Cubs | |
| 3006 ... 7/10/80 .. Rudy Law ............ Dodgers | | 3056 ... 8/24/80 .. Cliff Johnson ............. Cubs | |
| 3007 ... 7/10/80 .. Reggie Smith ....... Dodgers | | 3057 ... 8/24/80 .. Steve Dillard ............. Cubs | |
| 3008 ... 7/10/80 .. Steve Yeager ....... Dodgers | | 3058 ... 8/29/80 .. Mike Tyson ............... Cubs | |
| 3009 ... 7/10/80 .. Reggie Smith ....... Dodgers | | 3059 ... 8/29/80 .. Mike Tyson ............... Cubs | |
| 3010 ... 7/10/80 .. Dusty Baker ......... Dodgers | | 3060 ... 9/5/80 .... Tony Scott ......... Cardinals | |
| 3011 ... 7/15/80 .. Del Unser .............. Phillies | | 3061 ... 9/5/80 .... Keith Hernandez Cardinals | |
| 3012 ... 7/15/80 .. Bob Boone ............. Phillies | | 3062 ... 9/5/80 .... Dane Iorg .......... Cardinals | |
| 3013 ... 7/20/80 .. Rodney Scott .......... Expos | | 3063 ... 9/5/80 .... Ken Reitz .......... Cardinals | |
| 3014 ... 7/20/80 .. Andre Dawson ........ Expos | | 3064 ... 9/5/80 .... Mike Phillips ....... Cardinals | |
| 3015 ... 7/20/80 .. Ellis Valentine ......... Expos | | 3065 ... 9/5/80 .... Don Hood ........... Cardinals | |
| 3016 ... 7/20/80 .. Larry Parrish ........... Expos | | 3066 ... 9/5/80 .... Ken Reitz .......... Cardinals | |
| 3017 ... 7/20/80 .. Ron LeFlore ............ Expos | | 3067 ... 9/5/80 .... George Hendrick Cardinals | |
| 3018 ... 7/20/80 .. Ellis Valentine ......... Expos | | 3068 ... 9/5/80 .... Leon Durham ..... Cardinals | |
| 3019 ... 7/20/80 .. Steve Rogers .......... Expos | | 3069 ... 9/10/80 .. Davey Lopes ....... Dodgers | |
| 3020 ... 7/20/80 .. Rodney Scott .......... Expos | | 3070 ... 9/10/80 .. Derrel Thomas ..... Dodgers | |
| 3021 ... 7/20/80 .. Ellis Valentine ......... Expos | | 3071 ... 9/10/80 .. Burt Hooton ......... Dodgers | |
| 3022 ... 7/20/80 .. Warren Cromartie ... Expos | | 3072 ... 9/10/80 .. Davey Lopes ....... Dodgers | |
| 3023 ... 7/20/80 .. Larry Parrish ........... Expos | | 3073 ... 9/10/80 .. Derrel Thomas ..... Dodgers | |
| 3024 ... 7/25/80 .. Tim Raines .............. Expos | | 3074 ... 9/10/80 .. Burt Hooton ......... Dodgers | |
| 3025 ... 7/30/80 .. Mike Schmidt ......... Phillies | | 3075 ... 9/10/80 .. Jay Johnstone ..... Dodgers | |
| 3026 ... 7/30/80 .. Manny Trillo ........... Phillies | | 3076 ... 9/10/80 .. Mike Scioscia ...... Dodgers | |
| 3027 ... 7/30/80 .. Lonnie Smith ......... Phillies | | 3077 ... 9/10/80 .. Burt Hooton ......... Dodgers | |
| 3028 ... 8/4/80 .... Larry Herndon ........ Giants | | 3078 ... 9/15/80 .. Bob Shirley ............ Padres | |
| 3029 ... 8/4/80 .... Al Hargesheimer ..... Giants | | 3079 ... 9/15/80 .. Ozzie Smith ........... Padres | |
| 3030 ... 8/4/80 .... Larry Herndon ........ Giants | | 3080 ... 9/15/80 .. Randy Bass ........... Padres | |
| 3031 ... 8/4/80 .... Rennie Stennett ...... Giants | | 3081 ... 9/15/80 .. Tim Flannery .......... Padres | |
| 3032 ... 8/4/80 .... Max Venable .......... Giants | | 3082 ... 9/20/80 .. Joe Pettini .............. Giants | |
| 3033 ... 8/4/80 .... Rennie Stennett ...... Giants | | 3083 ... 9/20/80 .. Ed Whitson ............. Giants | |
| 3034 ... 8/4/80 .... Terry Whitfield ........ Giants | | 3084 ... 9/20/80 .. Terry Whitfield ........ Giants | |
| 3035 ... 8/9/80 .... Jerry Mumphrey ..... Padres | | 3085 ... 9/20/80 .. Joe Pettini .............. Giants | |
| 3036 ... 8/9/80 .... John Curtis ............ Padres | | 3086 ... 9/20/80 .. Guy Sularz .............. Giants | |
| 3037 ... 8/9/80 .... John D'Acquisto ..... Padres | | 3087 ... 9/20/80 .. Johnnie LeMaster ... Giants | |
| 3038 ... 8/14/80 .. Jerry Mumphrey ..... Padres | | 3088 ... 9/25/80 .. Gary Mathews ........ Braves | |
| 3039 ... 8/14/80 .. John Curtis ............ Padres | | 3089 ... 9/25/80 .. Bob Horner ............ Braves | |
| 3040 ... 8/14/80 .. Gene Richards ....... Padres | | 3090 ... 9/25/80 .. Rafael Ramirez ...... Braves | |
| 3041 ... 8/14/80 .. Jerry Mumphrey ..... Padres | | 3091 ... 9/25/80 .. Phil Niekro ............ Braves | |
| 3042 ... 8/14/80 .. Barry Evans ........... Padres | | 3092 ... 9/25/80 .. Rafael Ramirez ...... Braves | |
| 3043 ... 8/14/80 .. John Curtis ............ Padres | | 3093 ... 9/30/80 .. Gary Mathews ........ Braves | |
| 3044 ... 8/14/80 .. Dave Winfield ........ Padres | | 3094 ... 9/30/80 .. Dale Murphy ......... Braves | |
| 3045 ... 8/19/80 .. Mike Easler ............ Pirates | | 3095 ... 9/30/80 .. Glenn Hubbard ...... Braves | |
| 3046 ... 8/19/80 .. Ed Ott ................... Pirates | | 3096 ... 9/30/80 .. Doyle Alexander ..... Braves | |
| 3047 ... 8/19/80 .. John Candelaria ..... Pirates | | 3097 ... 9/30/80 .. Gary Mathews ........ Braves | |
| 3048 ... 8/19/80 .. Dave Parker .......... Pirates | | 3098 ... 9/30/80 .. Glenn Hubbard ...... Braves | |
| 3049 ... 8/19/80 .. Bill Madlock ........... Pirates | | 3099 ... 9/30/80 .. Doyle Alexander .... Braves | |
| 3050 ... 8/19/80 .. Ed Ott ................... Pirates | | 3100 ... 9/30/80 .. Terry Harper .......... Braves | |

| | | | |
|---|---|---|---|
| 3101 ... 10/4/80 .. Rick Monday ........ Dodgers | 3151 ... 5/16/81 .. Jim Tracy .................. Cubs |
| 3102 ... 10/4/80 .. Joe Ferguson ...... Dodgers | 3152 ... 5/21/81 .. Orlando Sanchez Cardinals |
| 3103 ... 10/4/80 .. Jerry Reuss ......... Dodgers | 3153 ... 5/21/81 .. John Martin ...... Cardinals |
| 3104 ... 10/4/80 .. Rick Monday ........ Dodgers | 3154 ... 5/21/81 .. Garry Templeton Cardinals |
| 3105 ... 10/4/80 .. Dusty Baker ......... Dodgers | 3155 ... 5/21/81 .. Ken Oberkfell .... Cardinals |
| 3106 ... 10/4/80 .. Pedro Guerrero ... Dodgers | 3156 ... 5/21/81 .. Orlando Sanchez Cardinals |
| 3107 ... 10/4/80 .. Joe Ferguson ...... Dodgers | 3157 ... 5/21/81 .. John Martin ...... Cardinals |
| 3108 ... 10/4/80 .. Jerry Reuss ......... Dodgers | 3158 ... 5/26/81 .. Juan Eichelberger .. Padres |
| 3109 ... 10/4/80 .. Jerry Reuss ......... Dodgers | 3159 ... 5/26/81 .. Broderick Perkins .. Padres |
| 3110 ... 4/15/81 .. Rafael Ramirez ...... Braves | 3160 ... 5/26/81 .. Terry Kennedy ....... Padres |
| 3111 ... 4/15/81 .. C. Washington ....... Braves | 3161 ... 5/26/81 .. Juan Eichelberger .. Padres |
| 3112 ... 4/15/81 .. Glenn Hubbard ..... Braves | 3162 ... 5/26/81 .. Ruppert Jones ....... Padres |
| 3113 ... 4/15/81 .. Dale Murphy ......... Braves | 3163 ... 5/26/81 .. Juan Eichelberger .. Padres |
| 3114 ... 4/15/81 .. Rafael Ramirez ...... Braves | 3164 ... 5/31/81 .. Larry Herndon ...... Giants |
| 3115 ... 4/15/81 .. C. Washington ....... Braves | 3165 ... 5/31/81 .. Tom Griffin ............. Giants |
| 3116 ... 4/15/81 .. Dale Murphy ......... Braves | 3166 ... 5/31/81 .. Darrell Evans .......... Giants |
| 3117 ... 4/15/81 .. Mike Lum ............... Braves | 3167 ... 5/31/81 .. Jerry Martin ............. Giants |
| 3118 ... 4/15/81 .. Tommy Doggs ....... Braves | 3168 ... 6/5/81 .... Mookie Wilson ......... Mets |
| 3119 ... 4/25/81 .. Bruce Berenyi ........... Reds | 3169 ... 6/5/81 .... Lee Mazzilli ............... Mets |
| 3120 ... 4/25/81 .. Dave Collins ............. Reds | 3170 ... 6/5/81 .... Randy Jones ............. Mets |
| 3121 ... 4/25/81 .. George Foster .......... Reds | 3171 ... 6/5/81 .... Mookie Wilson .......... Mets |
| 3122 ... 4/25/81 .. Dan Driessen ............ Reds | 3172 ... 6/5/81 .... Frank Taveras .......... Mets |
| 3123 ... 4/25/81 .. Joe Nolan ................. Reds | 3173 ... 6/5/81 .... Dave Kingman .......... Mets |
| 3124 ... 4/25/81 .. Ron Oester ............... Reds | 3174 ... 6/5/81 .... Mookie Wilson .......... Mets |
| 3125 ... 4/25/81 .. Bruce Berenyi ........... Reds | 3175 ... 6/5/81 .... Lee Mazzilli .............. Mets |
| 3126 ... 4/25/81 .. George Foster .......... Reds | 3176 ... 6/5/81 .... Mookie Wilson .......... Mets |
| 3127 ... 4/25/81 .. Ron Oester ............... Reds | 3177 ... 6/5/81 .... Dave Kingman .......... Mets |
| 3128 ... 4/25/81 .. Dave Collins ............. Reds | 3178 ... 6/10/81 .. Luis Aguayo .......... Phillies |
| 3129 ... 5/1/81 .... Rod Scurry ............. Pirates | 3179 ... 6/10/81 .. Steve Carlton ......... Phillies |
| 3130 ... 5/6/81 .... Tim Blackwell ............ Cubs | 3180 ... 6/10/81 .. Pete Rose ............. Phillies |
| 3131 ... 5/6/81 .... Bill Caudill ................. Cubs | 3181 ... 6/10/81 .. Luis Aguayo .......... Phillies |
| 3132 ... 5/6/81 .... Steve Henderson ...... Cubs | 3182 ... 6/10/81 .. Steve Carlton ......... Phillies |
| 3133 ... 5/11/81 .. Ken Griffey ................ Reds | 3183 ... 6/10/81 .. Pete Rose ............. Phillies |
| 3134 ... 5/11/81 .. Dave Concepcion ..... Reds | 3184 ... 6/10/81 .. Bob Boone ............. Phillies |
| 3135 ... 5/11/81 .. Johnny Bench ............ Reds | 3185 ... 6/10/81 .. Pete Rose ............. Phillies |
| 3136 ... 5/11/81 .. Ron Oester ............... Reds | 3186 ... 8/14/81 .. Randy Bass ........... Padres |
| 3137 ... 5/11/81 .. Ken Griffey ................ Reds | 3187 ... 8/14/81 .. Gene Richards ...... Padres |
| 3138 ... 5/11/81 .. Dave Collins ............. Reds | 3188 ... 8/14/81 .. Randy Bass ........... Padres |
| 3139 ... 5/11/81 .. Dave Concepcion ..... Reds | 3189 ... 8/19/81 .. Tim Raines ............. Expos |
| 3140 ... 5/11/81 .. George Foster .......... Reds | 3190 ... 8/19/81 .. Rodney Scott ......... Expos |
| 3141 ... 5/11/81 .. Dave Collins ............. Reds | 3191 ... 8/19/81 .. Andre Dawson ........ Expos |
| 3142 ... 5/11/81 .. Ray Knight ................. Reds | 3192 ... 8/19/81 .. Tim Wallach ............ Expos |
| 3143 ... 5/11/81 .. Ken Griffey ................ Reds | 3193 ... 8/19/81 .. Mike Phillips .......... Expos |
| 3144 ... 5/16/81 .. Steve Henderson ...... Cubs | 3194 ... 8/19/81 .. Scott Sanderson ... Expos |
| 3145 ... 5/16/81 .. Ken Reitz .................. Cubs | 3195 ... 8/19/81 .. Andre Dawson ........ Expos |
| 3146 ... 5/16/81 .. Tim Blackwell ............ Cubs | 3196 ... 8/19/81 .. Andre Dawson ........ Expos |
| 3147 ... 5/16/81 .. Randy Martz ............. Cubs | 3197 ... 8/25/81 .. Frank Taveras .......... Mets |
| 3148 ... 5/16/81 .. Steve Henderson ...... Cubs | 3198 ... 8/25/81 .. Lee Mazzilli .............. Mets |
| 3149 ... 5/16/81 .. Randy Martz ............. Cubs | 3199 ... 8/25/81 .. Greg Harris ............... Mets |
| 3150 ... 5/16/81 .. Scot Thompson ........ Cubs | 3200 ... 8/25/81 .. Hubie Brooks ............ Mets |

3201 ... 8/25/81 .. Mookie Wilson ........... Mets
3202 ... 8/25/81 .. Hubie Brooks ............. Mets
3203 ... 8/25/81 .. Mike Jorgensen ......... Mets
3204 ... 8/30/81 .. Lonnie Smith .......... Phillies
3205 ... 8/30/81 .. Dick Davis .............. Phillies
3206 ... 8/30/81 .. Dick Davis .............. Phillies
3207 ... 8/30/81 .. Luis Aguayo .......... Phillies
3208 ... 9/4/81 .... John Milner ............. Expos
3209 ... 9/4/81 .... Bill Gullickson .......... Expos
3210 ... 9/4/81 .... Tim Raines .............. Expos
3211 ... 9/4/81 .... Warren Cromartie ... Expos
3212 ... 9/4/81 .... Larry Parrish .......... Expos
3213 ... 9/4/81 .... Chris Speier ............ Expos
3214 ... 9/4/81 .... Rowland Office ........ Expos
3215 ... 9/9/81 .... Ed Miller ................. Braves
3216 ... 9/9/81 .... Brett Butler ............. Braves
3217 ... 9/9/81 .... Bruce Benedict ....... Braves
3218 ... 9/15/81 .. Paul Householder ..... Reds
3219 ... 9/15/81 .. Ray Knight .............. Reds
3220 ... 9/15/81 .. George Foster .......... Reds
3221 ... 9/15/81 .. Charlie Leibrandt ...... Reds
3222 ... 9/20/81 .. Milt May ................. Giants
3223 ... 9/20/81 .. Jack Clark .............. Giants
3224 ... 9/20/81 .. Billy Smith .............. Giants
3225 ... 9/20/81 .. Enos Cabell ........... Giants
3226 ... 9/20/81 .. Jeffrey Leonard ....... Giants
3227 ... 9/20/81 .. Darrell Evans ......... Giants
3228 ... 9/20/81 .. Dave Bergman ........ Giants
3229 ... 9/20/81 .. Jerry Martin ........... Giants
3230 ... 9/26/81 .. Ken Landreaux .... Dodgers
3231 ... 9/26/81 .. Pedro Guerrero ... Dodgers
3232 ... 9/26/81 .. Mike Scioscia ..... Dodgers
3233 ... 9/26/81 .. Ted Power .......... Dodgers
3234 ... 9/26/81 .. Davey Lopes ....... Dodgers
3235 ... 9/26/81 .. Steve Garvey ....... Dodgers
3236 ... 9/26/81 .. Mike Scioscia ...... Dodgers
3237 ... 9/26/81 .. Jack Perconte ..... Dodgers
3238 ... 9/26/81 .. Davey Lopes ....... Dodgers
3239 ... 9/26/81 .. Dusty Baker ........ Dodgers
3240 ... 9/26/81 .. Reggie Smith ....... Dodgers
3241 ... 10/1/81 .. Ken Griffey ................ Reds
3242 ... 10/1/81 .. Dave Concepcion ..... Reds
3243 ... 10/1/81 .. George Foster .......... Reds
3244 ... 10/1/81 .. Ron Oester .............. Reds
3245 ... 10/1/81 .. Bruce Berenyi .......... Reds
3246 ... 10/1/81 .. George Foster .......... Reds
3247 ... 10/1/81 .. Johnny Bench ........... Reds
3248 ... 10/1/81 .. Dave Collins ............. Reds
3249 ... 10/1/81 .. Paul Householder ..... Reds
3250 ... 4/6/82 .... Tommy Herr ....... Cardinals

3251 ... 4/6/82 .... Bob Forsch ........ Cardinals
3252 ... 4/6/82 .... Darrell Porter ..... Cardinals
3253 ... 4/6/82 .... Dane Iorg ........... Cardinals
3254 ... 4/6/82 .... Tommy Herr ....... Cardinals
3255 ... 4/11/82 .. Bob Horner ............ Braves
3256 ... 4/11/82 .. Rick Mahler ........... Braves
3257 ... 4/11/82 .. Brett Butler ............. Braves
3258 ... 4/16/82 .. Brett Butler ............. Braves
3259 ... 4/16/82 .. Bob Horner ............ Braves
3260 ... 4/16/82 .. Rufino Linares ........ Braves
3261 ... 4/16/82 .. Glenn Hubbard ...... Braves
3262 ... 4/16/82 .. Chris Chambliss ..... Braves
3263 ... 4/16/82 .. Rufino Linares ........ Braves
3264 ... 4/21/82 .. Pedro Guerrero ... Dodgers
3265 ... 4/21/82 .. Ken Landreaux .... Dodgers
3266 ... 4/21/82 .. Steve Garvey ....... Dodgers
3267 ... 4/21/82 .. Pedro Guerrero ... Dodgers
3268 ... 4/26/82 .. Keith Hernandez  Cardinals
3269 ... 4/26/82 .. Mark Littell ........ Cardinals
3270 ... 4/26/82 .. Jim Kaat ............. Cardinals
3271 ... 4/26/82 .. Steve Braun ....... Cardinals
3272 ... 4/26/82 .. George Hendrick Cardinals
3273 ... 5/1/82 .... Dale Berra ............ Pirates
3274 ... 5/1/82 .... Cecilio Guante ...... Pirates
3275 ... 5/1/82 .... Bill Madlock ........... Pirates
3276 ... 5/1/82 .... Mike Easler ........... Pirates
3277 ... 5/7/82 .... Bump Wills ................ Cubs
3278 ... 5/7/82 .... Junior Kennedy ....... Cubs
3279 ... 5/7/82 .... Ryne Sandberg ....... Cubs
3280 ... 5/7/82 .... Steve Henderson ...... Cubs
3281 ... 5/11/82 .. Dave Parker ........... Pirates
3282 ... 5/11/82 .. Willie Stargell ......... Pirates
3283 ... 5/11/82 .. Tom Griffin ............. Pirates
3284 ... 5/11/82 .. Dave Parker ........... Pirates
3285 ... 5/16/82 .. Keith Moreland ......... Cubs
3286 ... 5/16/82 .. Doug Bird .................. Cubs
3287 ... 5/16/82 .. Junior Kennedy ......... Cubs
3288 ... 5/16/82 .. Larry Cox .................. Cubs
3289 ... 5/16/82 .. Junior Kennedy ......... Cubs
3290 ... 5/16/82 .. Gary Woods .............. Cubs
3291 ... 5/22/82 .. Gary Rajsich ............. Mets
3292 ... 5/22/82 .. Ron Gardenhire ......... Mets
3293 ... 5/22/82 .. Pete Falcone ............ Mets
3294 ... 5/22/82 .. Pete Falcone ............ Mets
3295 ... 5/22/82 .. George Foster .......... Mets
3296 ... 5/22/82 .. Gary Rajsich ............. Mets
3297 ... 5/22/82 .. Wally Backman .......... Mets
3298 ... 5/22/82 .. Ron Gardenhire ......... Mets
3299 ... 5/22/82 .. Gary Rajsich ............. Mets
3300 ... 5/22/82 .. Mookie Wilson ........... Mets

| | | | |
|---|---|---|---|
| 3301 ... 5/28/82 .. John Stearns ............. Mets | 3351 ... 6/28/82 .. Dale Murphy ......... Braves |
| 3302 ... 5/28/82 .. Dave Kingman ........... Mets | 3352 ... 6/28/82 .. Rufino Linares ....... Braves |
| 3303 ... 5/28/82 .. Gary Rajsich ............. Mets | 3353 ... 6/28/82 .. Bob Horner ............ Braves |
| 3304 ... 5/28/82 .. Mookie Wilson ........... Mets | 3354 ... 7/4/82 .... Steve Sax ............. Dodgers |
| 3305 ... 5/28/82 .. John Stearns ............. Mets | 3355 ... 7/4/82 .... Ron Roenicke ...... Dodgers |
| 3306 ... 5/28/82 .. George Foster ........... Mets | 3356 ... 7/4/82 .... Ron Cey ............... Dodgers |
| 3307 ... 5/28/82 .. Dave Kingman ........... Mets | 3357 ... 7/4/82 .... Jorge Orta ............ Dodgers |
| 3308 ... 5/28/82 .. Gary Rajsich ............. Mets | 3358 ... 7/4/82 .... Steve Sax ............. Dodgers |
| 3309 ... 5/28/82 .. Wally Backman ......... Mets | 3359 ... 7/4/82 .... Ron Roenicke ...... Dodgers |
| 3310 ... 5/28/82 .. George Foster ........... Mets | 3360 ... 7/4/82 .... Jorge Orta ........... Dodgers |
| 3311 ... 5/28/82 .. Dave Kingman ........... Mets | 3361 ... 7/4/82 .... Steve Garvey ....... Dodgers |
| 3312 ... 6/2/82 .... Andre Dawson ........ Expos | 3362 ... 7/4/82 .... Ron Roenicke ...... Dodgers |
| 3313 ... 6/2/82 .... Andre Dawson ........ Expos | 3363 ... 7/4/82 .... Ron Cey ............... Dodgers |
| 3314 ... 6/2/82 .... Warren Cromartie ... Expos | 3364 ... 7/9/82 .... Lonnie Smith ...... Cardinals |
| 3315 ... 6/2/82 .... Scott Sanderson ..... Expos | 3365 ... 7/9/82 .... Tommy Herr ....... Cardinals |
| 3316 ... 6/2/82 .... Warren Cromartie ... Expos | 3366 ... 7/9/82 .... Ken Oberkfell ..... Cardinals |
| 3317 ... 6/8/82 .... Joe Morgan ............. Giants | 3367 ... 7/9/82 .... Willie McGee ...... Cardinals |
| 3318 ... 6/8/82 .... Jim Wohlford ........... Giants | 3368 ... 7/9/82 .... Keith Hernandez Cardinals |
| 3319 ... 6/8/82 .... Reggie Smith ........... Giants | 3369 ... 7/9/82 .... Dave LaPoint ..... Cardinals |
| 3320 ... 6/8/82 .... Tom O'Malley ......... Giants | 3370 ... 7/9/82 .... Dave LaPoint ..... Cardinals |
| 3321 ... 6/13/82 .. Garry Templeton .... Padres | 3371 ... 7/9/82 .... Willie McGee ...... Cardinals |
| 3322 ... 6/13/82 .. Ruppert Jones ....... Padres | 3372 ... 7/9/82 .... Ozzie Smith ....... Cardinals |
| 3323 ... 6/13/82 .. Tim Flannery ........... Padres | 3373 ... 7/9/82 .... Jeff Lahti ............. Cardinals |
| 3324 ... 6/13/82 .. John Montefusco .. Padres | 3374 ... 7/16/82 .. Jason Thompson ... Pirates |
| 3325 ... 6/13/82 .. Alan Wiggins .......... Padres | 3375 ... 7/16/82 .. Mike Easler ............ Pirates |
| 3326 ... 6/13/82 .. Garry Templeton .... Padres | 3376 ... 7/16/82 .. Larry McWilliams ... Pirates |
| 3327 ... 6/13/82 .. Terry Kennedy ....... Padres | 3377 ... 7/16/82 .. Omar Moreno ......... Pirates |
| 3328 ... 6/13/82 .. Luis Salazar ........... Padres | 3378 ... 7/16/82 .. Dave Parker .......... Pirates |
| 3329 ... 6/13/82 .. Sixto Lezcano ....... Padres | 3379 ... 7/16/82 .. Mike Easler ............ Pirates |
| 3330 ... 6/18/82 .. Garry Templeton .... Padres | 3380 ... 7/16/82 .. Larry McWilliams ... Pirates |
| 3331 ... 6/18/82 .. Ruppert Jones ....... Padres | 3381 ... 7/16/82 .. Mike Easler ............ Pirates |
| 3332 ... 6/18/82 .. Tim Flannery ........... Padres | 3382 ... 7/16/82 .. Tony Pena ............. Pirates |
| 3333 ... 6/18/82 .. Chris Welsh ........... Padres | 3383 ... 7/16/82 .. Dave Parker .......... Pirates |
| 3334 ... 6/18/82 .. Ruppert Jones ....... Padres | 3384 ... 7/16/82 .. Mike Easler ............ Pirates |
| 3335 ... 6/18/82 .. Terry Kennedy ....... Padres | 3385 ... 7/21/82 .. Ryne Sandberg ......... Cubs |
| 3336 ... 6/18/82 .. Chris Welsh ........... Padres | 3386 ... 7/21/82 .. Junior Kennedy ......... Cubs |
| 3337 ... 6/18/82 .. Terry Kennedy ....... Padres | 3387 ... 7/21/82 .. Keith Moreland ......... Cubs |
| 3338 ... 6/18/82 .. Tim Flannery ........... Padres | 3388 ... 7/21/82 .. Allen Ripley ............... Cubs |
| 3339 ... 6/18/82 .. Ruppert Jones ....... Padres | 3389 ... 7/27/82 .. Paul Householder ..... Reds |
| 3340 ... 6/18/82 .. Sixto Lezcano ........ Padres | 3390 ... 7/27/82 .. Ron Oester ............... Reds |
| 3341 ... 6/23/82 .. Chili Davis ............... Giants | 3391 ... 7/27/82 .. Charlie Leibrandt ...... Reds |
| 3342 ... 6/23/82 .. Dave Bergman ........ Giants | 3392 ... 7/27/82 .. Alex Trevino .............. Reds |
| 3343 ... 6/23/82 .. Chili Davis ............... Giants | 3393 ... 7/27/82 .. Charlie Leibrandt ...... Reds |
| 3344 ... 6/28/82 .. Chris Chambliss ...... Braves | 3394 ... 7/27/82 .. Cesar Cedeno .......... Reds |
| 3345 ... 6/28/82 .. Dale Murphy ......... Braves | 3395 ... 7/27/82 .. Dan Driessen ........... Reds |
| 3346 ... 6/28/82 .. C. Washington ....... Braves | 3396 ... 7/27/82 .. Paul Householder ..... Reds |
| 3347 ... 6/28/82 .. Dale Murphy ......... Braves | 3397 ... 7/27/82 .. Ron Oester ............... Reds |
| 3348 ... 6/28/82 .. Rafael Ramirez ....... Braves | 3398 ... 7/27/82 .. Alex Trevino .............. Reds |
| 3349 ... 6/28/82 .. Rick Mahler ............ Braves | 3399 ... 7/27/82 .. Charlie Leibrandt ...... Reds |
| 3350 ... 6/28/82 .. C. Washington ....... Braves | 3400 ... 7/27/82 .. Eddie Milner ............. Reds |

| | | | |
|---|---|---|---|
| 3401 ... 7/27/82 ... Cesar Cedeno .......... Reds | | 3451 ... 9/5/82 .... Pete Rose .............. Phillies | |
| 3402 ... 8/1/82 .... Joe Morgan ............. Giants | | 3452 ... 9/5/82 .... Mike Schmidt ....... Phillies | |
| 3403 ... 8/1/82 .... Chili Davis ............... Giants | | 3453 ... 9/5/82 .... Ozzie Virgil ............ Phillies | |
| 3404 ... 8/1/82 .... Reggie Smith .......... Giants | | 3454 ... 9/5/82 ... Ivan DeJesus ......... Phillies | |
| 3405 ... 8/1/82 .... Jeffrey Leonard ...... Giants | | 3455 ... 9/5/82 ... Len Matuszek ........ Phillies | |
| 3406 ... 8/1/82 .... Milt May .................. Giants | | 3456 ... 9/5/82 .... Pete Rose .............. Phillies | |
| 3407 ... 8/1/82 .... Reggie Smith .......... Giants | | 3457 ... 9/5/82 .... Manny Trillo .......... Phillies | |
| 3408 ... 8/6/82 .... Atlee Hammaker ..... Giants | | 3458 ... 9/10/82 .. Dusty Baker ........ Dodgers | |
| 3409 ... 8/6/82 .... Chili Davis ............... Giants | | 3459 ... 9/10/82 .. Rick Monday ........ Dodgers | |
| 3410 ... 8/6/82 .... Duane Kuiper ......... Giants | | 3460 ... 9/10/82 .. Bill Russell .......... Dodgers | |
| 3411 ... 8/6/82 .... Jeffrey Leonard ...... Giants | | 3461 ... 9/10/82 .. Burt Hooton .......... Dodgers | |
| 3412 ... 8/6/82 .... Atlee Hammaker ..... Giants | | 3462 ... 9/10/82 .. Ken Landreaux .... Dodgers | |
| 3413 ... 8/6/82 .... Chili Davis ............... Giants | | 3463 ... 9/10/82 .. Steve Garvey ....... Dodgers | |
| 3414 ... 8/6/82 .... Champ Summers .... Giants | | 3464 ... 9/10/82 .. Derrel Thomas ..... Dodgers | |
| 3415 ... 8/6/82 .... Duane Kuiper ......... Giants | | 3465 ... 9/10/82 .. Mike Scioscia ...... Dodgers | |
| 3416 ... 8/11/82 .. Broderick Perkins .. Padres | | 3466 ... 9/10/82 .. Jose Morales ....... Dodgers | |
| 3417 ... 8/11/82 .. Joe Pittman ............ Padres | | 3467 ... 9/15/82 .. C. Washington ....... Braves | |
| 3418 ... 8/11/82 .. Tony Gwynn ............ Padres | | 3468 ... 9/15/82 .. Glenn Hubbard ...... Braves | |
| 3419 ... 8/11/82 .. Luis Salazar ........... Padres | | 3469 ... 9/15/82 .. Terry Harper .......... Braves | |
| 3420 ... 8/11/82 .. Terry Kennedy ....... Padres | | 3470 ... 9/15/82 .. Bob Porter ............. Braves | |
| 3421 ... 8/11/82 .. Terry Kennedy ....... Padres | | 3471 ... 9/20/82 .. Dale Murphy .......... Braves | |
| 3422 ... 8/16/82 .. Tom Lawless ............ Reds | | 3472 ... 9/20/82 .. C. Washington ....... Braves | |
| 3423 ... 8/16/82 .. Dan Driessen ........... Reds | | 3473 ... 9/20/82 .. Glenn Hubbard ...... Braves | |
| 3424 ... 8/16/82 .. Bob Shirley ............... Reds | | 3474 ... 9/26/82 .. Duane Walker .......... Reds | |
| 3425 ... 8/16/82 .. Tom Lawless ............. Reds | | 3475 ... 9/26/82 .. Dan Driessen ........... Reds | |
| 3426 ... 8/16/82 .. Tom Lawless ............. Reds | | 3476 ... 9/26/82 .. Cesar Cedeno .......... Reds | |
| 3427 ... 8/16/82 .. Dan Driessen ........... Reds | | 3477 ... 9/26/82 .. Bob Shirley ............... Reds | |
| 3428 ... 8/16/82 .. Paul Householder ..... Reds | | 3478 ... 9/26/82 .. Duane Walker .......... Reds | |
| 3429 ... 8/21/82 .. Joel Youngblood ..... Expos | | 3479 ... 9/26/82 .. Bob Shirley ............... Reds | |
| 3430 ... 8/21/82 .. Andre Dawson ........ Expos | | 3480 ... 9/26/82 .. Duane Walker .......... Reds | |
| 3431 ... 8/21/82 .. Andre Dawson ........ Expos | | 3481 ... 9/26/82 .. Paul Householder ..... Reds | |
| 3432 ... 8/21/82 .. Al Oliver ................. Expos | | 3482 ... 9/26/82 .. Rafael Landestoy ..... Reds | |
| 3433 ... 8/21/82 .. Warren Cromartie ... Expos | | 3483 ... 9/26/82 .. Dave Concepcion ..... Reds | |
| 3434 ... 8/26/82 .. Andre Dawson ........ Expos | | 3484 ... 9/26/82 .. Ron Oester ............... Reds | |
| 3435 ... 8/26/82 .. Al Oliver .................. Expos | | 3485 ... 10/1/82 .. Duane Walker .......... Reds | |
| 3436 ... 8/26/82 .. Bill Gullickson .......... Expos | | 3486 ... 10/1/82 .. Paul Householder ..... Reds | |
| 3437 ... 8/26/82 .. Tim Raines .............. Expos | | 3487 ... 10/1/82 .. Ron Oester ............... Reds | |
| 3438 ... 8/26/82 .. Warren Cromartie ... Expos | | 3488 ... 10/1/82 .. Rafael Landestoy ...... Reds | |
| 3439 ... 8/26/82 .. Andre Dawson ........ Expos | | 3489 ... 10/1/82 .. Duane Walker .......... Reds | |
| 3440 ... 8/26/82 .. Doug Flynn .............. Expos | | 3490 ... 10/1/82 .. Duane Walker .......... Reds | |
| 3441 ... 8/31/82 .. Mookie Wilson ........... Mets | | 3491 ... 10/1/82 .. Bob Shirley ............... Reds | |
| 3442 ... 8/31/82 .. Dave Kingman ........... Mets | | 3492 ... 10/1/82 .. Gary Redus ............... Reds | |
| 3443 ... 8/31/82 .. Brian Giles ................ Mets | | 3493 ... 10/1/82 .. Duane Walker .......... Reds | |
| 3444 ... 8/31/82 .. Ed Lynch .................... Mets | | 3494 ... 10/1/82 .. Ron Oester ............... Reds | |
| 3445 ... 8/31/82 .. Mookie Wilson ........... Mets | | 3495 ... 4/17/83 .. Tim Raines .............. Expos | |
| 3446 ... 8/31/82 .. Ron Hodges .............. Mets | | 3496 ... 4/17/83 .. Andre Dawson ........ Expos | |
| 3447 ... 8/31/82 .. Ed Lynch .................... Mets | | 3497 ... 4/17/83 .. Warren Cromartie ... Expos | |
| 3448 ... 8/31/82 .. Mike Jorgensen ......... Mets | | 3498 ... 4/17/83 .. Gary Carter ............ Expos | |
| 3449 ... 8/31/82 .. Mookie Wilson ........... Mets | | 3499 ... 4/17/83 .. Terry Francona ....... Expos | |
| 3450 ... 9/5/82 .... Ozzie Virgil ............ Phillies | | 3500 ... 4/17/83 .. Andre Dawson ........ Expos | |

| | | | |
|---|---|---|---|
| 3501 ... 4/17/83 .. Warren Cromartie ... Expos | 3551 ... 6/28/83 .. Craig McMurtry ...... Braves |
| 3502 ... 4/22/83 .. Dick Ruthven ......... Phillies | 3552 ... 6/28/83 .. Rafael Ramirez ...... Braves |
| 3503 ... 4/22/83 ... Joe Morgan ............ Phillies | 3553 ... 6/28/83 ... Glenn Hubbard ...... Braves |
| 3504 ... 4/22/83 .. Bo Diaz .................. Phillies | 3554 ... 7/2/83 .... Pedro Guerrero ... Dodgers |
| 3505 ... 4/27/83 .. Tim Wallach ............ Expos | 3555 ... 7/2/83 .... Joe Beckwith ....... Dodgers |
| 3506 ... 4/27/83 .. Tim Blackwell ......... Expos | 3556 ... 7/2/83 .... Rafael Landestoy Dodgers |
| 3507 ... 4/27/83 .. Bryan Little ............. Expos | 3557 ... 7/2/83 .... Derrel Thomas ..... Dodgers |
| 3508 ... 4/27/83 .. Tim Blackwell ......... Expos | 3558 ... 7/2/83 .... Greg Brock ......... Dodgers |
| 3509 ... 4/27/83 .. Brad Mills ............... Expos | 3559 ... 7/2/83 .... Mike Marshall ...... Dodgers |
| 3510 ... 5/2/83 .... Hubie Brooks ............ Mets | 3560 ... 7/2/83 .... Ron Roenicke ...... Dodgers |
| 3511 ... 5/2/83 .... Danny Heep .............. Mets | 3561 ... 7/2/83 .... Derrel Thomas ..... Dodgers |
| 3512 ... 5/2/83 .... Wally Backman ......... Mets | 3562 ... 7/8/83 .... Hubie Brooks ............ Mets |
| 3513 ... 5/2/83 .... Brian Giles ................. Mets | 3563 ... 7/8/83 .... Keith Hernandez ....... Mets |
| 3514 ... 5/2/83 .... Mike Torrez .............. Mets | 3564 ... 7/8/83 .... Brian Giles ................. Mets |
| 3515 ... 5/2/83 .... Hubie Brooks ............ Mets | 3565 ... 7/8/83 .... Tom Gorman ............. Mets |
| 3516 ... 5/2/83 .... George Foster ........... Mets | 3566 ... 7/8/83 .... Mookie Wilson ........... Mets |
| 3517 ... 5/2/83 .... Wally Backman ......... Mets | 3567 ... 7/8/83 .... Darryl Strawberry ..... Mets |
| 3518 ... 5/2/83 .... Ronn Reynolds .......... Mets | 3568 ... 7/8/83 .... Ron Hodges .............. Mets |
| 3519 ... 5/2/83 .... Mike Torrez .............. Mets | 3569 ... 7/8/83 .... Brian Giles ................. Mets |
| 3520 ... 5/2/83 .... Hubie Brooks ............ Mets | 3570 ... 7/8/83 .... Hubie Brooks ............ Mets |
| 3521 ... 5/2/83 .... Wally Backman ......... Mets | 3571 ... 7/8/83 .... Keith Hernandez ....... Mets |
| 3522 ... 6/7/83 .... Chili Davis ............... Giants | 3572 ... 7/8/83 .... Darryl Strawberry ..... Mets |
| 3523 ... 6/7/83 .... Jeffrey Leonard ....... Giants | 3573 ... 7/8/83 .... Ron Hodges .............. Mets |
| 3524 ... 6/7/83 .... Atlee Hammaker ....... Giants | 3574 ... 7/13/83 .. Al Oliver ................... Expos |
| 3525 ... 6/12/83 .. Steve Garvey ......... Padres | 3575 ... 7/13/83 .. Terry Francona ....... Expos |
| 3526 ... 6/12/83 .. Kevin McReynolds . Padres | 3576 ... 7/13/83 .. Andre Dawson ........ Expos |
| 3527 ... 6/12/83 .. Luis Salazar ........... Padres | 3577 ... 7/13/83 .. Chris Speier ............ Expos |
| 3528 ... 6/12/83 .. Eric Show .............. Padres | 3578 ... 7/13/83 .. Bryan Little ............. Expos |
| 3529 ... 6/12/83 .. Eric Show .............. Padres | 3579 ... 7/17/83 .. Hubie Brooks ............ Mets |
| 3530 ... 6/12/83 .. Steve Garvey ......... Padres | 3580 ... 7/17/83 .. Darryl Strawberry ..... Mets |
| 3531 ... 6/12/83 .. Kevin McReynolds . Padres | 3581 ... 7/17/83 .. Keith Hernandez ....... Mets |
| 3532 ... 6/12/83 .. Luis Salazar ........... Padres | 3582 ... 7/17/83 .. Walt Terrell ................ Mets |
| 3533 ... 6/12/83 .. Mario Ramirez ....... Padres | 3583 ... 7/17/83 .. Jose Oquendo .......... Mets |
| 3534 ... 6/12/83 .. Jerry Turner ........... Padres | 3584 ... 7/21/83 .. Doug Flynn .............. Expos |
| 3535 ... 6/12/83 .. Terry Kennedy ....... Padres | 3585 ... 7/21/83 .. Tim Raines .............. Expos |
| 3536 ... 6/17/83 .. Kevin McReynolds . Padres | 3586 ... 7/26/83 .. Mike Schmidt ......... Phillies |
| 3537 ... 6/17/83 .. Eric Show .............. Padres | 3587 ... 7/26/83 .. Joe Lefebvre .......... Phillies |
| 3538 ... 6/17/83 .. Steve Garvey ......... Padres | 3588 ... 7/26/83 .. Charles Hudson ..... Phillies |
| 3539 ... 6/17/83 .. Kevin McReynolds . Padres | 3589 ... 7/26/83 .. Charles Hudson ..... Phillies |
| 3540 ... 6/17/83 .. Terry Kennedy ....... Padres | 3590 ... 7/26/83 .. Von Hayes .............. Phillies |
| 3541 ... 6/17/83 .. Ruppert Jones ....... Padres | 3591 ... 7/26/83 .. Charles Hudson ..... Phillies |
| 3542 ... 6/22/83 .. Chris Chambliss ..... Braves | 3592 ... 7/30/83 .. Dan Driessen ............ Reds |
| 3543 ... 6/22/83 .. Brett Butler ............ Braves | 3593 ... 7/30/83 .. Ron Oester .............. Reds |
| 3544 ... 6/22/83 .. Glenn Hubbard ...... Braves | 3594 ... 7/30/83 .. Dan Driessen ............ Reds |
| 3545 ... 6/22/83 .. Jerry Royster ......... Braves | 3595 ... 7/30/83 .. Duane Walker ........... Reds |
| 3546 ... 6/22/83 .. Chris Chambliss ..... Braves | 3596 ... 7/30/83 .. Nick Esasky .............. Reds |
| 3547 ... 6/22/83 .. Jerry Royster ......... Braves | 3597 ... 8/3/83 .... Ruppert Jones ....... Padres |
| 3548 ... 6/22/83 .. C. Washington ....... Braves | 3598 ... 8/3/83 .... Tim Lollar .............. Padres |
| 3549 ... 6/28/83 .. Craig McMurtry ...... Braves | 3599 ... 8/3/83 .... Bobby Brown ......... Padres |
| 3550 ... 6/28/83 .. Glenn Hubbard ...... Braves | 3600 ... 8/3/83 .... Terry Kennedy ....... Padres |

3601 ... 8/3/83 .... Bobby Brown ......... Padres
3602 ... 8/3/83 .... Alan Wiggins .......... Padres
3603 ... 8/3/83 .... Terry Kennedy ....... Padres
3604 ... 8/3/83 .... Luis Salazar ........... Padres
3605 ... 8/3/83 .... Tim Flannery .......... Padres
3606 ... 8/3/83 .... Kurt Bevacqua ....... Padres
3607 ... 8/7/83 .... Darrell Evans .......... Giants
3608 ... 8/7/83 .... Jeffrey Leonard ...... Giants
3609 ... 8/7/83 .... Chili Davis .............. Giants
3610 ... 8/7/83 .... Milt May ................. Giants
3611 ... 8/7/83 .... Mike Krukow ........... Giants
3612 ... 8/7/83 .... Chili Davis .............. Giants
3613 ... 8/7/83 .... Milt May ................. Giants
3614 ... 8/7/83 .... Jeffrey Leonard ...... Giants
3615 ... 8/12/83 .. Dave Bergman ........ Giants
3616 ... 8/12/83 .. Renie Martin ........... Giants
3617 ... 8/12/83 .. Chili Davis .............. Giants
3618 ... 8/12/83 .. Jack Clark .............. Giants
3619 ... 8/12/83 .. Jeffrey Leonard ...... Giants
3620 ... 8/17/83 .. Dave Concepcion ..... Reds
3621 ... 8/17/83 .. Frank Pastore .......... Reds
3622 ... 8/17/83 .. Nick Esasky ............. Reds
3623 ... 8/21/83 .. Dane Iorg ........... Cardinals
3624 ... 8/21/83 .. Darrell Porter ..... Cardinals
3625 ... 8/21/83 .. Danny Cox ......... Cardinals
3626 ... 8/21/83 .. Andy Van Slyke . Cardinals
3627 ... 8/21/83 .. Darrell Porter ..... Cardinals
3628 ... 8/26/83 .. Mel Hall .................... Cubs
3629 ... 8/26/83 .. Jody Davis ................ Cubs
3630 ... 9/1/83 .... Marvell Wynne ....... Pirates
3631 ... 9/1/83 .... Doug Frobel ........... Pirates
3632 ... 9/1/83 .... Rafael Belliard ........ Pirates
3633 ... 9/1/83 .... Lee Mazzilli ............ Pirates
3634 ... 9/1/83 .... Doug Frobel ........... Pirates
3635 ... 9/1/83 .... Richie Hebner ........ Pirates
3636 ... 9/1/83 .... Lee Tunnell ............. Pirates
3637 ... 9/1/83 .... Lee Mazzilli ............ Pirates
3638 ... 9/1/83 .... Dale Berra .............. Pirates
3639 ... 9/1/83 .... Joe Orsulak ............ Pirates
3640 ... 9/7/83 .... Alan Wiggins .......... Padres
3641 ... 9/7/83 .... Terry Kennedy ....... Padres
3642 ... 9/7/83 .... Ruppert Jones ....... Padres
3643 ... 9/7/83 .... Eric Show ............... Padres
3644 ... 9/7/83 .... Terry Kennedy ....... Padres
3645 ... 9/7/83 .... Garry Templeton ... Padres
3646 ... 9/11/83 .. Dan Gladden .......... Giants
3647 ... 9/11/83 .. Guy Sularz .............. Giants
3648 ... 9/11/83 .. Atlee Hammaker ..... Giants
3649 ... 9/11/83 .. Dan Gladden .......... Giants
3650 ... 9/11/83 .. Chili Davis .............. Giants

3651 ... 9/11/83 .. Chris Smith ............. Giants
3652 ... 9/11/83 .. Max Venable .......... Giants
3653 ... 9/11/83 .. Chili Davis .............. Giants
3654 ... 9/11/83 .. Darrell Evans .......... Giants
3655 ... 9/11/83 .. Chris Smith ............. Giants
3656 ... 9/11/83 .. Max Venable .......... Giants
3657 ... 9/15/83 .. Bill Russell ........... Dodgers
3658 ... 9/15/83 .. R.J. Reynolds ...... Dodgers
3659 ... 9/15/83 .. Alejandro Pena .... Dodgers
3660 ... 9/15/83 .. R.J. Reynolds ...... Dodgers
3661 ... 9/15/83 .. Alejandro Pena .... Dodgers
3662 ... 9/20/83 .. Steve Yeager ...... Dodgers
3663 ... 9/20/83 .. Rafael Landestoy  Dodgers
3664 ... 9/20/83 .. Steve Sax ............ Dodgers
3665 ... 9/20/83 .. R.J. Reynolds ...... Dodgers
3666 ... 9/20/83 .. Steve Yeager ....... Dodgers
3667 ... 9/20/83 .. Ken Landreaux .... Dodgers
3668 ... 9/20/83 .. Mike Marshall ...... Dodgers
3669 ... 9/25/83 .. Tom O'Malley ......... Giants
3670 ... 9/25/83 .. Joel Youngblood ..... Giants
3671 ... 9/25/83 .. Chili Davis .............. Giants
3672 ... 9/25/83 .. Chris Smith ............. Giants
3673 ... 9/29/83 .. Glenn Hubbard ...... Braves
3674 ... 9/29/83 .. Rafael Ramirez ...... Braves
3675 ... 9/29/83 .. Craig McMurtry ...... Braves
3676 ... 9/29/83 .. Chris Chambliss .... Braves
3677 ... 9/29/83 .. Brett Butler ............. Braves
3678 ... 4/4/84 .... Tim Raines ............. Expos
3679 ... 4/4/84 .... Andre Dawson ....... Expos
3680 ... 4/4/84 .... Argenis Salazar ....... Expos
3681 ... 4/4/84 .... Bill Gullickson .......... Expos
3682 ... 4/4/84 .... Tim Raines ............. Expos
3683 ... 4/4/84 .... Andre Dawson ....... Expos
3684 ... 4/10/84 .. Joe Lefebvre ........ Phillies
3685 ... 4/10/84 .. Von Hayes ............ Phillies
3686 ... 4/10/84 .. Bo Diaz .................. Phillies
3687 ... 4/10/84 .. Len Matuszek ........ Phillies
3688 ... 4/10/84 .. Joe Lefebvre ........ Phillies
3689 ... 4/10/84 .. Juan Samuel ......... Phillies
3690 ... 4/10/84 .. Mike Schmidt ........ Phillies
3691 ... 4/10/84 .. Joe Lefebvre ......... Phillies
3692 ... 4/10/84 .. Von Hayes ............ Phillies
3693 ... 4/10/84 .. Ivan DeJesus ........ Phillies
3694 ... 4/10/84 .. John Denny ........... Phillies
3695 ... 4/15/84 .. Nick Esasky ............ Reds
3696 ... 4/15/84 .. Dan Bilardello ........... Reds
3697 ... 4/15/84 .. Joe Price ................... Reds
3698 ... 4/15/84 .. Eddie Milner ............. Reds
3699 ... 4/15/84 .. Tony Perez ............... Reds
3700 ... 4/15/84 .. Dave Parker ............. Reds

| | | | |
|---|---|---|---|
| 3701 ... 4/15/84 .. Nick Esasky .............. Reds | 3751 ... 5/26/84 .. Marvell Wynne ....... Pirates |
| 3702 ... 4/15/84 .. Joe Price .................. Reds | 3752 ... 5/26/84 .. Lee Lacy ............... Pirates |
| 3703 ... 4/20/84 .. Bob Horner ............ Braves | 3753 ... 5/26/84 .. Tony Pena ............. Pirates |
| 3704 ... 4/20/84 .. C. Washington ....... Braves | 3754 ... 5/26/84 .. Bill Madlock ........... Pirates |
| 3705 ... 4/25/84 .. Terry Whitfield ..... Dodgers | 3755 ... 5/26/84 .. Lee Mazzilli ........... Pirates |
| 3706 ... 4/25/84 .. Pedro Guerrero ... Dodgers | 3756 ... 5/26/84 .. Dale Berra ............. Pirates |
| 3707 ... 4/25/84 .. Pedro Guerrero ... Dodgers | 3757 ... 5/26/84 .. Jason Thompson ... Pirates |
| 3708 ... 4/25/84 .. Mike Marshall ...... Dodgers | 3758 ... 5/26/84 .. Tony Pena ............. Pirates |
| 3709 ... 5/1/84 .... Ron Oester .............. Reds | 3759 ... 6/1/84 .... R.J. Reynolds ...... Dodgers |
| 3710 ... 5/1/84 .... Duane Walker .......... Reds | 3760 ... 6/1/84 .... Terry Whitfield ..... Dodgers |
| 3711 ... 5/1/84 .... Dave Concepcion ..... Reds | 3761 ... 6/1/84 .... Pedro Guerrero ... Dodgers |
| 3712 ... 5/1/84 .... Brad Gulden ............. Reds | 3762 ... 6/1/84 .... Rick Honeycutt ... Dodgers |
| 3713 ... 5/1/84 .... Jeff Russell .............. Reds | 3763 ... 6/17/84 .. Greg Brock ......... Dodgers |
| 3714 ... 5/1/84 .... Duane Walker .......... Reds | 3764 ... 6/17/84 .. Steve Sax ............ Dodgers |
| 3715 ... 5/1/84 .... Dave Parker ............. Reds | 3765 ... 6/17/84 .. Terry Whitfield ..... Dodgers |
| 3716 ... 5/1/84 .... Brad Gulden ............. Reds | 3766 ... 6/17/84 .. Steve Sax ............ Dodgers |
| 3717 ... 5/6/84 .... Wally Backman ....... Mets | 3767 ... 6/17/84 .. Pedro Guerrero ... Dodgers |
| 3718 ... 5/6/84 .... Darryl Strawberry .... Mets | 3768 ... 6/17/84 .. Terry Whitfield ..... Dodgers |
| 3719 ... 5/6/84 .... Ross Jones .............. Mets | 3769 ... 6/17/84 .. Mike Scioscia ...... Dodgers |
| 3720 ... 5/6/84 .... Wally Backman ......... Mets | 3770 ... 6/17/84 .. Dave Anderson .... Dodgers |
| 3721 ... 5/6/84 .... Darryl Strawberry ..... Mets | 3771 ... 6/17/84 .. Rick Monday ........ Dodgers |
| 3722 ... 5/6/84 .... Mookie Wilson ........... Mets | 3772 ... 7/3/84 .... Wally Backman ......... Mets |
| 3723 ... 5/6/84 .... Darryl Strawberry ..... Mets | 3773 ... 7/3/84 .... George Foster ......... Mets |
| 3724 ... 5/11/84 .. Garry Matthews ........ Cubs | 3774 ... 7/3/84 .... Hubie Brooks ............ Mets |
| 3725 ... 5/11/84 .. Mel Hall ..................... Cubs | 3775 ... 7/3/84 .... Mike Fitzgerald .......... Mets |
| 3726 ... 5/11/84 .. Jody Davis ................ Cubs | 3776 ... 7/3/84 .... Bruce Berenyi ........... Mets |
| 3727 ... 5/11/84 .. Ryne Sandberg ......... Cubs | 3777 ... 7/3/84 .... Danny Heep ............. Mets |
| 3728 ... 5/11/84 .. Dick Ruthven ............ Cubs | 3778 ... 7/3/84 .... Darryl Strawberry ...... Mets |
| 3729 ... 5/11/84 .. Bob Dernier .............. Cubs | 3779 ... 7/3/84 .... Hubie Brooks ............ Mets |
| 3730 ... 5/11/84 .. Leon Durham ............ Cubs | 3780 ... 7/8/84 .... Bill Gullickson .......... Expos |
| 3731 ... 5/11/84 .. Ron Cey .................... Cubs | 3781 ... 7/13/84 .. Von Hayes ............ Phillies |
| 3732 ... 5/16/84 .. Jason Thompson ... Pirates | 3782 ... 7/13/84 .. Shane Rawley ........ Phillies |
| 3733 ... 5/16/84 .. Amos Otis ............. Pirates | 3783 ... 7/13/84 .. Greg Gross ............ Phillies |
| 3734 ... 5/16/84 .. Jason Thompson ... Pirates | 3784 ... 7/13/84 .. Juan Samuel .......... Phillies |
| 3735 ... 5/16/84 .. Milt May ................. Pirates | 3785 ... 7/13/84 .. Glenn Wilson ......... Phillies |
| 3736 ... 5/16/84 .. Amos Otis ............. Pirates | 3786 ... 7/18/84 .. Ron Gardenhire ......... Mets |
| 3737 ... 5/16/84 .. Jason Thompson ... Pirates | 3787 ... 7/18/84 .. Walt Terrell ................ Mets |
| 3738 ... 5/16/84 .. Milt May ................. Pirates | 3788 ... 7/18/84 .. George Foster ........... Mets |
| 3739 ... 5/16/84 .. Amos Otis ............. Pirates | 3789 ... 7/18/84 .. Walt Terrell ................ Mets |
| 3740 ... 5/16/84 .. Lee Mazzilli ........... Pirates | 3790 ... 7/18/84 .. Darryl Strawberry ...... Mets |
| 3741 ... 5/16/84 .. Marvell Wynne ....... Pirates | 3791 ... 7/18/84 .. George Foster ........... Mets |
| 3742 ... 5/16/84 .. Johnny Ray ............ Pirates | 3792 ... 7/18/84 .. Mike Fitzgerald .......... Mets |
| 3743 ... 5/21/84 .. Tommy Herr ....... Cardinals | 3793 ... 7/24/84 .. Mark Davis ............. Giants |
| 3744 ... 5/21/84 .. Willie McGee ...... Cardinals | 3794 ... 7/24/84 .. Scot Thompson ....... Giants |
| 3745 ... 5/21/84 .. Andy Van Slyke . Cardinals | 3795 ... 7/24/84 .. Joel Youngblood ..... Giants |
| 3746 ... 5/21/84 .. Tommy Herr ....... Cardinals | 3796 ... 7/24/84 .. Chili Davis ............... Giants |
| 3747 ... 5/21/84 .. Willie McGee ...... Cardinals | 3797 ... 7/28/84 .. Steve Garvey ........ Padres |
| 3748 ... 5/21/84 .. George Hendrick Cardinals | 3798 ... 7/28/84 .. Carmelo Martinez .. Padres |
| 3749 ... 5/21/84 .. Ricky Horton ...... Cardinals | 3799 ... 7/28/84 .. Luis Salazar .......... Padres |
| 3750 ... 5/26/84 .. Tony Pena ............. Pirates | 3800 ... 7/28/84 .. Eric Show ............. Padres |

| | | | | |
|---|---|---|---|---|
| 3801 ... 7/28/84 .. Kevin McReynolds . Padres | | 3851 ... 8/31/84 .. Lonnie Smith ...... Cardinals |
| 3802 ... 7/28/84 .. Luis Salazar ........... Padres | | 3852 ... 8/31/84 .. David Green ....... Cardinals |
| 3803 ... 7/28/84 .. Eric Show .............. Padres | | 3853 ... 8/31/84 .. Darrell Porter ..... Cardinals |
| 3804 ... 7/28/84 .. Tony Gwynn .......... Padres | | 3854 ... 8/31/84 .. Terry Pendleton . Cardinals |
| 3805 ... 8/3/84 .... Garry Templeton .... Padres | | 3855 ... 9/5/84 .... Joel Youngblood ..... Giants |
| 3806 ... 8/3/84 .... Graig Nettles ......... Padres | | 3856 ... 9/5/84 .... Scot Thompson ...... Giants |
| 3807 ... 8/3/84 .... Carmelo Martinez .. Padres | | 3857 ... 9/5/84 .... Fran Mullins ............ Giants |
| 3808 ... 8/3/84 .... Eric Show .............. Padres | | 3858 ... 9/5/84 .... Chili Davis ............... Giants |
| 3809 ... 8/8/84 .... Manny Trillo ............ Giants | | 3859 ... 9/5/84 .... Scot Thompson ...... Giants |
| 3810 ... 8/8/84 .... Johnnie LeMaster ... Giants | | 3860 ... 9/5/84 .... Chris Brown ........... Giants |
| 3811 ... 8/8/84 .... Gene Richards ....... Giants | | 3861 ... 9/5/84 .... Fran Mullins ............ Giants |
| 3812 ... 8/8/84 .... Johnnie LeMaster ... Giants | | 3862 ... 9/5/84 .... Scot Thompson ...... Giants |
| 3813 ... 8/8/84 .... Bob Lacey .............. Giants | | 3863 ... 9/10/84 .. Milt Thompson ....... Braves |
| 3814 ... 8/12/84 .. Gary Redus .............. Reds | | 3864 ... 9/10/84 .. C. Washington ....... Braves |
| 3815 ... 8/12/84 .. Dave Parker .............. Reds | | 3865 ... 9/10/84 .. Dale Murphy .......... Braves |
| 3816 ... 8/12/84 .. Dave Van Gorder ...... Reds | | 3866 ... 9/10/84 .. Jerry Royster ......... Braves |
| 3817 ... 8/12/84 .. Ron Oester ............... Reds | | 3867 ... 9/10/84 .. C. Washington ....... Braves |
| 3818 ... 8/12/84 .. Dave Parker .............. Reds | | 3868 ... 9/10/84 .. Dale Murphy .......... Braves |
| 3819 ... 8/12/84 .. Eric Davis ................. Reds | | 3869 ... 9/10/84 .. Jerry Royster ......... Braves |
| 3820 ... 8/12/84 .. Tom Foley .................. Reds | | 3870 ... 9/10/84 .. Dale Murphy .......... Braves |
| 3821 ... 8/12/84 .. Skeeter Barnes ......... Reds | | 3871 ... 9/10/84 .. Zane Smith ............. Braves |
| 3822 ... 8/12/84 .. Dave Parker .............. Reds | | 3872 ... 9/15/84 .. Tony Gwynn ........... Padres |
| 3823 ... 8/12/84 .. Eric Davis ................. Reds | | 3873 ... 9/15/84 .. Steve Garvey ......... Padres |
| 3824 ... 8/12/84 .. Eddie Milner .............. Reds | | 3874 ... 9/20/84 .. Ken Landreaux .... Dodgers |
| 3825 ... 8/17/84 .. Denny Gonzalez .... Pirates | | 3875 ... 4/9/85 .... Mariano Duncan .. Dodgers |
| 3826 ... 8/17/84 .. Lee Mazzilli ,......... Pirates | | 3876 ... 4/9/85 .... Al Oliver .............. Dodgers |
| 3827 ... 8/17/84 .. Larry McWilliams ... Pirates | | 3877 ... 4/9/85 .... Mike Marshall ...... Dodgers |
| 3828 ... 8/17/84 .. Denny Gonzalez .... Pirates | | 3878 ... 4/9/85 .... Mike Marshall ...... Dodgers |
| 3829 ... 8/17/84 .. Lee Lacy ................. Pirates | | 3879 ... 4/14/85 .. Mike Schmidt ........ Phillies |
| 3830 ... 8/22/84 .. Leon Durham ............. Cubs | | 3880 ... 4/14/85 .. Mike Schmidt ........ Phillies |
| 3831 ... 8/22/84 .. Keith Moreland ......... Cubs | | 3881 ... 4/14/85 .. Bo Diaz .................. Phillies |
| 3832 ... 8/22/84 .. Ron Cey ................... Cubs | | 3882 ... 4/14/85 .. Steve Jeltz ............. Phillies |
| 3833 ... 8/22/84 .. Jody Davis ................ Cubs | | 3883 ... 4/14/85 .. Steve Carlton ......... Phillies |
| 3834 ... 8/22/84 .. Ron Cey ................... Cubs | | 3884 ... 4/14/85 .. Juan Samuel .......... Phillies |
| 3835 ... 8/22/84 .. Jay Johnstone .......... Cubs | | 3885 ... 4/14/85 .. Steve Jeltz ............. Phillies |
| 3836 ... 8/22/84 .. Garry Matthews ........ Cubs | | 3886 ... 4/14/85 .. Juan Samuel .......... Phillies |
| 3837 ... 8/22/84 .. Leon Durham ............. Cubs | | 3887 ... 4/14/85 .. Von Hayes .............. Phillies |
| 3838 ... 8/22/84 .. Bob Dernier .............. Cubs | | 3888 ... 4/19/85 .. Gerald Perry .......... Braves |
| 3839 ... 8/22/84 .. Ryne Sandberg ......... Cubs | | 3889 ... 4/24/85 .. Dave Parker ............. Reds |
| 3840 ... 8/22/84 .. Garry Matthews ........ Cubs | | 3890 ... 4/24/85 .. Tom Foley ................. Reds |
| 3841 ... 8/22/84 .. Leon Durham ............. Cubs | | 3891 ... 4/24/85 .. Duane Walker .......... Reds |
| 3842 ... 8/26/84 .. Tommy Herr ....... Cardinals | | 3892 ... 4/24/85 .. Tom Foley ................. Reds |
| 3843 ... 8/26/84 .. Terry Pendleton . Cardinals | | 3893 ... 4/24/85 .. Dave Van Gorder ...... Reds |
| 3844 ... 8/26/84 .. Kurt Kepshire ..... Cardinals | | 3894 ... 4/24/85 .. Pete Rose ................ Reds |
| 3845 ... 8/26/84 .. Willie McGee ...... Cardinals | | 3895 ... 4/24/85 .. Eddie Milner ............. Reds |
| 3846 ... 8/26/84 .. Lonnie Smith ...... Cardinals | | 3896 ... 4/28/85 .. Brad Komminsk ..... Braves |
| 3847 ... 8/26/84 .. Kurt Kepshire ..... Cardinals | | 3897 ... 4/28/85 .. Chris Chambliss .... Braves |
| 3848 ... 8/26/84 .. Terry Pendleton . Cardinals | | 3898 ... 4/28/85 .. Rick Cerone .......... Braves |
| 3849 ... 8/31/84 .. Dave LaPoint ...... Cardinals | | 3899 ... 4/28/85 .. Pascual Perez ........ Braves |
| 3850 ... 8/31/84 .. Willie McGee ...... Cardinals | | 3900 ... 4/28/85 .. C. Washington ........ Braves |

| | | | |
|---|---|---|---|
| 3901 ... 4/28/85 .. Chris Chambliss ..... Braves | 3951 ... 6/3/85 .... Jack Clark .......... Cardinals |
| 3902 ... 4/28/85 .. Ken Oberkfell ......... Braves | 3952 ... 6/3/85 .... Ozzie Smith ....... Cardinals |
| 3903 ... 5/3/85 .... Juan Samuel .......... Phillies | 3953 ... 6/3/85 .... Vince Coleman .. Cardinals |
| 3904 ... 5/3/85 .... Glenn Wilson ......... Phillies | 3954 ... 6/3/85 .... John Tudor ........ Cardinals |
| 3905 ... 5/3/85 .... Ozzie Virgil ........... Phillies | 3955 ... 6/8/85 .... Rick Adams ........... Giants |
| 3906 ... 5/3/85 .... Steve Jeltz ........... Phillies | 3956 ... 6/8/85 .... Rick Adams ........... Giants |
| 3907 ... 5/3/85 .... Steve Carlton ........ Phillies | 3957 ... 6/8/85 .... Chili Davis ............... Giants |
| 3908 ... 5/3/85 .... Tim Corcoran ........ Phillies | 3958 ... 6/8/85 .... Rob Deer ............... Giants |
| 3909 ... 5/3/85 .... Steve Carlton ........ Phillies | 3959 ... 6/8/85 .... Alex Trevino ........... Giants |
| 3910 ... 5/3/85 .... Juan Samuel .......... Phillies | 3960 ... 6/8/85 .... Bill Laskey .............. Giants |
| 3911 ... 5/3/85 .... Glenn Wilson ......... Phillies | 3961 ... 6/8/85 .... Rob Deer ............... Giants |
| 3912 ... 5/3/85 .... Kevin Gross .......... Phillies | 3962 ... 6/12/85 .. Terry Kennedy ...... Padres |
| 3913 ... 5/8/85 .... Mike Fitzgerald ....... Expos | 3963 ... 6/12/85 .. Carmelo Martinez .. Padres |
| 3914 ... 5/8/85 .... Joe Hesketh ........... Expos | 3964 ... 6/12/85 .. Eric Show .............. Padres |
| 3915 ... 5/8/85 .... Tim Raines .............. Expos | 3965 ... 6/12/85 .. Eric Show .............. Padres |
| 3916 ... 5/8/85 .... Joe Hesketh ........... Expos | 3966 ... 6/12/85 .. Kevin McReynolds . Padres |
| 3917 ... 5/8/85 .... Tim Raines .............. Expos | 3967 ... 6/17/85 .. Glenn Hubbard ...... Braves |
| 3918 ... 5/8/85 .... Vance Law ............... Expos | 3968 ... 6/17/85 .. Terry Harper .......... Braves |
| 3919 ... 5/8/85 .... Dan Driessen .......... Expos | 3969 ... 6/17/85 .. Larry Owen ........... Braves |
| 3920 ... 5/8/85 .... Tim Wallach ............. Expos | 3970 ... 6/17/85 .. Steve Shields ........ Braves |
| 3921 ... 5/8/85 .... Herm Winningham .. Expos | 3971 ... 6/17/85 .. Dale Murphy .......... Braves |
| 3922 ... 5/8/85 .... Joe Hesketh ........... Expos | 3972 ... 6/17/85 .. Larry Owen ........... Braves |
| 3923 ... 5/13/85 .. Joe Hesketh ........... Expos | 3973 ... 6/17/85 .. Brad Komminsk ...... Braves |
| 3924 ... 5/13/85 .. Herm Winningham .. Expos | 3974 ... 6/17/85 .. Ken Oberkfell ......... Braves |
| 3925 ... 5/13/85 .. Andre Dawson ........ Expos | 3975 ... 6/22/85 .. Dave Anderson .... Dodgers |
| 3926 ... 5/13/85 .. Hubie Brooks .......... Expos | 3976 ... 6/22/85 .. R.J. Reynolds ...... Dodgers |
| 3927 ... 5/13/85 .. Joe Hesketh ........... Expos | 3977 ... 6/27/85 .. Bob Horner ............ Braves |
| 3928 ... 5/13/85 .. Razor Shines ........... Expos | 3978 ... 6/27/85 .. C. Washington ....... Braves |
| 3929 ... 5/13/85 .. Herm Winningham .. Expos | 3979 ... 6/27/85 .. Glenn Hubbard ...... Braves |
| 3930 ... 5/18/85 .. Vince Coleman .. Cardinals | 3980 ... 6/27/85 .. Rafael Ramirez ...... Braves |
| 3931 ... 5/18/85 .. Tommy Herr ....... Cardinals | 3981 ... 6/27/85 .. C. Washington ....... Braves |
| 3932 ... 5/18/85 .. Andy Van Slyke . Cardinals | 3982 ... 6/27/85 .. Dale Murphy .......... Braves |
| 3933 ... 5/18/85 .. Jack Clark .......... Cardinals | 3983 ... 6/27/85 .. Terry Harper .......... Braves |
| 3934 ... 5/18/85 .. Terry Pendleton . Cardinals | 3984 ... 7/1/85 .... Terry Kennedy ...... Padres |
| 3935 ... 5/18/85 .. Terry Pendleton . Cardinals | 3985 ... 7/1/85 .... Carmelo Martinez .. Padres |
| 3936 ... 5/24/85 .. Ron Cey ................... Cubs | 3986 ... 7/1/85 .... Tony Gwynn .......... Padres |
| 3937 ... 5/24/85 .. Dick Ruthven ............ Cubs | 3987 ... 7/1/85 .... Terry Kennedy ...... Padres |
| 3938 ... 5/24/85 .. Keith Moreland ......... Cubs | 3988 ... 7/1/85 .... Graig Nettles ......... Padres |
| 3939 ... 5/24/85 .. Thad Bosley ............. Cubs | 3989 ... 7/1/85 .... Carmelo Martinez .. Padres |
| 3940 ... 5/24/85 .. Leon Durham ............ Cubs | 3990 ... 7/1/85 .... Bobby Brown ........ Padres |
| 3941 ... 5/24/85 .. Jody Davis ................ Cubs | 3991 ... 7/6/85 .... Dan Driessen ......... Expos |
| 3942 ... 5/24/85 .. Chico Walker ............ Cubs | 3992 ... 7/6/85 .... Mitch Webster ....... Expos |
| 3943 ... 5/29/85 .. Junior Ortiz ............ Pirates | 3993 ... 7/6/85 .... Joe Hesketh ............ Expos |
| 3944 ... 5/29/85 .. Jim Winn ................ Pirates | 3994 ... 7/11/85 .. Len Dykstra .............. Mets |
| 3945 ... 5/29/85 .. Lee Mazzilli ............ Pirates | 3995 ... 7/11/85 .. Rafael Santana ......... Mets |
| 3946 ... 5/29/85 .. Steve Kemp ........... Pirates | 3996 ... 7/11/85 .. Sid Fernandez ........... Mets |
| 3947 ... 5/29/85 .. Jim Morrison .......... Pirates | 3997 ... 7/11/85 .. Sid Fernandez ........... Mets |
| 3948 ... 5/29/85 .. Bill Almon .............. Pirates | 3998 ... 7/11/85 .. Darryl Strawberry ...... Mets |
| 3949 ... 5/29/85 .. Bill Almon .............. Pirates | 3999 ... 7/11/85 .. Gary Carter .............. Mets |
| 3950 ... 5/29/85 .. Jim Winn ................ Pirates | 4000 ... 7/11/85 .. Danny Heep .............. Mets |

| | | |
|---|---|---|
| 4001 ... 7/11/85 .. Rafael Santana ......... Mets | 4051 ... 8/23/85 .. Denny Gonzalez .... Pirates |
| 4002 ... 7/11/85 .. Sid Fernandez ........... Mets | 4052 ... 8/23/85 .. Lee Mazzilli ........... Pirates |
| 4003 ... 7/11/85 .. Wally Backman ......... Mets | 4053 ... 8/28/85 .. Garry Matthews ........ Cubs |
| 4004 ... 7/11/85 .. Danny Heep ............... Mets | 4054 ... 8/28/85 .. Leon Durham ............ Cubs |
| 4005 ... 7/20/85 .. Herm Winningham .. Expos | 4055 ... 8/28/85 .. Jay Baller .................. Cubs |
| 4006 ... 7/20/85 .. Bill Gullickson .......... Expos | 4056 ... 8/28/85 .. Garry Matthews ........ Cubs |
| 4007 ... 7/24/85 .. Von Hayes ............. Phillies | 4057 ... 8/28/85 .. Leon Durham ............ Cubs |
| 4008 ... 7/24/85 .. John Russell ........... Phillies | 4058 ... 8/28/85 .. Shawon Dunston ...... Cubs |
| 4009 ... 7/24/85 .. Rick Schu .............. Phillies | 4059 ... 8/28/85 .. Jay Baller .................. Cubs |
| 4010 ... 7/24/85 .. Juan Samuel ......... Phillies | 4060 ... 8/28/85 .. Leon Durham ............ Cubs |
| 4011 ... 7/24/85 .. Mike Schmidt ........ Phillies | 4061 ... 9/2/85 .... Thad Bosley ............. Cubs |
| 4012 ... 7/24/85 .. John Russell ........... Phillies | 4062 ... 9/15/85 .. Miguel Dilone ......... Padres |
| 4013 ... 7/24/85 .. Mike Schmidt ........ Phillies | 4063 ... 9/15/85 .. Graig Nettles ......... Padres |
| 4014 ... 7/30/85 .. Pete Rose ................. Reds | 4064 ... 9/15/85 .. LaMarr Hoyt ........... Padres |
| 4015 ... 7/30/85 .. Dan Bilardello ........... Reds | 4065 ... 9/15/85 .. Tony Gwynn ......... Padres |
| 4016 ... 7/30/85 .. Max Venable ............. Reds | 4066 ... 9/20/85 .. Dave Concepcion ..... Reds |
| 4017 ... 7/30/85 .. Buddy Bell ................ Reds | 4067 ... 9/20/85 .. Dave Parker .............. Reds |
| 4018 ... 7/30/85 .. Mario Soto ................ Reds | 4068 ... 9/25/85 .. Ken Landreaux .... Dodgers |
| 4019 ... 7/30/85 .. Pete Rose ................. Reds | 4069 ... 9/25/85 .. Bill Madlock ......... Dodgers |
| 4020 ... 7/30/85 .. Mario Soto ................ Reds | 4070 ... 9/25/85 .. Mike Marshall ...... Dodgers |
| 4021 ... 8/3/85 .... Terry Kennedy ....... Padres | 4071 ... 9/30/85 .. Dale Murphy ......... Braves |
| 4022 ... 8/3/85 .... Carmelo Martinez .. Padres | 4072 ... 9/30/85 .. Bob Horner ........... Braves |
| 4023 ... 8/3/85 .... Carmelo Martinez .. Padres | 4073 ... 9/30/85 .. C. Washington ....... Braves |
| 4024 ... 8/3/85 .... Tim Flannery .......... Padres | 4074 ... 9/30/85 .. Glenn Hubbard ...... Braves |
| 4025 ... 8/3/85 .... Tony Gwynn .......... Padres | 4075 ... 9/30/85 .. Pascual Perez ........ Braves |
| 4026 ... 8/3/85 .... Graig Nettles .......... Padres | 4076 ... 10/5/85 .. Terry Kennedy ....... Padres |
| 4027 ... 8/3/85 .... Terry Kennedy ....... Padres | 4077 ... 10/5/85 .. Kevin McReynolds . Padres |
| 4028 ... 8/3/85 .... Tim Flannery .......... Padres | 4078 ... 10/5/85 .. Tim Flannery .......... Padres |
| 4029 ... 8/9/85 .... Bruce Bochy .......... Padres | 4079 ... 10/5/85 .. Carmelo Martinez .. Padres |
| 4030 ... 8/9/85 .... Graig Nettles .......... Padres | 4080 ... 10/5/85 .. Kevin McReynolds . Padres |
| 4031 ... 8/9/85 .... Tim Flannery .......... Padres | 4081 ... 10/5/85 .. Mario Ramirez ....... Padres |
| 4032 ... 8/9/85 .... Bruce Bochy .......... Padres | 4082 ... 10/5/85 .. Miguel Dilone ......... Padres |
| 4033 ... 8/9/85 .... Dave Dravecky ....... Padres | 4083 ... 10/5/85 .. Carmelo Martinez .. Padres |
| 4034 ... 8/9/85 .... Miguel Dilone ........ Padres | 4084 ... 4/8/86 .... Bob Brenly ............. Giants |
| 4035 ... 8/9/85 .... Al Bumbry ............... Padres | 4085 ... 4/8/86 .... Robby Thompson ... Giants |
| 4036 ... 8/14/85 .. Brad Wellman ......... Giants | 4086 ... 4/8/86 .... Will Clark ................ Giants |
| 4037 ... 8/14/85 .. Jeffrey Leonard ....... Giants | 4087 ... 4/8/86 .... Mike Krukow .......... Giants |
| 4038 ... 8/14/85 .. Bob Brenly ............. Giants | 4088 ... 4/12/86 .. C. Washington ....... Braves |
| 4039 ... 8/14/85 .. Jim Gott ................. Giants | 4089 ... 4/12/86 .. Dale Murphy ......... Braves |
| 4040 ... 8/18/85 .. Pete Rose ................. Reds | 4090 ... 4/12/86 .. Rick Mahler ............ Braves |
| 4041 ... 8/18/85 .. Nick Esasky ............. Reds | 4091 ... 4/12/86 .. Dale Murphy ......... Braves |
| 4042 ... 8/18/85 .. Ron Oester ............... Reds | 4092 ... 4/12/86 .. Rick Mahler ............ Braves |
| 4043 ... 8/18/85 .. Jay Tibbs ................. Reds | 4093 ... 4/16/86 .. Will Clark ................ Giants |
| 4044 ... 8/18/85 .. Dave Parker .............. Reds | 4094 ... 4/16/86 .. Bob Brenly ............. Giants |
| 4045 ... 8/18/85 .. Bo Diaz ..................... Reds | 4095 ... 4/16/86 .. Roger Mason .......... Giants |
| 4046 ... 8/18/85 .. Cesar Cedeno .......... Reds | 4096 ... 4/16/86 .. Dan Gladden .......... Giants |
| 4047 ... 8/23/85 .. Bill Madlock ........... Pirates | 4097 ... 4/16/86 .. Bob Melvin .............. Giants |
| 4048 ... 8/23/85 .. Mike Brown .......... Pirates | 4098 ... 4/16/86 .. Roger Mason .......... Giants |
| 4049 ... 8/23/85 .. Sammy Khalifa ....... Pirates | 4099 ... 4/16/86 .. Will Clark ................ Giants |
| 4050 ... 8/23/85 .. Lee Tunnell ............. Pirates | 4100 ... 4/16/86 .. Jeffrey Leonard ....... Giants |

4101 ... 4/16/86 .. Bob Brenly .............. Giants
4102 ... 4/21/86 .. Omar Moreno ......... Braves
4103 ... 4/21/86 .. Joe Johnson ............ Braves
4104 ... 4/21/86 .. Rafael Ramirez ..... Braves
4105 ... 4/21/86 .. Glenn Hubbard ...... Braves
4106 ... 4/25/86 .. Dave Concepcion ..... Reds
4107 ... 4/25/86 .. Tom Browning .......... Reds
4108 ... 4/25/86 .. Ron Oester ............... Reds
4109 ... 4/25/86 .. Dave Concepcion ..... Reds
4110 ... 4/25/86 .. Max Venable ............ Reds
4111 ... 4/25/86 .. Dave Parker ............. Reds
4112 ... 4/25/86 .. Bo Diaz ..................... Reds
4113 ... 4/29/86 .. Glenn Wilson ....... Phillies
4114 ... 4/29/86 .. Steve Jeltz ........... Phillies
4115 ... 5/3/86 ... Tim Raines .............. Expos
4116 ... 5/3/86 .... Vance Law .............. Expos
4117 ... 5/3/86 .... Andre Dawson ........ Expos
4118 ... 5/3/86 .... Dann Bilardello ...... Expos
4119 ... 5/7/86 ... Len Dykstra ............... Mets
4120 ... 5/7/86 ... Darryl Strawberry ...... Mets
4121 ... 5/7/86 .... Howard Johnson ....... Mets
4122 ... 5/11/86 .. Trench Davis ......... Pirates
4123 ... 5/11/86 .. Junior Ortiz ........... Pirates
4124 ... 5/11/86 .. Johnny Ray ............ Pirates
4125 ... 5/15/86 .. Len Dykstra ............... Mets
4126 ... 5/15/86 .. Gary Carter ............... Mets
4127 ... 5/15/86 .. Ray Knight ................. Mets
4128 ... 5/15/86 .. Ron Darling .............. Mets
4129 ... 5/15/86 .. Len Dykstra ............... Mets
4130 ... 5/15/86 .. Keith Hernandez ....... Mets
4131 ... 5/15/86 .. Tim Teufel ................. Mets
4132 ... 5/20/86 .. Sammy Khalifa ...... Pirates
4133 ... 5/20/86 .. R.J. Reynolds ........ Pirates
4134 ... 5/20/86 .. Johnny Ray ............ Pirates
4135 ... 5/20/86 .. Mike Brown ........... Pirates
4136 ... 5/20/86 .. Jim Morrison .......... Pirates
4137 ... 5/20/86 .. Sammy Khalifa ...... Pirates
4138 ... 5/20/86 .. R.J. Reynolds ........ Pirates
4139 ... 5/20/86 .. Sid Bream .............. Pirates
4140 ... 5/20/86 .. Jim Morrison .......... Pirates
4141 ... 5/31/86 .. Al Newman .............. Expos
4142 ... 5/31/86 .. Mitch Webster ........ Expos
4143 ... 6/24/86 .. Ron Oester ............... Reds
4144 ... 6/24/86 .. Dave Parker ............. Reds
4145 ... 6/24/86 .. Eddie Milner ............ Reds
4146 ... 6/24/86 .. Eric Davis ................. Reds
4147 ... 6/29/86 .. Len Matuszek ...... Dodgers
4148 ... 6/29/86 .. Jeff Hamilton ....... Dodgers
4149 ... 6/29/86 .. Craig Shipley ....... Dodgers
4150 ... 6/29/86 .. Len Matuszek ...... Dodgers

4151 ... 6/29/86 .. Jeff Hamilton ....... Dodgers
4152 ... 6/29/86 .. Reggie Williams ... Dodgers
4153 ... 6/29/86 .. Steve Sax .......... Dodgers
4154 ... 6/29/86 .. Jeff Hamilton ....... Dodgers
4155 ... 7/4/86 .... Darryl Strawberry ...... Mets
4156 ... 7/4/86 .... Gary Carter ............... Mets
4157 ... 7/4/86 .... Keith Hernandez ....... Mets
4158 ... 7/4/86 .... Darryl Strawberry ...... Mets
4159 ... 7/4/86 .... Howard Johnson ....... Mets
4160 ... 7/4/86 .... Rafael Santana ...... Mets
4161 ... 7/8/86 .... Andre Dawson ........ Expos
4162 ... 7/8/86 .... Hubie Brooks .......... Expos
4163 ... 7/8/86 .... Tim Wallach ............. Expos
4164 ... 7/8/86 .... Al Newman ............... Expos
4165 ... 7/8/86 .... Jay Tibbs ................. Expos
4166 ... 7/8/86 .... Tim Raines .............. Expos
4167 ... 7/8/86 .... Tim Wallach ............. Expos
4168 ... 7/8/86 .... Mike Fitzgerald ........ Expos
4169 ... 7/8/86 .... Jay Tibbs ................. Expos
4170 ... 7/12/86 .. Juan Samuel .......... Phillies
4171 ... 7/12/86 .. Ronn Reynolds ...... Phillies
4172 ... 7/12/86 .. Ron Roenicke ....... Phillies
4173 ... 7/12/86 .. Steve Jeltz ............ Phillies
4174 ... 7/12/86 .. Juan Samuel .......... Phillies
4175 ... 7/12/86 .. Mike Schmidt ......... Phillies
4176 ... 7/12/86 .. Ronn Reynolds ...... Phillies
4177 ... 7/12/86 .. Tom Foley .............. Phillies
4178 ... 7/17/86 .. Gary Carter ............... Mets
4179 ... 7/17/86 .. Danny Heep ............... Mets
4180 ... 7/17/86 .. Ray Knight ................. Mets
4181 ... 7/17/86 .. Wally Backman ......... Mets
4182 ... 7/17/86 .. Darryl Strawberry ...... Mets
4183 ... 7/17/86 .. Ray Knight ................. Mets
4184 ... 7/17/86 .. Bob Ojeda ................. Mets
4185 ... 7/17/86 .. Darryl Strawberry ...... Mets
4186 ... 7/22/86 .. Tim Raines .............. Expos
4187 ... 7/22/86 .. Mitch Webster ........ Expos
4188 ... 7/22/86 .. Andre Dawson ........ Expos
4189 ... 7/22/86 .. Mike Fitzgerald ...... Expos
4190 ... 7/22/86 .. Floyd Youmans ....... Expos
4191 ... 7/22/86 .. Tim Raines .............. Expos
4192 ... 7/22/86 .. Andre Dawson ........ Expos
4193 ... 7/22/86 .. Wayne Krenchicki ... Expos
4194 ... 7/22/86 .. Mitch Webster ........ Expos
4195 ... 7/22/86 .. Andre Dawson ........ Expos
4196 ... 7/22/86 .. Tim Wallach ............. Expos
4197 ... 7/22/86 .. Rene Gonzales ....... Expos
4198 ... 7/22/86 .. Al Newman ............... Expos
4199 ... 7/22/86 .. Mitch Webster ........ Expos
4200 ... 7/27/86 .. Gary Redus ........... Phillies

| | | | | |
|---|---|---|---|---|
| 4201 ... 7/27/86 .. Glenn Wilson ......... Phillies | | 4251 ... 9/13/86 .. Terry Kennedy ....... Padres |
| 4202 ... 7/27/86 .. John Russell .......... Phillies | | 4252 ... 9/13/86 .. Tim Flannery ......... Padres |
| 4203 ... 7/27/86 .. Steve Jeltz ............. Phillies | | 4253 ... 9/19/86 .. Tim Flannery ......... Padres |
| 4204 ... 7/27/86 .. Kevin Gross ........... Phillies | | 4254 ... 9/19/86 .. Graig Nettles ......... Padres |
| 4205 ... 7/27/86 .. Gary Redus ........... Phillies | | 4255 ... 9/19/86 .. Gary Green ............ Padres |
| 4206 ... 7/27/86 .. Jeff Stone .............. Phillies | | 4256 ... 9/19/86 .. Tim Flannery ......... Padres |
| 4207 ... 7/27/86 .. Mike Schmidt ......... Phillies | | 4257 ... 9/19/86 .. Benito Santiago ..... Padres |
| 4208 ... 7/27/86 .. John Russell .......... Phillies | | 4258 ... 9/19/86 .. Andy Hawkins ....... Padres |
| 4209 ... 7/27/86 .. Kevin Gross ........... Phillies | | 4259 ... 9/19/86 .. Tony Gwynn .......... Padres |
| 4210 ... 8/12/86 .. Mike Scioscia ...... Dodgers | | 4260 ... 9/24/86 .. Robby Thompson ... Giants |
| 4211 ... 8/12/86 .. Len Matuszek ...... Dodgers | | 4261 ... 9/24/86 .. Bob Brenly ............. Giants |
| 4212 ... 8/12/86 .. Reggie Williams ... Dodgers | | 4262 ... 9/24/86 .. Candy Maldonado .. Giants |
| 4213 ... 8/12/86 .. Rick Honeycutt .... Dodgers | | 4263 ... 9/24/86 .. Bob Melvin ............ Giants |
| 4214 ... 8/12/86 .. Greg Brock ......... Dodgers | | 4264 ... 9/24/86 .. Candy Maldonado .. Giants |
| 4215 ... 8/12/86 .. Len Matuszek ...... Dodgers | | 4265 ... 9/24/86 .. Bob Melvin ............ Giants |
| 4216 ... 8/17/86 .. Dale Murphy ......... Braves | | 4266 ... 9/24/86 .. Jose Uribe ............. Giants |
| 4217 ... 8/17/86 .. Ken Griffey ............ Braves | | 4267 ... 9/24/86 .. Robby Thompson ... Giants |
| 4218 ... 8/17/86 .. Dale Murphy ......... Braves | | 4268 ... 9/24/86 .. Candy Maldonado .. Giants |
| 4219 ... 8/17/86 .. Glenn Hubbard ..... Braves | | 4269 ... 9/24/86 .. Brad Gulden .......... Giants |
| 4220 ... 8/17/86 .. Zane Smith ............ Braves | | 4270 ... 9/24/86 .. Rick Lancellotti ...... Giants |
| 4221 ... 8/22/86 .. Terry Pendleton . Cardinals | | 4271 ... 9/24/86 .. Will Clark ................ Giants |
| 4222 ... 8/22/86 .. Ozzie Smith ....... Cardinals | | 4272 ... 10/3/86 .... Dale Murphy ......... Braves |
| 4223 ... 8/22/86 .. Clint Hurdle ....... Cardinals | | 4273 ... 10/3/86 .... Glenn Hubbard ...... Braves |
| 4224 ... 8/22/86 .. Vince Coleman .. Cardinals | | 4274 ... 10/3/86 .... Jim Acker .............. Braves |
| 4225 ... 8/22/86 .. Ozzie Smith ....... Cardinals | | 4275 ... 10/3/86 .... Ken Griffey ............ Braves |
| 4226 ... 8/22/86 .. Andy Van Slyke . Cardinals | | 4276 ... 10/3/86 .... Jim Acker .............. Braves |
| 4227 ... 8/27/86 .. Ryne Sandberg ......... Cubs | | 4277 ... 10/3/86 .... Dale Murphy ......... Braves |
| 4228 ... 8/27/86 .. Shawon Dunston ...... Cubs | | 4278 ... 4/8/87 .... Steve Sax .......... Dodgers |
| 4229 ... 8/27/86 .. Chris Speier ............. Cubs | | 4279 ... 4/8/87 .... Mike Marshall ...... Dodgers |
| 4230 ... 8/27/86 .. Jerry Mumphrey ........ Cubs | | 4280 ... 4/8/87 .... Rick Honeycutt .... Dodgers |
| 4231 ... 8/27/86 .. Keith Moreland ......... Cubs | | 4281 ... 4/8/87 .... Mike Ramsey ....... Dodgers |
| 4232 ... 9/2/86 .... Jamie Moyer ............. Cubs | | 4282 ... 4/8/87 .... Franklin Stubbs ... Dodgers |
| 4233 ... 9/2/86 .... Jerry Mumphrey ........ Cubs | | 4283 ... 4/8/87 .... Dave Anderson ... Dodgers |
| 4234 ... 9/2/86 .... Leon Durham ............ Cubs | | 4284 ... 4/8/87 .... Rick Honeycutt .... Dodgers |
| 4235 ... 9/2/86 .... Dave Martinez .......... Cubs | | 4285 ... 4/8/87 .... Mike Ramsey ....... Dodgers |
| 4236 ... 9/2/86 .... Jody Davis ................ Cubs | | 4286 ... 4/8/87 .... Mike Marshall ...... Dodgers |
| 4237 ... 9/8/86 .... Eric Davis ................. Reds | | 4287 ... 4/8/87 .... Franklin Stubbs ... Dodgers |
| 4238 ... 9/8/86 .... Bo Diaz ..................... Reds | | 4288 ... 4/13/87 .... Mike Ramsey ....... Dodgers |
| 4239 ... 9/8/86 .... Nick Esasky .............. Reds | | 4289 ... 4/13/87 .. Pedro Guerrero .. Dodgers |
| 4240 ... 9/8/86 .... Ron Oester ................ Reds | | 4290 ... 4/13/87 .. Mariano Duncan .. Dodgers |
| 4241 ... 9/8/86 .... Chris Welsh .............. Reds | | 4291 ... 4/13/87 .. Rick Honeycutt .... Dodgers |
| 4242 ... 9/8/86 .... Dave Parker .............. Reds | | 4292 ... 4/13/87 .. Steve Sax ............ Dodgers |
| 4243 ... 9/8/86 .... Eric Davis ................. Reds | | 4293 ... 4/13/87 .. Mike Ramsey ....... Dodgers |
| 4244 ... 9/8/86 .... Eddie Milner .............. Reds | | 4294 ... 4/13/87 .. Pedro Guerrero .. Dodgers |
| 4245 ... 9/8/86 .... Chris Welsh .............. Reds | | 4295 ... 4/13/87 .. Mariano Duncan .. Dodgers |
| 4246 ... 9/8/86 .... Eric Davis ................. Reds | | 4296 ... 4/13/87 .. Len Matuszek ...... Dodgers |
| 4247 ... 9/13/86 .. Tim Flannery ......... Padres | | 4297 ... 4/18/87 .. Dave Parker .............. Reds |
| 4248 ... 9/13/86 .. Steve Garvey ........ Padres | | 4298 ... 4/18/87 .. Ron Oester ............... Reds |
| 4249 ... 9/13/86 ..John Kruk .............. Padres | | 4299 ... 4/18/87 .. Kal Daniels ............... Reds |
| 4250 ... 9/13/86 .. Steve Garvey ........ Padres | | 4300 ... 4/18/87 .. Terry Francona ......... Reds |

| | | |
|---|---|---|
| 4301 ... 4/18/87 .. Dave Parker .............. Reds | 4351 ... 5/22/87 .. Tim Conroy ........ Cardinals |
| 4302 ... 4/18/87 .. Eric Davis ................. Reds | 4352 ... 5/27/87 .. Andy Van Slyke ..... Pirates |
| 4303 ... 4/25/87 .. Tracy Jones .............. Reds | 4353 ... 5/27/87 .. Johnny Ray ........... Pirates |
| 4304 ... 4/25/87 .. Kurt Stillwell .............. Reds | 4354 ... 5/27/87 .. Jim Morrison .......... Pirates |
| 4305 ... 4/25/87 .. Eric Davis ................. Reds | 4355 ... 5/27/87 .. Mike Lavalliere ....... Pirates |
| 4306 ... 4/25/87 .. Ron Oester ............... Reds | 4356 ... 5/27/87 .. Rafael Belliard ........ Pirates |
| 4307 ... 4/25/87 .. Eric Davis ................. Reds | 4357 ... 5/27/87 .. Sid Bream .............. Pirates |
| 4308 ... 4/25/87 .. Bo Diaz .................... Reds | 4358 ... 5/27/87 .. Jim Morrison .......... Pirates |
| 4309 ... 4/25/87 .. Ron Oester ............... Reds | 4359 ... 6/2/87 .... Jerry Mumphrey ........ Cubs |
| 4310 ... 4/25/87 .. Ted Power ................ Reds | 4360 ... 6/2/87 .... Jody Davis ................ Cubs |
| 4311 ... 4/25/87 .. Dave Parker .............. Reds | 4361 ... 6/2/87 .... Mike Mason ............. Cubs |
| 4312 ... 4/25/87 .. Eric Davis ................. Reds | 4362 ... 6/7/87 .... Chili Davis .............. Giants |
| 4313 ... 4/25/87 .. Ted Power ................ Reds | 4363 ... 6/7/87 .... Bob Brenly ............. Giants |
| 4314 ... 5/1/87 .... Glenn Hubbard ...... Braves | 4364 ... 6/7/87 .... Ivan DeJesus .......... Giants |
| 4315 ... 5/1/87 .... Dion James ............ Braves | 4365 ... 6/7/87 .... Atlee Hammaker ..... Giants |
| 4316 ... 5/1/87 .... Glenn Hubbard ...... Braves | 4366 ... 6/7/87 .... Chris Speier ........... Giants |
| 4317 ... 5/1/87 .... Rafael Ramirez ...... Braves | 4367 ... 6/7/87 .... Bob Brenly ............. Giants |
| 4318 ... 5/6/87 .... Juan Samuel ........ Phillies | 4368 ... 6/7/87 .... Ivan DeJesus .......... Giants |
| 4319 ... 5/6/87 .... Von Hayes ............ Phillies | 4369 ... 6/7/87 .... Chris Speier ........... Giants |
| 4320 ... 5/6/87 .... Miko Schmidt ........ Phillies | 4370 ... 6/7/87 .... Will Clark ................ Giants |
| 4321 ... 5/6/87 .... Milt Thompson ....... Phillies | 4371 ... 6/7/87 .... Jeffrey Leonard ....... Giants |
| 4322 ... 5/6/87 .... Von Hayes ............ Phillies | 4372 ... 6/7/87 .... Bob Brenly ............. Giants |
| 4323 ... 5/6/87 .... Lance Parrish ........ Phillies | 4373 ... 6/7/87 .... Robby Thompson ... Giants |
| 4324 ... 5/6/87 .... Don Carman .......... Phillies | 4374 ... 6/12/87 .. John Shelby ........ Dodgers |
| 4325 ... 5/11/87 .. Mike Schmidt ........ Phillies | 4375 ... 6/12/87 .. Pedro Guerrero ... Dodgers |
| 4326 ... 5/11/87 .. Jeff Stone .............. Phillies | 4376 ... 6/12/87 .. Ralph Bryant ........ Dodgers |
| 4327 ... 5/11/87 .. Don Carman .......... Phillies | 4377 ... 6/12/87 .. Bob Welch .......... Dodgers |
| 4328 ... 5/11/87 .. Jeff Stone .............. Phillies | 4378 ... 6/12/87 .. Franklin Stubbs ... Dodgers |
| 4329 ... 5/11/87 .. Juan Samuel ........ Phillies | 4379 ... 6/12/87 .. Dave Anderson ... Dodgers |
| 4330 ... 5/11/87 .. Von Hayes ............ Phillies | 4380 ... 6/12/87 .. Bob Welch .......... Dodgers |
| 4331 ... 5/11/87 .. Luis Aguayo ........... Phillies | 4381 ... 6/12/87 .. Mickey Hatcher .... Dodgers |
| 4332 ... 5/16/87 .. Ryne Sandberg ........ Cubs | 4382 ... 6/12/87 .. Pedro Guerrero ... Dodgers |
| 4333 ... 5/16/87 .. Jerry Mumphrey ........ Cubs | 4383 ... 6/12/87 .. Franklin Stubbs ... Dodgers |
| 4334 ... 5/16/87 .. Andre Dawson .......... Cubs | 4384 ... 6/12/87 .. Alex Trevino ........ Dodgers |
| 4335 ... 5/16/87 .. Shawon Dunston ...... Cubs | 4385 ... 6/17/87 .. Dave Parker ............. Reds |
| 4336 ... 5/16/87 .. Jerry Mumphrey ........ Cubs | 4386 ... 6/17/87 .. Kurt Stillwell ............. Reds |
| 4337 ... 5/16/87 .. Shawon Dunston ...... Cubs | 4387 ... 6/23/87 .. Benito Santiago ..... Padres |
| 4338 ... 5/16/87 .. Dave Martinez ......... Cubs | 4388 ... 6/23/87 .. Stan Jefferson ....... Padres |
| 4339 ... 5/16/87 .. Jamie Moyer ............. Cubs | 4389 ... 6/23/87 .. Ed Whitson ........... Padres |
| 4340 ... 5/16/87 .. Shawon Dunston ...... Cubs | 4390 ... 6/23/87 .. Carmelo Martinez .. Padres |
| 4341 ... 5/22/87 .. Vince Coleman .. Cardinals | 4391 ... 6/28/87 .. Jeffrey Leonard ....... Giants |
| 4342 ... 5/22/87 .. Jack Clark .......... Cardinals | 4392 ... 6/28/87 .. Chili Davis .............. Giants |
| 4343 ... 5/22/87 .. Curt Ford ........... Cardinals | 4393 ... 6/28/87 .. Mike Aldrete ........... Giants |
| 4344 ... 5/22/87 .. Tim Conroy ........ Cardinals | 4394 ... 6/28/87 .. Matt Williams ......... Giants |
| 4345 ... 5/22/87 .. Vince Coleman .. Cardinals | 4395 ... 6/28/87 .. Atlee Hammaker ..... Giants |
| 4346 ... 5/22/87 .. Willie McGee ...... Cardinals | 4396 ... 6/28/87 .. Robby Thompson ... Giants |
| 4347 ... 5/22/87 .. Tommy Herr ....... Cardinals | 4397 ... 6/28/87 .. Chris Speier ........... Giants |
| 4348 ... 5/22/87 .. Tim Conroy ........ Cardinals | 4398 ... 6/28/87 .. Matt Williams .......... Giants |
| 4349 ... 5/22/87 .. Jack Clark .......... Cardinals | 4399 ... 6/28/87 .. Atlee Hammaker ..... Giants |
| 4350 ... 5/22/87 .. Willie McGee ...... Cardinals | 4400 ... 6/28/87 .. Robby Thompson ... Giants |

| | | |
|---|---|---|
| 4401 ... 6/28/87 .. Robby Thompson ... Giants | 4451 ... 8/13/87 .. Candy Maldonado .. Giants |
| 4402 ... 7/3/87 .... Juan Samuel ......... Phillies | 4452 ... 8/13/87 .. Will Clark ................ Giants |
| 4403 ... 7/3/87 .... Greg Gross ............ Phillies | 4453 ... 8/13/87 .. Bob Brenly .............. Giants |
| 4404 ... 7/3/87 .... Luis Aguayo .......... Phillies | 4454 ... 8/13/87 .. Mike Aldrete ........... Giants |
| 4405 ... 7/3/87 .... Bruce Ruffin .......... Phillies | 4455 ... 8/13/87 .. Candy Maldonado .. Giants |
| 4406 ... 7/3/87 .... Juan Samuel ......... Phillies | 4456 ... 8/13/87 .. Will Clark ................ Giants |
| 4407 ... 7/3/87 .... Milt Thompson ....... Phillies | 4457 ... 8/13/87 .. Bob Brenly .............. Giants |
| 4408 ... 7/3/87 .... Lance Parrish ........ Phillies | 4458 ... 8/13/87 .. Harry Spilman ......... Giants |
| 4409 ... 7/3/87 .... Glenn Wilson ......... Phillies | 4459 ... 8/18/87 .. Vince Coleman .. Cardinals |
| 4410 ... 7/3/87 .... Bruce Ruffin .......... Phillies | 4460 ... 8/18/87 .. Willie McGee ...... Cardinals |
| 4411 ... 7/3/87 .... Juan Samuel ......... Phillies | 4461 ... 8/18/87 .. Vince Coleman .. Cardinals |
| 4412 ... 7/8/87 .... Jeff Reed ................. Expos | 4462 ... 8/18/87 .. Ozzie Smith ....... Cardinals |
| 4413 ... 7/8/87 .... Floyd Youmans ....... Expos | 4463 ... 8/18/87 .. Jack Clark .......... Cardinals |
| 4414 ... 7/8/87 .... Tim Raines .............. Expos | 4464 ... 8/18/87 .. Vince Coleman .. Cardinals |
| 4415 ... 7/8/87 .... Hubie Brooks .......... Expos | 4465 ... 8/18/87 .. Ozzie Smith ....... Cardinals |
| 4416 ... 7/8/87 .... Floyd Youmans ....... Expos | 4466 ... 8/18/87 .. Jack Clark .......... Cardinals |
| 4417 ... 7/8/87 .... Tim Wallach ............ Expos | 4467 ... 8/18/87 .. Tony Pena .......... Cardinals |
| 4418 ... 7/8/87 .... Andres Galarraga .... Expos | 4468 ... 8/23/87 .. Ryne Sandberg ........ Cubs |
| 4419 ... 7/8/87 .... Jeff Reed ................. Expos | 4469 ... 8/23/87 .. Leon Durham ............ Cubs |
| 4420 ... 7/8/87 .... Casey Candaele ..... Expos | 4470 ... 8/23/87 .. Andre Dawson .......... Cubs |
| 4421 ... 7/19/87 .. Lance Parrish ........ Phillies | 4471 ... 8/23/87 .. Dave Martinez .......... Cubs |
| 4422 ... 7/19/87 .. Greg Gross ............ Phillies | 4472 ... 8/23/87 .. Ryne Sandberg ........ Cubs |
| 4423 ... 7/19/87 .. Juan Samuel ......... Phillies | 4473 ... 8/23/87 .. Shawon Dunston ...... Cubs |
| 4424 ... 7/24/87 .. Lee Mazzilli .............. Mets | 4474 ... 8/23/87 .. Jim Sundberg ........... Cubs |
| 4425 ... 7/24/87 .. Gary Carter .............. Mets | 4475 ... 8/29/87 .. John Cangelosi ...... Pirates |
| 4426 ... 7/29/87 .. Bruce Benedict ...... Braves | 4476 ... 8/29/87 .. Jose Lind ............... Pirates |
| 4427 ... 7/29/87 .. Glenn Hubbard ...... Braves | 4477 ... 8/29/87 .. R.J. Reynolds ........ Pirates |
| 4428 ... 7/29/87 .. Charlie Puleo ......... Braves | 4478 ... 8/29/87 .. Al Pedrique ........... Pirates |
| 4429 ... 7/29/87 .. Dale Murphy ......... Braves | 4479 ... 8/29/87 .. Mike Bielecki ......... Pirates |
| 4430 ... 7/29/87 .. Ken Griffey ............. Braves | 4480 ... 8/29/87 .. R.J. Reynolds ........ Pirates |
| 4431 ... 8/3/87 .... Jeffrey Leonard ....... Giants | 4481 ... 8/29/87 .. Mike Lavalliere ...... Pirates |
| 4432 ... 8/3/87 .... Robby Thompson ... Giants | 4482 ... 9/4/87 .... Bobby Bonilla ........ Pirates |
| 4433 ... 8/3/87 .... Mike Krukow ........... Giants | 4483 ... 9/4/87 .... Mike Bielecki ......... Pirates |
| 4434 ... 8/3/87 .... Chili Davis .............. Giants | 4484 ... 9/4/87 .... John Cangelosi ...... Pirates |
| 4435 ... 8/3/87 .... Bob Brenly .............. Giants | 4485 ... 9/4/87 .... Andy Van Slyke ..... Pirates |
| 4436 ... 8/3/87 .... Robby Thompson ... Giants | 4486 ... 9/4/87 .... Mike Lavalliere ...... Pirates |
| 4437 ... 8/3/87 .... Mike Krukow ........... Giants | 4487 ... 9/4/87 .... Al Pedrique ........... Pirates |
| 4438 ... 8/3/87 .... Jeffrey Leonard ....... Giants | 4488 ... 9/9/87 .... Eddie Milner ............ Giants |
| 4439 ... 8/3/87 .... Bob Brenly .............. Giants | 4489 ... 9/9/87 .... Will Clark ................ Giants |
| 4440 ... 8/3/87 .... Robby Thompson ... Giants | 4490 ... 9/9/87 .... Jose Uribe .............. Giants |
| 4441 ... 8/3/87 .... Jose Uribe .............. Giants | 4491 ... 9/9/87 .... Atlee Hammaker ..... Giants |
| 4442 ... 8/3/87 .... Mike Krukow ........... Giants | 4492 ... 9/9/87 .... Matt Williams .......... Giants |
| 4443 ... 8/8/87 .... Stan Jefferson ........ Padres | 4493 ... 9/9/87 .... Francisco Melendez Giants |
| 4444 ... 8/8/87 .... Mark Grant ............. Padres | 4494 ... 9/9/87 .... Candy Maldonado .. Giants |
| 4445 ... 8/8/87 .... Stan Jefferson ........ Padres | 4495 ... 9/9/87 .... Will Clark ................ Giants |
| 4446 ... 8/8/87 .... John Kruk .............. Padres | 4496 ... 9/9/87 .... Bob Brenly .............. Giants |
| 4447 ... 8/8/87 .... Benito Santiago ..... Padres | 4497 ... 9/9/87 .... Chili Davis .............. Giants |
| 4448 ... 8/8/87 .... James Steels ......... Padres | 4498 ... 9/9/87 .... Jessie Reid ............. Giants |
| 4449 ... 8/13/87 .. Mike Krukow ........... Giants | 4499 ... 9/9/87 .... Chris Speier ........... Giants |
| 4450 ... 8/13/87 .. Jeffrey Leonard ....... Giants | 4500 ... 9/9/87 .... Mike Aldrete ........... Giants |

4501 ... 9/9/87 .... Candy Maldonado .. Giants
4502 ... 9/9/87 .... Will Clark ................ Giants
4503 ... 9/9/87 .... Bob Brenly ............. Giants
4504 ... 9/14/87 .. Ralph Bryant ........ Dodgers
4505 ... 9/14/87 .. Phil Garner .......... Dodgers
4506 ... 9/14/87 .. John Shelby ........ Dodgers
4507 ... 9/14/87 .. Ralph Bryant ........ Dodgers
4508 ... 9/14/87 .. Phil Garner .......... Dodgers
4509 ... 9/14/87 .. Chris Gwynn ........ Dodgers
4510 ... 9/14/87 .. Ralph Bryant ........ Dodgers
4511 ... 9/14/87 .. Ken Landreaux .. Dodgers
4512 ... 9/14/87 .. Mike Deveraux .. Dodgers
4513 ... 9/19/87 .. John Kruk ............. Padres
4514 ... 9/19/87 .. Tim Flannery ......... Padres
4515 ... 9/19/87 .. Garry Templeton .... Padres
4516 ... 9/19/87 .. Garry Templeton .... Padres
4517 ... 9/19/87 .. Tony Gwynn .......... Padres
4518 ... 9/19/87 .. John Kruk ............. Padres
4519 ... 9/19/87 .. Garry Templeton .... Padres
4520 ... 9/19/87 .. Stan Jefferson ....... Padres
4521 ... 9/19/87 .. John Kruk ............. Padres
4522 ... 9/19/87 .. Carmelo Martinez .. Padres
4523 ... 9/19/87 .. Benito Santiago ..... Padres
4524 ... 9/24/87 .. Albert Hall ............. Braves
4525 ... 9/24/87 .. Ozzie Virgil ............. Braves
4526 ... 9/24/87 .. Ron Gant ............... Braves
4527 ... 9/24/87 .. Ozzie Virgil ............. Braves
4528 ... 9/24/87 .. Graig Nettles .......... Braves
4529 ... 9/29/87 .. John Shelby ........ Dodgers
4530 ... 9/29/87 .. Ralph Bryant ........ Dodgers
4531 ... 9/29/87 .. Glenn Hoffman .... Dodgers
4532 ... 9/29/87 .. Ralph Bryant ........ Dodgers
4533 ... 9/29/87 .. Glenn Hoffman .... Dodgers
4534 ... 9/29/87 .. Mike Sharperson . Dodgers
4535 ... 9/29/87 .. Steve Sax ........... Dodgers
4536 ... 9/29/87 .. Mike Marshall ...... Dodgers
4537 ... 9/29/87 .. Glenn Hoffman .... Dodgers
4538 ... 10/4/87 .. Dave Collins ............. Reds
4539 ... 10/4/87 .. Jeff Treadway ........... Reds
4540 ... 10/4/87 .. Tracy Jones ............... Reds
4541 ... 10/4/87 .. Buddy Bell ................ Reds
4542 ... 10/4/87 .. Kurt Stillwell ............. Reds
4543 ... 10/4/87 .. Tom Browning .......... Reds
4544 ... 10/4/87 .. Paul O'Neill ............... Reds
4545 ... 10/4/87 .. Terry McGriff ............. Reds
4546 ... 10/4/87 .. Tom Browning .......... Reds
4547 ... 10/4/87 .. Jeff Treadway ........... Reds
4548 ... 4/8/88 .... Eric Davis ................. Reds
4549 ... 4/8/88 .... Paul O'Neill ............... Reds
4550 ... 4/8/88 .... Nick Esasky ............. Reds

4551 ... 4/8/88 .... Terry McGriff ............. Reds
4552 ... 4/8/88 .... Tom Browning .......... Reds
4553 ... 4/8/88 .... Eric Davis ................. Reds
4554 ... 4/8/88 .... Nick Esasky ............. Reds
4555 ... 4/8/88 .... Tom Browning .......... Reds
4556 ... 4/8/88 .... Paul O'Neill ............... Reds
4557 ... 4/8/88 .... Terry McGriff ............. Reds
4558 ... 4/8/88 .... Tom Browning .......... Reds
4559 ... 4/12/88 .. Ken Oberkfell ........ Braves
4560 ... 4/12/88 .. Zane Smith ............ Braves
4561 ... 4/12/88 .. Dale Murphy .......... Braves
4562 ... 4/12/88 .. Ken Griffey ............ Braves
4563 ... 4/12/88 .. Bruce Benedict ...... Braves
4564 ... 4/12/88 .. Zane Smith ............ Braves
4565 ... 4/12/88 .. Damaso Garcia ...... Braves
4566 ... 4/12/88 .. Dale Murphy .......... Braves
4567 ... 4/17/88 .. Kal Daniels ............. Reds
4568 ... 4/17/88 .. Paul O'Neill ............... Reds
4569 ... 4/17/88 .. Danny Jackson ......... Reds
4570 ... 4/17/88 .. Kal Daniels ............. Reds
4571 ... 4/17/88 .. Frank Williams .......... Reds
4572 ... 4/17/88 .. Paul O'Neill ............... Reds
4573 ... 4/17/88 .. Leo Garcia ................ Reds
4574 ... 4/17/88 .. Barry Larkin .............. Reds
4575 ... 4/17/88 .. Eric Davis ................. Reds
4576 ... 4/22/88 .. Keith Moreland ...... Padres
4577 ... 4/22/88 .. Benito Santiago .... Padres
4578 ... 4/22/88 .. Roberto Alomar ..... Padres
4579 ... 4/22/88 .. Carmelo Martinez .. Padres
4580 ... 4/22/88 .. Garry Templeton .... Padres
4581 ... 4/22/88 .. Jimmy Jones .......... Padres
4582 ... 4/22/88 .. Tony Gwynn .......... Padres
4583 ... 4/22/88 .. Garry Templeton .... Padres
4584 ... 4/27/88 .. Kevin Gross ........ Phillies
4585 ... 4/27/88 .. Juan Samuel ......... Phillies
4586 ... 4/27/88 .. Chris James ........... Phillies
4587 ... 4/27/88 .. Milt Thompson ....... Phillies
4588 ... 4/27/88 .. Juan Samuel ......... Phillies
4589 ... 4/27/88 .. Lance Parrish ........ Phillies
4590 ... 4/27/88 .. Chris James ........... Phillies
4591 ... 4/27/88 .. Mike Young ............ Phillies
4592 ... 4/27/88 .. Juan Samuel ......... Phillies
4593 ... 5/2/88 .... Von Hayes ............ Phillies
4594 ... 5/2/88 .... Phil Bradley .......... Phillies
4595 ... 5/2/88 .... Luis Aguayo .......... Phillies
4596 ... 5/7/88 .... Tim Wallach ........... Expos
4597 ... 5/7/88 .... Mike Fitzgerald ........ Expos
4598 ... 5/7/88 .... Tom Foley ................ Expos
4599 ... 5/7/88 .... Pascual Perez ......... Expos
4600 ... 5/7/88 .... Hubie Brooks ........ Expos

| | | | |
|---|---|---|---|
| 4601 ... 5/7/88 .... Mitch Webster ......... Expos | 4651 ... 6/24/88 .. Mike Aldrete ............ Giants |
| 4602 ... 5/7/88 .... Andres Galarraga .... Expos | 4652 ... 6/24/88 .. Kevin Mitchell ......... Giants |
| 4603 ... 5/13/88 .. Dave Martinez ......... Cubs | 4653 ... 6/24/88 .. Jose Uribe ............. Giants |
| 4604 ... 5/13/88 .. Damon Berryhill ........ Cubs | 4654 ... 6/24/88 .. Candy Maldonado .. Giants |
| 4605 ... 5/13/88 .. Shawon Dunston ...... Cubs | 4655 ... 6/24/88 .. Kelly Downs ............ Giants |
| 4606 ... 5/13/88 ...Jamie Moyer ............. Cubs | 4656 ... 6/29/88 .. John Shelby ......... Dodgers |
| 4607 ... 5/13/88 .. Shawon Dunston ...... Cubs | 4657 ... 6/29/88 .. Jeff Hamilton ....... Dodgers |
| 4608 ... 5/13/88 .. Jamie Moyer ............. Cubs | 4658 ... 6/29/88 .. John Shelby ......... Dodgers |
| 4609 ... 5/13/88 .. Dave Martinez .......... Cubs | 4659 ... 6/29/88 .. Jeff Hamilton ....... Dodgers |
| 4610 ... 5/13/88 .. Damon Berryhill ........ Cubs | 4660 ... 6/29/88 .. Dave Anderson .... Dodgers |
| 4611 ... 5/13/88 .. Shawon Dunston ...... Cubs | 4661 ... 6/29/88 .. Kirk Gibson .......... Dodgers |
| 4612 ... 5/13/88 .. Mark Grace ............... Cubs | 4662 ... 6/29/88 .. Mike Marshall ...... Dodgers |
| 4613 ... 5/13/88 .. Vance Law ................ Cubs | 4663 ... 6/29/88 .. John Shelby ......... Dodgers |
| 4614 ... 5/18/88 .. Barry Bonds ........... Pirates | 4664 ... 6/29/88 .. Jeff Hamilton ....... Dodgers |
| 4615 ... 5/18/88 .. Andy Van Slyke ..... Pirates | 4665 ... 6/29/88 .. Orel Hershiser ..... Dodgers |
| 4616 ... 5/24/88 .. R.J. Reynolds ........ Pirates | 4666 ... 7/3/88 .... Darryl Strawberry ...... Mets |
| 4617 ... 5/24/88 .. Barry Bonds ....:..... Pirates | 4667 ... 7/3/88 .... Mookie Wilson ........... Mets |
| 4618 ... 5/24/88 .. R.J. Reynolds ........ Pirates | 4668 ... 7/3/88 .... Mackey Sasser .......... Mets |
| 4619 ... 5/24/88 .. Mike Diaz .............. Pirates | 4669 ... 7/3/88 .... Kevin Elster ............. Mets |
| 4620 ... 5/24/88 .. Barry Bonds ........... Pirates | 4670 ... 7/3/88 .... Wally Backman ......... Mets |
| 4621 ... 5/29/88 .. Ryne Sandberg ......... Cubs | 4671 ... 7/3/88 .... Mookie Wilson ........... Mets |
| 4622 ... 5/29/88 .. Rafael Palmeiro ........ Cubs | 4672 ... 7/3/88 .... Wally Backman ......... Mets |
| 4623 ... 5/29/88 .. Shawon Dunston ...... Cubs | 4673 ... 7/9/88 .... Howard Johnson ....... Mets |
| 4624 ... 5/29/88 .. Jerry Mumphrey ....... Cubs | 4674 ... 7/9/88 .... Dave Magadan .......... Mets |
| 4625 ... 6/4/88 .... Robby Thompson ... Giants | 4675 ... 7/9/88 .... Rick Aguilera ............. Mets |
| 4626 ... 6/4/88 .... Candy Maldonado .. Giants | 4676 ... 7/9/88 .... Howard Johnson ....... Mets |
| 4627 ... 6/4/88 .... Chris Speier ............ Giants | 4677 ... 7/9/88 .... Mackey Sasser .......... Mets |
| 4628 ... 6/4/88 .... Matt Williams .......... Giants | 4678 ... 7/16/88 .. Juan Samuel ......... Phillies |
| 4629 ... 6/4/88 .... Robby Thompson ... Giants | 4679 ... 7/16/88 .. Don Carman .......... Phillies |
| 4630 ... 6/4/88 .... Will Clark ................ Giants | 4680 ... 7/16/88 .. Don Carman .......... Phillies |
| 4631 ... 6/4/88 .... Chris Speier ............ Giants | 4681 ... 7/21/88 .. Juan Samuel .......... Phillies |
| 4632 ... 6/4/88 .... Matt Williams .......... Giants | 4682 ... 7/21/88 .. Mike Schmidt ........ Phillies |
| 4633 ... 6/4/88 .... Candy Maldonado .. Giants | 4683 ... 7/21/88 .. Darren Daulton ...... Phillies |
| 4634 ... 6/4/88 .... Kirt Manwaring ....... Giants | 4684 ... 7/21/88 .. Juan Samuel .......... Phillies |
| 4635 ... 6/9/88 .... Franklin Stubbs ... Dodgers | 4685 ... 7/21/88 .. Milt Thompson ....... Phillies |
| 4636 ... 6/9/88 .... Kirk Gibson .......... Dodgers | 4686 ... 7/21/88 .. Chris James ........... Phillies |
| 4637 ... 6/13/88 ... Albert Hall .............. Braves | 4687 ... 7/21/88 .. Milt Thompson ....... Phillies |
| 4638 ... 6/13/88 .. Kevin Coffman ....... Braves | 4688 ... 7/21/88 .. Chris James ........... Phillies |
| 4639 ... 6/13/88 .. Ron Gant ................ Braves | 4689 ... 7/21/88 .. Milt Thompson ....... Phillies |
| 4640 ... 6/13/88 .. Gerald Perry .......... Braves | 4690 ... 7/27/88 .. Stan Jefferson ........ Padres |
| 4641 ... 6/13/88 .. Paul Runge ............. Braves | 4691 ... 7/27/88 .. Chris Brown ........... Padres |
| 4642 ... 6/13/88 .. Ron Gant ................. Braves | 4692 ... 7/27/88 .. Chris Brown ........... Padres |
| 4643 ... 6/13/88 .. Dale Murphy ........... Braves | 4693 ... 7/27/88 .. Roberto Alomar ...... Padres |
| 4644 ... 6/13/88 .. Andres Thomas ..... Braves | 4694 ... 8/1/88 .... Mike Aldrete ............ Giants |
| 4645 ... 6/18/88 .. Gerald Perry .......... Braves | 4695 ... 8/1/88 .... Bob Melvin ............. Giants |
| 4646 ... 6/18/88 .. Kevin Coffman ....... Braves | 4696 ... 8/1/88 .... Jose Uribe .............. Giants |
| 4647 ... 6/18/88 .. Ron Gant ................ Braves | 4697 ... 8/1/88 .... Atlee Hammaker ..... Giants |
| 4648 ... 6/18/88 .. Kevin Coffman ....... Braves | 4698 ... 8/1/88 .... Atlee Hammaker ..... Giants |
| 4649 ... 6/18/88 .. Ron Gant ................. Braves | 4699 ... 8/1/88 .... Kevin Mitchell ......... Giants |
| 4650 ... 6/18/88 .. Ken Oberkfell ......... Braves | 4700 ... 8/1/88 .... Jose Uribe .............. Giants |

| | | | |
|---|---|---|---|
| 4701 ... 8/1/88 .... Atlee Hammaker ..... Giants | 4751 ... 9/3/88 .... Mike Laga .......... Cardinals |
| 4702 ... 8/1/88 .... Brett Butler .............. Giants | 4752 ... 9/8/88 .... Steve Sax ............ Dodgers |
| 4703 ... 8/1/88 .... Will Clark ................ Giants | 4753 ... 9/8/88 .... Kirk Gibson .......... Dodgers |
| 4704 ... 8/1/88 .... Kevin Mitchell ......... Giants | 4754 ... 9/8/88 .... John Shelby .......... Dodgers |
| 4705 ... 8/6/88 .... Pedro Guerrero ... Dodgers | 4755 ... 9/8/88 .... Mike Davis ........... Dodgers |
| 4706 ... 8/6/88 .... Alfredo Griffin ...... Dodgers | 4756 ... 9/8/88 .... Kirk Gibson .......... Dodgers |
| 4707 ... 8/6/88 .... Tim Belcher .......... Dodgers | 4757 ... 9/8/88 .... Mickey Hatcher .... Dodgers |
| 4708 ... 8/6/88 .... John Shelby ......... Dodgers | 4758 ... 9/8/88 .... Jeff Hamilton ....... Dodgers |
| 4709 ... 8/6/88 .... Pedro Guerrero ... Dodgers | 4759 ... 9/14/88 .. Chris Sabo ................ Reds |
| 4710 ... 8/6/88 .... Tracy Woodson ... Dodgers | 4760 ... 9/14/88 .. Dave Collins ............. Reds |
| 4711 ... 8/11/88 .. Bob Melvin .............. Giants | 4761 ... 9/14/88 .. Nick Esasky .............. Reds |
| 4712 ... 8/11/88 .. Atlee Hammaker ..... Giants | 4762 ... 9/14/88 .. Danny Jackson ......... Reds |
| 4713 ... 8/11/88 .. Ernest Riles ............ Giants | 4763 ... 9/14/88 .. Eric Davis ................. Reds |
| 4714 ... 8/11/88 .. Atlee Hammaker ..... Giants | 4764 ... 9/14/88 .. Dave Collins ............. Reds |
| 4715 ... 8/11/88 .. Candy Maldonado .. Giants | 4765 ... 9/14/88 .. Nick Esasky .............. Reds |
| 4716 ... 8/11/88 .. Brett Butler .............. Giants | 4766 ... 9/14/88 .. Jeff Reed ................... Reds |
| 4717 ... 8/15/88 .. Marvell Wynne ....... Padres | 4767 ... 9/14/88 .. Van Snider ................ Reds |
| 4718 ... 8/15/88 .. Andy Hawkins ........ Padres | 4768 ... 9/14/88 .. Eric Davis ................. Reds |
| 4719 ... 8/20/88 .. Andy Van Slyke ..... Pirates | 4769 ... 9/14/88 .. Jeff Reed ................... Reds |
| 4720 ... 8/20/88 .. Mike Lavalliere ....... Pirates | 4770 ... 9/14/88 .. Ron Oester ................ Reds |
| 4721 ... 8/20/88 .. Al Pedrique ............ Pirates | 4771 ... 9/14/88 .. Kal Daniels ............... Reds |
| 4722 ... 8/20/88 .. John Smiley ........... Pirates | 4772 ... 9/19/88 .. Alfredo Griffin ...... Dodgers |
| 4723 ... 8/20/88 .. Bobby Bonilla ......... Pirates | 4773 ... 9/19/88 .. Steve Sax ............ Dodgers |
| 4724 ... 8/24/88 .. Rafael Palmeiro ........ Cubs | 4774 ... 9/19/88 .. Mike Marshall ....... Dodgers |
| 4725 ... 8/24/88 .. Shawon Dunston ...... Cubs | 4775 ... 9/19/88 .. John Shelby .......... Dodgers |
| 4726 ... 8/24/88 .. Mitch Webster .......... Cubs | 4776 ... 4/6/89 .... Ken Williams ........... Tigers |
| 4727 ... 8/24/88 .. Ryne Sandberg ........ Cubs | 4777 ... 4/6/89 .... Torey Lovullo .......... Tigers |
| 4728 ... 8/24/88 .. Andre Dawson .......... Cubs | 4778 ... 4/6/89 .... Alan Trammell ......... Tigers |
| 4729 ... 8/24/88 .. Vance Law ................ Cubs | 4779 ... 4/6/89 .... Matt Nokes ............. Tigers |
| 4730 ... 8/24/88 .. Mitch Webster .......... Cubs | 4780 ... 4/6/89 .... Billy Bean ................ Tigers |
| 4731 ... 8/24/88 .. Mark Grace ............... Cubs | 4781 ... 4/6/89 .... Fred Lynn ................ Tigers |
| 4732 ... 8/24/88 .. Damon Berryhill ....... Cubs | 4782 ... 4/6/89 .... Matt Nokes ............. Tigers |
| 4733 ... 8/29/88 .. Ryne Sandberg ........ Cubs | 4783 ... 4/6/89 .... Pat Sheridan ........... Tigers |
| 4734 ... 8/29/88 .. Mark Grace ............... Cubs | 4784 ... 4/12/89 .. B.J. Surhoff .......... Brewers |
| 4735 ... 8/29/88 .. Mitch Webster .......... Cubs | 4785 ... 4/12/89 .. Robin Yount ......... Brewers |
| 4736 ... 8/29/88 .. Andre Dawson .......... Cubs | 4786 ... 4/12/89 .. Rob Deer ............. Brewers |
| 4737 ... 8/29/88 .. Vance Law ................ Cubs | 4787 ... 4/12/89 .. Glenn Braggs ....... Brewers |
| 4738 ... 8/29/88 .. Shawon Dunston ...... Cubs | 4788 ... 4/12/89 .. Terry Francona .... Brewers |
| 4739 ... 8/29/88 .. Mitch Webster .......... Cubs | 4789 ... 4/12/89 .. Joey Meyer ......... Brewers |
| 4740 ... 8/29/88 .. Vance Law ................ Cubs | 4790 ... 4/12/89 .. B.J. Surhoff .......... Brewers |
| 4741 ... 8/29/88 .. Shawon Dunston ...... Cubs | 4791 ... 4/12/89 .. Robin Yount ......... Brewers |
| 4742 ... 8/29/88 .. Greg Maddux ........... Cubs | 4792 ... 4/12/89 .. Glenn Braggs ....... Brewers |
| 4743 ... 8/29/88 .. Mitch Webster .......... Cubs | 4793 ... 4/12/89 .. Joey Meyer ......... Brewers |
| 4744 ... 9/3/88 .... Vince Coleman .. Cardinals | 4794 ... 4/12/89 .. Gus Polidor ......... Brewers |
| 4745 ... 9/3/88 .... Pedro Guerrero .. Cardinals | 4795 ... 4/12/89 .. Bill Spiers ........... Brewers |
| 4746 ... 9/3/88 .... Tom Brunansky .. Cardinals | 4796 ... 4/12/89 .. Jim Gantner ......... Brewers |
| 4747 ... 9/3/88 .... Terry Pendleton . Cardinals | 4797 ... 4/12/89 .. Rob Deer ............. Brewers |
| 4748 ... 9/3/88 .... John Morris ........ Cardinals | 4798 ... 4/12/89 .. Joey Meyer ......... Brewers |
| 4749 ... 9/3/88 .... Vince Coleman .. Cardinals | 4799 ... 4/17/89 .. Paul Molitor ......... Brewers |
| 4750 ... 9/3/88 .... Jim Lindeman .... Cardinals | 4800 ... 4/17/89 .. Glenn Braggs ....... Brewers |

| | | | |
|---|---|---|---|
| 4801 ... 4/17/89 .. Rob Deer ............. Brewers | | 4851 ... 5/23/89 .. Bob Boone ............. Royals | |
| 4802 ... 4/23/89 .. George Bell ....... Blue Jays | | 4852 ... 5/23/89 .. Kevin Seitzer .......... Royals | |
| 4803 ... 4/23/89 .. Fred McGriff ...... Blue Jays | | 4853 ... 5/23/89 .. Bo Jackson ............ Royals | |
| 4804 ... 4/23/89 .. Ernie Whitt ........ Blue Jays | | 4854 ... 5/23/89 .. Danny Tartabull ...... Royals | |
| 4805 ... 4/23/89 .. Jesse Barfield .... Blue Jays | | 4855 ... 5/29/89 .. Brady Anderson ..... Orioles | |
| 4806 ... 4/23/89 .. Manny Lee ........ Blue Jays | | 4856 ... 5/29/89 .. Cal Ripken ............. Orioles | |
| 4807 ... 4/23/89 .. Ernie Whitt ........ Blue Jays | | 4857 ... 5/29/89 .. Randy Milligan ....... Orioles | |
| 4808 ... 4/23/89 .. Rance Mulliniks . Blue Jays | | 4858 ... 5/29/89 .. Randy Milligan ....... Orioles | |
| 4809 ... 4/23/89 .. Manny Lee ........ Blue Jays | | 4859 ... 5/29/89 .. Craig Worthington .. Orioles | |
| 4810 ... 4/23/89 .. Nelson Liriano ... Blue Jays | | 4860 ... 5/29/89 .. Bill Ripken ............. Orioles | |
| 4811 ... 4/23/89 .. Fred McGriff ...... Blue Jays | | 4861 ... 5/29/89 .. Brady Anderson ..... Orioles | |
| 4812 ... 4/23/89 .. Jesse Barfield ... Blue Jays | | 4862 ... 5/29/89 .. Mickey Tettleton .... Orioles | |
| 4813 ... 4/23/89 .. Rob Ducey ......... Blue Jays | | 4863 ... 5/29/89 .. Joe Orsulak ........... Orioles | |
| 4814 ... 4/30/89 .. Nick Esasky ........ Red Sox | | 4864 ... 5/29/89 .. Larry Sheets .......... Orioles | |
| 4815 ... 4/30/89 .. Wade Boggs ........ Red Sox | | 4865 ... 6/3/89 .... Scott Bradley ....... Mariners | |
| 4816 ... 4/30/89 .. Danny Heep ........ Red Sox | | 4866 ... 6/3/89 .... Jeffrey Leonard ... Mariners | |
| 4817 ... 4/30/89 .. Nick Esasky ........ Red Sox | | 4867 ... 6/3/89 .... Jim Presley ......... Mariners | |
| 4818 ... 4/30/89 .. Rich Gedman ...... Red Sox | | 4868 ... 6/3/89 .... Jay Buhner .......... Mariners | |
| 4819 ... 4/30/89 .. Jody Reed ........... Red Sox | | 4869 ... 6/3/89 .... Harold Reynolds . Mariners | |
| 4820 ... 4/30/89 .. Jim Rice ............... Red Sox | | 4870 ... 6/3/89 .... Jim Presley ......... Mariners | |
| 4821 ... 4/30/89 .. Nick Esasky ........ Red Sox | | 4871 ... 6/3/89 .... Jay Buhner .......... Mariners | |
| 4822 ... 4/30/89 .. Rich Gedman ...... Red Sox | | 4872 ... 6/3/89 .... Greg Briley .......... Mariners | |
| 4823 ... 4/30/89 .. Randy Kutcher .... Red Sox | | 4873 ... 6/3/89 .... "Ken Griffey, Jr." .. Mariners | |
| 4824 ... 4/30/89 .. Jim Rice ............... Red Sox | | 4874 ... 6/3/89 .... Jim Presley ......... Mariners | |
| 4825 ... 5/5/89 .... Rich Gedman ...... Red Sox | | 4875 ... 6/3/89 .... Jay Buhner .......... Mariners | |
| 4826 ... 5/5/89 .... Jim Rice ............... Red Sox | | 4876 ... 6/8/89 .... Dave Gallagher . White Sox | |
| 4827 ... 5/5/89 .... Nick Esasky ........ Red Sox | | 4877 ... 6/8/89 .... Ron Kittle .......... White Sox | |
| 4828 ... 5/11/89 .. Willie Wilson .......... Royals | | 4878 ... 6/8/89 .... Dan Pasqua ...... White Sox | |
| 4829 ... 5/11/89 .. Jim Eisenreich ........ Royals | | 4879 ... 6/8/89 .... Carlton Fisk ...... White Sox | |
| 4830 ... 5/11/89 .. Danny Tartabull ...... Royals | | 4880 ... 6/8/89 .... Ron Kittle .......... White Sox | |
| 4831 ... 5/11/89 .. Bo Jackson ............ Royals | | 4881 ... 6/8/89 .... Ivan Calderon ... White Sox | |
| 4832 ... 5/11/89 .. Bill Buckner ............ Royals | | 4882 ... 6/8/89 .... Ron Kittle .......... White Sox | |
| 4833 ... 5/11/89 .. Bo Jackson ............ Royals | | 4883 ... 6/14/89 .. Claudell WashingtonAngels | |
| 4834 ... 5/11/89 .. Willie Wilson .......... Royals | | 4884 ... 6/14/89 .. Jack Howell ............ Angels | |
| 4835 ... 5/11/89 .. Jim Eisenreich ........ Royals | | 4885 ... 6/14/89 .. Johnny Ray ............ Angels | |
| 4836 ... 5/11/89 .. Bo Jackson ............ Royals | | 4886 ... 6/14/89 .. Bill Schroeder ......... Angels | |
| 4837 ... 5/11/89 .. Kurt Stillwell ........... Royals | | 4887 ... 6/14/89 .. Kent Anderson ....... Angels | |
| 4838 ... 5/11/89 .. Bo Jackson ............ Royals | | 4888 ... 6/14/89 .. Dick Schofield ........ Angels | |
| 4839 ... 5/18/89 .. Gary Gaetti ............. Twins | | 4889 ... 6/14/89 .. Claudell WashingtonAngels | |
| 4840 ... 5/18/89 .. Jim Dwyer ................ Twins | | 4890 ... 6/14/89 .. Devon White ........ Red Sox | |
| 4841 ... 5/18/89 .. Gene Larkin ............. Twins | | 4891 ... 6/20/89 .. Mike Greenwell ... Red Sox | |
| 4842 ... 5/18/89 .. Randy Bush .............. Twins | | 4892 ... 6/20/89 .. Nick Esasky ......... Red Sox | |
| 4843 ... 5/18/89 .. Gene Larkin ............. Twins | | 4893 ... 6/20/89 .. Jody Reed ........... Red Sox | |
| 4844 ... 5/18/89 .. Greg Gagne ............. Twins | | 4894 ... 6/20/89 .. Mike Greenwell ... Red Sox | |
| 4845 ... 5/18/89 .. Dan Gladden ............ Twins | | 4895 ... 6/20/89 .. Nick Esasky ......... Red Sox | |
| 4846 ... 5/18/89 .. Randy Bush .............. Twins | | 4896 ... 6/20/89 .. Randy Kutcher .... Red Sox | |
| 4847 ... 5/18/89 .. Kirby Puckett ........... Twins | | 4897 ... 6/25/89 .. Dave Clark ............. Indians | |
| 4848 ... 5/18/89 .. Tim Laudner ............. Twins | | 4898 ... 6/25/89 .. Pete O'Brien .......... Indians | |
| 4849 ... 5/23/89 .. Kurt Stillwell ........... Royals | | 4899 ... 6/25/89 .. Brook Jacoby ......... Indians | |
| 4850 ... 5/23/89 .. Bo Jackson ............ Royals | | 4900 ... 6/25/89 .. Joe Carter ............. Indians | |

| | | |
|---|---|---|
| 4901 ... 6/25/89 .. Felix Fermin ........... Indians | 4951 ... 7/25/89 .. Tony Fernandez  Blue Jays |
| 4902 ... 6/25/89 .. Pete O'Brien .......... Indians | 4952 ... 7/25/89 .. Pat Borders ....... Blue Jays |
| 4903 ... 6/25/89 .. Oddibe McDowell .. Indians | 4953 ... 7/25/89 .. Lloyd Moseby .... Blue Jays |
| 4904 ... 6/30/89 .. "Ken Griffey, Jr." .. Mariners | 4954 ... 7/25/89 .. Nelson Liriano ... Blue Jays |
| 4905 ... 6/30/89 .. Darnell Coles ...... Mariners | 4955 ... 7/25/89 .. Tony Fernandez  Blue Jays |
| 4906 ... 6/30/89 .. Edgar Martinez .... Mariners | 4956 ... 7/30/89 .. Paul Molitor .......... Brewers |
| 4907 ... 6/30/89 .. Greg Briley ......... Mariners | 4957 ... 7/30/89 .. Jim Gantner .......... Brewers |
| 4908 ... 6/30/89 .. Jeffrey Leonard ... Mariners | 4958 ... 7/30/89 .. Greg Brock .......... Brewers |
| 4909 ... 6/30/89 .. Darnell Coles ...... Mariners | 4959 ... 7/30/89 .. Bill Spiers ............. Brewers |
| 4910 ... 6/30/89 .. Omar Vizquel ...... Mariners | 4960 ... 7/30/89 .. Charlie O'Brien .... Brewers |
| 4911 ... 6/30/89 .. Jeffrey Leonard ... Mariners | 4961 ... 7/30/89 .. Mike Felder .......... Brewers |
| 4912 ... 7/6/89 .... Brian Downing ........ Angels | 4962 ... 7/30/89 .. Bill Spiers ............. Brewers |
| 4913 ... 7/6/89 .... Tony Armas ............. Angels | 4963 ... 7/30/89 .. Paul Molitor .......... Brewers |
| 4914 ... 7/6/89 .... Kent Anderson ....... Angels | 4964 ... 7/30/89 .. Mike Felder .......... Brewers |
| 4915 ... 7/6/89 .... Devon White .......... Angels | 4965 ... 7/30/89 .. Bill Spiers ............. Brewers |
| 4916 ... 7/6/89 .... Tony Armas ............. Angels | 4966 ... 8/5/89 .... Joe Orsulak ........... Orioles |
| 4917 ... 7/6/89 .... Kent Anderson ....... Angels | 4967 ... 8/5/89 .... Bob Melvin ............. Orioles |
| 4918 ... 7/6/89 .... Dick Schofield ........ Angels | 4968 ... 8/5/89 .... Bill Ripken ............. Orioles |
| 4919 ... 7/6/89 .... Chili Davis .............. Angels | 4969 ... 8/5/89 .... Cal Ripken ............. Orioles |
| 4920 ... 7/6/89 .... Tony Armas ............. Angels | 4970 ... 8/5/80 .... Larry Sheets .......... Orioles |
| 4921 ... 7/6/89 .... Dick Schofield ........ Angels | 4971 ... 8/5/89 .... Randy Milligan ....... Orioles |
| 4922 ... 7/6/89 .... Devon White .......... Angels | 4972 ... 8/5/89 .... Bill Ripken ............. Orioles |
| 4923 ... 7/6/89 .... Wally Joyner .......... Angels | 4973 ... 8/5/89 .... Phil Bradley ........... Orioles |
| 4924 ... 7/15/89 .. Paul Zuvella .......... Indians | 4974 ... 8/10/89 .. Fred Lynn ................. Tigers |
| 4925 ... 7/15/89 .. Brad Komminsk ..... Indians | 4975 ... 8/10/89 .. Matt Nokes ............... Tigers |
| 4926 ... 7/15/89 .. Andy Allanson ....... Indians | 4976 ... 8/10/89 .. Mike Heath .............. Tigers |
| 4927 ... 7/15/89 .. Joe Carter .............. Indians | 4977 ... 8/10/89 .. Fred Lynn ................. Tigers |
| 4928 ... 7/15/89 .. Joey Belle .............. Indians | 4978 ... 8/10/89 .. Chet Lemon .............. Tigers |
| 4929 ... 7/15/89 .. Jerry Browne ......... Indians | 4979 ... 8/10/89 .. Doug Strange .......... Tigers |
| 4930 ... 7/15/89 .. Dion James ............ Indians | 4980 ... 8/10/89 .. Mike Heath .............. Tigers |
| 4931 ... 7/20/89 .. Steve Sax ............. Yankees | 4981 ... 8/10/89 .. Fred Lynn ................. Tigers |
| 4932 ... 7/20/89 .. Luis Polonia ......... Yankees | 4982 ... 8/10/89 .. Doug Strange .......... Tigers |
| 4933 ... 7/20/89 .. Jesse Barfield ...... Yankees | 4983 ... 8/10/89 .. Mike Heath .............. Tigers |
| 4934 ... 7/20/89 .. Alvaro Espinoza .. Yankees | 4984 ... 8/10/89 .. Gary Pettis .............. Tigers |
| 4935 ... 7/20/89 .. Luis Polonia ......... Yankees | 4985 ... 8/10/89 .. Lou Whitaker ........... Tigers |
| 4936 ... 7/20/89 .. Mel Hall ................. Yankees | 4986 ... 8/10/89 .. Fred Lynn ................. Tigers |
| 4937 ... 7/20/89 .. Jesse Barfield ..... Yankees | 4987 ... 8/16/89 .. Alvin Davis .......... Mariners |
| 4938 ... 7/20/89 .. Don Slaught .......... Yankees | 4988 ... 8/16/89 .. Darnell Coles ...... Mariners |
| 4939 ... 7/20/89 .. Don Mattingly ...... Yankees | 4989 ... 8/16/89 .. Greg Briley ......... Mariners |
| 4940 ... 7/20/89 .. Jesse Barfield ..... Yankees | 4990 ... 8/16/89 .. Jeffrey Leonard ... Mariners |
| 4941 ... 7/20/89 .. Mike Pagliarulo ... Yankees | 4991 ... 8/16/89 .. Jim Presley ......... Mariners |
| 4942 ... 7/25/89 .. Kelly Gruber ...... Blue Jays | 4992 ... 8/16/89 .. Greg Briley ......... Mariners |
| 4943 ... 7/25/89 .. George Bell ....... Blue Jays | 4993 ... 8/16/89 .. Jim Presley ......... Mariners |
| 4944 ... 7/25/89 .. Fred McGriff ...... Blue Jays | 4994 ... 8/16/89 .. Greg Briley ......... Mariners |
| 4945 ... 7/25/89 .. Ernie Whitt ......... Blue Jays | 4995 ... 8/22/89 .. Jose Canseco .............. A's |
| 4946 ... 7/25/89 .. Kelly Gruber ...... Blue Jays | 4996 ... 8/22/89 .. Dave Henderson .......... A's |
| 4947 ... 7/25/89 .. George Bell ....... Blue Jays | 4997 ... 8/22/89 .. Tony Phillips ................. A's |
| 4948 ... 7/25/89 .. Ernie Whitt ......... Blue Jays | 4998 ... 8/22/89 .. Rickey Henderson ........ A's |
| 4949 ... 7/25/89 .. Lloyd Moseby .... Blue Jays | 4999 ... 8/22/89 .. Ron Hassey ................. A's |
| 4950 ... 7/25/89 .. Junior Felix ........ Blue Jays | 5000 ... 8/22/89 .. Rickey Henderson ........ A's |

| | | | |
|---|---|---|---|
| 5001 ... 8/22/89 .. Ron Hassey .................. A's | 5051 ... 9/12/89 .. Willie Wilson ........... Royals |
| 5002 ... 8/22/89 .. Dave Henderson .......... A's | 5052 ... 9/12/89 .. Bo Jackson ............ Royals |
| 5003 ... 8/22/89 .. Mark McGwire .............. A's | 5053 ... 9/18/89 .. Greg Briley .......... Mariners |
| 5004 ... 8/22/89 .. Tony Phillips ................. A's | 5054 ... 9/18/89 .. Darnell Coles ...... Mariners |
| 5005 ... 8/22/89 .. Terry Steinbach ............ A's | 5055 ... 9/24/89 .. Carlos Martinez  White Sox |
| 5006 ... 8/22/89 .. Jose Canseco .............. A's | 5056 ... 9/24/89 .. Robin Ventura ... White Sox |
| 5007 ... 8/22/89 .. Ron Hassey .................. A's | 5057 ... 9/24/89 .. Ozzie Guillen ... White Sox |
| 5008 ... 8/27/89 .. C. Washington ....... Angels | 5058 ... 9/24/89 .. Lance Johnson . White Sox |
| 5009 ... 8/27/89 .. Devon White .......... Angels | 5059 ... 9/24/89 .. Steve Lyons ...... White Sox |
| 5010 ... 8/27/89 .. Brian Downing ........ Angels | 5060 ... 9/24/89 .. Robin Ventura ... White Sox |
| 5011 ... 8/27/89 .. John Orton ............ Angels | 5061 ... 9/24/89 .. Ron Karkovice ... White Sox |
| 5012 ... 8/27/89 .. Glenn Hoffman ....... Angels | 5062 ... 9/24/89 .. Steve Lyons ...... White Sox |
| 5013 ... 8/27/89 .. C. Washington ....... Angels | 5063 ... 9/24/89 .. Ivan Calderon ... White Sox |
| 5014 ... 8/27/89 .. Jack Howell ............ Angels | 5064 ... 9/30/89 .. Chili Davis .............. Angels |
| 5015 ... 8/27/89 .. C. Washington ....... Angels | 5065 ... 9/30/89 .. Jack Howell ............ Angels |
| 5016 ... 8/27/89 .. Bobby Rose ............ Angels | 5066 ... 9/30/89 .. John Orton ............ Angels |
| 5017 ... 8/27/89 .. Chili Davis .............. Angels | 5067 ... 9/30/89 .. Devon White .......... Angels |
| 5018 ... 8/27/89 .. John Orton ............ Angels | 5068 ... 9/30/89 .. Mark McLemore ..... Angels |
| 5019 ... 9/2/89 .. Willie Wilson ......... Royals | 5069 ... 9/30/89 .. Jack Howell ............ Angels |
| 5020 ... 9/2/89 .... Bo Jackson ............ Royals | 5070 ... 9/30/89 .. John Orton ............. Angels |
| 5021 ... 9/2/89 .... Kurt Stillwell .......... Royals | 5071 ... 9/30/89 .. Dick Schofield ........ Angels |
| 5022 ... 9/2/89 .... Brad Wellman ........ Royals | 5072 ... 9/30/89 .. Mark McLemore ..... Angels |
| 5023 ... 9/2/89 .... Kurt Stillwell .......... Royals | 5073 ... 9/30/89 .. Jack Howell ............ Angels |
| 5024 ... 9/2/89 .... Brad Wellman ........ Royals | 5074 ... 9/30/89 .. Jack Eppard ........... Angels |
| 5025 ... 9/2/89 .... Willie Wilson ........... Royals | 5075 ... 9/30/89 .. Dick Schofield ........ Angels |
| 5026 ... 9/2/89 .... George Brett ......... Royals | 5076 ... 9/30/89 .. Devon White .......... Angels |
| 5027 ... 9/2/89 .... Bob Boone ............ Royals | 5077 ... 4/9/90 .... George Bell ....... Blue Jays |
| 5028 ... 9/2/89 .... George Brett ......... Royals | 5078 ... 4/9/90 .... John Olerud ...... Blue Jays |
| 5029 ... 9/2/89 .... Bo Jackson ............ Royals | 5079 ... 4/9/90 .... Junior Felix ........ Blue Jays |
| 5030 ... 9/7/89 .... Phil Bradley .......... Orioles | 5080 ... 4/9/90 .... Junior Felix ........ Blue Jays |
| 5031 ... 9/7/89 .... Steve Finley .......... Orioles | 5081 ... 4/14/90 .. Luis Polonia ....... Yankees |
| 5032 ... 9/7/89 .... Craig Worthington .. Orioles | 5082 ... 4/14/90 .. Mel Hall ................ Yankees |
| 5033 ... 9/7/89 .... Bob Melvin ............ Orioles | 5083 ... 4/14/90 .. Steve Sax ........... Yankees |
| 5034 ... 9/7/89 .... Steve Finley .......... Orioles | 5084 ... 4/14/90 .. Deion Sanders .... Yankees |
| 5035 ... 9/7/89 .... Craig Worthington .. Orioles | 5085 ... 4/20/90 .. Alvaro Espinoza .. Yankees |
| 5036 ... 9/7/89 .... Bob Melvin ............ Orioles | 5086 ... 4/20/90 .. Dave Winfield ...... Yankees |
| 5037 ... 9/7/89 .... Phil Bradley .......... Orioles | 5087 ... 4/20/90 .. Jesse Barfield ..... Yankees |
| 5038 ... 9/7/89 .... Craig Worthington .. Orioles | 5088 ... 4/20/90 .. Roberto Kelly ...... Yankees |
| 5039 ... 9/7/89 .... Phil Bradley .......... Orioles | 5089 ... 4/20/90 .. Alvaro Espinoza .. Yankees |
| 5040 ... 9/12/89 .. Kevin Seitzer .......... Royals | 5090 ... 4/20/90 .. Jesse Barfield ..... Yankees |
| 5041 ... 9/12/89 .. Kurt Stillwell .......... Royals | 5091 ... 4/20/90 .. Roberto Kelly ...... Yankees |
| 5042 ... 9/12/89 .. Frank White ........... Royals | 5092 ... 4/20/90 .. Randy Velarde .... Yankees |
| 5043 ... 9/12/89 .. Willie Wilson ......... Royals | 5093 ... 4/20/90 .. Jesse Barfield ..... Yankees |
| 5044 ... 9/12/89 .. Bo Jackson ............ Royals | 5094 ... 4/26/90 .. Lance Johnson . White Sox |
| 5045 ... 9/12/89 .. Jim Eisenreich ........ Royals | 5095 ... 4/26/90 .. Sammy Sosa .... White Sox |
| 5046 ... 9/12/89 .. Danny Tartabull ...... Royals | 5096 ... 4/26/90 .. Carlton Fisk ...... White Sox |
| 5047 ... 9/12/89 .. Willie Wilson ........... Royals | 5097 ... 4/26/90 .. Robin Ventura ... White Sox |
| 5048 ... 9/12/89 .. Danny Tartabull ...... Royals | 5098 ... 4/26/90 .. Lance Johnson . White Sox |
| 5049 ... 9/12/89 .. Kurt Stillwell .......... Royals | 5099 ... 4/26/90 .. Sammy Sosa .... White Sox |
| 5050 ... 9/12/89 .. Frank White ........... Royals | 5100 ... 4/26/90 .. Ivan Calderon ... White Sox |

| | | | |
|---|---|---|---|
| 5101 ... 4/26/90 .. Carlton Fisk ...... White Sox | 5151 ... 6/11/90 .. Carney Lansford .......... A's |
| 5102 ... 4/26/90 .. Steve Lyons ...... White Sox | 5152 ... 6/11/90 ... Ken Phelps ................... A's |
| 5103 ... 4/26/90 .. Scott Fletcher ... White Sox | 5153 ... 6/16/90 ... Greg Briley ....... Mariners |
| 5104 ... 4/26/90 .. Ron Kittle .......... White Sox | 5154 ... 6/16/90 .. Jeffrey Leonard ... Mariners |
| 5105 ... 4/26/90 .. Carlton Fisk ...... White Sox | 5155 ... 6/16/90 .. Edgar Martinez .... Mariners |
| 5106 ... 4/26/90 .. Steve Lyons ...... White Sox | 5156 ... 6/16/90 .. Brian Giles ......... Mariners |
| 5107 ... 4/26/90 .. Robin Ventura ... White Sox | 5157 ... 6/16/90 .. Matt Sinatro ....... Mariners |
| 5108 ... 4/26/90 .. Scott Fletcher ... White Sox | 5158 ... 6/16/90 .. Jay Buhner ......... Mariners |
| 5109 ... 4/26/90 .. Dan Pasqua ...... White Sox | 5159 ... 6/16/90 .. Edgar Martinez .... Mariners |
| 5110 ... 5/1/90 .... Sammy Sosa .... White Sox | 5160 ... 6/16/90 .. Matt Sinatro ....... Mariners |
| 5111 ... 5/1/90 .... Ivan Calderon ... White Sox | 5161 ... 6/16/90 .. Harold Reynolds . Mariners |
| 5112 ... 5/1/90 .... Dan Pasqua ...... White Sox | 5162 ... 6/22/90 .. Greg Briley ....... Mariners |
| 5113 ... 5/1/90 .... Carlos Martinez White Sox | 5163 ... 6/22/90 .. Alvin Davis ........ Mariners |
| 5114 ... 5/1/90 .... Ron Karkovice .. White Sox | 5164 ... 6/22/90 .. Jeffrey Leonard ... Mariners |
| 5115 ... 5/1/90 .... Dan Pasqua ...... White Sox | 5165 ... 6/22/90 .. Jeffrey Leonard ... Mariners |
| 5116 ... 5/1/90 .... Carlos Martinez White Sox | 5166 ... 6/22/90 .. Pete O'Brien ...... Mariners |
| 5117 ... 5/1/90 .... Scott Fletcher ... White Sox | 5167 ... 6/22/90 .. Dave Valle ......... Mariners |
| 5118 ... 5/8/90 .... Russ Morman ......... Royals | 5168 ... 6/22/90 .. Pete O'Brien ...... Mariners |
| 5119 ... 5/11/90 .. Dion James .......... Indians | 5169 ... 6/22/90 .. Edgar Martinez .... Mariners |
| 5120 ... 5/11/90 .. Brook Jacoby ......... Indians | 5170 ... 6/22/90 .. Dave Valle .......... Mariners |
| 5121 ... 5/11/90 .. Mitch Webster ....... Indians | 5171 ... 6/27/90 .. Paul Sorrento ........... Twins |
| 5122 ... 5/11/90 .. Brook Jacoby ......... Indians | 5172 ... 6/27/90 .. Greg Gagne ........... Twins |
| 5123 ... 5/11/90 .. Keith Hernandez ... Indians | 5173 ... 6/27/90 .. Kent Hrbek .............. Twins |
| 5124 ... 5/11/90 .. Cory Snyder .......... Indians | 5174 ... 7/2/90 .... Wade Boggs ...... Red Sox |
| 5125 ... 5/11/90 .. "Sandy Alomar, Jr." Indians | 5175 ... 7/2/90 .... Kevin Romine ...... Red Sox |
| 5126 ... 5/17/90 .. Cecil Fielder ............ Tigers | 5176 ... 7/2/90 .... Carlos Quintana .. Red Sox |
| 5127 ... 5/17/90 .. Matt Nokes .............. Tigers | 5177 ... 7/2/90 .... Wade Boggs ...... Red Sox |
| 5128 ... 5/17/90 .. Mike Heath .............. Tigers | 5178 ... 7/2/90 .... Tom Brunansky .... Red Sox |
| 5129 ... 5/17/90 .. Lloyd Moseby .......... Tigers | 5179 ... 7/2/90 .... Tony Pena ........... Red Sox |
| 5130 ... 5/17/90 .. Mike Heath .............. Tigers | 5180 ... 7/2/90 .... Wade Boggs ...... Red Sox |
| 5131 ... 6/6/90 .... Rickey Henderson ........ A's | 5181 ... 7/7/90 .... Jody Reed .......... Red Sox |
| 5132 ... 6/6/90 .... Mark McGwire .......... A's | 5182 ... 7/7/90 .... Carlos Quintana .. Red Sox |
| 5133 ... 6/6/90 .... Doug Jennings ............ A's | 5183 ... 7/7/90 .... Wade Boggs ...... Red Sox |
| 5134 ... 6/6/90 .... Walt Weiss ................ A's | 5184 ... 7/7/90 .... Jody Reed .......... Red Sox |
| 5135 ... 6/6/90 .... Carney Lansford .......... A's | 5185 ... 7/7/90 .... Tom Brunansky ... Red Sox |
| 5136 ... 6/6/90 .... Mark McGwire .......... A's | 5186 ... 7/7/90 .... Dwight Evans ...... Red Sox |
| 5137 ... 6/6/90 .... Mark McGwire .......... A's | 5187 ... 7/7/90 .... Kevin Romine ...... Red Sox |
| 5138 ... 6/6/90 .... Doug Jennings ............ A's | 5188 ... 7/7/90 .... Luis Rivera .......... Red Sox |
| 5139 ... 6/11/90 .. Willie Randolph .......... A's | 5189 ... 7/7/90 .... Jody Reed .......... Red Sox |
| 5140 ... 6/11/90 .. Doug Jennings ............ A's | 5190 ... 7/7/90 .... Dwight Evans ...... Red Sox |
| 5141 ... 6/11/90 .. Ron Hassey ................ A's | 5191 ... 7/7/90 .... Kevin Romine ...... Red Sox |
| 5142 ... 6/11/90 .. Rickey Henderson ........ A's | 5192 ... 7/7/90 .... Luis Rivera .......... Red Sox |
| 5143 ... 6/11/90 .. Doug Jennings ............ A's | 5193 ... 7/14/90 .. Lou Whitaker ........... Tigers |
| 5144 ... 6/11/90 .. Felix Jose ...................... A's | 5194 ... 7/14/90 .. Cecil Fielder ............ Tigers |
| 5145 ... 6/11/90 .. Dave Henderson .......... A's | 5195 ... 7/14/90 .. Lloyd Moseby .......... Tigers |
| 5146 ... 6/11/90 .. Jamie Quirk .................. A's | 5196 ... 7/14/90 .. Dave Bergman ........ Tigers |
| 5147 ... 6/11/90 .. Walt Weiss .................. A's | 5197 ... 7/14/90 .. Chet Lemon ............ Tigers |
| 5148 ... 6/11/90 .. Ron Hassey ................ A's | 5198 ... 7/14/90 .. Larry Sheets ............ Tigers |
| 5149 ... 6/11/90 .. Felix Jose ...................... A's | 5199 ... 7/20/90 .. Alan Trammell .......... Tigers |
| 5150 ... 6/11/90 .. Dave Henderson .......... A's | 5200 ... 7/20/90 .. Lloyd Moseby .......... Tigers |

| | | | |
|---|---|---|---|
| 5201 ... 7/20/90 .. Mike Heath .............. Tigers | | 5251 ... 8/28/90 .. Dante Bichette ....... Angels | |
| 5202 ... 7/20/90 .. Lloyd Moseby .......... Tigers | | 5252 ... 8/28/90 .. Dick Schofield ........ Angels | |
| 5203 ... 7/25/90 .. Matt Nokes .......... Yankees | | 5253 ... 8/28/90 .. Dave Winfield ........ Angels | |
| 5204 ... 7/25/90 .. Jim Leyritz ............ Yankees | | 5254 ... 8/28/90 .. Lance Parrish ...... Angels | |
| 5205 ... 7/25/90 .. Bob Geren ........... Yankees | | 5255 ... 8/28/90 .. Dick Schofield ........ Angels | |
| 5206 ... 7/25/90 .. Alvaro Espinoza .. Yankees | | 5256 ... 8/28/90 .. Luis Polonia ........... Angels | |
| 5207 ... 7/25/90 .. Bob Geren ........... Yankees | | 5257 ... 8/28/90 .. Devon White ........... Angels | |
| 5208 ... 7/25/90 .. Deion Sanders .... Yankees | | 5258 ... 9/3/90 .... Jerry Browne ...... Indians | |
| 5209 ... 7/25/90 .. Kevin Maas .......... Yankees | | 5259 ... 9/3/90 .... Candy Maldonado . Indians | |
| 5210 ... 7/25/90 .. Kevin Maas .......... Yankees | | 5260 ... 9/3/90 .... Brook Jacoby ......... Indians | |
| 5211 ... 7/25/90 .. Alvaro Espinoza .. Yankees | | 5261 ... 9/3/90 .... Joel Skinner ........... Indians | |
| 5212 ... 7/31/90 .. Paul Molitor .......... Brewers | | 5262 ... 9/3/90 .... Dion James ........... Indians | |
| 5213 ... 7/31/90 .. Gary Sheffield ..... Brewers | | 5263 ... 9/3/90 .... Candy Maldonado . Indians | |
| 5214 ... 7/31/90 .. Greg Vaughn ....... Brewers | | 5264 ... 9/3/90 .... Brook Jacoby ......... Indians | |
| 5215 ... 7/31/90 .. Paul Molitor .......... Brewers | | 5265 ... 9/3/90 .... Cory Snyder .......... Indians | |
| 5216 ... 7/31/90 .. Robin Yount ......... Brewers | | 5266 ... 9/8/90 .... Kevin Seitzer ......... Royals | |
| 5217 ... 7/31/90 .. Greg Vaughn ....... Brewers | | 5267 ... 9/8/90 .... Jim Eisenreich ....... Royals | |
| 5218 ... 7/31/90 .. Charlie O'Brien .... Brewers | | 5268 ... 9/8/90 .... Bo Jackson ............ Royals | |
| 5219 ... 7/31/90 .. Bill Spiers ............. Brewers | | 5269 ... 9/8/90 .... Gerald Perry .......... Royals | |
| 5220 ... 8/5/90 .... Greg Myers ........ Blue Jays | | 5270 ... 9/8/90 .... Kurt Stillwell ........ Royals | |
| 5221 ... 8/5/90 .... Kelly Gruber ...... Blue Jays | | 5271 ... 9/8/90 .... Kevin Seitzer ......... Royals | |
| 5222 ... 8/5/90 .... George Bell ....... Blue Jays | | 5272 ... 9/8/90 .... Jim Eisenreich ....... Royals | |
| 5223 ... 8/5/90 .... Mookie Wilson ... Blue Jays | | 5273 ... 9/8/90 .... Kurt Stillwell ......... Royals | |
| 5224 ... 8/5/90 .... Greg Myers ........ Blue Jays | | 5274 ... 9/14/90 .. Robin Yount ......... Brewers | |
| 5225 ... 8/10/90 .. Lance Johnson . White Sox | | 5275 ... 9/14/90 .. Rob Deer ............. Brewers | |
| 5226 ... 8/10/90 .. Steve Lyons ...... White Sox | | 5276 ... 9/14/90 .. Robin Yount ......... Brewers | |
| 5227 ... 8/17/90 .. Dan Pasqua ..... White Sox | | 5277 ... 9/14/90 .. Rob Deer ............. Brewers | |
| 5228 ... 8/17/90 .. Frank Thomas ... White Sox | | 5278 ... 9/14/90 .. Bill Spiers ............. Brewers | |
| 5229 ... 8/17/90 .. Ron Karkovice .. White Sox | | 5279 ... 9/14/90 .. Jim Gantner ......... Brewers | |
| 5230 ... 8/17/90 .. Scott Fletcher ... White Sox | | 5280 ... 9/14/90 .. Dave Parker ........ Brewers | |
| 5231 ... 8/17/90 .. Ivan Calderon ... White Sox | | 5281 ... 9/14/90 .. Rob Deer ............. Brewers | |
| 5232 ... 8/17/90 .. Frank Thomas ... White Sox | | 5282 ... 9/14/90 .. B.J. Surhoff ......... Brewers | |
| 5233 ... 8/17/90 .. Ron Karkovice .. White Sox | | 5283 ... 9/14/90 .. Greg Vaughn ....... Brewers | |
| 5234 ... 8/17/90 .. Sam Sosa .......... White Sox | | 5284 ... 9/14/90 .. Dave Parker ........ Brewers | |
| 5235 ... 8/17/90 .. Craig Grebeck .. White Sox | | 5285 ... 9/19/90 .. Alvin Davis .......... Mariners | |
| 5236 ... 8/17/90 .. Dan Pasqua ...... White Sox | | 5286 ... 9/19/90 .. Greg Briley .......... Mariners | |
| 5237 ... 8/17/90 .. Frank Thomas ... White Sox | | 5287 ... 9/24/90 .. Donnie Hill .............. Angels | |
| 5238 ... 8/17/90 .. Craig Grebeck .. White Sox | | 5288 ... 9/24/90 .. Brian Downing ....... Angels | |
| 5239 ... 8/17/90 .. Ivan Calderon ... White Sox | | 5289 ... 9/24/90 .. Dave Winfield ........ Angels | |
| 5240 ... 8/17/90 .. Frank Thomas .. White Sox | | 5290 ... 9/24/90 .. Jack Howell .......... Angels | |
| 5241 ... 8/17/90 .. Ron Karkovice .. White Sox | | 5291 ... 9/24/90 .. Dick Schofield ........ Angels | |
| 5242 ... 8/22/90 .. Alvin Davis .......... Mariners | | 5292 ... 9/24/90 .. Lee Stevens ........... Angels | |
| 5243 ... 8/22/90 .. Henry Cotto ........ Mariners | | 5293 ... 9/24/90 .. Dick Schofield ........ Angels | |
| 5244 ... 8/22/90 .. Jeff Schaefer ....... Mariners | | 5294 ... 9/24/90 .. Devon White ........ Angels | |
| 5245 ... 8/22/90 .. "Ken Griffey, Jr." .. Mariners | | 5295 ... 9/24/90 .. Brian Downing ....... Angels | |
| 5246 ... 8/22/90 .. Henry Cotto ........ Mariners | | 5296 ... 9/24/90 .. Dave Winfield ........ Angels | |
| 5247 ... 8/28/90 .. Devon White .......... Angels | | 5297 ... 9/24/90 .. Lee tevens ............ Angels | |
| 5248 ... 8/28/90 .. Lee Stevens ........... Angels | | 5298 ... 9/30/90 .. Dave Henderson ......... A's | |
| 5249 ... 8/28/90 .. Lance Parrish ......... Angels | | 5299 ... 9/30/90 .. Carney Lansford .......... A's | |
| 5250 ... 8/28/90 .. Lance Parrish ......... Angels | | 5300 ... 9/30/90 .. Ron Hassey ................. A's | |

| | | | |
|---|---|---|---|
| 5301 ... 9/30/90 .. Mike Gallego ................ A's | 5351 ... 5/1/91 .... Devon White ...... Blue Jays |
| 5302 ... 9/30/90 .. Dave Henderson .......... A's | 5352 ... 5/1/91 .... Roberto Alomar . Blue Jays |
| 5303 ... 9/30/90 .. Harold Baines .............. A's | 5353 ... 5/1/91 .... Joe Carter .......... Blue Jays |
| 5304 ... 9/30/90 .. Dann Howitt ................. A's | 5354 ... 5/1/91 .... Glenallen Hill ..... Blue Jays |
| 5305 ... 9/30/90 .. Dann Howitt ................. A's | 5355 ... 5/1/91 .... Greg Myers ....... Blue Jays |
| 5306 ... 9/30/90 .. Mike Bordick ................ A's | 5356 ... 5/1/91 .... Devon White ...... Blue Jays |
| 5307 ... 9/30/90 .. Mike Gallego ................ A's | 5357 ... 5/1/91 .... Roberto Alomar . Blue Jays |
| 5308 ... 9/30/90 .. Doug Jennings ............. A's | 5358 ... 5/1/91 .... Kelly Gruber ...... Blue Jays |
| 5309 ... 4/8/91 .... Dante Bichette ..... Brewers | 5359 ... 5/1/91 .... Glenallen Hill ..... Blue Jays |
| 5310 ... 4/8/91 .... Jim Gantner ......... Brewers | 5360 ... 5/1/91 .... Greg Myers ....... Blue Jays |
| 5311 ... 4/8/91 .... Franklin Stubbs .... Brewers | 5361 ... 5/1/91 .... Roberto Alomar . Blue Jays |
| 5312 ... 4/8/91 .... Candy Maldonado Brewers | 5362 ... 5/8/91 .... Devon White ...... Blue Jays |
| 5313 ... 4/8/91 .... Dante Bichette ..... Brewers | 5363 ... 5/8/91 .... Mark Whiten ...... Blue Jays |
| 5314 ... 4/8/91 .... Jim Gantner ......... Brewers | 5364 ... 5/8/91 .... Greg Myers ....... Blue Jays |
| 5315 ... 4/8/91 .... Paul Molitor ......... Brewers | 5365 ... 5/8/91 .... Mookie Wilson ... Blue Jays |
| 5316 ... 4/8/91 .... Franklin Stubbs .... Brewers | 5366 ... 5/8/91 .... John Olerud ...... Blue Jays |
| 5317 ... 4/8/91 .... Jim Gantner ......... Brewers | 5367 ... 5/8/91 .... Manuel Lee ....... Blue Jays |
| 5318 ... 4/14/91 .. Ernie Whitt ............. Orioles | 5368 ... 5/13/91 .. Travis Fryman ......... Tigers |
| 5319 ... 4/14/91 .. Brady Anderson ..... Orioles | 5369 ... 5/13/91 .. Milt Cuyler .............. Tigers |
| 5320 ... 4/14/91 .. Joe Orsulak ........... Orioles | 5370 ... 5/13/91 .. Mickey Tettleton ...... Tigers |
| 5321 ... 4/14/91 .. Ernie Whitt ............. Orioles | 5371 ... 5/13/91 .. Pete Incaviglia ........ Tigers |
| 5322 ... 4/14/91 .. Brady Anderson ..... Orioles | 5372 ... 5/29/91 .. Chuck Knoblauch .... Twins |
| 5323 ... 4/14/91 .. Randy Milligan ....... Orioles | 5373 ... 5/29/91 .. Chuck Knoblauch .... Twins |
| 5324 ... 4/14/91 .. Glenn Davis ........... Orioles | 5374 ... 5/29/91 .. Chili Davis ............... Twins |
| 5325 ... 4/14/91 .. Sam Horn ............... Orioles | 5375 ... 5/29/91 .. Brian Harper ............ Twins |
| 5326 ... 4/14/91 .. Ernie Whitt ............. Orioles | 5376 ... 6/6/91 .... Kirk Gibson ............ Royals |
| 5327 ... 4/20/91 .. Mike Devereaux ..... Orioles | 5377 ... 6/6/91 .... Danny Tartabull ...... Royals |
| 5328 ... 4/20/91 .. Randy Milligan ....... Orioles | 5378 ... 6/6/91 .... Warren Cromartie .. Royals |
| 5329 ... 4/20/91 .. Sam Horn ............... Orioles | 5379 ... 6/6/91 .... Brent Mayne ........... Royals |
| 5330 ... 4/20/91 .. Joe Orsulak ........... Orioles | 5380 ... 6/6/91 .... David Howard ........ Royals |
| 5331 ... 4/20/91 .. Chris Hoiles ........... Orioles | 5381 ... 6/6/91 .... Danny Tartabull ...... Royals |
| 5332 ... 4/20/91 .. Randy Milligan ....... Orioles | 5382 ... 6/6/91 .... Kevin Seitzer .......... Royals |
| 5333 ... 4/20/91 .. Glenn Davis ........... Orioles | 5383 ... 6/6/91 .... David Howard ........ Royals |
| 5334 ... 4/20/91 .. Sam Horn ............... Orioles | 5384 ... 6/6/91 .... Brian McRae .......... Royals |
| 5335 ... 4/20/91 .. Craig Worthington .. Orioles | 5385 ... 6/11/91 .. Dan Pasqua ...... White Sox |
| 5336 ... 4/20/91 .. Chris Hoiles ........... Orioles | 5386 ... 6/11/91 .. Sam Sosa ......... White Sox |
| 5337 ... 4/26/91 .. Jerry Browne ......... Indians | 5387 ... 6/11/91 .. Tim Raines ........ White Sox |
| 5338 ... 4/26/91 .. Albert Belle .......... Indians | 5388 ... 6/11/91 .. Dan Pasqua ...... White Sox |
| 5339 ... 4/26/91 .. Sandy Alomar ........ Indians | 5389 ... 6/11/91 .. Lance Johnson . White Sox |
| 5340 ... 4/26/91 .. Brook Jacoby ......... Indians | 5390 ... 6/11/91 .. Frank Thomas .. White Sox |
| 5341 ... 4/26/91 .. Beau Allred ............ Indians | 5391 ... 6/11/91 .. Dan Pasqua ...... White Sox |
| 5342 ... 4/26/91 .. Mark Lewis ............ Indians | 5392 ... 6/11/91 .. Sam Sosa ......... White Sox |
| 5343 ... 4/26/91 .. Jerry Browne ......... Indians | 5393 ... 6/11/91 .. Tim Raines ........ White Sox |
| 5344 ... 4/26/91 .. Albert Belle .......... Indians | 5394 ... 6/11/91 .. Frank Thomas .. White Sox |
| 5345 ... 4/26/91 .. Chris James .......... Indians | 5395 ... 6/16/91 .. Jesse Barfield ..... Yankees |
| 5346 ... 5/1/91 .... Devon White ...... Blue Jays | 5396 ... 6/16/91 .. Steve Sax ............ Yankees |
| 5347 ... 5/1/91 .... John Olerud ...... Blue Jays | 5397 ... 6/16/91 .. Mel Hall ............... Yankees |
| 5348 ... 5/1/91 .... Mark Whiten ...... Blue Jays | 5398 ... 6/16/91 .. Roberto Kelly ...... Yankees |
| 5349 ... 5/1/91 .... Glenallen Hill ..... Blue Jays | 5399 ... 6/16/91 .. Jesse Barfield ..... Yankees |
| 5350 ... 5/1/91 .... Manuel Lee ........ Blue Jays | 5400 ... 6/16/91 .. Roberto Kelly ...... Yankees |

| | | |
|---|---|---|
| 5401 ... 6/21/91 .. Dan Pasqua ...... White Sox | 5451 ... 7/28/91 .. Rob Deer ................. Tigers |
| 5402 ... 6/21/91 .. Sam Sosa ......... White Sox | 5452 ... 7/28/91 .. Tony Phillips ............ Tigers |
| 5403 ... 6/21/91 .. Frank Thomas .. White Sox | 5453 ... 7/28/91 .. Scott Livingstone ..... Tigers |
| 5404 ... 6/21/91 .. Craig Grebeck .. White Sox | 5454 ... 8/19/91 .. Mike Devereaux ..... Orioles |
| 5405 ... 6/21/91 .. Sam Sosa ......... White Sox | 5455 ... 8/19/91 .. Randy Milligan ....... Orioles |
| 5406 ... 7/2/91 .... Jose Canseco .............. A's | 5456 ... 8/19/91 .. Chito Martinez ....... Orioles |
| 5407 ... 7/2/91 .... Mike Gallego ................ A's | 5457 ... 8/19/91 .. Leo Gomez ............ Orioles |
| 5408 ... 7/2/91 .... Willie Wilson ............... A's | 5458 ... 8/19/91 .. Bill Ripken ............. Orioles |
| 5409 ... 7/2/91 .... Vance Law .................. A's | 5459 ... 8/19/91 .. Randy Milligan ....... Orioles |
| 5410 ... 7/2/91 .... Harold Baines .............. A's | 5460 ... 8/19/91 .. Leo Gomez ............ Orioles |
| 5411 ... 7/7/91 .... Max Venable .......... Angels | 5461 ... 8/24/91 .. Brent Mayne ........... Royals |
| 5412 ... 7/7/91 .... Dave Winfield ......... Angels | 5462 ... 8/30/91 .. Brian McRae .......... Royals |
| 5413 ... 7/7/91 .... Lance Parrish ......... Angels | 5463 ... 8/30/91 .. Danny Tartabull ...... Royals |
| 5414 ... 7/7/91 .... Donnie Hill .............. Angels | 5464 ... 8/30/91 .. Kirk Gibson ........... Royals |
| 5415 ... 7/7/91 .... Luis Sojo ................ Angels | 5465 ... 8/30/91 .. Danny Tartabull ...... Royals |
| 5416 ... 7/7/91 .... Luis Polonia ........... Angels | 5466 ... 9/6/91 .... Warren Newson White Sox |
| 5417 ... 7/7/91 .... Max Venable .......... Angels | 5467 ... 9/6/91 .... Ron Karkovice .. White Sox |
| 5418 ... 7/7/91 .... Wally Joyner ........... Angels | 5468 ... 9/6/91 .... Joey Cora ....... White Sox |
| 5419 ... 7/7/91 .... Dave Winfield ......... Angels | 5469 ... 9/6/91 .... Joey Cora ......... White Sox |
| 5420 ... 7/7/91 .... Dave Parker ........... Angels | 5470 ... 9/6/91 .... Ozzie Guillen .... White Sox |
| 5421 ... 7/7/91 .... Donnie Hill .............. Angels | 5471 ... 9/6/91 .... Bo Jackson ....... White Sox |
| 5422 ... 7/7/91 .... Luis Sojo ................ Angels | 5472 ... 9/12/91 .. Dan Gladden ........... Twins |
| 5423 ... 7/7/91 .... Max Venable .......... Angels | 5473 ... 9/12/91 .. Kirby Puckett ........... Twins |
| 5424 ... 7/7/91 .... Lance Parrish ......... Angels | 5474 ... 9/12/91 .. Kent Hrbek .............. Twins |
| 5425 ... 7/13/91 .. Joe Carter .......... Blue Jays | 5475 ... 9/12/91 .. Chili Davis ................ Twins |
| 5426 ... 7/13/91 .. Greg Myers ........ Blue Jays | 5476 ... 9/12/91 .. Chili Davis ................ Twins |
| 5427 ... 7/13/91 .. Rene Gonzales .. Blue Jays | 5477 ... 9/12/91 .. Shane Mack ............. Twins |
| 5428 ... 7/13/91 .. John Olerud ....... Blue Jays | 5478 ... 9/12/91 .. Greg Gagne ............ Twins |
| 5429 ... 7/13/91 .. Rance Mulliniks . Blue Jays | 5479 ... 9/12/91 .. Kirby Puckett ........... Twins |
| 5430 ... 7/13/91 .. Greg Myers ........ Blue Jays | 5480 ... 9/12/91 .. Chili Davis ................ Twins |
| 5431 ... 7/13/91 .. Rob Ducey ......... Blue Jays | 5481 ... 9/19/91 .. Dave Gallagher ...... Angels |
| 5432 ... 7/18/91 .. Devon White ...... Blue Jays | 5482 ... 9/19/91 .. Wally Joyner .......... Angels |
| 5433 ... 7/18/91 .. Kelly Gruber ...... Blue Jays | 5483 ... 9/19/91 .. Dave Gallagher ...... Angels |
| 5434 ... 7/18/91 .. Kelly Gruber ...... Blue Jays | 5484 ... 9/19/91 .. Lee Stevens .......... Angels |
| 5435 ... 7/18/91 .. Greg Myers ........ Blue Jays | 5485 ... 9/19/91 .. Lee Stevens .......... Angels |
| 5436 ... 7/18/91 .. Roberto Alomar . Blue Jays | 5486 ... 9/19/91 .. Luis Sojo ................ Angels |
| 5437 ... 7/23/91 .. Mo Vaughn ......... Red Sox | 5487 ... 9/19/91 .. John Orton ............ Angels |
| 5438 ... 7/23/91 .. Jody Reed ........... Red Sox | 5488 ... 9/25/91 .. "Ken Griffey, Jr." . Mariners |
| 5439 ... 7/23/91 .. Jack Clark .......... Red Sox | 5489 ... 9/25/91 .. Dave Cochrane ... Mariners |
| 5440 ... 7/23/91 .. Ellis Burks .......... Red Sox | 5490 ... 9/25/91 .. Edgar Martinez .... Mariners |
| 5441 ... 7/23/91 .. Luis Rivera ......... Red Sox | 5491 ... 9/25/91 .. Pete O'Brien ....... Mariners |
| 5442 ... 7/23/91 .. Steve Lyons ........ Red Sox | 5492 ... 9/25/91 .. Tino Martinez ...... Mariners |
| 5443 ... 7/23/91 .. Luis Rivera ......... Red Sox | 5493 ... 9/25/91 .. Omar Vizquel ...... Mariners |
| 5444 ... 7/28/91 .. Tony Phillips ......... Tigers | 5494 ... 9/25/91 .. Edgar Martinez .... Mariners |
| 5445 ... 7/28/91 .. Scott Livingstone ..... Tigers | 5495 ... 9/25/91 .. "Ken Griffey, Jr." . Mariners |
| 5446 ... 7/28/91 .. Lloyd Moseby .......... Tigers | 5496 ... 9/30/91 .. Edgar Martinez .... Mariners |
| 5447 ... 7/28/91 .. Rob Deer ................. Tigers | 5497 ... 9/30/91 .. Edgar Martinez .... Mariners |
| 5448 ... 7/28/91 .. Milt Cuyler ............... Tigers | 5498 ... 9/30/91 .. Pete O'Brien ....... Mariners |
| 5449 ... 7/28/91 .. Lloyd Moseby .......... Tigers | 5499 ... 9/30/91 .. Pete O'Brien ........ Mariners |
| 5450 ... 7/28/91 .. Cecil Fielder ............ Tigers | 5500 ... 9/30/91 .. Tino Martinez ...... Mariners |

| | | | |
|---|---|---|---|
| 5501 ... 9/30/91 .. David Valle .......... Mariners | 5551 ... 5/27/92 .. Frank Thomas .. White Sox |
| 5502 ... 10/6/91 .. Harold Baines .............. A's | 5552 ... 6/6/92 .... Chuck Knoblauch .... Twins |
| 5503 ... 10/6/91 .. Mike Gallego ................ A's | 5553 ... 6/6/92 .... Shane Mack ............. Twins |
| 5504 ... 10/6/91 .. Mike Bordick ................ A's | 5554 ... 6/6/92 .... Greg Gagne ............. Twins |
| 5505 ... 10/6/91 .. Harold Baines .............. A's | 5555 ... 6/6/92 .... Gene Larkin ............. Twins |
| 5506 ... 10/6/91 .. Dave Henderson ......... A's | 5556 ... 6/6/92 .... Randy Bush ............. Twins |
| 5507 ... 10/6/91 .. Terry Steinbach ........... A's | 5557 ... 6/12/92 .. Jose Canseco .............. A's |
| 5508 ... 10/6/91 .. Mike Gallego ................ A's | 5558 ... 6/12/92 .. Mark McGwire .............. A's |
| 5509 ... 10/6/91 .. Mike Bordick ................ A's | 5559 ... 6/12/92 .. Jamie Quirk ................. A's |
| 5510 ... 10/6/91 .. Jose Canseco .............. A's | 5560 ... 6/12/92 .. Mike Bordick ................ A's |
| 5511 ... 10/6/91 .. Terry Steinbach ........... A's | 5561 ... 6/12/92 .. Mark McGwire .............. A's |
| 5512 ... 4/6/92 .... Edgar Martinez .... Mariners | 5562 ... 6/12/92 .. Walt Weiss ................... A's |
| 5513 ... 4/6/92 .... David Valle .......... Mariners | 5563 ... 6/17/92 .. Luis Polonia .......... Angels |
| 5514 ... 4/6/92 .... Edgar Martinez .... Mariners | 5564 ... 6/17/92 .. John Orton ............ Angels |
| 5515 ... 4/6/92 .... David Valle .......... Mariners | 5565 ... 6/17/92 .. Von Hayes ............. Angels |
| 5516 ... 4/30/92 .. Frank Thomas .. White Sox | 5566 ... 6/17/92 .. Junior Felix ............ Angels |
| 5517 ... 4/30/92 .. Dan Pasqua ...... White Sox | 5567 ... 6/17/92 .. Hubie Brooks .......... Angels |
| 5518 ... 4/30/92 .. Dan Pasqua ...... White Sox | 5568 ... 6/17/92 .. Lee Stevens ........... Angels |
| 5519 ... 5/5/92 .... Chris Hoiles .......... Orioles | 5569 ... 6/17/92 .. Luis Polonia .......... Angels |
| 5520 ... 5/5/92 .... Joe Orsulak .......... Orioles | 5570 ... 6/17/92 .. Von Hayes ............. Angels |
| 5521 ... 5/9/92 .... Paul Molitor ......... Brewers | 5571 ... 6/28/92 .. Dan Gladden .......... Tigers |
| 5522 ... 5/9/92 .... Pat Listach ........... Brewers | 5572 ... 6/28/92 .. Travis Fryman ........ Tigers |
| 5523 ... 5/9/92 .... Robin Yout ............ Brewers | 5573 ... 6/28/92 .. Mickey Tettleton ...... Tigers |
| 5524 ... 5/9/92 .... Greg Vaughn ....... Brewers | 5574 ... 6/28/92 .. Milt Cuyler ............. Tigers |
| 5525 ... 5/9/92 .... Franklin Stubbs .... Brewers | 5575 ... 6/28/92 .. Cecil Fielder ............ Tigers |
| 5526 ... 5/9/92 .... Pat Listach ........... Brewers | 5576 ... 6/28/92 .. Mickey Tettleton ...... Tigers |
| 5527 ... 5/9/92 .... Jim Gantner .......... Brewers | 5577 ... 6/28/92 .. Tony Phillips ........... Tigers |
| 5528 ... 5/9/92 .... Dante Bichette ..... Brewers | 5578 ... 7/4/92 .... Danny Tartabull ... Yankees |
| 5529 ... 5/9/92 .... Kevin Seitzer ........ Brewers | 5579 ... 7/4/92 .... Kevin Maas .......... Yankees |
| 5530 ... 5/16/92 .. Paul Molitor ......... Brewers | 5580 ... 7/4/92 .... Matt Nokes .......... Yankees |
| 5531 ... 5/16/92 .. Greg Vaughn ....... Brewers | 5581 ... 7/4/92 .... Charlie Hayes ..... Yankees |
| 5532 ... 5/16/92 .. Paul Molitor ......... Brewers | 5582 ... 7/4/92 .... Mel Hall ............... Yankees |
| 5533 ... 5/16/92 .. Dante Bichette ..... Brewers | 5583 ... 7/4/92 .... Matt Nokes .......... Yankees |
| 5534 ... 5/16/92 .. Dante Bichette ..... Brewers | 5584 ... 7/4/92 .... Charlie Hayes ..... Yankees |
| 5535 ... 5/16/92 .. Franklin Stubbs .... Brewers | 5585 ... 7/4/92 .... Mike Gallego ....... Yankees |
| 5536 ... 5/21/92 .. Gary Thurman ........ Royals | 5586 ... 7/4/92 .... Roberto Kelly ...... Yankees |
| 5537 ... 5/21/92 .. Brian McRae .......... Royals | 5587 ... 7/4/92 .... Don Mattingly ...... Yankees |
| 5538 ... 5/21/92 .. Terry Shumpert ...... Royals | 5588 ... 7/4/92 .... Kevin Maas ......... Yankees |
| 5539 ... 5/21/92 .. Gary Thurman ........ Royals | 5589 ... 7/4/92 .... Matt Nokes .......... Yankees |
| 5540 ... 5/21/92 .. Brian McRae .......... Royals | 5590 ... 7/4/92 .... Roberto Kelly ...... Yankees |
| 5541 ... 5/21/92 .. George Brett .......... Royals | 5591 ... 7/9/92 .... Mark Lewis ........... Indians |
| 5542 ... 5/21/92 .. Mike Macfarlane ..... Royals | 5592 ... 7/9/92 .... Reggie Jefferson ... Indians |
| 5543 ... 5/21/92 .. Gary Thurman ........ Royals | 5593 ... 7/9/92 .... Jim Thome ............ Indians |
| 5544 ... 5/27/92 .. Robin Ventura ... White Sox | 5594 ... 7/9/92 .... Kenny Lofton ......... Indians |
| 5545 ... 5/27/92 .. Frank Thomas .. White Sox | 5595 ... 7/9/92 .... Albert Belle .......... Indians |
| 5546 ... 5/27/92 .. Time Raines ..... White Sox | 5596 ... 7/9/92 .... Mark Lewis ........... Indians |
| 5547 ... 5/27/92 .. Robin Ventura ... White Sox | 5597 ... 7/9/92 .... JimThome .............. Indians |
| 5548 ... 5/27/92 .. Frank Thomas .. White Sox | 5598 ... 7/9/92 .... Albert Belle .......... Indians |
| 5549 ... 5/27/92 .. Matt Merullo ...... White Sox | 5599 ... 7/16/92 .. Jeff Tackett ............ Orioles |
| 5550 ... 5/27/92 .. Lance Johnson . White Sox | 5600 ... 7/16/92 .. Sam Horn ............. Orioles |

| | | | |
|---|---|---|---|
| 5601 ... 7/16/92 .. Chito Martinez ....... Orioles | 5635 ... 8/11/92 .. Scott Leius ............... Twins |
| 5602 ... 7/16/92 .. Leo Gomez ............. Orioles | 5636 ... 8/11/92 .. Greg Gagne ............. Twins |
| 5603 ... 7/21/92 .. Greg Vaughn ....... Brewers | 5637 ... 8/11/92 .. Greg Gagne ............. Twins |
| 5604 ... 7/21/92 .. John Jaha ............ Brewers | 5638 ... 8/16/92 .. Mark Carreon .......... Tigers |
| 5605 ... 7/21/92 .. Robin Yout ........... Brewers | 5639 ... 8/16/92 .. Chad Kreuter .......... Tigers |
| 5606 ... 7/21/92 .. Robin Yout ........... Brewers | 5640 ... 8/16/92 .. Mark Carreon .......... Tigers |
| 5607 ... 7/26/92 .. Brady Anderson ..... Orioles | 5641 ... 8/16/92 .. Chad Kreuter .......... Tigers |
| 5608 ... 7/26/92 .. Cal Ripken ............. Orioles | 5642 ... 8/16/92 .. Tony Phillips ............ Tigers |
| 5609 ... 7/26/92 .. Leo Gomez ............. Orioles | 5643 ... 8/21/92 .. Junior Ortiz ............ Indians |
| 5610 ... 7/26/92 .. Mike Devereaux ..... Orioles | 5644 ... 8/27/92 .. Juan Samuel .......... Royals |
| 5611 ... 7/26/92 .. Leo Gomez ............. Orioles | 5645 ... 8/27/92 .. Jeff Conine ............. Royals |
| 5612 ... 8/1/92 .... Junior Felix ............ Angels | 5646 ... 8/27/92 .. David Howard ........ Royals |
| 5613 ... 8/1/92 .... Gary Gaetti ............. Angels | 5647 ... 8/27/92 .. Juan Samuel .......... Royals |
| 5614 ... 8/1/92 .... Greg Myers ............ Angels | 5648 ... 8/27/92 .. Kevin Koslofski ....... Royals |
| 5615 ... 8/1/92 .... Gary Gartti ............. Angels | 5649 ... 9/1/92 .... Kevin Koslofski ....... Royals |
| 5616 ... 8/1/92 .... Ken Oberkfell .......... Angels | 5650 ... 9/1/92 .... Brian McRae ........... Royals |
| 5617 ... 8/1/92 .... Junior Felix ............ Angels | 5651 ... 9/1/92 .... Gary Thurman ......... Royals |
| 5618 ... 8/1/92 .... Chad Curtis ............ Angels | 5652 ... 9/1/92 .... Gregg Jefferies ...... Royals |
| 5619 ... 8/6/92 .... Jerry Browne ................ A's | 5653 ... 9/1/92 .... George Brett ........... Royals |
| 5620 ... 8/6/92 .... Carney Lansford ......... A's | 5654 ... 9/7/92 .... Billy Hatcher ........ Red Sox |
| 5621 ... 8/6/92 .... Jose Canseco ............. A's | 5655 ... 9/7/92 .... Mo Vaughn .......... Red Sox |
| 5622 ... 8/6/92 .... Willie Wilson ................ A's | 5656 ... 9/7/92 .... Jody Reed ............ Red Sox |
| 5623 ... 8/6/92 .... Eric Fox ........................ A's | 5657 ... 9/7/92 .... Billy Hatcher ........ Red Sox |
| 5624 ... 8/6/92 .... Jose Canseco ............. A's | 5658 ... 9/7/92 .... Jody Reed ............ Red Sox |
| 5625 ... 8/6/92 .... Randy Ready ............... A's | 5659 ... 9/7/92 .... Wade Boggs ........ Red Sox |
| 5626 ... 8/6/92 .... Eric Fox ........................ A's | 5660 ... 9/22/92 .. Shane Mack ............. Twins |
| 5627 ... 8/6/92 .... Jerry Browne ................ A's | 5661 ... 9/22/92 .. Shane Mack ............. Twins |
| 5628 ... 8/6/92 .... Jose Canseco ............. A's | 5662 ... 9/22/92 .. Kirby Puckett ........... Twins |
| 5629 ... 8/6/92 .... Eric Fox ........................ A's | 5663 ... 9/22/92 .. Pedro Munoz .......... Twins |
| 5630 ... 8/6/92 .... Mike Bordick ................ A's | 5664 ... 9/27/92 .. Henry Cotto ......... Mariners |
| 5631 ... 8/11/92 .. Shane Mack ............. Twins | 5665 ... 9/27/92 .. Lance Parrish ...... Mariners |
| 5632 ... 8/11/92 .. Kirby Puckett ........... Twins | 5666 ... 9/27/92 .. Greg Briley .......... Mariners |
| 5633 ... 8/11/92 .. Kirby Puckett ........... Twins | 5667 ... 9/27/92 .. Lance Parrish ...... Mariners |
| 5634 ... 8/11/92 .. Kent Hrbek ............... Twins | 5668 ... 9/27/92 .. Greg Briley .......... Mariners |

PSIms